W9-CTT-905

SOME CALL
IT UTOPIA

"Arrabus is the beating heart of Wyst. Despite rumor to the contrary, Arrabus functions; Arrabus is real; Arrabus, in fact, is an amazing experience. Whoever doubts can come to Wyst and learn for himself. Immigrants are no longer welcome additions to the over-crowded social facilities; still, anyone with a sufficiently thick skin can participate either temporarily or permanently in a fantastic social experiment, where food and shelter, like air, are considered the natural right of all men.

"The newcomer will find himself suddenly relieved of anxieties. He works two brief periods of 'drudge' each week, with another two hours of 'maintenance' at the block where he resides. He will find himself immediately caught up in a society dedicated to self-fulfillment, pleasure and frivolity. He will dance, sing, gossip, engage in countless love affairs, endlessly ride the 'man-rivers' to no special destination, and waste hours in that obsessive occupation of the Arrabins, people-watching. . . .

"Every visitor to Wyst expects shocks and surprises, but never can he prepare himself for the sheer bogglement inflicted upon him by reality!"

—from the confidential files
of the Connatic.

WYST: ALASTOR 1716

by

Jack Vance

DAW Books, Inc.
Donald A. Wollheim, Publisher

1633 Broadway, New York, N.Y. 10019

Copyright ©, 1978, by Jack Vance

All Rights Reserved.

Cover art by David Mattingly.

FIRST PRINTING, NOVEMBER 1978

3 4 5 6 7 8 9

 DAW TRADEMARK REGISTERED
U.S. PAT. OFF. MARCA
REGISTRADA. HECHO EN U.S.A.

PRINTED IN U.S.A.

Chapter 1

◦◦●━━━━◆▶━━━━●◦◦

Alastor Cluster, a node of thirty thousand live stars, uncounted dead hulks and vast quantities of interstellar detritus, clung to the inner rim of the galaxy with the Unfortunate Waste before, the Nonestic Gulf beyond and the Gaean Reach a sparkling haze to the side. For the space traveler, no matter which his angle of approach, a remarkable spectacle was presented: constellations blazing white, blue and red; curtains of luminous stuff, broken here, obscured there by black storms of dust; star streams wandering in and out; whorls and spatters of phosphorescent gas.

Should Alastor Cluster be considered a segment of the Gaean Reach? The folk of the Cluster seldom reflected upon the matter, and indeed considered themselves neither Gaean nor Alastrid. The typical inhabitant, when asked about his origin, might perhaps cite his native world or, more usually, his local district, as if this place were so extraordinary, so special and widely famed that its reputation hung on every tongue of the galaxy.

Parochialism dissolved before the glory of the Connatic who ruled Alastor Cluster from his palace Lusz on the world Numenes: a structure famed across the human universe. Five pylons veered up from five islets to a groined arch a thousand feet above the ocean, supporting first a series of promenade decks; then a bank of administrative offices, ceremonial halls and the core of the Alastrid Communications System; then the Ring of Worlds; then further offices and residential suites for distinguished visitors; and finally, ten thousand feet above the ocean, the Connatic's private quarters. The highest pinnacle penetrated the clouds, sometimes piercing through to the upper sky. When sunlight glistened on its iridescent surfaces Lusz was a wonderful sight, and often considered the most inspiring artifact yet created by the human race.

Aloft in his eyrie, the Connatic lived without formality. For public appearances he arrayed himself in a severe black uniform and a black casque, in order to project an image of austerity, vigilance and inflexible authority: so he was known to his subjects. On more casual occasions—alone in his eyrie, as a high official on the Connatic's service, as an anonymous wanderer in the odd corners of the Cluster—he seemed a far easier man, of rather ordinary appearance, notable only for his manner of unobtrusive competence.

At Lusz, his workroom occupied the highest tip of the eyrie: a cupola with an outlook in all directions. The furnishings were constructed of massive dark wood: a pair of cushioned chairs, a work table, a sideboard supporting a clutter of souvenirs, photographs, curios and oddments, including a globe of Old Earth. To one side of the work table a panel displayed a conventionalized chart of the Cluster with three thousand glittering lights of various colors* to represent the inhabited worlds.

The work room served the Connatic as his most familiar and comfortable retreat. The time was now evening; plumblue twilight suffused the room. The Connatic stood before the western window, watching the passing of the afterglow and the coming of the stars.

The quiet was broken by a brief clear sound: Tink! Like a drop of water into a basin.

The Connatic spoke without turning: "Esclavade?"

A voice replied: "A deputation of four persons has arrived from Arrabus on Wyst. They announce themselves as 'The Whispers' and request a conference at your convenience."

The Connatic, still gazing out across the afterglow, reflected a moment, then said: "I will meet them in an hour. Take them to the Black Chamber, and provide suitable refreshment."

"As you say, sir."

Turning from the window, the Connatic went to his work table. He spoke a number: "1716." Three cards fell into a

---

* The colors served as a code to local conditions. By adjusting a switch, the Connatic might select any of several categories of reference. With the switch in its ordinary position, at *General*, the Connatic at a glance could gauge the circumstances in aggregate of three trillion people. When the Connatic touched one of the lights, its name and number appeared on a pane. If he should increase the pressure, information cards detailing recent and significant local events dropped into a slot. Should he speak a number, the world so designated showed a brief burst of white light and again the cards were produced.

hopper. The first, dated two weeks previously at Waunisse, a city of Arrabus, read:

Sir:

My previous reports upon the subject at hand are identified by the codes appended below. In gist: Arrabus shortly celebrates a Centenary Festival, to mark a hundred years under the aegis of the so-called "Egalistic Manifold." If I may presume to refresh your memory, this document enjoins all men, and specifically all Arrabins, to a society based upon human equality in a condition of freedom from toil, want and coercion.

The realization of these ideals has not been without dislocation. I refer you to my previous reports.

The Whispers, an executive committee of four, have come to take a very serious view of the situation. Their projections convince them that certain fundamental changes are necessary. At the Centenary they will announce a program to revitalize the Arrabin economy, which may not be popular: the Arrabin folk, like any others, hope for and expect augmentation rather than constriction of their lives. The present work week comprises thirteen hours of more or less uncomplicated routine, which the Arrabins nevertheless hope to reduce.

To dramatize the need for change, the Whispers will be coming to Lusz. They intend to consult with you on a realistic basis, and they hope that you will appear at the Centenary Festival, to identify yourself with the new program and perhaps provide economic assistance. I have been in consultation with the Whispers at Waunisse. Tomorrow they return to Uncibal, and will immediately depart for Numenes.

In my opinion they have made a realistic assessment of conditions, and I recommend that you listen to them with sympathetic attention.

> Bonamico,
> Connatic's Cursar at Uncibal, Arrabus.

The Connatic read the card with care, then turned to the second card, which had been dated at Waunisse on the day after the first message.

To the Connatic at Lusz:
 Greetings from the Whispers of Arrabus.
 We will presently arrive at Lusz, where we hope to
confer with you upon matters of great scope and urgency. We will also convey to you an invitation to our
Centenary Festival, which signalizes a hundred years of
egalism. There is much to be said on this subject, and at
our conference we will disclose our thoughts regarding
the next hundred years, and the adjustments which must
inevitably be made. At this time we will solicit your advice and constructive assistance.
 In all respect, we are,

                              the Whispers of Arrabus.

The Connatic had studied the two messages previously and
was familiar with their contents. The third message, arriving
subsequent to the first two, was new to him.

The Connatic at Lusz:
From the Alastor Centrality at Uncibal, Arrabus.
 It becomes my duty to report upon an odd and disturbing situation. A certain Jantiff Ravensroke has
presented himself to the Centrality, with information
which he declares to be of the most absolute urgency.
Cursar Bonamico is unaccountably absent and I can
think only to request that you immediately send an in-
vestigative officer, that he may learn the truth of what
may be a serious matter.

                              Clode Morre, Clerk,
                              The Alastor Centrality,
                              Uncibal.

Even as the Connatic brooded upon this third message, a
fourth dropped into the hopper.

To the Connatic at Lusz:
 Events are flying in all directions here, to my great
distress and consternation. Specifically, I fear for poor
Jantiff Ravensroke, who is in terrible danger; unless
someone puts a stop, they'll have his blood or worse. He
is accused of a vile crime but he is surely as inocent as
a child. Clerk Morre has been murdered and Cursar
Bonamico cannot be located; therefore I have ordered
Jantiff south into the Weirdlands, despite the rigors of
the way.

I send this off in agitation, and with the hope that
help is on the way.

> Aleida Gluster, Clerk,
> The Alastor Centrality,
> Uncibal.

The Connatic stood motionless, frowning down at the card.
After a moment he turned away and by a twisting wooden
staircase descended to the level below. A door slid aside; he
entered a car, dropped to the Ring of Worlds, and, by one of
the radial slideways reserved to his private use, rode to
Chamber 1716.

In the vestibule a placard provided basic data regarding
Wyst—the single planet of the white star Dwan, was small,
cool, dense, and populated by over three billion persons. He
continued into the main chamber. At the center floated a
seven-foot globe: a replica in miniature of Wyst, although
physiographic relief had been exaggerated by a factor of ten
in the interests of clarity. The Connatic touched the surface
and the globe rotated under his hand. The opposed continents
Trembal and Tremora appeared; the Connatic stopped the ro-
tation. The continents together extended four thousand miles
around the flank of Wyst, from the Northern Gulf to the
Moaning Ocean in the south, to resemble a rather thick-waist-
ed hourglass. At the equator, or the narrowest section of the
hourglass, the continents were split apart by the Salaman Sea, a
drowned rift averaging a hundred miles in width. That strip
of littoral, never more than twenty miles wide, between sea
and the flanking scarps to north and south, comprised the
land of Arrabus. To the south were the cities Uncibal and
Serce, to the north Propunce and Waunisse, each pair merg-
ing indistinguishably: in effect Arrabus was a single metropolitan area. Beyond the north and south extended the so-
called "Weirdlands," one-time civilized domains, now a pair
of wildernesses shrouded under dark forest.

The Connatic turned the globe a half-revolution and briefly
inspected Zumer and Pombal, island continents opposed
across the equator: each an uninviting terrain of mountain
crags and half-frozen swamps, supporting a minimal population.

Moving away from the globe, the Connatic studied an array of effigies. Closest at hand stood a pair of Arrabins,
dressed alike in gaily patterned smocks, short trousers and
sandals of synthetic fiber. They wore their hair teased out into

extravagant puffs and fringes, evidently to the prompting of individual whim. Their expressions were cheerful if rather distrait, like those of children contemplating a pleasant bit of mischief. Their complexions were pale to medium in tone, and their ethnic type seemed to be mixed. Nearby stood folk from Pombal and Zumer, men and women of a more distinctive character: tall, large-boned, with long beaked noses, bony jaws and chins. They wore padded garments studded with copper ornaments, boots and brimless hats of crumpled leather. On the wall behind a photograph depicted a Zur shunk-rider on his awesome mount*, both caparisoned for the sport known as "shunkery." Somewhat apart from the other effigies crouched a middle-aged woman in a hooded gown striped vertically in yellow, orange and black; her fingernails gleamed as if gilded. *Weirdland Witch* read the identifying plaque.

Moving to the information register, the Connatic studied a synopsis of Arrabin history**, with which he was familiar only in outline. As he read he nodded slowly, as if in validation of a private opinion. Turning from the register he went to examine three large photographs on the wall. The first, an aerial view of Uncibal, might have been a geometrical exercise in which rows of many-colored blocks dwindled to a point at the horizon. The second photograph depicted the interior of the 32nd District Stadium. Spectators encrusted the interior; a pair of shunk confronted each other across the field. The third photograph presented a view along one of the great Arrabin slideways: a moving strip something more than a hundred feet wide, choked with humanity, extending into the distance as far as lens could see.

The Connatic studied the photographs with a trace of awe. The idea of human beings in vast numbers was familiar to him as an abstraction; in the photographs the abstraction was made real.

He glanced through a file of cursar's*** reports; one of these, ten years old, read:

* Shunk: monstrous creatures indigenous to the Pombal swamps, notably cantankerous and unpredictably vicious. They refuse to thrive on Zumer, though the Zur are considered the most adept riders. At the Arrabin stadia spectacles involving shunk are, along with the variety of hussade, the most popular of entertainments.

** See Glossary #1.

*** Cursar: the Connatic's local representative, usually based in an enclave known as "Alastor Centrality."

Arrabus is the beating heart of Wyst. Despite rumor to the contrary, Arrabus functions; Arrabus is real; Arrabus, in fact, is an amazing experience. Whoever doubts can come to Wyst and learn for himself. Immigrants are no longer welcome additions to the overcrowded social facilities; still, anyone with a sufficiently thick skin can participate either temporarily or permanently in a fantastic social experiment, where food and shelter, like air, are considered the natural right of all men.

The newcomer will find himself suddenly relieved of anxieties. He works two brief periods of "drudge" each week, with another two hours of "maintenance" at the block where he resides. He will find himself immediately caught up in a society dedicated to self-fulfillment, pleasure and frivolity. He will dance, sing, gossip, engage in countless love affairs, endlessly ride the "man-rivers" to no special destination, and waste hours in that obsessive occupation of the Arrabins, people-watching. He will make his breakfast, lunch and dinner upon wholesome "gruff" and nutritious "deedle," with a dish of "wobbly," as the expression goes, "to fill up the cracks." If he is wise he will learn to tolerate, and even enjoy, the diet, since there is nothing else to eat.

"Bonter," or natural food, is almost unknown on Arrabus. The problems involved in growing, distributing and preparing "bonter" for three billion persons is quite beyond the capacity of those who have resolutely eliminated toil from their lives. Occasionally "bonter" is a subject of wistful speculation but no one seems seriously troubled by its lack. A certain opprobrium attaches to the person who concerns himself overmuch with food. The casual visitor will refrain from grumbling unless he wishes to become known as a "guttrick." So much for the high cuisine of Arrabus; it fails to exist. A final note: intoxicants are not produced by any of the public agencies. Disselberg, who drank no wine, beer or spirit, declared against them as "social waste." Nevertheless, every day on every level of every block someone will be brewing a jug or two of "swill" from fragments of left-over gruff.

And another:

Every visitor to Wyst expects shocks and surprises, but never can he prepare himself for the sheer bogglement inflicted upon him by reality. He observes the endless blocks dwindling in strict conformity to the laws of perspective until finally they disappear; he stands on an overpass watching the flow of a hundred-foot man-river, with its sensitive float of white faces; he visits Disjerferact on the Uncibal mud flats, a place of carnival, whose attractions include a death house where folk so inclined deliver eloquent orations, then die by suicide to the applause of casual passersby; he watches a parade of shunk lurch fatefully toward the stadium. He asks himself, is any of this truly real, or even possible? He blinks; all is as before. But the incredibility still persists!

Perhaps he may depart the confines of Arrabus, to wander the misty forests to north and south: the so-called Weirdlands. As soon as he crosses the scarps, he finds himself in another world, which apparently exists only to reassure the Arrabins that their lot is truly a fortunate one. Hard to imagine that a thousand years ago these wastes were the provinces of dukes and princes. Trees conceal every trace of the former splendor. Wyst is a small world, only five thousand miles in diameter; a relatively few miles of travel takes one far around the horizons. If one travels south beyond the Weirdlands he comes at last to the shore of the Moaning Ocean, to find a land with a character all its own. Merely to watch the opal light of Dwan reflecting from the cold gray waves makes the journey well worth the effort.

The casual visitor to Wyst, however, seldom departs the cities of Arrabus, where he may presently feel an almost overpowering suffocation of numbers, a psychic claustrophobia. The subtle person becomes aware of a deeper darker presence, and he looks about him in fascination, with a crawling of the viscera, like a primeval man watching a cave mouth, certain that a horrid beast waits inside.

The Connatic smiled at the somewhat perfervid style of the report; he looked to see who had submitted it: Bonamico, the current cursar, a rather emotional man. Still—who could say? The Connatic himself had never visited Wyst; perhaps he might share Bonamico's comprehensions. He glanced at a final note, which was also signed by Bonamico:

Zumer and Pombal, the small continents, are mountainous and half frozen; they deserve mention only because they are home to the ill-natured shunk and the no less irascible folk who manage them.

Time pressed: in a few minutes the Connatic must meet with the Whispers. He gave the globe a final glance and set it spinning; so it would turn for days, until air friction brought it to a halt.

Returning aloft, the Connatic went directly to his dressing room, where he created that version of himself which he saw fit to present to the people of the Cluster: first a few touches of skin toner to accentuate the bones of jaw and temple; then film which darkened his eyes and enhanced their intensity; then a clip of simulated cartilege to raise the bridge of his nose and produce a more incisive thrust to his profile. He donned an austere suit of black, relieved only by a silver button at each shoulder, and finally pulled a casque of black fabric over his close-cropped mat of hair.

He touched a button; across the room appeared the holographic image of himself: a spare saturnine man of indeterminate age, with an aspect suggesting force and authority. With neither approval nor dissatisfaction he considered the image; he was, so to speak, dressed for work, in the uniform of his calling.

Esclavade's quiet voice issued from an unseen source. "The Whispers have arrived in the Black Parlor."

"Thank you." The Connatic stepped into the adjoining chamber: a replica of the Black Parlor, exact to the images of the Whispers themselves: three men and a woman dressed in that informal, rather frivolous, style current in contemporary Arrabus. The Connatic examined the images with care: a reconnaissance he made of almost every deputation, to offset, at least in part, the careful strategems by which the visitors hoped to further their aims. Uneasiness, rigidity, anger, easy calm, desperation, fatalistic torpor: the Connatic had learned to recognize the indicators and to judge the mood in which the delegations came to meet him.

In the Connatic's estimation, this seemed a particularly disparate group, despite the uniformity of their garments. Each presented a different psychological aspect, which frequently signaled disunity, or perhaps mutual antagonism. In the case of the Whispers, who were selected by an almost random process, such lack of inner cohesion might be without significance, or so the Connatic reflected.

The oldest of the group, a gray-haired man of no great stature, at first glance appeared the least effectual of the four. He sat awry: neck twisted, head askew, legs splayed, elbows cocked at odd angles: a man sinewy and gaunt, with a long-nosed vulpine face. He spoke in a restless, peevish voice: "— heights give me to fret; even here between four walls I know that the soil lies far below; we should have requested a conference at low altitude."

"Water lies below, not soil," growled another of the Whispers, a massive man with a rather surly expression. His hair, hanging in lank black ringlets, made no concession to the fashionable Arrabin puff; of the group he seemed the most forceful and resolute.

The third man said: "If the Connatic trusts his skin to these floors, never fear! Your own far less valuable pelt is safe."

"I fear nothing!" declared the old man. "Did I not climb the Pedestal? Did I not fly in the *Sea Disk* and the space ship?"

"True, true," said the third. "Your valor is famous." This was a man somewhat younger than the other two and notably well-favored, with a fine straight nose and a smiling debonair expression. He sat close beside the fourth Whisper, a round-faced woman with a pale, rather coarse, complexion and a square assertive jaw.

Esclavade entered the room. "The Connatic will give you his attention shortly. He suggests that meanwhile you might care to take refreshment." He waved toward the back wall; a buffet slid into the parlor. "Please serve yourselves; you will find that we have taken your preferences into account." Only the Connatic noticed the twitch at the corner of Esclavade's mouth.

Esclavade departed the parlor. The crooked old Whisper at once jumped to his feet. "Let's see what we have here." He sidled toward the buffet. "Eh? Eh? What's this? Gruff and deedle! Can the Connatic afford a trifle of bonter for our poor deprived jaws?"

The woman said in an even voice: "Surely he thinks it only courteous to serve familiar victuals to his guests."

The handsome man uttered a sardonic laugh. "The Connatic is hardly of egalistic persuasion. By definition he is the elite of the elite. There may be a message here."

The massive man went to the buffet and took a cake of gruff. "I eat it at home; I shall eat it here, and give the matter no thought."

The crooked man poured a cup of the viscous white liquid; he tasted, and made a wry grimace. "The deedle isn't all that good."

Smiling, the Connatic went to sit in a heavy wooden chair. He touched a button and his image appeared in the Black Parlor. The Whispers jerked around. The two men at the buffet slowly put down their food; the handsome man started to rise, then changed his mind and remained in his place.

Esclavade entered the Black Parlor and addressed the image.

"Sir, these are the Whispers of Arrabus Nation on Wyst. From Waunisse, the lady Fausgard." Then he indicated the massive man. "From Uncibal, the gentleman Orgold." The handsome man: "From Serce, the gentleman Lemiste." The crooked man: "From Propunce, the gentleman Delfin."

The Connatic said: "I welcome you to Lusz. You will notice that I appear before you in projection; this is my invariable precaution, and many uncertainties are circumvented."

Fausgard said somewhat tartly, "As a monomarch, and the elite of the elite, I suppose you go in constant fear of assassination."

"It is a very real risk. I see hundreds of folk, of every condition. Some, inevitably, prove to be madmen who fancy me a cruel and luxurious tyrant. I use an entire battery of techniques to avoid their murderous, if well-meant, assaults."

Fausgard gave her head a stubborn shake. The Connatic thought: Here is a woman of rock-hard conviction. Fausgard said: "Still, as absolute master of several trillion persons, you must recognize that yours is a position of unnatural privilege."

The Connatic thought: She is also of a somewhat contentious disposition. Aloud he said, "Naturally! The knowledge is never far from my mind, and is balanced, or neutralized, only by the fact of its total irrelevance."

"I fear that you leave me behind."

"The idea is complex, yet simple. I am I, who by reason of events beyond my control am Connatic. If I were someone else, I would not be Connatic; this is indisputable. The corol-

lary is also clear: there would be a Connatic who was not I.
He, like I, would ponder the singularity of his condition. So,
you see, I as Connatic discover no more marvelous privilege
to my life than you in your condition as Fausgard the Whisper."

Fausgard laughed uncertainly. She started to reply only to
be preceded by the suave Lemiste. "Sir, we are here not to
analyze your person, or your status, or the chances of fate. In
fact, as pragmatic egalists, we deny the existence of Fate, as
a supernormal or ineffable entity. Our mission is more specific."

"I shall be interested to hear it."

"Arrabus has existed one hundred years as an egalistic nation. We are unique in the Cluster, perhaps across the Gaean
universe. In a short time, at our Centenary festival, we
celebrate a century of achievement."

The Connatic reflected in some puzzlement: They take a
tone rather different from what I had expected! Once more:
take nothing, ever, for granted! He said: "I am of course
aware of the Centenary, and I am considering your kind invitation to be on hand."

Lemiste continued, in a voice somewhat quick and stac-
cato: "As you know we have constructed an enlightened society, dedicated to full egalism and individual fulfillment. We
are naturally anxious to advertise our achievements, both for
glory and for material benefit: hence our invitation. But let
me explain. Ordinarily the Connatic's presence at an egalistic
festival might be considered anomalous, even a compromise
of principle. We hope, however, that, should you choose to
attend, you will put aside your elitist role and for a period
become one with us: residing in our blocks, riding the man-
ways, attending the public spectacles. You will thereby apprehend our institutions on a personal basis."

After a moment's thoughtful silence the Connatic said:
"This is an interesting proposal. I must give it serious attention. You have taken refreshment? I could have offered you
more elaborate fare, but in view of your principles I
desisted."

Delfin, who had restlessly restrained his tongue, at last
broke forth. "Our principles are real enough! That is why we
are here: to advance them, but yet to protect them from their
own success. Everywhere in the Cluster live jackals and inter-
lopers, by the millions; they consider Arrabus a charitable
hospice, where they flock by the myriads to batten upon the

good things which we have earned through toil and sacrifice. It is done in the name of immigration, which we want to stop, but always we are thwarted by the Law of Free Movement. We have therefore certain demands that we feel—"

Fausgard quickly interrupted: "More properly: 'requests.' "

Delfin waved his arm in the air. "Demands, requests, it all comes out the same end! We want, first, a stop to immigration; second, Cluster funds to feed the hordes already on hand; third, new machinery to replace the equipment worn out nurturing the pests."

Delfin apparently was not popular with his fellow Whispers; each sought to suggest disassociation from Delfin's rather vulgar manners.

Fausgard spoke in a tone of brittle facetiousness: "Well then, Delfin; let's not bore the Connatic with a tirade."

Delfin slanted her a crooked grin. "Tirade, is it? When one talks of wolves, one does not describe mice. The Connatic values plain talk, so why sit here simpering with our fingers up our arses? Yes, yes, as you like. I'll hold my tongue." He squinted toward the Connatic. "I warn you, she'll use an hour to repeat what I gave you in twenty seconds."

Fausgard ignored the remark. "Sir, the Whisper Lemiste has spoken of our Centenary: this has been the primary purpose of our deputation. But other problems, to which Whisper Delfin has alluded, also exist, and perhaps we might also consider them at this time."

"By all means," said the Connatic. "It is my function to mitigate difficulties, if effectuation is fair, feasible and countenanced by Allastrid Basic Law."

Fausgard said earnestly, "Our problems can be expressed in very few words—"

Delfin could not restrain himself. "A single word is enough: immigrants! A thousand each week! Apes and lizards, airy aesthetes, languid ne'er-do-wells with nothing on their minds but girls and bonter. We are not allowed to halt them! Is it not absurd?"

Lemiste said smoothly: "Whisper Delfin is exuberant in his terms; many of the immigrants are worthy idealists. Still, many others are little better than parasites."

Delfin would not be denied. "Were they all saints, the flow must be halted! Would you believe it? An immigrant excluded me from my own apartment!"

Fausgard said wryly: "Here may be the source of Whisper Delfin's fervor."

Orgold spoke for the first time, in plangent disgust: "We sound like a gaggle of cackshaws."

The Connatic said reflectively: "A thousand a week in a population of three billion is not a large percentage."

Orgold replied in a business-like manner, which affected the Connatic more favorably than did Orgold's coarse and vaguely untidy appearance. "Our facilities already are overextended. At this moment we need eighteen new sturge plants—"

Lemiste helpfully inserted an annotation: " 'Sturge' is raw food-slurry."

"—a new deep layer of drains, tanks and feeders, a thousand new blocks. The toil involved is tremendous. The Arrabins do not wish to devote whole lifetimes to toil. So steps must be taken. First, and perhaps least—if only to quiet Delfin—the influx of immigrants must be halted."

"Difficult," said the Connatic. "Basic Law guarantees freedom of movement."

Delfin cried out: "Egalism is envied across the Cluster! Since all Alastor cannot come to Arrabus, then egalism must be spread across the Cluster. This should be your immediate duty!"

The Connatic showed the trace of a somber smile. "I must study your ideas with care. At the moment their logic eludes me."

Delfin muttered under his breath, and swung sulkily sideways in his chair. He snapped across his shoulder: "The logic is the immigrants' feet; in their multitudes they march on Arrabus!"

"A thousand a week? Ten times as many Arrabins commit suicide."

"Nothing is thereby proved!"

The Connatic gave an indifferent shrug and turned a dispassionate inspection around the group. Odd, he reflected, that Orgold, Lemiste and Fausgard, while patently uninterested in Delfin's views, should allow him to act as spokesman, and to present absurd demands, thereby diminishing the dignity of them all. Lemiste's perceptions were perhaps the keenest of the group. He managed a deprecatory smile. "The Whispers are necessarily strong-minded, and we do not always agree on how best to solve our problems."

Fausgard said shortly: "Or even to identify them, for that matter."

Lemiste paid her no heed. "In essence, our machinery is

obsolescent. We need new equipment, to produce more goods more efficiently."

"Are you then requesting a grant of money?"

"This certainly would help, on a continuing basis."

"Why not reclaim the lands to north and south? At one time they supported a population."

Lemiste gave his head a dubious shake. "Arrabins are an urban folk; we know nothing of agriculture."

The Connatic rose to his feet. "I will send expert investigators to Arrabus. They will analyze your situation and make recommendations."

Tension broke loose in Fausgard; she exclaimed sharply: "We don't want investigators or study commissions; they'll tell us: 'Do this! Do that!'—all contra-egalistic! We want no more competition and greed; we can't abandon our gains!"

"Be assured that I will personally study the matter," said the Connatic.

Orgold dropped his air of stolid detachment. "Then you will come to Wyst?"

"Remember," Lemiste called out cheerfully, "you are invited to participate at the Centenary!"

"I will consider the invitation most carefully. Now then, I noticed you showed only small interest in the collation I set forth; you might prefer a more adventurous cuisine, and I wish you to be my guests. Along the lower promenades are hundreds of excellent restaurants; please dine where you like and instruct the attendant to place all charges to the Connatic's account."

"Thank you," said Fausgard rather tersely. "That is most gracious."

The Connatic turned to go, then halted as if on sudden thought. "By the way, who is Jantiff Ravensroke?"

The Whispers stared at him in frozen attitudes of doubt and wonder. Lemiste said at last: "Jantiff Ravensroke? I do not recognize the name."

"Nor I!" cried Delfin, hoarse and truculent.

Fausgard numbly shook her head and Orgold merely gazed impassively at a point above the Connatic's head.

Lemiste asked: "Who is this 'Jantiff'?"

"A person who has corresponded with me; it is no great matter. If I visit Arrabus I will take the trouble to look him up. Good evening to you all."

His image moved into the shadows at the side of the room, and faded.

In the dressing room the Connatic removed his casque. "Esclavade?"

"Sir?"

"What do you think of the Whispers?"

"An odd group. I detect voice tremor in Fausgard and Lemiste. Orgold's assurance is impervious to tension. Delfin lacks all restraint. The name 'Jantiff Ravensroke' may not be unfamiliar to them."

"There is a mystery here," said the Connatic. "Certainly they did not travel all the way from Wyst to make a series of impossible proposals, quite at odds to their stated purposes."

"I agree. Something has altered their viewpoint."

"I wonder if there is a connection with Jantiff Ravensroke?"

Chapter 2

••••⟶◆⟵••••

Jantiff Ravensroke had been born in comfortable circumstances at Frayness on Zeck, Alastor 503. His father, Lile Ravensroke, calibrated micrometers at the Institute of Molecular design; his mother held a part-time job as technical analyst at Orion Instruments. Two sisters, Ferfan and Juille, specialized respectively in a sub-phase of condaptery* and the carving of mooring posts.**

At the junior academy Jantiff, a tall thin young man with a long bony face and lank black hair, trained first in graphic design, then, after a year, reoriented himself into chromatics and perceptual psychology. At senior school he threw himself into the history of creative imagery, despite the opinion of his

---

* From the Gaean *condaptriol:* the science of information management, which includes the more restricted field of cybernetics.

** Zeck is a world of a hundred thousand islands scattered across a hundred seas, inlets and channels; the single continent is mottled with lakes and waterways. Many families live aboard houseboats, and often own a sea-sailer as well. Mooring posts are ornate constructions, symbolic of status, profession, or special interests.

family that he was spreading himself too thin. His father pointed out that he could not forever delay taking a specialty, that unrelated enthusiasms, while no doubt entertaining, would seem to merge into frivolity and even irresponsibility.

Jantiff listened with dutiful attention, but soon thereafter he chanced upon an old manual of landscape painting, which insisted that only natural pigments could adequately depict natural objects; and, further, that synthetic substances, being bogus and unnatural, subconsciously influenced the craftsman and inevitably falsified his work. Jantiff found the argument convincing and began to collect, grind and blend umbers and ochers, barks, roots, berries, the glands of fish and the secretions of nocturnal rodents, while his family looked on in amusement.

Lile Ravensroke again felt obliged to correct Jantiff's instability. He took an oblique approach to the topic. "I take it that you are not reconciled to a life of abject poverty?"

Jantiff, naturally mild and guileless, with occasional lapses into absent-mindedness, responded without hesitation: "Certainly not! I very much enjoy the good things of life!"

Lile Ravensroke went on, in a casual voice: "I expect that you intend to earn these good things not by crime or fraud but through your own good efforts?"

"Of course!" said Jantiff, now somewhat puzzled. "That goes without saying."

"Then how do you expect to profit from your training to date: which is to say, a smattering of this and an inkling of that? 'Expertise' is the word you must concentrate upon! Sure control over a special technique: this is how you put coin in your pocket!"

In a subdued voice Jantiff stated that he had not yet discovered a specialty which he felt would interest him across the entire span of his existence. Lile Ravensroke replied that to his almost certain knowledge no divine fiat had ever ordained that toil must be joyful or interesting. Aloud Jantiff acknowledged the rightness of his father's views, but privately clung to the hope that somehow he might turn his frivolity to profit.

Jantiff finished his term at senior school with no great distinction, and the summer recess lay before him. During these few brief months he must define the course of his future: specialized study at the lyceum, or perhaps apprenticeship as a technical draftsman. It seemed that youth, with all its joyful vagaries, lay definitely behind! In a morose mood Jantiff hap-

pened to pick up the old treatise on the depiction of landscapes, and there he encountered a tantalizing passage:

> For certain craftsmen, the depiction of landscapes be-
> comes a lifelong occupation. Many interesting examples
> of the craft exist. Remember: the depiction reflects not
> only the scene itself but the craftsman's private point of
> view!
> Another aspect to the craft must at least be men-
> tioned: sunlight. The basic adjunct to the visual process
> varies from world to world, from a murky red glow to a
> crackling purple-white glare. Each of these lights makes
> necessary a different adjustment of the subjective-objec-
> tive tension. Travel, especially trans-planetary travel, is a
> most valuable training for the depictive craftsman. He
> learns to look with a dispassionate eye; he clears away
> films of illusion and sees objects as they are.
> There is one world where sun and atmosphere cooper-
> ate to produce an absolutely glorious light, where every
> surface quivers with its true and just color. The sun is
> the white star Dwan and the fortunate world is Wyst,
> Alastor 1716.

Juille and Ferfan decided to cure Jantiff of his wayward
moods. They diagnosed his problem as shyness, and introduced him to a succession of bold and sometimes boisterous
girls, in the hope of enhancing his social life. The girls quickly
became either bored, puzzled or uneasy. Jantiff was neither
ill-favored, with his black hair, blue-green eyes and almost
aquiline profile, nor shy; nevertheless he lacked talent for
small talk, and he suspected, justly enough, that his unconventional yearnings would only excite derision were he rash
enough to discuss them.

To avoid a fashionable social function, Jantiff, without in-
forming his sisters, took himself off to the family houseboat,
which was moored at a pier on the Shard Sea. Fearful that
either Juille or Ferfan or both might come out to fetch him,
Jantiff immediately cast off the mooring lines and drove
across Fallas Bay to the shallows, where he anchored his boat
among the reeds.

Solitude the peace at last, thought Jantiff. He boiled up a
pot of tea, then settled into a chair on the foredeck and
watched the orange sun Mur settle toward the horizon. Late-
afternoon breeze rippled the water; a million orange corusca-

tions twinkled among the slender black reeds. Jantiff's mood loosened; the quiet, wide sky, the play of sunlight on the water were balm to his uncertain soul. If only he could capture the peace of this moment and maintain it forever! Sadly he shook his head: life and time were inexorable; the moment must pass. A photograph was useless, and pigment could never reproduce such space, such glitter and glow. Here in fact was the very essence of his yearnings: he wanted to control that magic linkage between the real and the unreal, the felt and the seen. He wanted to pervade himself with the secret meaning of things and use this lore as the mood took him. These "secret meanings" were not necessarily profound or subtle; they simply were what they were. Like the present circumstances for instance: the mood of late afternoon, the boat among the reeds, with—perhaps most important of all—the lonely figure on the deck. In his mind Jantiff composed a depiction, and went so far as to select pigments. . . . He sighed and shook his head. An impractical idea. Even were he able to achieve such a representation, what could he do with it? Hang it on a wall? Absurd. Successive viewings would neutralize the effect as fast as repetition of a joke.

The sun sank; water moths fluttered among the reeds. From seaward came the sound of quiet voices in measured discussion. Jantiff listened intently, eerie twinges coursing along his skin. No one could explain the sea-voices. If a person tried to drift stealthily near in a boat the sounds ceased. And the meaning, no matter how intently one listened, always just evaded intelligibility. The sea voices had always haunted Jantiff. Once, he had recorded the sounds, but when he played them back, the sense was even more remote. Secret meanings, mused Jantiff. . . . He strained to listen. If he could comprehend, only a word so as to pick up the gist, then he might understand everything. As if becoming aware of the eavesdropper, the voices fell silent, and night darkened the sea.

Jantiff went into the cabin. He dined on bread, meat and beer, then returned to the deck. Stars blazed across the sky; Jantiff sat watching, his mind adrift among the far places, naming those stars he recognized, speculating about others.*

* For the folk of Alastor Cluster, the stars are near and familiar, and "astronomy" (star-naming) is taught to all children. A knowledgeable person can name a thousand stars or more, with as many apposite anecdotes. Such star-namers in the olden times commanded great fame and prestige.

So much existed: so much to be felt and seen and known! A single life was not enough. . . . Across the water drifted a murmur of voices, and Jantiff imagined pale shapes floating in the dark, watching the stars. . . . The voices dwindled and faded. Silence. Once more Jantiff retreated into the cabin, where he boiled up another pot of tea.

Someone had left a copy of the *Transvoyer* on the table. Leafing through the pages Jantiff's attention was caught by a heading:

THE ARRABIN CENTENARY: *A Remarkable Era of Social Innovation on the Planet Wyst: Alastor 1716*

Your Transvoyer correspondent visits Uncibal, the mighty city beside the sea. Here he discovers a dynamic society, propelled by novel philosophical energies. The Arrabin goal is human fulfillment, in a condition of leisure and amplitude. How has this miracle been accomplished? By a drastic revision of traditional priorities. To pretend that racks and stress do not exist would cheapen the Arrabin achievement, which shows no signs of flagging. The Arrabins are about to celebrate their first century. Our correspondent supplies the fascinating details.

Jantiff read the article with more than casual interest; Wyst rejoiced in the remarkable light of the sun Dwan, where— how did the phrase go?—"every surface quivers with its true and just color." He put the magazine aside, and went once more out upon the deck. The stars had moved somewhat across the sky; that constellation known locally as the "Shamizade" had risen in the east and was reflected on the sea. Jantiff inspected the heavens, wondering which star was Dwan. Stepping back into the cabin, he consulted the local edition of the Alastor Almanac, where Dwan was identified as a dim white star in the Turtle constellation, along the edge of the carapace.*

---

* It is no doubt unnecessary to point out that constellations as seen from one world of the Cluster differ from those of every other; accordingly, each world uses its local nomenclature. On the other hand, certain structural features of the Cluster—for instance, the Fiamifer, the Crystal Eel, Koon's Hole, the Goodby Place—are terms in the common usage.

Jantiff climbed to the top deck of the houseboat and scanned the sky. There, to the north, under the Stator hung the Turtle, and there shone the pale flicker of Dwan. Perhaps imagination played Jantiff tricks, but the star indeed seemed charged with color.

The information regarding Wyst might have been only of idle interest, had not Jantiff on the very next day noticed an advertisement sponsored by Central Space Transport Systems, announcing a promotional competition. For that depiction best illustrating the scenic charm of Zeck, the System would provide transportation to and from any world of the Cluster, with an additional three hundred ozols spending money. Jantiff instantly assembled panel and pigments and from memory rendered the shallows of the Shard Sea, with the houseboat at anchor among the reeds. Time was short; he worked in a fury of concentrated energy, and submitted the composition to the agency only minutes before the deadline.

Three days later he was notified, not altogether to his surprise, that he had won the grand prize.

Jantiff waited until evening to break the news to his family. They were astounded both that Jantiff's daubings could command value and that he yearned for far strange worlds. Jantiff tried earnestly to explain his motives. "Naturally I'm not unhappy at home; how could I be? I'm just at loose ends. I can't settle myself. I have the feeling that just out of sight, just past the corner of my eye, something new and shimmering and wonderful waits for me—if only I knew where to look!"

His mother sniffed. "Really, Jantiff, you're so fanciful."

Lile Ravenstroke asked sadly: "Haven't you any ambition for a normal and ordinary life? No shimmering flapdoodle, just honest work and a happy home?"

"I don't know what my ambitions are! That's the entire difficulty. My best hope is to get away for a bit and see something of the Cluster. Then perhaps I'll be able to settle down."

His mother in distress cried, "You'll go far from here and make your career, and we'll never see you again!"

Jantiff gave an uneasy laugh. "Of course not! I plan nothing so stern! I'm restless and uneasy; I want to see how other people live so that I can decide how I want to live myself."

Lile Ravensroke said somberly: "When I was young I had similar notions. For better or worse, I put them aside and now I feel sure that I acted for the best. There's nothing out there that isn't better at home."

Ferfan said to Jantiff, "There'll never be sour-grass pie, or brunts, or shushings the way mother cooks."

"I'm prepared to rough it for a bit. I might even like the exotic foods."

"Ugh," said Juille. "They all sound so odd and rank."

The group sat silent for a moment. Then: "If you feel you must go," said Juille's father, "our arguments won't dissuade you."

"It's really for the best," said Jantiff hollowly. "Then, when I come back, with the wander-dust off my heels, I'll hopefully be settled and definite, and you'll be proud of me."

"But Janty, we're proud of you now," said Ferfan without any great conviction.

Juille asked: "Where will you go, and what will you do?"

Jantiff spoke with spurious joviality: "Where will I go? Here, there, everywhere! And what will I do? Everything! Anything! All for the sake of experience. I'll try the carbuncle mines on Arcady; I'll visit the Connatic at Lusz; perhaps I'll drop at Arrabus and spend a few weeks with the emancipated folk."

" 'Emancipated folk' ?" growled Lile Ravensroke. "A twittering brook of dilly-bugs is more likely."

"Well, that's their claim. They only work thirteen hours a week, and it seems to agree with them."

Juille cried: "You'll settle in Arrabus and become emancipated and we'll never see you again!"

"My dear girl, there is not the slightest chance of such a thing."

"Then don't go to Wyst! The Transvoyer article said that people arrive from everywhere and never leave."

Ferfan, who also cherished secret dreams of travel, said wistfully: "If it's such a wonderful place, perhaps we'd all better go there."

Her father laughed humorlessly. "I can't spare the time from work."

Chapter 3

Arriving at Uncibal on a rainy night Jantiff was reminded of a paragraph in the *Alastrid Gazeteer*: "Across many years wise travelers have learned to discount their first impression of a new environment. Such judgments are derived from previous experience in previous places and are infallibly distorted." On this dismal evening Uncibal Space-port lacked every quaint or charming quality, and Jantiff wondered why a system which for a century had gratified uncounted Arrabins could not better promote the comfort of a relatively few visitors.

Two hundred and fifty passengers, debarking from the spaceships, found themselves alone in the gloom, a quarter-mile from a line of low blue lights which presumably marked the terminal building. Muttering and grumbling the passengers squelched off through the puddles.*

Jantiff walked to the side of the straggling troop, thrilling to contact with alien soil. From the direction of Uncibal drifted a waft of odor, oddly sour and heavy, yet half-familiar, which only served to emphasize the strangeness of the world Wyst.

At the terminal a droning voice addressed the newcomers: "Welcome to Arrabus. We distinguish three types of visitors: first, commercial representatives and tourists intending brief visits; second, persons planning sojourns of less than a year; third, immigrants. Please form orderly queues at the designated doorways. Attention: the import of food-stuffs is prohibited. All such items must be surrendered at the Contraband Property desk. Welcome to Arrabus. We distinguish three types of visitors. . . ."

Jantiff pushed through the crowds; apparently several hundred arrivals from a previous ship still waited in the reception hall. Eventually he discovered the file marked 2,

* See Glossary, No. 2.

which snaked back and forth across the room in a most confusing manner, and took his place in the line. Most arriving persons, he noted, intended immigration, and the queue in File 3 stretched several times as far as that in File 2. The queue in File 1 was very short indeed.

Step by sidling step Jantiff crossed the room. At the far end an array of eight wickets controlled the movement of the new arrivals, but only two of these wickets were in operation. A corpulent man, immediately behind Jantiff, thought to hasten the motion of the line by standing close to Jantiff and pressing with his belly. When Jantiff, to avoid the contact, moved as close as convenient to the person ahead, the corpulent man promptly inched forward, to squeeze Jantiff even more closely. The man ahead at last looked around at Jantiff and said in a cold voice: "Really, sir, I am as anxious as you to negotiate this file; no matter how you press the line moves no faster."

Jantiff could offer no explanation which would not offend the corpulent man, who now stood so close that his breath warmed Jantiff's cheek. Finally, when the man ahead stepped forward, Jantiff resolutely held his ground, despite the fat man's breathing and jostling.

Ultimately Jantiff arrived at the wicket, where he presented his landing pass. The clerk, a young woman with extravagant puffs of blond hair over her ear, thrust it aside. "That's not correct! Where is your green clearance card?"

Jantiff fumbled through his pockets. "I don't seem to have any green card. They gave me no such document."

"Sir, you'll have to go back to the ship for your green clearance card."

Jantiff chanced to notice that the fat man carried a white card similar to his own. In desperation he said: "This man here has no green card either."

"That's a matter of no relevance. I can't allow you entry unless you present the proper documents."

"This was all they gave me; surely it's sufficient?"

"Sir, please, you're obstructing the line."

In numb dismay Jantiff stared at his white card. "It says here, 'Landing pass and clearance card.' "

The clerk looked at it sidelong, and made a clicking sound with her tongue. She went to the second booth and conferred with the clerk, who made a telephone call.

The blond girl returned to the wicket. "This is a new form; it was introduced only last month. I haven't drudged this office for a year and I've been sending everyone back to the ship. Your questionnaire, please—no, the blue sheet."

Jantiff produced the proper document: an intricate form which he had painstakingly completed.

"Hm . . . Jantiff Ravensroke . . . Frayness, on Zeck. Occupation: technical graphics expert. Reason for visit: curiosity." She glanced at him with raised eyebrows. "Curiosity? About what?"

Jantiff hurriedly said: "I want to study the Arrabin social system."

"Then you should have written 'study.' "

"I'll change it."

"No, you can't alter the document; you'll have to fill out a new form. Somewhere in the outer chambers you'll find blank forms and a desk; at least that's how it went a year ago."

"Wait!" cried Jantiff. "After 'curiosity' I'll write: 'about Arrabin social system.' There's plenty of room, and that's not alteration."

"Oh, very well. It's not regular, of course."

Jantiff quickly made the entry and the clerk reached for the validation stamp. A gong sounded; she dropped the stamp, rose to her feet and went to the back of the wicket where she tossed a cape around her shoulders. A young man entered the wicket: round-faced, boyish, his eyelids drooping as if from lack of sleep. "Here I am!" he told the blond girl. "A trifle late, but that's not too bad; I've only just returned from a swill at Serce and directly to drudge. Still, I might as well recover on drudge as off. Come to think, it's the best way."

"Lucky you. I'm low tomorrow. I'll probably draw sanitation or greasing the rollers."

"I drew a shoe machine last week; it's really rather amusing once you learn which handles to pull. Halfway through my stint the circuits went wrong and the shoes all came away with funny big toes. I sent them on anyway, in hopes of launching a new style. Think of it! Maybe I'll be famous!"

"Small chance. Who wants to wear funny shoes with big toes?"

"Somebody had better want to wear them; they've gone into boxes."

The fat man called over Jantiff's shoulder: "Can't we hurry things just a bit? Everyone's anxious to rest and have a bite of food."

The two clerks turned him identical stares of blank incomprehension. The girl picked up her handbag. "Off to bed for me. I'm too tired even to copulate."

"I know those days. . . . Well, I suppose I'd better be earning my gruff." He stepped forward and picked up Jantiff's papers. "Now then, let's see . . . . First, I'll need your green entry card."

"I don't have any green card."

"No green card? Then, my friend, you'd better get one. I know that much, at least. Just run back to the ship and locate the purser; he'll fix you up in a jiffy."

"This white card supercedes the green card."

"Oh, is that how they do it now? Good enough then. So now, what else? The blue questionnaire: I won't bother with that; it's boring for both of us. You'll want a housing assignment. Do you have any preferences?"

"Not really. Where would you suggest?"

"Uncibal, of course. Here's a decent location." He gave Jantiff a metal disk. "Go to Block 17-882 and show this disk to the floor clerk." He lifted the stamp and gave Jantiff's papers a resounding blow. "There you are, my friend! I wish you the enjoyment of your bed, the digestion of your gruff and lucky draws from the drudge barrel."

"Thank you. Can I spend the night in the hotel? Or must I go to Block 17-whatever-it-is?"

"The Travelers Inn by all means, if you've got the ozols.* The man-ways are wet tonight. It's no time to be seeking out a block."

The Travelers Inn, an ancient bulk with a dozen wings and annexes, stood directly opposite the terminal exit. Jantiff entered the lobby and applied at the desk for a chamber. The clerk handed him a key: "That will be seven ozols, sir."

Jantiff leaned back aghast. "Seven ozols? For one room with one bed? For a single night?"

"Correct, sir."

Jantiff reluctantly paid over the money. When he saw the chamber he became more indignant than ever; in Frayness such a room would be considered minimal and rent for an ozol or less.

Returning downstairs to the restaurant, Jantiff seated him-

---

* Ozols: a monetary unit roughly equivalent to the Gaean SVU: the value of an adult's unskilled labor under standard conditions for the duration of an hour.

self at one of the enameled concrete counters. An attendant placed a covered tray in front of him.

"Not so fast," said Jantiff. "Let me look at the menu."

"No menu here, my friend. It's gruff and deedle, with a bit of wobbly to fill in the chinks. We all eat alike."

Jantiff lifted the cover from the tray; he found four cakes of baked brown dough, a mug of white liquid and a bowl of yellow paste. Jantiff tasted the "gruff"; the flavor was mild and not unpleasant. The "deedle" was tart and faintly astringent, while the "wobbly" seemed a simple custard.

Jantiff finished his meal and the attendant gave him a slip of paper. "Please pay at the main desk."

Jantiff glanced at the slip in wonder. "Two ozols. Can this price be correct?"

"The price may not be 'correct,'" said the attendant. "Still it's the price we exact here at the Travelers Inn."

A cavernous bathroom was shared by both sexes, personal modesty having succumbed to egalism. Jantiff diffidently made use of the facilities, wondering what his mother would say, then thankfully retired to his chamber.

In the morning, after Wyst's short night, Jantiff rose from his bed to find Dwan already halfway up the sky. Jantiff looked out across the city in great interest, studying the play of light among the blocks and along the man-ways. Each of the blocks showed a different color, and, possibly because Jantiff was bringing to bear an expectant vision, the colors seemed peculiarly rich and clean, as if they had just been washed.

Jantiff dressed and, descending to the ground floor, took advice from the desk clerk as to the location of Block 17-882. Giving the restaurant and its two-ozol breakfast a wide berth, Jantiff set off along the man-way: a sliding surface thronged with Arrabins, rapid toward the center, slow at the edges.

Dwan-light illuminated the city-scape to either side in a manner Jantiff found entrancing, and his spirits rose.

The man-way curved westward; the blocks in lines to right and left marched away to the horizon, dwindling to points. Laterals poured human streams upon the man-way; Jantiff had never imagined such vast crowds: a marvelous spectacle in itself! The city Uncibal must be reckoned one of the wonders of the Gaean universe! Across his course at right angles slid another of the mighty Arrabin man-rivers: a pair of boulevards flowing in opposite directions. Jantiff glimpsed

rank behind rank of men and women riding with faces curiously serene.

The man-way swerved and joined another, larger, man-
way. Jantiff began to watch the overhanging signs which gave
warning of lead-offs. He diverted to a slow neighborhood
feeder and presently stepped off in front of a weathered pink
block, two hundred feet square and twenty-three stories high.
Block 17-882, his designated home.

Jantiff paused to inspect the face of the structure. The surface paint, peeling off in areas, showed blotches of pink, old
rose and pale pink which gave the block a raffish and restless
air, in contrast to its neighbor, which was painted a supercili-
ous blue. Jantiff found the color congenial and congratulated
himself on the lucky chance of his allotment. Like all the
other blocks, the walls showed no windows, nor any openings
except for the entrance. Over the parapet surrounding the
roof hung foliage from the roof garden. Constant traffic
passed in and out of the portal: men, women and a few children, in identical garments, of colors somewhat too garish for
Jantiff's taste, as if the folk were dressed for a carnival. Their
faces likewise were gay; they laughed and chattered and
walked jauntily; Jantiff's spirits rose to look at them, and his
misgivings began to dwindle.

Jantiff passed into the lobby and approached the desk. He
presented his requisition to the clerk, a short round-bodied
man with gingery hair arranged in ear-puffs and elaborate
love-locks. The round cheerful face instantly became petulant. "My aching bowels! Is it yet another immigrant?"

"No, indeed," said Jantiff with dignity. "I am a visitor."

"What's the odds? You're one more cup of water in the
full bucket. Why don't you start an Egalism Society on your
own world?"

Jantiff replied politely: "People aren't so inclined on Zeck."

"Neither Zeck nor the whole elitist covey! We can't absorb
their ne'er-do-wells indefinitely. Our machines break down, so
what happens when the sturge stops and there's no more
wump? We'll all go hungry together."

Jantiff's jaw dropped. "Are there really that many immigrants?"

"Too true! A thousand each and every week!"

"But surely some of them leave?"

"Not enough! Only six hundred, or hopefully seven; still,
hope won't mend machines." He handed Jantiff a key. "Your

roommate will show you the wumper, and explain the rules. You'll receive a drudge schedule this afternoon."

Jantiff said tentatively: "I'd prefer a single apartment, if any are available."

"You've got a single apartment," said the clerk. "It comes with two beds. If the population rises another billion we'll put in hammocks. Floor 19, Apartment D 18. I'll call up and mention that you're coming."

The ascensor conveyed Jantiff to the nineteenth floor. He found Corridor D and presently arrived at Apartment 18. He hesitated, raised his hand to knock, then decided that under the circumstances he was entitled to effect his own entry; accordingly he touched his key to the latch plate. The door slid aside to reveal a sitting room furnished with a pair of low couches, a table, a set of cases and a wall screen. A patterned beige and black rug covered the floor; from the ceiling hung a dozen globes fashioned from wire and colored paper. On one of the couches sat a man and a woman, both considerably older than Jantiff.

Jantiff stepped forward, feeling a trifle sheepish. "I'm Jantiff Ravensroke, and I've been assigned to this apartment."

The man and the woman showed gracious smiles and jumped smartly to their feet. (Later, when Jantiff recalled his sojourn at Uncibal, he never failed to reflect upon the careful etiquette by which the Arrabins eased the circumstances of their lives.)

The man was tall and elegant, with a fine straight nose and flashing eyes. He wore his black hair in glossy ear-puffs, with artful cusps down the forehead; of the two he seemed the more forthright. He gave Jantiff a friendly salute which conveyed nothing of the desk clerk's disapproval. "Welcome to Arrabus, Jantiff! Welcome to Old Pink and to this excellent apartment!"

"Thank you very much," said Jantiff. This affable and intelligent man was evidently to be his roommate and Jantiff's misgivings dissolved.

"Allow me to perform the introductions. This lady is the miraculous Skorlet, a person of charm and capability, and I am Esteban."

Skorlet spoke in a quick husky voice: "You seem clean and quiet, and I'm sure that we'll have no difficulties. Please don't whistle in the apartment, or inquire the purpose of my work more than once, or belch loudly. I can't abide a belching man."

With an effort Jantiff maintained his sangfroid. Here was a situation which he had not anticipated. With desperate facility he said: "I'll keep your remarks very much in mind." He surveyed Skorlet from the corner of his eye. An introverted woman, he thought, perhaps a bit tense. She stood almost as tall as he was with rather heavy arms and legs. Her face was pale and round; her features were unremarkable except for the eyes glowing under strong black eyebrows. She wore her ear-puffs small, with black curls piled in a heap above: a woman neither comely nor yet repulsive. She might not be so easy a roommate as Esteban, however. He said: "I hope you won't find me too difficult."

"I'm sure not. You seem a nice lad. Esteban, borrow three mugs from the wumper; I'll pour out a taste of swill* to mark the occasion. You brought in a pack or two of bonter, or so I hope?"

"Sorry," said Jantiff. "The idea never occurred to me."

Esteban went off on his errand; Skorlet rummaged under the case and brought out a jug. "Please don't think me non-mutual.** I just can't believe that an occasional jug of swill will destroy Arrabus. You're sure there's not even a trace of bonter in your luggage?"

"I don't carry any luggage; only this handbag."

"Pity. There's nothing like pickles and pepper sausage to advance the swill. While we're waiting, I'll show you your bed."

Jantiff followed her into a small square chamber, furnished with two wardrobes, two cases, a table, now cluttered with Skorlet's small belongings, and two cots separated by a flimsy curtain. Skorlet brushed the trinkets to one side of the table. "Your half," she said, "and your bed." She jerked her thumb. "During my drudge the apartment is at your disposal, should you wish to entertain a friend, and vice versa. Things work out well unless we draw the same stint, but that's not too often."

"Aha, yes, I see," said Jantiff.

Esteban returned with three blue glass mugs; Skorlet solemnly poured them full. "To the Centenary!" she called in a brassy voice. "May the Connatic do his duty!"

Jantiff drank down the murky liquid and controlled a gri-

* The illicit Arrabin intoxicant: a heavy beer prepared from salvaged gruff, industrial glucose and sometimes tar-pods from the roof garden.
** Mutuality: the Arrabin code of conduct, with force deriving not from abstraction, or tradition, but from mutuality of interest.

mace at the aftertaste, which he associated with mice and old mattresses.

"Very bold," said Esteban approvingly. "Very bold indeed. You have an active thumb for the swill!"

"Yes, very good," said Jantiff. "And when does the Centenary occur?"

"Shortly—a matter of a few months. There's to be a simply explosive festival, with free games and dancing along the ways, and probably no end of swill. I'll surely put down a good supply. Esteban, can't you scrounge me a dozen jugs?"

"My dear, I've drawn the vitamin stint only once, and the Mutual stood right on top of me, watching my every move. I was lucky to capture the two of them."

"Then we must do without swill."

"Can't you use a plastic bag?" Jantiff suggested. "After all, the container need not be rigid."

Esteban ruefully shook his head. "It's been tried many times; our plastic bags all leak."

Skorlet said: "Old Sarp has a jug which he's too parsimonious to use. I'll have Kedidah put the snerge on it. That's three jugs at least. Now where's the gruff?"

"I'll contribute from lunch," said Esteban.

"If it's needed," said Jantiff, "I will too."

Skorlet looked at him approvingly. "That the spirit! Who said the immigrants are lampreys sucking our juices? Not the case with Jantiff!"

Esteban said meditatively: "I know a chap in Purple Vendetta who taps sturge from the pipe and he makes a very fierce swill indeed. I might just promote a bucket or two of raw sturge; it's worth the experiment."

Jantiff asked: "What is 'sturge'?"

"Simple food pulp. It's piped out from the central plant. In the kitchen it magically becomes gruff, deedle and wobbly. No reason why it shouldn't make good swill."

Skorlet carefully poured each of the three mugs half full. "Well—once again to the Festival, and may the Connatic put all would-be immigrants to work making pickles and pepper sausage, for consignment to Uncibal!"

"And let the Propuncers gnaw last week's gruff!"

"Save some for the Connatic. He can be as egal as the rest of us."

"Oh, he'll dine on bonter at the Travelers Inn; no fear of that."

Jantiff asked: "Is the Connatic actually coming to the Festival?"

Skorlet shrugged. "The Whispers are going out to Lusz to invite him, but who knows what he'll say?"

"He won't come," said Esteban. "Total fool he'd feel at the ceremony, with everybody screaming 'Hurrah for egalism!' and 'Egalism for the Cluster!' "

"And 'Low drudge for the Connatic, just like the rest of us!' "

"Exactly. What could he say?"

"Oh, something like, 'My dear subjects, I'm disappointed that you haven't laid red velvet along Uncibal River for my delicate feet. Now it's not well known, and I'd never reveal it anywhere but here on Arrabus, but I'm actually a chwig.* I command that you fill me a tank with your best bonter.' "

Half amused, half scandalized, Jantiff protested: "Really, you do him injustice! He lives a most sedate life!"

Skorlet sneered. "That's all smarm from his Bureau of Acclamation. Who knows what the Connatic's really like?"

Esteban drained his blue glass mug and looked in calculation toward the jug.

"We all know that the Connatic often disappears from Lusz. Now I've heard—this is admittedly rumor, but where there's smoke there's fire—that during these exact intervals, and only during these intervals, Bosko Boskowitz** makes his depredations. This correspondence has been thoroughly researched, so I've heard, and there's no doubt about it."

"Interesting!" said Skorlet. "Doesn't Bosko Boskowitz maintain a secret palace among the starments staffed only with beautiful children, who must obey his every whim?"

"That's the case! And isn't it odd that the Whelm never interferes with Bosko Boskowitz?"

"More than odd! That's why I say: 'Egalism across the Cluster!' "

Jantiff said in disgust: "I don't believe a word of it."

Skorlet laughed her gloomy laugh. "You're young and naïve."

"As to that I can't say."

"No matter." Skorlet peered into the jug. "I suppose we might as well put a term to it."

* Reference to a peculiar vice associated with food, encountered almost exclusively on Wyst.

** An almost fabulous starmenter, guilty of the most atrocious ravages. See Glossary #3.

"Excellent idea!" declared Esteban. "The strength is always at the bottom of the jug."

Skorlet raised her head. "No time now; there goes the gong. Let's go for wump. Then, afterwards, why not conduct our new friend around the city?"

"Certainly! I'm always ready for a promenade! It's a fine day after the rain. And what of Tanzel? We could pick her up along the way."

"Yes, of course. Poor little dear; I haven't seen her for days. I'll call her right now." She went to the screen, but pushed buttons in vain. "It still won't go! Idiotic thing! There's been maintenance on it twice!"

Jantiff went to the screen, touched the buttons, listened. He slipped up the retainer ring and lowered the screen upon its hinge.

Skorlet and Esteban came to look over his shoulder. "Do you understand these things?"

"Not really. As children, we're trained to elementary circuits, but I haven't gone much further. Still, this is very simple equipment; all plug-ins, and the telltale shows when they're bad. . . . Hm. These are all in order. Look here; this filter bank isn't slotted accurately. Try now."

The screen glowed. Skorlet said bitterly: "The maintenance fellow studied his instruction book for two hours and still couldn't do the job."

"Oh well," said Esteban, "he was just someone like me on high drudge."

Skorlet merely gave a sour grunt. She touched buttons, and spoke to the woman whose face appeared. "Tanzel, please."

A girl nine or ten years old looked forth from the screen. "Hello, Mother. Hello, Father."

"We're dropping by in about an hour, and we'll go for a nice promenade. Will you be ready?"

"Oh, yes! I'll wait in front."

"Good! In just about an hour."

The three turned to go. Jantiff stopped short. "I'll just put my bag in the wardrobe; no harm starting out tidy at least."

Esteban clapped Jantiff on the shoulder. "I think you've got a jewel here, Skorlet."

"Oh, I suppose he'll do."

As they walked along the corridor Jantiff asked, "What happened to your last roommate?"

"I don't know," said Skorlet. "She went out one day and never came back."

"How strange!"

"I suppose so. No one ever knows what's in another person's mind. Here's the wumper."

The three entered a long wide room, lined with tables and benches, and already filled with chattering residents of Level 19. An attendant punched their apartment numbers into a register; the three took covered trays from a dispenser and went to a table. The tray contained exactly the same rations Jantiff had been served the previous evening at the Travelers Inn.

Skorlet put a cake of gruff to the side. "For our next swill."

Esteban with an expression of whimsical grief did likewise. "For swill, any sacrifice is worthy."

"Here's mine," said Jantiff. "I insist on contributing."

Skorlet gathered the three cakes together. "I'll take them back to the apartment, and we'll all just pretend that we've eaten them."

Esteban jumped to his feet. "A good idea, but let me! I'll be glad to run the errand."

"Don't be silly," said Skorlet. "It's only a step or two."

Esteban said, laughing, "We'll both go, if you're so stubborn."

Jantiff looked from one to the other, bemused, "Is it really such a point of courtesy? I'll come too, in that case."

Esteban sighed and shook his head. "Of course not. Skorlet is merely a wayward person. . . . None of us will go."

Skorlet shrugged. "As you wish."

Jantiff said, "We can easily restrain our appetites. At least I can. And we'll drop off the gruff on our way out."

"Of course," said Esteban. "That's the fair way."

Jantiff wondered at the exquisite nicety of Esteban's politesse.

"Eat the wump and shut up," said Skorlet.

The meal was taken in silence. Jantiff inspected his fellow residents with interest. There was no reserve and anonymity; everyone seemed to know everyone else; cheerful greetings, banter, allusion to social events and mutual friends rang around the room. A slender girl with fine honey-colored hair paused beside Skorlet and whispered something in her ear, with an arch side glance toward Jantiff. Skorlet gave a dreary laugh. "Go on with you! It's all nonsense, as well you know!"

The girl went on to a nearby table, where she joined friends. Jantiff thought her slender round body, her charming features and her saucy spontaneity all attractive, but made no comment.

Skorlet noticed the direction of his gaze. "That's Kedidah. The old sandpiper yonder is Sarp, her roommate. He tries to copulate a dozen times a day, which makes for an inconvenient roommate; after all, one's social life is usually elsewhere. She just offered to trade you for Sarp, but I wouldn't hear of it. Esteban is always handy when I'm in the mood, which perhaps isn't as often as it should be."

Jantiff, spooning up his wobbly, forbore comment.

Upon leaving the refectory, the three stopped by the apartment where Skorlet dropped off the three cakes of gruff. Skorlet turned to Jantiff. "Are you ready?"

"I'm just debating whether to bring my camera. My family wants photographs by the dozen."

"Better not this time," said Esteban. "Wait till you know the ropes. Then you can get some really dramatic photographs. And also you'll have learned to cope with the, alas, all too prevalent snergery."

" 'Snergery'? What is that?"

"Theft, to put it bluntly. Arrabus abounds with snerges. Haven't you heard?"

Jantiff shook his head. "I can't understand why anyone should steal under egalism."

Esteban laughed. "Snerging ensures egalism. It's a very direct remedy against anyone accumulating goods. In Arrabus we share and share alike."

"I can't understand the logic in all this," said Jantiff, but neither Esteban nor Skorlet showed any interest in pursuing the topic.

The three proceeded to the man-way and rode half a mile to the district crèche, where Tanzel waited: a pretty wisp of a girl with Skorlet's round face, Esteban's fine features and a thoughtful intelligence all her own. She greeted Skorlet and Esteban with restrained affection, and Jantiff with quite obvious curiosity. After a few moments of covert inspection, she told him: "Really, you look much like the rest of us!"

"Of course! How did you expect me to look?"

"Like a cannibal, or an exploiter, or maybe one of their victims."

"What odd ideas!" said Jantiff. "On Zeck at least no one would care to be thought an exploiter, much less a victim."

"Then why did you come to Arrabus?"

"That's a hard question," said Jantiff somberly. "I'm not

sure that I know the answer myself. At home too much pressed on me, while all the time I searched for something I couldn't find. I needed to get away and order my mind."

Esteban and Skorlet had been listening to the conversation with distant half-smiles. Esteban inquired in a light voice: "And then, when your mind has been ordered?"

"This is what I don't know. In essence I want to create something remarkable and beautiful, something that is my very own. . . . I want to indicate the mysteries of life. I don't hope to explain them, mind you; I wouldn't, even if I could. I want to reveal their dimensions and their wonder, for people who are interested or even people who aren't. . . . I'm afraid I don't explain myself very well."

Skorlet said in a rather cool voice, "You explain well enough, but no one quite understands."

Tanzel, listening with knitted eyebrow, said: "I understand a little of what he's saying, I wonder about these mysteries too. For instance, why am I me, and not somebody else?"

Skorlet said roughly: "You'll wear your brain out, thinking along those lines."

Esteban told her earnestly: "Remember, my dear, that Jantiff isn't an egalist like the rest of us; he wants to do something quite extraordinary and individualistic."

"Yes, partly that," said Jantiff, wishing that he had never ventured an opinion. "But it's more like this: here I am, born into life with certain capabilities. If I don't use these capabilities and achieve my utmost then I'm cheating myself, and living a soiled life."

"Hmm," said Tanzel sagely. "If everyone were like you, the world would be a very nervous place."

Jantiff gave an embarrassed laugh. "No cause for worry; there don't seem to be many people like me."

Tanzel gave her shoulders a jerk of somber disinterest, and Jantiff was pleased to drop the subject. A moment later her mood changed; she tugged at Jantiff's sleeve and pointed ahead. "There's Uncibal River! I do so love watching from the bridge! Oh, please come, everyone! Over to the deck!"

Tanzel ran out upon the prospect deck. The others followed more sedately, and all stood leaning on the rail as Uncibal River passed below; a pair of slideways, each a hundred feet wide, crowded close with the folk of Arrabus. Tanzel told Jantiff excitedly: "If you stand here long enough you'll see everyone in the world!"

"That of course isn't true," said Skorlet crisply, as if she did not altogether approve of Tanzel's fancies.

Below passed the Arrabins: folk of all ages, faces serene and easy, as if they walked alone, rapt in contemplation. Occasionally someone might raise his eyes to look at the line of faces along the deck; for the most part the crowds passed below oblivious to those who watched from above.

Esteban began to show signs of restlessness. He straightened, slapped the rails and, with a thoughtful glance toward the sky, said: "Perhaps I'd better be moving along. My friend Hester will be expecting me."

Skorlet's black eyes glittered. "There is no need whatever for you to rush off."

"Well, in a way—"

"Which route do you go?"

"Oh—just along the River."

"We'll all go together and take you to Hester's block. She's at the Tesseract, I believe."

Dignity struggling with annoyance, Esteban said curtly, "Shall we move along then?"

A ramp curved down and around to the boarding platform; they stepped out into the crowd and were carried away to the west. As they moved across to the faster lanes, Jantiff discovered an odd effect. When he looked over his shoulder to the right, faces in his immediate vicinity receded and fell away into the blur. When he looked back to his left, the faces surged up from nowhere, drew abreast and passed ahead into an equally anonymous beyond. The effect was disturbing for reasons he could not precisely define; he began to feel vertigo and turned away to face forward, to watch the blocks move past, each a different color: pinks and browns and yellows; greens of every description: moss, mottled green-white, cadaverous blue-green, black-green; faded reds and orange-purples: all augmented to a state of clarity by the Dwan-light.

Jantiff became interested in the colors. Each no doubt exerted a symbolic influence upon those who lived with them. Peach, blotched with stump-water tan—who chose these colors? What canons were involved? Lavender-white, blue, acid green—on and on, each color no doubt dear to the folk who lived there. . . Tanzel tugged at his elbow. Jantiff looked around to see Esteban moving swiftly away to the right. Tanzel said somberly: "He just remembered an important engagement; he asked me to express his regrets to you."

Skorlet, her face flushed with annoyance, stepped smartly

past. "Something I've got to do! I'll see you later!" She likewise was gone through the crowd, and Jantiff was left with
Tanzel. He looked at her in bewilderment. "Where did they go
so suddenly?"

"I don't know, but let's go on. I could ride Uncibal River
forever!"

"I think we'd better go back. Do you know the way?"

"Of course! We just revert to Disselberg River, then cross
to 112th Lateral."

"You show me the way. I've had enough promenading for
the day. Strange that both Esteban and Skorlet decided to
leave so suddenly!"

"I suppose so," said Tanzel. "But I've come to expect
strange things. . . . Well, if you want to go back, we'll take
the next turnaround."

As they rode Jantiff gave his attention to Tanzel: An appealing little creature, so he decided. He asked if she enjoyed
her school. Tanzel shrugged. "I'd have to drudge otherwise,
so I learn counting, reading and ontology. Next year I'll be
into personal dynamics, and that's more fun. We learn how
to express ourselves and dramatize. Did you go to school?"

"Yes, indeed: sixteen long years."

"What did you learn?"

"An amazing variety of facts and topics."

"And then you went out to drudge?"

"No, not yet. I haven't found anything I really want to do."

"I don't suppose you live at all egalistically."

"Not as you do here. Everyone works much harder; but
most everyone enjoys his work."

"But not you."

Jantiff gave an embarrassed laugh. "I'm willing to work
very hard, but I don't quite know how. My sister Ferfan
carves mooring posts. Perhaps I'll do something like that."

Tanzel nodded. "Someday let's talk again. There's the
crèche; I'll turn off here. Your block is straight along; it's Old
Pink, on the left. Good-bye."

Jantiff proceeded along the man-way and presently saw
ahead that block which he now must consider "home": Old
Pink.

He entered, ascended to Level 19 and sauntered around
the corridor to his apartment. He opened the door and tact-
fully called out: "I'm home. It's Jantiff!"

No response. The apartment was empty. Jantiff entered
and slid the door shut. He stood for a moment wondering

what to do with himself. Still two hours until dinner. Another ration of gruff, deedle, and wobbly. Jantiff grimaced. The globes of paper and wire caught his eye; he went to examine them. Their function was not at all clear. The paper was green flimsy, the wire had been salvaged from another operation. Perhaps Skorlet intended to decorate the apartment with gay green bubbles. If so, thought Jantiff, her achievement was remarkably slipshod.* Well, so long as they pleased Skorlet, it was none of his affair. He looked into the bedroom, to appraise the two cots and the not-too-adequate curtain. Jantiff wondered what his mother would say. Certainly nothing congratulatory. Well, this was why he had come traveling, to explore other ways and other customs. Though for a fact, since matters were so casual he would definitely have preferred the young woman—what was her name? Kedidah?—whom he had noticed in the refectory.

He decided to unpack his satchel and went to the wardrobe where he had left it. He looked down in consternation. The lock was broken; the lid was askew. Opening the case, Jantiff examined the contents. His few clothes apparently had not been molested, except for his spare shoes, of fine gray lantile. These were missing, as well as his pigments and pad, his camera and recorder, a dozen other small implements. Jantiff went slowly into the sitting room and sank into a chair.

A brief few minutes later Skorlet entered the apartment. Jantiff thought that she looked in a very bad mood, with her black eyes glittering, and her mouth set in a hard line. Her voice crackled as she spoke: "How long have you been here?"

"Five or ten minutes."

"Kindergoff Lateral was down to the contractors," she said bitterly. "I had to walk an entire mile."

"While we were gone someone broke into my case and stole most of my things."

The news seemed to drive Skorlet close to the limits of self-control. "And what do you expect?" she snapped in an unpleasantly harsh voice. "This is an egalistic country; why should you have more than anyone else?"

---

* Jantiff would later learn that many folk furnished their apartments in unique, or even bizarre, styles, scrounging and pilfering materials over a period of years, and spending immense effort to achieve some special effect. Such apartments were generally considered unegalistic, and those who lived there often incurred derision.

"I have been over-egalized," said Jantiff dryly. "To the effect that I now have less than anyone else."

"Those are problems you must learn to cope with," said Skorlet and marched into the bedroom.

A few days later Jantiff wrote a letter to his family:

"My dearest mother, father and sisters:

I am now established in what must be the most remarkable nation of Alastor Cluster: Arrabus of Wyst. I inhabit a two-room apartment in close contiguity to a handsome woman with strong views on egalism. She doesn't approve of me particularly. However, she is civil and on occasion helpful. Her name is Skorlet. You may wonder at this unconventional arrangement; it is really quite simple. Egalism refuses to recognize sexual differences. One person is considered equal to every other, in all respects. To emphasize sexual differences is called "sexivation." For a girl to primp or show her figure to best advantage is "sexivation" and it is considered a serious offense.

The apartments were originally intended to house male or female couples, or mated couples, but the philosophy was denounced as "sexivationist," and apartment assignments are now made at random, though often persons will trade about. Anyone coming to Arrabus must leave his prejudices behind! Already I have learned that, no matter what the apparent similarities of a new place to one's home, the stranger must not be misled! *Things are never what they seem!* Think of this! And think of all the Cluster worlds and all the Gaean Reach, and the Erdic Realms, and the Primarchic! Think of these trillions of folk, each with his singular face! A frightening thought, really. Still I am much impressed by Arrabus. The system works; there is no desire for change. The Arrabins seem happy and content, or at the very least, passive. They place their highest value upon leisure, at the expense of personal possessions, good food, and a certain degree of freedom. They are far from well educated, and no one has expertise in any specific field. Maintenance and repairs are done by whomever is assigned the job, or in serious cases, to contracting firms from the Weirdlands. (These are the provinces to north and south. They are not nations; I doubt if they have any formal government whatever, but I don't know much about them.)

I have not been able to do any serious work because my apparatus has been stolen. Skorlet considers this quite normal and cannot understand my distress. She jeers at my "anti-egalism." Well, so be it. As I say, the Arrabins are a strange folk, who become excited only by food—not their usual "wump" but good natural food; in fact an acquaintance by the name of Esteban has mentioned one or two vices so odd and repellent as to be unspeakable, and I will say no more.

The block where I live is known as "Old Pink" because of its eczematous color. Each block, ostensibly identical to all others, is vividly distinctive, at least in the minds of the folk who live there, and they will characterize the blocks as "dreary," "frivolous," "teeming with sly snerges," "serves good wump," "serves bad wump," "too many pranksters," "sexivationist." Each block has it's own legends, songs and special jargon. "Old Pink" is considered easy-going and faintly raffish, which of course describes me very well, too.

You ask, What is a "snerge"? A thief. I have already suffered the attentions of a snerge, and my camera is missing so I can't send photographs. Luckily I was carrying my ozols with me. Please send me by return mail new pigments, vehicle, applicators and a big pad of matrix. Ferfan will tell you what I need. Send them insured; if they came by ordinary delivery, they might be egalized.

Later: I have done my first stint of drudge, at an export factory, for which I receive what is called "drivet": ten tokens for each hour worked. My weekly drivet is a hundred and thirty tokens, of which eighty-two must immediately be paid to the block, for food and lodging. The remainder is not too useful, since there is not much to buy: garments, shoes, stadium tickets, toasted seaweed at Disjerferact. I now dress like an Arrabin, so as not to be conspicuous. Certain shops at the space-port sell imported goods—tools, toys, occasional trifles of "bonter," at the most astonishing prices! In tokens, of course, which have almost no exchange value against the ozol—something like five hundred tokens to the ozol.

Absurd, of course. On second thought, not so absurd. Who wants tokens? There is nothing to buy.

Still, this way of life, peculiar as it seems, is not necessarily a bad system. I suspect that every style of life works out to be a trade off between various kinds of freedoms. There are naturally many different freedoms, and sometimes one freedom implies the absence of another.

In any event I've been getting ideas for depictions, which I know you don't take seriously. The light here is absolutely ravishing: a deceptively pale light, which seems to diffract everywhere into colored fringes.

I have much more to tell you, but I'll reserve something for my next. I won't ask you to send in "bonter"; I'd be—well, to tell the truth, I don't know what would happen, but I don't want to learn.

Immigrants and visitors are not well liked, yet I find that my fame as a "fixer" has already spread far and wide. Isn't this a joke? I know only what we were taught at school and what I learned at home. Still, everyone who has a bad screen insists that I fix it for him. Sometimes utter strangers! And when I do these favors, do they thank me? Verbally, yes, but there is a most peculiar expression on their faces: I can't describe it. Contempt, distaste, antipathy? Because I so easily command this (to them) recondite skill. I have on this instant come to a decision. No longer will I perform favors free. I will demand tokens or hours of drudge. They will sneer and make remarks, but they will respect me more.

Here are some of my ideas for depictions:

The blocks of Uncibal, in the colors which hold so much meaning for the Arrabins.

The view along Uncibal River from a prospect deck, with the oncoming sea of faces, all blank and serene.

The games, the shunk battles, the Arrabin version of hussade.*

Disjerferact, the carnival along the mudflats. More of this later.

Just a word or two about the local version of hussade, and I hope no one in the family will be shocked or dismayed. The game is played to standard rules; the defeated sheirl, however, must undergo a most distressing

---

* Hussade: See Glossary, #4.

experience. She is disrobed and placed upon a cart with a repulsive wooden effigy, which is so controlled as to commit an unnatural act upon the sheirl; meanwhile, the losing team must pull this cart around the stadium. The wonder never leaves me: how are sheirls recruited? Each must realize that sooner or later her team must lose, yet none ever seems to consider this contingency.

They are either very brave or very foolish, or perhaps they are impelled by some dark human inclination which rejoices at public degradation.

Well, enough on this subject. I think I mentioned that my camera has been stolen: hence no photographs. In fact, I'm not sure that there is any agency at Uncibal to make prints from my matrix.

I will report further in my next letter.

From your loving,
Jantiff.

Chapter 4

One morning Esteban came by Jantiff's apartment with a friend. "Attention, please, Janty Ravensroke! This is Olin, a dear good fellow, for all his portly abdomen. It signifies sound sleep and a peaceful conscience, or so Olin assures me; he owns no magic bonter cabinet."

Jantiff politely acknowledged the introduction, and offered a pleasantry of his own: "Please don't consider me guilt-ridden because I am thin!"

Olin and Esteban were provoked to hearty laughs. Esteban said: "Olin's screen has developed a most curious ailment; it spits up plumes of red fire, even at amusing messages. He naturally suffers agonies of distress. I told him: Be of good cheer! My friend Jantiff is a Zeck technician who likes nothing better than setting such things right."

Jantiff attempted a bright tone. "I have rather a good idea along these lines. Suppose I conduct a seminar on small repairs, at a charge per session, say, of fifty tokens a student. Everyone—you and Olin included—can learn all I know, and

then you can do your own repairs and also oblige those of
your friends who lack the skills."

Olin's smile trembled uncertainly; Esteban's handsome eyebrows peaked emphatically. "My dear fellow!" exclaimed Esteban. "Are you really in earnest?"

"Of course! Everyone gains. I earn extra tokens and also
avoid the nuisance of running about performing favors. You
in turn augment your capabilities."

For a moment Esteban stood speechless. Then, half-laugh-
ing, he said: "But Jantiff, dear naïve Jantiff! I don't want to
augment my capabilities! This implies a predisposition for
work. For civilized men work is an unnatural occupation!"

"I suppose there is no inherent virtue in work," Jantiff
conceded. "Unless, of course, it is performed by someone
else."

"Work is the useful function of machines," said Esteban.
"Let the machines augment their capabilities! Let the automatons ponder and drudge! The span of existence is oh! so
brief; why should a single second be wasted?"

"Yes, yes, of course," said Jantiff. "An ideal concept and
all very well. In practice however both you and Olin already
have wasted two or three hours inspecting Olin's screen, exclaiming at the flaw, formulating plans and coming here. Assume that I agreed to look into the matter, then you and Olin
must return to Olin's apartment to watch me make the repair.
Let us say a total of four hours apiece. Eight man-hours as a
grand total, not even counting my time, when Olin probably
could have set the matter to rights in ten minutes. Isn't this a
case where capabilities saves time?"

Esteban gave his head a grave shake. "Jantiff, above all
you are a master of casuistry. This 'capability' implies a point
of view quite at odds with the beatific* life."

"I feel that I must agree to this," said Olin.

"You'd rather lose the use of your screen than fix it yourself?"

Esteban's versatile eyebrows performed another feat, this
time indicating quizzical distaste. "It goes without saying!
This practicality of yours is a backward step. I also might
mention that your proposed class is exploitative, and would
surely excite the Monitors."

"I hadn't thought in those terms," said Jantiff. "Well, in all
candor, I find that these little favors are taking too much of

---

* An arbitrary rendering of a word in the Arrabin dialect, expressing
the quality of leisurely, luxurious and well-arranged existence.

my time and destroying the beatitude of my life. If Olin wants to work my next drudge, I'll fix his screen."

Olin and Esteban exchanged amused glances. Both shrugged, turned away and departed the apartment.

From Zeck came a parcel for Jantiff, containing pigments, applicators, papers and mats. Jantiff immediately set to work making real the images which haunted his imagination. Skorlet occasionally watched him, making no comments and asking no questions; Jantiff did not trouble to ask her opinion.

In the refectory one day, the girl whom Jantiff previously had admired plumped herself down opposite him. With her lips twitching against a grin of sheer exuberance, she pointed a finger toward Jantiff. "Explain something: do! Every time I come to the wumper you stare at me first from one side of your face and them the other. Why should this be? Am I so outrageously attractive and extraordinarily beautiful."

Jantiff grinned sheepishly. "I find you outrageously attractive and extraordinarily beautiful."

"Sh!" The girl glanced mischievously right and left. "Already I'm considered a sexivationist. You'll absolutely confirm the general suspicion!"

"Well, be that as it may, I can't keep my eyes off of you, and that's the truth of it."

"And all you do is look? How odd! But then, you're an immigrant."

"Just a visitor. I hope that my coarse behavior hasn't disturbed you."

"Not in the slightest. I've always thought you rather pleasant. We'll copulate if you like; you can show me some new and amusing antics. No, not now; low drudge awaits me, curse all of it. Another time, if you're of a mind."

"Well, yes," said Jantiff. "I suppose it boils down to that. Your name, I believe, is Kedidah."

"How did you know?"

"Skorlet told me."

Kedidah made a wry face. "Skorlet doesn't like me. She says I'm flippant, and an arrant sexivator, as I mentioned."

"I'm bewildered. Why?"

"Oh—I don't really know. I like to tease and play. I arrange my hair to suit my mood. I like men to like me and I'm not concerned about women."*

---

* A more or less accurate paraphrase. The Arrabin dialect avoids distinction of gender. Masculine and feminine pronouns are suppressed

"These aren't flagrant crimes."

"Aha! Ask Skorlet!"

"I'm not concerned for Skorlet's opinions. In fact, I find her overly intense. My name, incidentally, is Jantiff Ravensroke."

"What an odd name! No doubt you're an ingrained elitist. How are you adapting to egalism?"

"Quite well. Although I'm still perplexed by certain of the Arrabin customs."

"Understandably. We're a most complicated people, maybe to compensate for our egalism."

"I suppose that's possible. Would you like to visit other worlds?"

"Of course, unless I had to toil constantly, in which case I'll stay here where life is gay. I have friends and clubs and games; I never gloom because I think only of pleasure. In fact, some of us are going out on forage in a day or so; you're welcome to come along if you like."

"What's a 'forage'?"

"An expedition into the primitive! We ride up into the hills, then maraud south into the Weirdlands. This time it's to be Pamatra Valley, where we know secret places. We'll hope to find some very good bonter; but even if not, it's always a lark."

"I'd like to go, if I'm not on drudge."

"We'll start Twisday morning, right after wump and return Fyrday night, or even Dwanday morning."

"That suits me very well."

"Good. We'll meet here. Bring some sort of robe, since we'll probably sleep in the open. With luck we'll find all kinds of tasty things."

Early Twisday morning, as soon as the refectory opened its doors, Jantiff went to take his breakfast. On Skorlet's advice he carried a knapsack containing a blanket, a towel and two days advance ration of gruff. Skorlet had spoken brusquely of the expedition, with something of a sneer: "You'll get wet in the fog and scratch yourself on brambles and run through the night until you're exhausted and if you're lucky you'll build a

in favor of the neutral pronoun. "Parent" replaces "mother" and "father"; "sibling" serves for both "brother" and "sister." When distinctions must be made, as in the conversation transcribed above, colloquialisms are used, almost brutally offensive in literal translation, reference being made to the genital organs.

fire if someone thinks to bring along matches. Still, by all means, go out and flounder through the forest and dodge the man-traps and who knows? Maybe you'll find a berry or two or a bit of toasted meat. Where are you going?"

"Kedidah spoke of secret places in Pamatra Valley."

"Pah. What does she know of secret places, or anything else for that matter? Esteban is planning a real bonterfest before long; save your appetite for that."

"Well, I've already agreed to go with Kedidah's group."

Skorlet shrugged and sniffed. "Do as you like. Here, take these matches and be prepared, and don't eat toad-wort, otherwise you'll never return to Uncibal. As for Kedidah, she's never been right about anything, and I'm told she doesn't clean herself, when you copulate you never know what you're wading around in."

Jantiff mumbled something incoherent and busied himself with his painting. Skorlet came to look over his shoulder. "Who are those people?"

"They're the Whispers, receiving a committee of contractors in Serce."

Skorlet gave him a searching scrutiny. "You're never been to Serce."

"I used a photograph from the *Concept*. Didn't you see it?"

"No one sees anything in the *Concept* except hussade announcments." She studied another picture: a view along Uncibal River. She gave her head a shake of distaste. "All those faces, each so exact! It quite makes me uneasy!"

"Look carefully," Jantiff suggested. "Are there any you recognize?"

After a moment's silence Skorlet said: "To be sure! There's Esteban! And can this be me? Very clever; you have a remarkable knack!" She took up another sheet. "And what is this? the wumper? All these faces again; they seem so blank." She turned Jantiff another searching look. "What effect is this?"

Jantiff said hurriedly: "Arrabins seem, somehow, composed, let us say."

"Composed? What a thought! We're fervent, idealistic, reckless—when we have the opportunity—mutable, passionate. All these, yes. Composed? No."

"No doubt you're right," said Jantiff. "Somehow I haven't captured this quality."

Skorlet turned away, then spoke over her shoulder. "I wonder if you could spare some of that blue pigment? I'd like to paint symbols on my cult globes."

Jantiff looked first up at the constructions of paper and wire, each a foot in diameter, then to the wide coarse brush which Skorlet habitually employed, and finally with eyebrows ruefully raised, to the rather small capsule of blue pigment. "Really, Skorlet, I don't see how this is possible. Can't you use house paint or ink, or something similar?"

Skorlet went pink in the face. "And how or where can I get house paint? Or ink? I know nothing of these things; they aren't available to just anyone, and I've never been on a drudge where I could snerge any."

"I think I saw ink for sale on Counter 5 at the Area Store," Jantiff said cautiously. "Perhaps—"

Skorlet made a vehement gesture, expressing rejection and disgust. "At a hundred tokens the dram? You foreigners are all alike, so pampered by your wealth, yet heartless and selfish beneath it all!"

"Oh, very well," said Jantiff despondently. "Take the pigment if you really need it. I'll use another color."

But Skorlet, flouncing away, went to the mirror and began to change the decoration of her ears. Jantiff heaved a sigh and continued with his painting.

The foragers gathered in the lobby of Old Pink; eight men and five women. Jantiff's knapsack instantly aroused jocular attention. "Ha, where does Jantiff think we're off to, the Far Edge?"

"Jantiff, dear fellow, we're only going on a bit of a forage, not a migration!"

"Jantiff is an optimist! He takes trays and bags and baskets to bring home his bonter!"

"Bah, I'll bring mine home, too, but on the inside!"

A young man named Garrace, portly and blond, asked: "Jantiff, tell us really and in truth: what are you carrying?"

Jantiff, grinning apologetically, said: "Actually, nothing of any consequence: a change of clothes, a few cakes of gruff, my sketch pad, and, if you must know the truth, some toilet paper."

"Good old Jantiff! He is at least candid!"

"Well then, let's be off, toilet paper and all!"

The group proceeded to the man-way, rode to Uncibal River, moved west for an hour, changed to a lateral which took them south into the hills.

Jantiff had studied a map the day previously, and now tried to identify features of the landscape. He pointed to a great granite abutment looming over the way ahead. "That must be the Solitary Witness; am I right?"

"Exactly," said Thworn, an assertive young man with russet hair. "Over and beyond is the Near Wold and a spate of bonter if we're lucky. See that notch? That's Hebron Gap; it will take us into Pamatra Valley and that's where we're bound."

"I suspect we'd do better out on the Middle Wold, toward Fruberg," said a saturnine young man named Uwser. "Some people I know worked Pamatra Valley two or three months ago and came home hungry."

"Nonsense," scoffed Thworn. "I can smell the vat-berries dripping from here! And don't forget the Frubergers: a stone-throwing gang of villains!"

"The Valley folk are no better," declared Sunover, a girl as tall as Jantiff and of far more impressive girth. "On the whole, they're fat and smelly, and I don't like to copulate with them."

"In that case, run," said Uwser. "Have you no imagination?"

"Eat, copulate, run," intoned Garrace. "The three dynamics of Sunover's existence."

Jantiff asked Sunover: "Why either copulate or run, if you're not of a mind to do so?"

Sunover merely made an impatient clucking sound. Kedidah gave Jantiff a pat on the cheek. "They're both good for the soul, dear boy, and sometimes they aid one's comfort as well."

Jantiff said in a worried voice: "I'd like to know what's expected of me. Do I copulate or do I run? What are the signals? And where do we find the bonter?"

"Everything happens at once," said Garrace with an impish grin.

"All in good time, Jantiff!" spoke the imperious Thworn. "Don't become anxious at this stage of the game!"

Jantiff shrugged and gave his attention to a set of industrial buildings toward which most of the traffic on the man-way seemed to be directed. In response to his question Garrace informed him that here those hormones which figured largely in Arrabin exports were extracted, refined and packaged. "You'll get your notice before long," Garrace told him. "It's our common fate. Into the plant like so many automatons, down on the pallet, along the operation line. They milk your glands, distill your blood, tap your spinal ducts, and in general have their way with all your most private parts. Don't worry; you'll have your turn."

Jantiff had not previously known of this aspect to life in Arrabus. He frowned over his shoulder toward the cluster of pale brown buildings. "How long does all this take?"

"Two days, and for another two or three days you are totally addled. Still, export we must, to pay for maintenance, and what, after all, is two days a year in the interests of egalism?"

The man-way ended at a depot, where the group boarded an ancient omnibus. Swaying and wallowing perilously, the omnibus slid them up the road between slopes overgrown with blue canker-wort and black dendrons studded with poisonous scarlet seed balls.

After an hour's ride the bus arrived at the head of Hebron Gap. "End of the road, all out!" cried Thworn. "Now we must march off on foot, like the adventurers of old!"

The troop set off along a lane leading downhill through a stand of kirkash trees smelling strong and sweet of resin. Ahead the land flattened to become Pamatra Valley; beyond stretched the Weirdlands under a smoke-colored shroud of forest.

Garrace called over his shoulder: "Jantiff, shake a leg there; you'll have to keep up. What are you doing?"

"Just making a sketch of that tree. Look at the way the branches angle out! They're like dancing maenads!"

"No time for sketching!" Thworn called back. "We've still got five or ten miles to go."

Jantiff reluctantly put away his sketch pad and caught up with the others.

The lane swung out on a meadow and broke into a half-dozen trails leading off in various directions. Here the group encountered another set of foragers. "Hello there!" called Uwser, "what's your house?"

"We're desperadoes from Bumbleville in Two-twenty."

"That's a long way from us. "We're all Old Pinkers, from Seventeen—except Woble and Vich; they're denizens of the infamous White Palace. What luck are you having?"

"Nothing to speak of. We heard a rumor of a lovely bitternut tree, but we couldn't find it. We ate a few sweet-hops and looked into an orchard, but the locals warned us off and sent a boy to spy us clear of the premises. What are you for?"

"Bonter of all sorts, and we're a determined group. We'll probably push south five or ten miles before we start our forage."

"Good luck to you!"

Thworn led the Old Pinkers south along a trail which took them at once into a dense forest of black mace trees. The air in the shade was dank and chill and smelled strong of mouldering vegetation. Thworn called out: "Everyone watch for bitternuts and remember there's a wild plum tree somewhere in the vicinity!"

A mill passed with no evidence either of nuts or plums, and the trail came to a fork. Thworn hesitated. "I don't recall this fork. . . . I wonder if we set off along the wrong trail? Well, no matter; the bonter is out there somewhere! So then—the right-hand fork!"

Ernaly, a rather frail girl with a fastidious manner, said plaintively: "How far must we go? I'm really not all that keen on hiking, especially if you don't know the way."

Thworn said sternly: "My dear girl, naturally we've got to hike! We're in the middle of the forest with nothing to eat but skane bark."

"Please don't talk about eating," cried Rehilmus, a blonde kitten-faced girl with small feet and a ripe figure displayed almost to the point of sexivation, "I'm ravenous right now."

Thworn swung his arm in a gesture of command. "No complaints! Up and away and after the bonter!"

The group set out along the right-hand path, which presently dwindled to a trail winding this way and that under the lowering mace trees. Kedidah, walking at the rear with Jantiff, grumbled under her breath. "Thworn doesn't know where he's going any more than I do."

"What, exactly, are we looking for?" Jantiff asked.

"These Wold farms are the richest of Weirdland, because they fringe on the Pleasant Zone. The farmers are mad for copulation; they give baskets of bonter for a bit of fondling. You can't imagine the tales I've heard: roasted fowl, fried salt-side, pickled batracher, baskets of fruit! All for a brisk bit of copulation."

"It seems too good to be true."

Kedidah laughed. "Only if there's fair play. It's not unknown that while the girls are copulating the men are eating until there's nothing left, and the walk home is apt to be moody."

"So I would imagine," said Jantiff. "Sunover, for instance, would never accept such a situation without protest."

"I suspect not. Look, Thworn has discovered something!"

In response to Thworn's signals the group fell silent. They advanced cautiously, at last to peer through the foliage out upon a small farmstead. To one side a half-dozen cattle grazed the meadow; to the other grew rows of bantock and mealie-bush and tall racks of vat-berries. At the center stood a rambling structure of timber and petrified soil.

Garrace pointed: "Look—yonder! Lyssum vines! Is anyone about?"

"The place seems deserted," Uwser muttered. "Notice the fowl roost to the side!"

"Well then, I'm for being bold," said Garrace. "They're all within, gulping down their noon bonter, and here stand we with our mouths open. I accept the unspoken invitation!"

He stepped out from the forest and advanced upon the lyssum vines, followed by Colcho, Hasken, Vich, Thworn and the others, with Jantiff thoughtfully keeping to the rear. Garrace uttered a startled cry as the ground gave way under his feet; he disappeared from view. The others paused uncertainly, then went forward to peer down at Garrace, where he floundered among sodden brambles. "Get me out of here," he roared. "Don't just stand there gaping!"

"No need to be offensive," said Thworn. "Here; give me your hand!" He pulled and Garrace was dragged up to solid ground.

"What a vile trick!" exclaimed Rehilmus. "You might have been seriously hurt!"

"I'm not at all comfortable," growled Garrace. "I'm full of thorns and they've poured a year's worth of slops down there. But I'm still for that lyssum, and now I'll have it for sure."

"Do be careful!" cried Maudel, another of the girls. "These folk are obviously unfriendly."

"And now I'm unfriendly too!" Garrace proceeded toward the vines, testing the ground ahead of him. After a moment's hesitation the others followed.

Twenty yards short of the vines he stumbled and almost fell. He looked down: "A trip wire!"

From the farmhouse issued two men, a stout woman and a pair of striplings. They picked up cudgels and one of the boys raised a hatch in the side of the structure. Out rushed four black delps of that sort known as "mouthers." Baying and moaning, they charged the foragers, followed by the farm folk with their cudgels. With one accord the foragers turned and ran toward the forest, led by Jantiff who had not ventured any great distance into the meadow.

The slowest of the foragers was the amiable Colcho, who had the misfortune to fall. The delps were upon him, but the farm folk called them off and sent them after the other fugitives while they beat Colcho with their cudgels, until Colcho finally managed to break away, and running faster than ever, gained the relative security of the forest. The delps leapt upon Rehilmus and Ernaly and might have done them damage had not Thworn and Jantiff beaten them away with dead branches.

The group returned the way they had come. Reaching the fork they found that Colcho had evidently fled in a direction different from their own and was now missing. Everyone called, "Colcho! Colcho! Where are you?" But Colcho failed to reply, and no one felt in any mood to return along the trail looking for him. "He should have stayed with the group," said Uwser.

"He had no chance," Kedidah pointed out. "The farm folk were beating him and he was lucky to get away at all."

"Poor Colcho," sighed Maudel.

" 'Poor Colcho?' " cried Garrace in outrage. "What about me? I've been scratched and stabbed; I'm stinking with nameless muck! I've got to do something for myself!"

"There's a stream yonder; go bathe," Thworn suggested. "You'll feel much better."

"Not if I have to get back into these clothes; they're absolutely befouled."

"Well, Jantiff is carrying a spare outfit: you're about of a size and I'm sure he'll let you have them. Right, Jantiff? It's all for one and one for all among the jolly Old Pinkers!"

Jantiff reluctantly brought the garments from his knapsack, and Garrace went off to bathe.

Kedidah demanded of Thworn: "What now? Have you any notion of where we are?"

"Of course. We take the left fork instead of the right; I had a momentary lapse of memory; there's really no problem."

Rehilmus said crossly: "Except that it's time for wump, and I'm famished. In fact I can't go another step."

"We're all hungry," said Hasken. "You're not really alone."

"Yes, I am," declared Rehilmus. "No one becomes as hungry as I do, because I just can't function without food."

"Oh, the devil," said Thworn in disgust. "Jantiff, give her a bite or two of gruff, to keep her on her feet."

"I'm hungry too," said Ernaly peevishly.

"Oh, don't pout so," said Rehilmus. "I'll share with you."

Jantiff brought out his four cakes of gruff and placed them upon a stump. "This is all I have. Divide it as you like."

Rehilmus and Ernaly each took a cake; Thworn and Uwser shared the third; Kedidah and Sunover shared the fourth.

Garrace returned from washing in the stream. "Feeling better?" asked Rehilmus brightly.

"To some extent, although I wish Jantiff's clothes came a size larger. Still, far better than these befouled rags." He held them away from him with exaggerated disgust. "I won't carry them with me; I guess I'll just leave them here."

"Don't give up good clothes," Thworn advised. "There's room in Jantiff's knapsack, just drop them in."

"That would solve everything," said Garrace, and he turned to Jantiff. "You're sure you don't mind?"

"Quite sure," said Jantiff in a gloomy voice.

Thworn rose to his feet. "Everybody ready? Away we go!"

The foragers set off along the trail, Thworn again in the lead. Presently he made a clenched-fist sign of jubilation and swung around. "This is the trail; I recognized that knob of rock. There's bonter ahead; I smell it from here!"

"How much farther?" demanded Rehilmus. "Quite candidly, my feet hurt."

"Patience, patience! A few miles farther, over that far ridge. This is my secret place, so everyone must pledge absolute discretion!"

"Whatever you say. Just show us the bonter."

"Come along then; don't delay."

The group, enlivened, jogged forward and even sang jocular songs, of gluttony, legendary forages and chwig.

The countryside became more open as they climbed the slope. At the ridge a vast panorama extended to the south: dark forests, a line of river and a dramatic sky, leaden violet at the horizon, pearl white on high, mottled with shoals of white, gray and black clouds. Jantiff halted to absorb the scene and reached for his pad to make a rough sketch, but his hand encountered Garrace's dank garments and he gave up the idea.

The others had gone ahead; Jantiff hurried to catch up. As they descended the trees grew thickly over the trail.

Thworn called a halt. "From here on quiet and caution; let's not create any more fiascos."

Sunover, peering ahead, said: "I don't see anything whatever. Are you sure this is the right trail?"

"Dead sure. We're at the far edge of Pamatra Valley, where the best limequats grow, and the river flat-fish cook up sweet as nuts. That's further south, to be sure, but the first farms are just below us, so caution all. Jantiff, what in the world are you mooning at?"

"Nothing of consequence: just the lichens on this old log. Notice how the oranges contrast with the blacks and browns!"

"Charming and quaint, but we can't spare time for poetic ecstasies. Onward all, with caution!"

The foragers proceeded in utter silence: a half-mile, a mile. Once again Rehilmus became restive, but Thworn furiously signaled her to silence. A moment later he brought the group to a halt. "Look yonder now, but don't let yourselves be seen."

"Everyone be vigilant," Uwser cautioned. "Spy out the trip-wires, pitfalls, electric pounces and other such nuisances."

Peering through the trees Jantiff saw another farmstead not a great deal different from the first they had encountered.

Thworn, Garrace, Uwser and the others conferred, pointing here and there. Then all armed themselves with stout sticks, in the event delps should again be encountered.

Thworn told the group: "We'll go quietly yonder, where there don't seem to be any trip-wires, then make for the fowl-run at the rear of the house. So now, keep low to the ground. Good luck and good bonter!"

He hunched himself almost double and ran off at a curious wobbling shuffle; the others followed. As before Garrace was the boldest. He ventured into the vegetable garden, to pull up the root crops, cramming some in his mouth, some in his pockets. Doble, Vich and Sunover busied themselves at the vatberry arbor, but the season was past and only a few husks remained. Thworn proceeded toward the fowl-run.

Someone blundered into a trip-wire. A dismal clanking sound issued from a belfry on top of the house. The door opened and out ran an old man, an old woman and a small boy. The old man picked up a stick and attacked Garrace,

Maudel and Hasken, who were among his radishes; they
flung him to the ground and did the same for the old woman.
The boy ran into the house and emerged with an axe; flaming-eyed he lunged for the foragers. Thworn raised his voice
in a shout: "Everybody off and away, on the double!"

Snatching up a few last radishes the foragers departed the
way they had come, Thworn and Uwser exultant in the possession of a pair of rather thin old fowl, the necks of which
they had already wrung.

The group halted, panting and triumphant in the lane. "We
should have stayed longer," Rehilmus protested. "I saw a
really choice melon."

"Not with that alarm going! We were away in good time;
let's be gone before their reinforcements arrive. This way
down the trail!"

In a clearing beside a small stream the group halted.
Thworn and Uwser plucked and eviscerated the fowl while
Garrace built a fire; the meat was skewered upon sharp
sticks and toasted.

Kedidah looked this way and that. "Where is Jantiff?"

No one seemed interested.

"He seems to have gotten lost," said Rehilmus.

Garrace glanced down the path. "Nowhere in sight. He's
back there somewhere gazing raptly at an old stump."

"Well, no great loss," said Thworn. "So much more for the
rest of us."

The foragers began their feast.

"Ah! This is good stuff!" declared Garrace. "We should do
this more often."

"Ah!" sighed Rehilmus. "Marvelous! Throw a few of those
radishes this way; they're ideal!"

"The Connatic himself never ate better," declared Sunover.

"A pity there's not just a bit more," said Rehilmus. "I
could eat on for hours and never stop; I love it so!"

Thworn reluctantly rose to his feet. "We'd better be starting back; it's a long march over the hills."

Chapter 5

On the following day Kedidah, entering the refectory, discovered Jantiff sitting unobtrusively alone in a far corner. She marched across the room and plumped herself down beside him. "What happened to you yesterday? You missed all the fun."

"Yes, I suppose so. I decided that I wasn't all that hungry."

"Oh, come now, Jantiff. I can see through you. You're annoyed and sulky."

"Not really. I just don't feel right stealing from other people."

"What nonsense!" declared Kedidah loftily. "They've got plenty; why can't they share a bit with us?"

"There wouldn't be much to share among three billion people."

"Perhaps not." She reached out and took his hand. "I must say that you acted very nicely yesterday. I was quite pleased with you."

Jantiff flushed. "Do you really mean that?"

"Of course!"

Jantiff said haltingly, "I've—been thinking."

"About what?"

"That old man in your apartment; what's his name?"

"Sarp."

"Yes. I wonder if he would trade apartments with me. Then we could be together constantly."

Kedidah laughed. "Old sarp wouldn't dream of moving, and anyway, there's no fun when people live together and see each other at their worst. Isn't that really true?"

"Oh, I don't know. If you're fond of someone, you like to be with him or her as much as possible."

"Well, I'm fond of you and I see you as much as possible."

"But that isn't enough!"

"Besides, I've got lots of friends, and all of them make demands upon me."

Jantiff started to speak, then decided to hold his tongue. Kedidah picked up his portfolio. "What have you here? Pictures? Oh, please, may I look?"

"Of course."

Kedidah turned the sketches exclaiming in pleasure. "Jantiff, how exciting! I recognize this; it's our foraging group on the trail. This is Thworn, and here's Garrace, and—this is me! Jantiff! Do I look like that? All stiff and pale and staring, as if I'd seen a goblin? Don't answer me; I'll only be annoyed. If only you'd do a nice drawing of me that I could hang on the wall!" She returned to the sketch. "Sunover—Uwser—Rehilmus—everybody! And this glimpse of a person at the rear—that's you!"

Skorlet and Esteban came into the refectory, and with them that sprite of contradictory moods who was their daughter Tanzel. Kedidah called out: "Come look at Jantiff's wonderful pictures! Here's our forage party; we're on the trail! It's so real you can smell the kerkash balm!"

Esteban examined the sketch with an indulgent smile. "You don't seem overloaded with bonter."

"Naturally not! It's still morning and we're on our way south. And don't worry about bonter; we dined in style, all of us. Roast fowl, a salad of fresh herbs, buckets of fruit—all magnificent!"

"Oh!" exclaimed Tanzel. "I wish I'd been there!"

"Moderation, please," said Esteban, "I've gone foraging myself."

Kedidah said with dignity: "Next time come along with us and make certain how we fare."

"Which reminds me," mused Jantiff. "Did Colcho ever find his way home?"

No one troubled to answer. Esteban said: "I'm as keen for bonter as the next, but nowadays I pay the tokens and the gypsies provide the feast. Indeed, I have plans afoot at this very moment. Join the group, if you like. You'll have to pay your share, of course."

"How much? I just might go."

"Five hundred tokens, which includes air transport into the Weirdlands."

Kedidah clapped at her golden brown ear-puffs in shock. "Do you take me for a contractor? I can't fetch any such sum!"

Tanzel said sadly, "I don't have five hundred tokens either."

Skorlet turned a sharp glance toward Esteban, another at Jantiff. "Don't worry, dear. You'll be included."

Esteban, ignoring the remarks, continued to turn through Jantiff's sketches. "Very good. . . . A bit over-ambitious, this one. Too many faces. . . . Aha! I recognize someone here."

Kedidah looked. "That's myself and Sarp sitting in our chairs. Jantiff, when did you do this?"

"A few days ago. Skorlet, would you trade apartments with Kedidah?"

Skorlet gave an ejaculation of startled amusement. "Whatever for?"

"I'd like to share an apartment with her."

"And I'd share with that muttering old madman? Not on your life!"

Esteban offered advice: "Never share with someone you fancy; when the edge wears off, irritation wears on."

"It's not sensible to copulate too much with one person," said Kedidah.

"In fact, I don't like copulation," said Tanzel. "It's quite tiresome."

Esteban turned over the sketches. "Well, well! Whom do we have here?"

Tanzel pointed excitedly. "That's you and that's Skorlet, and that's old Sarp. I don't know that big man."

Esteban laughed. "Not quite. I see a resemblance, but only because Jantiff draws all his faces with the same expression."

"By no means," said Jantiff. "A face is the symbol—the graphic image—of a personality. Consider! Written characters represent spoken words. Depicted features represent personalities! I depict faces still and at rest so as not to confuse their meaning."

"Far, far beyond my reach," sighed Esteban.

"Not at all! Consider once more! I might depict two men laughing at a joke. One is really cantankerous, the other is good-natured. Since both are laughing, you might believe both to be good-natured. When the features are still, the personality is free to reveal itself."

Esteban held up his hands. "Enough! I submit! And I'll be the last to deny that you've a great knack for this sort of stuff."

"It's not a knack at all," said Jantiff. "I've had to practice for years."

Tanzel said brightly: "Isn't it elitism when someone tries to do something better than everyone else?"

"Theoretically, yes," said Skorlet, "but Jantiff is an Old Pinker and certainly not an elitist."

Esteban chuckled. "Any other crimes we can lay upon Jantiff's head?"

Tanzel thought a moment. "He's a monopolist who hoards his time and won't share with me, and I like him very much."

Skorlet snorted. "Jantiff's tit-willow mannerisms are actually arrant sexivation. He even affects poor little Tanzel."

"He's also an exploiter, because he wants to use up Kedidah."

Jantiff opened his mouth to roar an indignant rebuttal, but words failed him. Kedidah patted him on the shoulder. "Don't worry, Tanzel; I like him too and today he can monopolize me all he likes, because I want to go to the games and we'll go together."

"I'd like to go myself," said Esteban. "That great new Shkooner is fighting the piebald Wewark: both awesome beasts."

"Perhaps so, but I'm mad for Kizzo in the second event. He's mounted on the blue Jamouli, and he's so absolutely gallant I swoon to watch him."

Esteban pursed his lips. "He's really too exuberant in his flourishes, and I can't approve of his knee action. Still, he's reckless to a fault, and makes poor Lamar and Kelchaff seem a pair of fearful old ladies."

"Oh, dear," said Skorlet. "I've got drudge and can't go!"

"Save your tokens for the gypsies," said Esteban. "If you're planning to join the feast, that is to say."

"True. I must work on my globes. I wonder where I can find more pigment?" Her gaze rested speculatively on Jantiff, who said hurriedly, "I can't possibly spare any more. I'm very low on everything."

Esteban spoke to Jantiff: "What of you? Are you for this bonterfest?"

Jantiff hesitated. "I've just been foraging, and I'm not sure I enjoy it."

"My dear fellow, it's not the same thing at all! Do you have ozols?"

"Well, a few. Safely locked away, of course."

"Then you can afford the bonterfest. I'll mark you down for a place."

"Oh—very well. Where and when does the event take place?"

"When? As soon as I make proper arrangements. Everything must be right! Where? Out in the Weirdlands where we can enjoy the countryside. I have recently become acquainted with Contractor Shubart; he'll allow us use of an air-car."

Jantiff gave a hollow laugh. "Who now is the exploiter, monopolist, elitist tycoon and all the rest? What of egalism now?"

Esteban retorted in a debonair, if somewhat edgy, voice: "Egalism is all very well, and I subscribe to it! Still: why deny the obvious? Everyone wants to make the most of their life. If I were able, I'd be a contractor; perhaps I'll become one yet."

"You've picked the wrong time," said Kedidah. "Did you read the *Concept*? The Whispers insist that the contractors cost too much and that changes must be made. Perhaps there'll be no more contractors."

"Ridiculous!" snorted Skorlet. "Who'll do the work?"

"I've no idea," said Kedidah. "I'm neither a Whisper nor a contractor."

"I'll ask my friend Shubart," said Esteban. "He'll know all about it."

"I don't understand!" said Tanzel plaintively. "I thought contractors were all ignorant outsiders, vulgar and mean, who did our nasty work for us. Would you really want to be someone like that?"

Esteban gave a gay laugh. "I'd be a very nice contractor, as polite and clever as I am now!"

Kedidah jumped to her feet. "Come, Jantiff! Let's be off, if we're to get good seats. And bring along a few extra tokens; this week I'm totally bankrupt."

Late in the afternoon Jantiff returned home along Disselberg River. The shunk contests* had exceeded all his expectations; his mind seethed with sensations and images.

The crowds had early obtruded themselves, choking all man-ways leading to the stadium. Jantiff had noted the vivacity of their faces, the wet shine of their eyes, the tremulous flexibility of their mouths as they talked and laughed: these were not the folk, serene and bland, who promenaded along Uncibal River! The stadium itself was a gigantic place, rearing high in a succession of levels: bank on bank, buttress over buttress, balcony after balcony, closing off the sky, with

---

* A pallid rendering of the Arrabin term which translates into something like: "confrontations of fateful glory."

the spectators a crusted blur. From everywhere came a pervasive whisper, hoarse as the sea, waxing and waning to the movement of events.

The preliminary ceremonies Jantiff found rather tedious: an hour of marching and countermarching by musicians in purple and brown uniforms to music of horns, grumbling bass resonators and three-foot cymbals. At last eight portals slid aside; eight men rode forth, erect and somber on the pedestals of power-chariots. They circled the field, gazing straight ahead, as if oblivious to all but their own fateful thoughts. Staring directly ahead, the riders departed the field.

The stadium-sound rose and fell, reflecting the consonance of moods of half a million people in close proximity, and Jantiff wondered at the psychological laws governing such phenomena.

Abruptly, responding to an influence beyond Jantiff's perception, the sounds halted and the air became tense with silence.

The portals to east and west slid apart; out lurched a pair of shunk. They rumbled in rage, stamped the turf, reared thirty feet into the air as if to fling away those calm and indomitable riders who stood on their shoulders. So began the contests.

The hulks collided with awesome impacts; the poise of the riders transcended belief. Even though the fact occurred before Jantiff's eyes. Time and time again they evaded the great pads, to remount with calm authority as the shunk lurched to its feet. He communicated his wonder to Kedidah: "What a miracle they stay alive!"

"Sometimes two or even three are killed. Today—they're lucky." Jantiff turned her a curious side glance; was the wistful note in her voice for the crushed riders or for those who managed to evade death?

"They train for years and years," Kedidah told him as they left the stadium. "They live in the stink and noise and feel of the beasts; then they come to Arrabus and hope to ride at ten contests; then they can return to Zonder with their fortunes." Kedidah fell silent and seemed to become distrait. Where the lateral joined Disselberg River she said abruptly: "I'll leave you here, Janty; there's an appointment I simply must keep."

Jantiff's jaw sagged. "I thought we could spend the evening together; maybe at your apartment—"

Kedidah smilingly shook her head. "Impossible, Janty. Now excuse me, please; I've got to hurry."

"But I wanted to discuss moving in with you!"

"No, no, no! Janty, behave yourself! I'll see you in the wumper."

Jantiff returned to Old Pink with hurt feelings. He found Skorlet busy with her globes, daubing the last of his blue, black, dark green and umber pigments upon the paper contrivances.

Jantiff stared in shock. "Whatever are you up to? Really, Skorlet, that isn't a decent thing to do!"

Skorlet flung him a glance, and in her white face he saw a desperation he had never previously noticed. She turned back to her work, then after a moment found words and spoke through gritted teeth. "It's not fair that you should have everything and me nothing."

"But I don't have everything!" Jantiff bleated. "I have nothing! You've taken them all! Brown, black, green, blue! I have a few reds, true, and orange and ocher and yellow—no, now you've deprived me of my yellow as well—"

"Listen, Jantiff! I need tokens to take myself and Tanzel on the bonterfest. She's never been anywhere and seen nothing, much less tasted bonter. I don't care if I use all your pigments! You are so rich, you can get more, and I must make these cult-globes, dog defile them!"

"Why doesn't Esteban pay for Tanzel? He never seems to lack tokens."

Skorlet gave a bitter snort. "Esteban is too self-important to spare tokens for anyone. In all candor, he should have lived out in the Bad Worlds where he could be a tycoon. Or an exploiter. For certain he's no egalist. And you'd never imagine the wild schemes that throng his mind."

Surprised by Skorlet's vehemence, Jantiff went to his chair. Skorlet continued to daub grimly at her contrivances and Jantiff growled: "What good are those things that you're wasting my pigments on?"

"I don't know what good they are! I take them down to Disjerferact and people pay good tokens for them and that's all I care. Now I need just a bit of that orange—Jantiff, it's no use showing me that mulish expression!"

"Here, take it! This is the last time! From now on I'm locking everything up in my case!"

"Jantiff, you're a very small person."

"And you're very large—with other people's belongings!"

"Control your tongue, Jantiff! You have no right to hector

me! Now turn on the screen. The Whispers are making an important speech and I want to hear it."

"Bah," muttered Jantiff. "Just more of the same." Nevertheless, upon meeting Skorlet's lambent gaze, he rose to his feet and did her bidding.

Jantiff wrote a letter home:

Dearest family:

First my inevitable requests. I don't want to be a nuisance, but circumstances are against me. Please send me another selection of pigments, of double size. They cannot be obtained here, like everything else. Still, life progresses. The food of course is deadly dull; everyone is obsessed with "bonter." Some friends are planning a "gypsy banquet," whatever that is. I've been invited, and I'll probably attend, if only to get away from gruff and deedle for a few hours.

I fear that I'm developing a fragmented personality. I wonder sometimes if I'm not living in a dreamland, where white is black and black is not white, which would be too simple, but something totally absurd like, say, ten dead dogfish or the smell of gilly-flowers. Mind you, Arrabus was at one time a very ordinary industrialized nation. Is this the inevitable sequence? The ideas succeed each other with a frightening logic. Life is short; why waste a second on thankless drudgery? Technology exists for this purpose! Therefore, technology must be augmented and extended, to dispel as much drudgery as possible. Let the machines toil! Leisure, the rich flavor of sheer existence, is the goal! Very good, if only the machines could do everything. But they won't repair themselves, and they won't perform human services, so even Arrabins must drudge: a sour thirteen hours a week. Next, the machines are unkind enough to break down. Contractors must be hired, from compounds in Blale and Froke and other places at the back of the Weirdlands. Needless to say, the contractors refuse to work on the cheap. In fact, or so I am told, they absorb almost the whole of the gross Arrabin product. The Arrabins could relieve the situation by training persons so inclined to be technicians and mechanics, but egalists assert that specialization is the first step toward elitism. No doubt they are right. It never occurs to anyone that the

contractors are elitists of the very finest water, who grow
rich exploiting the Arrabins—if exploiting is the proper
word.

I wrote "never occurs to anyone," but perhaps this
isn't quite accurate. The other night I heard a public
address by the Whispers. I made some sketches as they
appeared on the screen; I enclose one of them. The
Whispers are chosen by a random process. On each level
of every block someone, selected by lot, becomes a monitor. The twenty-three monitors choose by lot, a Block
Warden. From the Block Wardens of each district a Del-
egate is selected, by lot of course. Each of the four great
metropolitan divisions: Uncibal, Propunce, Waunisse
and Serce, is represented by its Panel of Delegates. By
lot one of these Delegates becomes a Whisper. The
Whispers are expected to wield their authority, such as it
is, in a subdued, egalistic manner: hence the title "Whispers" which developed, so I am told, from a jocular conversation many years ago.

In any event the Whispers appeared on the screen the
other night. They spoke very guardedly, and made dutiful obeisance to the glories of egalism. Still, the effect
was hardly optimistic. Even I apprehended the hints, and
my ears are not as keen in this regard as those of the
Arrabins. The woman Fausgard read out statistics making no comment, but everyone could hear that the equi-
librium was failing, that capital deterioration exceeded
repair and replacement, from which everyone could
draw whatever conclusion they chose. The Whispers announced that they will shortly visit the Connatic at Lusz
to discuss the situation. These ideas aren't popular; the
Arrabins reject them automatically, and I have heard
grumbling that the expedition to Numenes is just a
junket in search of high living. Remember, the Whispers
live in the same apartments and eat the same gruff,
deedle and wobbly as anyone else; however, they do no
drudge. At the Centenary they will make a further announcement, undoubtedly to the effect that the contractors must be phased out. This idea in itself hurts no
Arrabin feelings. The contractors live baronial lives on
their country estates, and the Arrabins know them (en-
viously?) for elitists.

Items of incidental intelligence: Blade, at the south
edge of "Weirdland," is warmed by an equatorial cur-

rent and is not as cold as its latitude suggests. Remember, Wyst is a very small world! The folk who live in Froke, to the west of Blale, are called Frooks. Nomads wander Weirdland forests; some are called "gypsies" and others "witches," for reasons past my comprehension. The gypsies range closer to Arrabus and provide feasts of bonter for a fee. The Arrabins lack all interest in music. None play musical instruments, presumably because of the drudgery involved. Indeed this is a strange place! Shocking, disturbing, uncomfortable, hungry, but fascinating! I never tire of watching the great crowds: everywhere people! There is sheer magnificence to these numbers; it is marvelous to stand above Uncibal River, gazing down at the faces. Invent a face: any face you like. Big nose, little ears, round eyes, long chin—sooner or later you'll see it in Uncibal River! And do these numbers create a drabness? or uniformity? To the contary! Every Arrabin desperately asserts his individuality, with personal tricks and fads. A futile kind of life, no doubt, but isn't all life futile? The Arrabins enter life from nowhere and when they die no one remembers them. They produce nothing substantial; in fact—so it now occurs to me—the only commodity they produce is leisure!

Enough for now. I'll write soon again.

As usual all my affection,

Jantiff.

Jantiff had locked away those pigments remaining to him. Skorlet perforce decided that her cult-globes were complete and began to tie them into clusters of six. Jantiff's restless activities at last attracted her notice. She looked up from her work and uttered a peevish complaint. "Why in the name of all perversity must you flutter here and there like a bird with a broken wing? Settle yourself, I beg you!"

Jantiff responded with quiet dignity. "I made certain sketches of the Whispers the other night. I wanted to send one or two to my family, but they have disappeared. I am beginning to suspect snergery."

Skorlet gave a bark of rude laughter. "If this is the case, you should be flattered!"

"I am merely annoyed."

"You make such an absurd fuss over nothing! Draw up another sketch, or send off others. The affair is quite inconsequential and you cannot imagine how you distract me."

"Excuse me," said Jantiff. "As you suggest, I will send another sketch, and please convey my compliments to the snerge."

Skorlet only shrugged and finished her work. "Now, Jantiff, please help me carry the globes down to Esteban's apartment; he knows the dealer who sells for the best price."

Jantiff started to protest but Skorlet cut him short: "Really, Jantiff, I'm dumbfounded! In your life you've enjoyed every known luxury, yet you won't help poor Tanzel to a single taste of bonter!"

"That's not true," cried Jantiff hotly. "I took her to Disjerferact the other day and bought her all the poggets* and water-puffs and eel-pies she could eat!"

"Never mind all that! Just bear a hand now; I'm not asking anything unreasonable of you."

Jantiff sullenly allowed himself to be loaded down with cult-globes. Skorlet gathered up the rest and they proceeded around the corridors to Esteban's apartment. In response to Skorlet's kick at the door, Esteban peered out into the corridor. He saw the globes without show of enthusiasm. "So many?"

"Yes, so many! I've made them and you can trade them, and please bring back whatever old wire you can salvage."

"It's really an enormous inconvenience—"

Skorlet tried to make a furious gesture but, impeded by the globes, managed only to flap her elbows. "You and Jantiff are both insufferable! I intend to go to the feast and Tanzel is coming as well. Unless you care to pay for her bonter, then you must help me with these globes!"

Esteban gave a groan of annoyance. "An abominable nuisance! Well, dog defile it, what must be, must be. Let's count them out."

While they worked Jantiff seated himself upon the couch, which Esteban had upholstered with a fine thick cloth, patterned in a dramatic orange, brown and black geometry. The other furnishings showed similar evidence of taste and discrimination. Upon an end table Jantiff noticed a camera of familiar aspect. He picked it up, looked at it closely and put it in his pocket.

Skorlet and Esteban finished the count. "Kibner is not the

---

* Shredded seaweed, wound around a twig and fried in hot oil.

effusively generous person you take him for," said Esteban. "He'll want at least thirty percent of the gross."

Skorlet gave a poignant contralto cry of distress. "That's utterly exorbitant! Think of the scrounging, the work, the inconvenience I've suffered! Ten percent is surely enough!"

Esteban laughed dubiously. "I'll start with five and settle as low as I can."

"Be steadfast! Also you must carefully impress values upon Kibner! He seems to think we don't know the worth of money."

"Creeping elitism there!" Esteban warned her facetiously. "Curb that tendency!"

"Yes, of course," said Skorlet sarcastically. "Come along, Jantiff. It's almost time for evening wump."

Esteban's gaze brushed the end table, stopped short, veered around the room, returned briefly to the end table, then came to rest upon Jantiff. "Just a moment. There's snergery going on, and I don't care to be a party to it."

"What are you talking about?" snapped Skorlet. "You have nothing worth attention."

"What of my camera? Come now, Jantiff, disgorge. You were sitting on the couch, and I even saw you make the move."

"This is embarrassing," said Jantiff.

"No doubt. The camera is missing. Do you have it?"

"As a matter of fact I have my own camera with me, the one I brought from Zeck. I haven't so much as seen yours."

Esteban took a menacing step forward and extended his hand. "No snerging here, please. You took my camera; give it back."

"No, this is definitely my own camera."

"It's mine! It was on the table and I saw you take it."

"Can you identify it?"

"Naturally! Beyond all equivocation! I could even describe the pictures on the matrix." He hesitated and added: "If I chose to do so."

"Mine has the name Jantiff Ravensroke engraved beside the serial number in twisted reed Old Mish characters. Does yours?"

Esteban stared at Jantiff with hot round brown eyes. He spoke in a harsh voice: "I don't know what's engraved beside the serial number."

Jantiff wrote in elegant flourishes on a piece of paper. "This is Old Mish. Do you care to inspect my camera?"

Esteban made an incomprehensible sound and turned his back.

Jantiff and Skorlet left the apartment. As they walked the corridor Skorlet said: "That was both childish and unnecessary. What do you gain by antagonizing Esteban?"

Jantiff stopped short in shock and astonishment. Skorlet strode grimly forward without slackening her pace. Jantiff ran to catch up. "You can't be serious!"

"Naturally I'm serious!"

"But I only reclaimed the property he stole from me! Isn't that a reasonable act?"

"You should use the word 'snerge'; it's far more polite."

"I was quite polite to Esteban, under the circumstances."

"Not really. You know how fastidiously proud he is."

"Hmmf. I don't understand how any Arrabin can be proud."

Skorlet swung around and briskly slapped Jantiff's face. Jantiff stood back, then shrugged. In silence they returned to their apartment. Skorlet flung open the door and marched into the sitting room. Jantiff closed the door with exaggerated care.

Skorlet swung around to face him. Jantiff retreated, but Skorlet now was remorseful. In a throbbing voice she cried: "It was wrong to strike you; please forgive me."

"My fault, really," mumbled Jantiff. "I should not have mentioned the Arrabins."

"Let's not talk about it; we're both tired and troubled. In fact, let's go to bed and copulate, to restore our equanimity; I simply must relax."

"That's an odd notion but—oh, I suppose so, if you're of a mind."

Arriving at Kedidah's apartment, Jantiff found only Sarp on the premises. Sarp announced gruffly that Kedidah would be back shortly "—with noise and confusion and jerking about this way and that. Not an easy one to share with, I'll tell you!"

"A pity!" said Jantiff. "Why don't you trade apartments with someone?"

"Easier said than done! Who'd choose to burden their lives with such a hity-tity waloonch? And will she pick up behind herself? Never. She creates disorder out of the thin air!"

"As a matter of fact I find my own roommate just a bit too quietly self-contained," said Jantiff. "One hardly knows she is about, and she has an almost geometrical sense of tidiness. Perhaps I might be persuaded to trade with you."

Sarp cocked his head to the side, and squinted dubiously at Jantiff. "It's always a gamble. Who is this paragon of yours?"

"Her name is Skorlet."

Sarp emitted a wild hoot of derision. "Skorlet! Neat? With her incessant cult-globes? And 'quietly self-contained'? She is not only talkative but meddlesome and domineering! She hectored poor Wissilim so that he not only changed levels but moved clear out of Old Pink! What kind of fool do you take me for?"

"You misunderstand her; she is actually quite mild. Look here; I'll even include an inducement."

"Such as what?"

"Well, I'll paint your portrait, in several colors."

"Ha! Yonder hangs the mirror; what else do I need?"

"Well—here is a fine stylus I brought from Zeck: a scientific marvel. It draws carbon and water and nitrogen from the air to formulate a soft ink which it then burns permanently upon paper. It never fails and lasts a lifetime."

"I write very little. What else can you offer?"

"I don't have a great deal else. A jade and silver medallion for your cap?"

"I'm not a vain man; I'd only trade it out on the mud flats for a mouthful of bonter, so what's the odds? Good old gruff and deedle with wobbly to fill in the chinks: that'll do for me."

"I thought Kedidah was such a trial."

"Compared to Skorlet she's an angel of mercy. A bit noisy and over-gregarious; who could deny it? And now she's taken up with Garch Darskin of the Ephthalotes . . . In fact, here she comes now."

The door swung aside; into the apartment burst Kedidah with three muscular young men. "Good, kind Sarp!" cried Kedidah. "I knew I'd find him home! Bring out your jug of swill and pour us all a toddy; Garch has been at practice and I'm exhausted watching him."

"The swill is gone," growled Sarp. "You finished it yesterday." Kedidah took heed of Jantiff. "Here's an obliging fellow! Jantiff, fetch us in your jug of swill. Hussade is a taxing occupation and we're all in need of a toddy!"

"Sorry," said Jantiff rather stiffly. "I'm not able to oblige you."

"What a bore. Garch, Kirso, Rambleman; this is Janty

Ravensroke, from Zeck. Janty, you are meeting the cutting edge of the Ephthalotes: the most efficient team on Wyst!"

"I am honored to make your acquaintance," said Jantiff in his most formal voice.

"Jantiff is very talented," said Kedidah. "He produces the most fascinating drawings! Jantiff, do us a picture!"

Jantiff shook his head in embarrassment. "Really, Kedidah, I just don't knock out these things on the spur of the moment. Furthermore, I don't have my equipment with me."

"You're just modest! Come now, Janty, produce something witty and amusing! Look, there's your stylus, and somewhere, somewhere, somewhere, a scrap of paper . . . Use the back of this registration form."

Jantiff reluctantly took the materials. "What shall I draw?"

"Whatever suits you. Me, Garch, or even old Sarp."

"Don't bother with me," said Sarp. "Anyway I'm going out to meet Esteban. He's got some mysterious proposal to communicate."

"It's probably just his bonterfest; I'd go instantly if I had the tokens. Jantiff, perform for us! Do Rambleman; he's the most picturesque! Notice his nose; it's like the fluke of an anchor: pure North Pombal for you!"

With stiff fingers Jantiff set to work. The others watched a moment or two then fell to talking and paid him no further heed. In disgust Jantiff rose to his feet and left the apartment. No one seemed so much as to notice his going.

Dear all of you:

Thanks forever for the pigments; I'll guard these with great care. Skorlet snerged my last set to paint designs upon her cult-globes. She hoped to sell them for a large sum, but now she thinks Kibven, the Disjerferact booth-tender, cheated her. She's dreadfully exasperated, so I walk very carefully around the apartment. She's become abstracted and distant; I can't understand why. Something is hanging in the air. The bonterfest? This is a big event both for herself and for Tanzel. I don't pretend to understand Skorlet; still I can't evade the impression that she's disturbed and unsettled. Tanzel is a pleasant little creature. I took her to Disjerferact and spent all of half an ozol buying her such delicacies as toasted seaweed and sour eel tarts. The Disjerferact traders are none of them Arrabins, and a more curious collection you never saw. Disjerferact covers a large area and there are thou-

sands of them: folk from I don't know where. Monte-
banks, junk dealers, prestidigitators, gamblers, pup-
peteers and clown-masters, illusionists and marvel-makers,
tricksters, grotesques, musicians, acrobats, clairvoyants,
and of course the food-sellers. Disjerferact is pathetic,
sordid, pungent, fascinating and a tumult of color and
noise. Most amazing of all are the Pavilions of Rest,
which must be unique in the Gaean universe. To the
Pavilions come Arrabins who wish to die. Proprietors of
the various pavilions vie in making their services attractive. There are five currently in operation. The most
economical operation is conducted upon a cylindrical
podium ten feet high. The customer mounts the podium
and there delivers a valedictory declamation, sometimes
spontaneous, sometimes rehearsed over a period of
months. These declamations are of great interest and
there is always an attentive audience, cheering, applaud-
ing or uttering groans of sympathy. Sometimes the sentiments are unpopular, and the speech is greeted with
cat-calls. Meanwhile a snuff of black fur descends from
above. Eventually it drops over the postulant and his ex-
planations are heard no more. An enterprising Gaean
from one of the Home Worlds has recorded a large
number of these speeches and published them in a book
entitled *Before I Forget*.

Nearby is Halcyon House. The person intent upon
surcease, after paying his fee, enters a maze of prisms.
He wanders here and there in a golden shimmer, while
friends watch from the outside. His form becomes indistinct among the reflections and then is seen no more.

At the next pavilion, the Perfumed Boat floats in a
channel. The voyager embarks and reclines upon a
couch. A profusion of paper flowers is arranged over his
body; he is tendered a goblet of cordial and sent floating
away into a tunnel from which issue strains of ethereal
music. The boat eventually floats back to the dock clean
and empty. What occurs in the tunnel is not made clear.

The services provided by the Happy Way-Station are
more convivial. The wayfarer arrives with all his boon
companions. In a luxurious wood-paneled hall they are
served whatever delicacies and tipple the wayfarer's
purse can afford. All eat, drink, reminisce; exchange
pleasantries, until the lights begin to dim, whereupon the
friends take their leave and the room goes dark. Some-

times the wayfarer changes his mind at the last minute and departs with his friends. On other occasions (so I am told) the party becomes outrageously jolly and mistakes may be made. The wayfarer manages to crawl away on his hands and knees, his friends remaining in a drunken daze around the table while the room goes dark.

The fifth pavilion is a popular place of entertainment, and is conducted like a game of chance. Five participants each wager a stipulated sum and are seated in iron chairs numbered one through five. Spectators also pay an admission fee and are allowed to make wagers. An index spins into motion, slows and stops upon a number. The person in the chair so designated wins five times his stake. The other four drop through trap doors and are seen no more. A tale—perhaps apocryphal—is told of a certain desperate man named Bastwick, who took Seat Two on a stake of only twenty tokens. He won and remained seated, his stake now a hundred tokens. Two won again, and again Bastwick remained seated, his stake now five hundred tokens. Again Two won, and Bastwick had gained twenty-five hundred tokens. In a nervous fit he fled the pavilion. Seat Two won twice more running. Had Bastwick remained seated, he would have won 62,500 tokens!

I visited the pavilions with Tanzel, who is very knowing; in fact my information is derived from her. I asked what happened to the cadavers, and I learned rather more than I wanted to know! The objects are macerated and flushed into a drain, along with all other wastes and slops. The slurry, known as "spent sturge," is piped to a central processing plant, along with "spent sturge" from everywhere in the city. Here it is processed, renewed and replenished and piped back to all the blocks of the city as "ordinary sturge." In the block kitchens the sturge becomes the familiar and nutritious gruff, deedle and wobbly.

While I am on the subject, let me recount a rather odd event which took place one morning last week. Skorlet and I chanced to be up on the roof garden when a corpse was discovered behind some thimble-pod bushes. Apparently he had been stabbed in the throat. People stood around muttering, Skorlet and I included, until eventually the Block Warden arrived. He dragged the body to the descensor, and that was that.

I was naturally perplexed by all this. I mentioned to Skorlet that no one on Zeck would touch the corpse until the police had investigated thoroughly.

Skorlet gave me her customary sneer. "This is an egalistic nation; we need no police, we have our Mutuals to advise us and to restrain crazy people."

"Evidently the Mutuals aren't enough!" I told her. "We've just seen a murdered man!"

Skorlet became annoyed. "That was Tango, a boisterous fellow and a cheat! He notoriously trades his drudge, then never finds time to work off the stint. He won't be missed by anyone."

"Do you mean to say that there won't be an investigation of any kind?"

"Not unless someone files a report with the Warden."

"Surely that's unnecessary! The Warden hauled the body away."

"Well, he can hardly write out a report to himself, can he? Be practical!"

"I am practical! There's a murderer among us, perhaps on our very own level!"

"Quite likely, but who wants to make the report? The Warden would then be obliged to interrogate everyone, and take endless depositions; we would hear no end of disgraceful disclosures and everyone would be upset, to what real end?"

"So poor Tango is murdered, and no one cares."

"He's not 'poor Tango'! He was a boor and a pest!"

I pursued the subject no further. I speculate that every society has a means of purging itself and ejecting offensive elements. This is how it is accomplished under egalism.

There's so much to tell you that I can't come to a stopping place. The public entertainments are prodigious. I have attended what they call a "shunkery," which is beyond belief. Hussade is also very popular here; in fact, a friend of mine is acquainted with certain of the Ephthalotes, a team from Port Cass on the north coast of Zumer. None of the Arrabins play hussade. All the players hail from other parts of Wyst or offplanet. I understand that the games are rather more intense here than—

A tap-tap-tap. Jantiff put aside his letter and went to the door. Kedidah stood in the corridor. "Hello, Jantiff. Can I come in?"

Jantiff moved aside; Kedidah sauntered into the room. She gave Jantiff a look of mock-severe accusation. "Where have you been? I haven't seen you for a week! You're never even in the wumper!"

"I've been going late," said Jantiff.

"Well, I've missed you. When one gets used to a person, he has no right to slink off into hiding."

"You seem preoccupied with your Ephthalotes," said Jantiff.

"Yes! Aren't they wonderful? I adore hussade! They play today as a matter of fact. I was supposed to have a pass but I've lost it. Wouldn't you like to go?"

"Not particularly. I'm rather busy—"

"Come, Janty, don't be harsh with me. I believe that you're jealous. How can you worry about a whole hussade team?"

"Very easily. There's exactly nine times the worry, not counting substitutes. Nor the sheirl."

"How silly! After all, a person can't be split or diminished merely because she's very busy."

"It depends upon what she's busy at," muttered Jantiff.

Kedidah only laughed. "Are you going with me to the hussade game? Please, Janty!"

Jantiff sighed in resignation. "When do you want to go?"

"Right now; in fact this very minute, or we'll be late. When I couldn't find my pass, I was frantic until I thought of you, dear good boy that you are. Incidentally, you'll have to pay my way in. I'm utterly bereft of tokens."

Jantiff turned to face her, mouth quivering in speechless indignation. At the sight of her smiling face he gave a sour shrug. "I simply don't understand you."

"And I don't understand you, Janty, so we're in balance. What if we did? How would we benefit? Better the way we are. Come along now or we'll be late."

Jantiff returned to his letter:

—elsewhere.

By the strangest coincidence, I have just escorted my friend to the hussade game. The Ephthalotes played a team known as the Dangsgot Bravens, from the Caradas Islands. I am still shaken. Hussade at Uncibal is not like

hussade at Frayness. The stadium is absolutely vast, and
engorged with unbelievable hordes. Nearby one sees human faces and can even hear individual voices, but in
the distance the crowd becomes a palpitating crust.

The game itself is standard, with a few local modifica-
tions not at all to my liking. The initial ceremonies are
stately, elaborate and prolonged; after all, everyone has
plenty of time. The players parade in splendid costumes,
and are introduced one at a time. None, incidentally, are
Arrabin. Each performs a number of ritual posture,
then retires. The two sheirls appear at each end of the
field, and ascend into their temples while a pair of or-
chestras play *Glory to the Virgin Sheirls*. At the same
time a great wooden effigy is brought out on the field: a
twelve-foot representation of the karkoon* Claubus,
which the sheirls pointedly ignore, for reasons you will
presently understand. A third orchestra plays blatant
braying "karkoon" music, in antiphony to the two *Glo-
rys*. I took note of the folk nearby; all were uneasy and
restless, shuddering at the discords, yet earnest and intent and keyed taut for the drama to come. The sheirls
at this point stand quietly in their temples, enveloped in
Dwanlight and a wonderful psychic haze, each the em-
bodiment of all the graces and beauties; yet, certainly,
through the minds of each whirl the thrilling questions:
Will I be glorified? Will I be given to Claubus?

The game proceeds, until one of the teams can pay no
more ransom. Their sheirl thereupon is defiled by Claubus in a most revolting and unnatural manner; in this
condition she and Claubus are trundled around the field
in a cart pulled by the defeated team, to the accompa-
niment of the coarse braying music. The victors enjoy a
splendid feast of bonter; the spectators undergo a catharsis and presumably are purged of their tensions. As for
the humiliated sheirl, she has forever lost her beauty and
dignity. She becomes an outcast and, in her desperation,
may attempt almost anything. As you will perceive, hussade at Uncibal is not a merry pastime; it is a grim and
poignant spectacle: an immensely popular public rite.
Under the circumstances, it seems very odd that the

---

* In the Alastrid myths karkoons are a tribe of quasi-demonic beings,
characterized by hatred of mankind and insatiable lust.

teams never lack for beautiful sheirls, who are drawn to
danger as a moth to flame. The Arrabins are indeed an
odd people, who like to toy with the most morbid possi-
bilities. For instance: at the shunk contests the barriers
are quite low, and the shunk in their mad antics often
charge over and into the spectators. Dozens are crushed.
Are the barriers raised? Are those lower seats empty?
Never! In such a way the Arrabins participate in these
rituals of life and death. Needless to say, none *expects* to
be torn to bits, just as no sheirl expects to be defiled. It
is all sheer egocentricity: the myth of self triumphant
over destiny! I believe that as folk become urbanized,
just so intensely are they individuated, and not to the
contrary. From this standpoint the crowds flowing along
Uncibal River quite transcend the imagination. Try to
think of it! Row after row, rank after rank of faces,
each the node of a distinct and autonomous universe.

On this note I will close my letter. I wish I could inform you of definite plans, but for a fact I have none; I
am torn between fascination and revulsion for this
strange place.

Now I must go to drudge: I have traded stints with a
certain Arsmer from an apartment along the hall. This
week is unusually busy! Still, by Zeck standards, an idyll
of leisure!

With my dearest love to all: your wayward

Jantiff

Chapter 6

••••———◆———••••

Jantiff became ever more aware of Skorlet's strange new
manner. Never had he thought her placid or stolid, but now
she alternated between fits of smouldering silence and a peculiar nervous gaiety. Twice Jantiff discovered her in close colloquy with Esteban, and the discussions came to such an
abrupt halt that Jantiff was made to feel an intruder. Another
time he found her pacing the apartment, shaking her hands

as if they were wet. This was a new manifestation which Jantiff felt impelled to notice. "What is bothering you now?"

Skorlet stopped short, turned Jantiff an opaque black glance, then blurted forth her troubles. "It's Esteban and his cursed bonterfest. Tanzel is sick with excitement, and Esteban wants full payment. I don't have the tokens."

"Why doesn't he pay for Tanzel himself?"

"Hah! You should know Esteban by this time! He's absolutely heartless when it comes to money."*

Jantiff began to sense a possible trend to the conversation. He gave his head a sympathetic shake and sidled away toward the bedroom. Skorlet caught his arm, and Jantiff's fears were quickly realized. Skorlet spoke in a throaty voice: "Jantiff, I have a hundred tokens; I need five hundred more for the bonterfest. Won't you lend me that much? I'll do something nice for you."

Jantiff winced and shifted his gaze around the room. "There's nothing nice I need just now."

"But Jantiff, it's only an ozol or two. You've got a whole sheaf."

"I'll need those ozols on the way home."

"You already have your ticket! You told me so!"

"Yes, yes! I have my ticket! But I might want to stop off along the way, and then there'll be no money because I squandered it at Esteban's bonterfest."

"But you're squandering money on your own place in the group."

"I also squandered my pigments on your cult-globes."

"Must you be so petty?" snarled Skorlet, suddenly furious. "You're too paltry to bother with! Give thanks that I convinced Esteban of this!"

"I don't know what you're talking about," said Jantiff stiffly. "It's not Esteban's affair whether I'm paltry or petty or anything else."

Skorlet started to speak, then suppressed her remarks and said merely: "I'll say no more on that subject."

"Exactly so," said Jantiff frigidly. "In fact, nothing more need be said on any subject whatever."

Skorlet's face twisted askew in a darkling leer. "No? I thought you wanted to move in with that slang** Kedidah."

---

* Among the arrabins paternity is always in doubt, but even when an acknowledged fact, incurs no burden of obligation.

** A hairless rodent, long and slender, capable of producing a variety of odors at will.

"I spoke along those lines," said Jantiff in a measured voice. "Evidently it can't be done, and that seems to be the end of it."

"But it can be done, and quite easily, if I choose to do it."

"Oh? How will you accomplish this miracle?"

"Please, Jantiff, don't analyze my every statement. What I undertake to do, I achieve, and never doubt it. Old Sarp will move here if Tanzel will copulate with him from time to time, and she's very anxious for the feast so everything works out nicely."

Jantiff turned away in disgust. "I don't want to be part of any such arrangement."

Skorlet stared at him, her brows two black bars of puzzlement. "And why not? Everyone gets what he wants; why should you object?"

Jantiff tried to formulate a lofty remark, but none of his sentiments seemed appropriate. He heaved a sigh. "First, I want to discuss the matter with Kedidah. After all—"

"No! Kedidah has no force in this affair. What's it to her? She's busy with her hussade team; she cares not a whit whether you're here or there!"

Jantiff, looking up at the ceiling, composed an incisive rejoinder, but at the end held his tongue. Skorlet's concepts and his own were incommensurable; why incite her into a new tirade?

Skorlet needed no stimulation. "Frankly, Jantiff, I'll be pleased to have you out of here. You and your precious posturings! Piddling little sketches hung up everywhere to remind us of your talents! You'll never forget your elitism, will you? This is Arrabus, Jantiff! You're here on sufferance, so never forget it!"

"Nothing of the sort!" stormed Jantiff. "I've paid all my fees and I do my own drudge."

Skorlet's round white face underwent a sly and cunning contortion. "Those sketches, they're very strange! It gives me to wonder, these endless faces! Why do you do it? What or whom are you looking for? I want the truth!"

"I draw faces because it suits me to do so. And now, unless I'm to be late for drudge—"

"And now: bah! Give me the money and I'll make the arrangements."

"Absolutely not. You make the arrangements first. In any event, I don't have so many tokens; I'll have to change ozols at the space-port."

Skorlet gave him a long grim look. "So long as I can make Esteban a definite answer, and I'm seeing him directly."

"Be as definite as you like."

Skorlet marched from the apartment. Jantiff changed into his work overalls and descended to the street where suddenly he recalled that today Arsmer had taken over his stint. Feeling foolish he returned up the ascensor to his apartment. Stepping into the bedroom he removed boots and coveralls, and took them to the cabinet. At this moment the outer door opened and several people entered. Heavy footsteps approached the bedroom; someone pushed aside the door and looked in, but failed to notice Jantiff by the cabinet. "He's not here," said a voice Jantiff recognized as that of Esteban.

"He's gone off to drudge," said Skorlet. "Sit, and I'll see if the swill is fit to drink."

"Don't bother so far as I'm concerned," said a husky-harsh voice which Jantiff failed to recognize. "I can't abide the stuff."

Sarp's plangent rasp sounded in reply: "Easy for you to say, with all your wines and fructifers!"

"Never fear, soon you'll say the same!" declared Esteban in a voice of reckless enthusiasm. "Just give us a couple months."

"You're either a genius or a lunatic," said the unknown voice.

"Use the word 'visionary'!" said Esteban. "Isn't this how great events have gone in the past? The visionary seizes upon an idle reverie; he constructs an irresistible scheme and topples an empire! From Jantiff's miserable little sketch comes this notion of a lifetime."

" 'Lifetime': that is apt usage," said the unknown man drily. "The word reverberates."

"Here and now we abandon negativity!" exclaimed Esteban. "It's only a hindrance. We succeed by our very boldness!"

"Still, let's not be rash. I can point out a hundred avenues into disaster."

"Very good! We'll consider each in turn and give them all wide berths. Skorlet, where is the swill? Pour with a loose hand."

"Don't neglect me," said Sarp.

Jantiff went to sit on the bed. He uttered a tentative cough, just as Esteban spoke out. "Success to our venture!"

"I'm still not altogether attuned to your frequency,"

grumbled the unknown man. "To me it sounds implausible, improbable, even unreal."

"Not at all," declared Esteban gaily. "Break the affair into seperate steps. Each is simplicity in itself. In your case especially; how can you choose to act otherwise?"

The unknown man gave a sour grunt. "There's something in what you say. Let me see that sketch again . . . Yes; it's really most extraordinary."

Skorlet spoke in a sardonic aside. "Perhaps we should drink our toast to Jantiff."

"Quite so," said Esteban. "We must think very carefully about Jantiff."

Jantiff stretched himself out on the bed and considered crawling underneath.

"He only typifies the basic problem," said the unknown voice. "In simple terms: how do we avoid recognition?"

"This is where you become indispensable," said Esteban.

Sarp gave a rasping chuckle. "By definition, we're all indispensable."

"True," said Esteban. "For one of us to succeed, all must succeed."

"One thing is certain," mused Skorlet. "Once we commit ourselves there's no turning back."

Jantiff could not help reflecting that Skorlet's voice, cool and steady, was far different from the voice she had used during their recent quarrel.

"Back to the basic problem," said the husky-harsh voice. "Your absence from Old Pink will certainly be noticed."

"We'll have transferred to other blocks!"

"Well and good, until someone looks at the screen and says: 'Why, there's Sarp! And dog defile us all, that's surely Skorlet! And Esteban!' "

"I've considered this at length," said Esteban. "The problem is surmountable. Our acquaintances, after all, are not innumberable."

Sarp asked: "Are you forgetting Loudest Bombah?* The Whispers are inviting him to the Centenary."

"He's invited, but I can't believe that he'll come."

"You never know," said the unknown voice. "Stranger

---

* Bombah: Arrabin slang for a wealthy off-worlder: by extension a tourist.
Loud Bombah: an important and powerful off-worlder.
Loudest Bombah: the Connatic.

things have happened. I insist that we leave nothing to chance."

"Agreed! In fact I've considered the matter. Think! If he's on hand he'll be sure to mount the monkey-pole*; correct?"

"A possibility, but not a certainty."

"Well, he's either on hand or he isn't."

"That is definitely true."

"If someone gave you a bag of poggets and you knew one might be deadly poisonous, what would you do?"

"Throw away the whole bag."

"That's certainly one possibility. A good number of poggets are wasted, of course."

"Hmmf . . . Well, we'll discuss it another time. Are you still planning your bonterfest?"

"Most definitely," said Skorlet. "I've promised Tanzel and there's no reason to disappoint her."

"It makes us all conspicuous, after a fashion."

"Not really. Bonterfests aren't uncommon."

"Still, why not cancel the affair? There'll be opportunities in the future."

"But I'm not confident of the future! It's a spinning top which can totter in any direction!"

"Whatever you like. It's not a critical matter."

Skorlet, for one reason or another, chose to enter the bedroom. She went to her cabinet, then, turning, saw Jantiff. She gave a croak of astonishment. "What are you doing here?"

Jantiff feigned the process of awakening. "Eh? What? Oh, hello, Skorlet. Is it time for wump?"

"I thought you were at drudge."

"Arsmer took my drudge today. Why? What's the problem? Are you having guests?" Jantiff sat up and swung his legs to the floor. From the sitting room came a mutter of voices, then the outer door slid open and shut. Esteban sauntered into the bedroom.

"Hello, Jantiff. Did we disturb you?"

"Not at all," said Jantiff. He looked up uneasily at Esteban's looming bulk. "I was sound asleep." He rose to his feet. Esteban stood aside as Jantiff went into the sitting room, which was now empty.

Esteban's voice came softly against his back. "Skorlet tells me that you are advancing her money for the bonterfest."

"Yes," said Jantiff shortly. "I agreed to this."

* Monkey-pole: the Pedestal overlooking the Field of Voices.

"When can I have the money? Sorry to be abrupt, but I've got to meet my commitments."

"Will tomorrow do?"

"Very well indeed. Until tomorrow, then."

Esteban turned a significant glance toward Skorlet and left the apartment. Skorlet followed him into the corridor.

Jantiff went to the wall where he had pinned up certain of his sketches. He studied each in turn; none, to Jantiff's eyes at least, seemed in the slightest degree inflammatory. A most peculiar situation!

Skorlet returned. Jantiff quickly moved away from the sketches. Skorlet went to the table and rearranged her few trifles of bric-a-brac. In an airy voice she said: "Esteban is such an extravagant man! I never take him seriously. Especially after a mug or two of swill, when he fantasizes most outrageously. I don't know if you heard him talking—" She paused and looked sideways, dense black eyebrows arched in question.

Jantiff said hurriedly, "I was dead asleep; I didn't even know he was there."

Skorlet gave a curt nod. "You can't imagine the intrigues and plots I've heard over the years! None ever amounted to anything, of course."

"Oh? What of the bonterfest? Is that a fantasy too?"

Skorlet laughed in brittle merriment. "Definitely not! That's quite real! In fact you'd better go change your money and I'll make arrangements with Sarp."

Chapter 7

••••————◆————••••

Jantiff departed Old Pink and walked slowly to the manway. The day was cool, clear and crisp. Dwan hung in the sky, coruscating like a molten pearl, but for once Jantiff paid no heed to chromatic effects. He rode the lateral to Uncibal River, and diverted east toward the space-port. Odd, most decidedly odd, this affair. What could it all mean? Certainly nothing constructive.

A mile east of the space-port a lateral led north past the Alastor Centrality and on to the Field of Voices. Almost without conscious intent Jantiff diverted upon the lateral and rode to the Centrality: a structure of black stone, set to the back of a compound paved with slabs of lavender porphyry and planted with twin rows of lime trees.

Jantiff crossed the compound, passed through an air curtain into a foyer. Behind a counter sat a slender dark-haired young man, apparently no Arrabin by evidence both of his hair style and an indefinable off world manner. He addressed Jantiff politely: "What are your needs, sir?"

"I wish a few moments with the cursar," said Jantiff. "May I inquire his name?"

"He is Bonamico, and I believe that he is presently disengaged. May I ask your name?"

"I am Jantiff Ravensroke, from Frayness on Zeck."

"This way, if you please."

The clerk touched a button and spoke: "The Respectable Jantiff Ravensroke of Zeck, is here, sir."

A voice responded: "Very good, Clode; I'll see him at once."

Clode made a sign to Jantiff and conducted him across the foyer. A door slid aside; they entered a study paneled in white wood with a green rug upon the floor. A massive table at the center of the room supported a variety of objects: books, charts, photographs, cubes of polished wood, a small hologram stage, a six-inch sphere of rock crystal which seemed to function as a clock. Against the table leaned the cursar: a short sturdy man with pleasant blunt features and blond hair cropped close.

Clode performed a formal introduction: "Cursar Bonamico, this is the Respectable Jantiff Ravensroke."

"Thank you, Clode," said the cursar. He spoke to Jantiff: "Will you be pleased to take a cup of tea?"

"By all means," said Jantiff. "That is very kind of you."

"Clode, would you see to it? Be seated, sir, and tell me how I can be of service."

Jantiff lowered himself into a cushioned chair. The cursar remained by the table. "You are a recent arrival?"

"Quite true," said Jantiff. "But how did you know?"

"Your shoes tell the tale," said the cursar with a faint smile. "They are of better quality than one sees about the ways of Arrabus."

"Yes, of course." Jantiff gripped the arms of his chair and

leaned forward. "What I have to tell you is so odd that I don't quite know where to begin. Perhaps I should mention that at Frayness on Zeck I trained in dimensional drafting and pictorial composition, so that I have some small skill at depiction. Since arriving here I've made dozens of sketches: folk along the man-ways and at my block, which is Old Pink, 17-882."

The cursar nodded. "Proceed, please."

"My roommate is a certain Skorlet. Today, one of her friends, Esteban, arrived at the apartment with a man named Sarp and a fourth man whom I don't know. They were not aware that I was in the bedroom and held a colloquy which I could not help but overhear." To the best of his ability Jantiff reproduced the conversation. "Eventually Skorlet found me in the bedroom and became very disturbed. Sarp and the fourth man left instantly. The episode impressed me very unfavorably. In fact, I regard it as rather sinister." He paused to sip the tea which Clode had brought in during his account.

The cursar considered a moment. "You have no inkling as to the identity of the fourth man?"

"None whatever. I glimpsed his back through the door as he left the apartment; he seemed large, with heavy shoulders and black hair. This is my impression, at least."

The cursar gave his head a dubious shake. "I don't quite know what to tell you. The tone of the conversation certainly suggests something more than idle mischief."

"That was my definite impression."

"Still, no overt acts have been committed. I can't exert the Connatic's authority on the basis of a conversation which, after all, might be only wild talk. The Arrabins, as you may have noticed, are prone to extravagance."

Jantiff frowned in dissatisfaction. "Can't you make inquiries, or perform an investigation?"

"How? The Centrality here is a very minor affair, to an extraordinary degree. We're like an enclave on foreign soil. I have a staff of two: Clode and Aleida. They're underworked, but neither qualifies as a secret operative; no more, in fact, do I. There's not even an Arrabin police agency to deal with."

"Still, something must be done!"

"I agree, but first let's assemble some facts. Try to discover the identity of the fourth man. Can you do this?"

Jantiff said reluctantly, "I suppose this is possible. Esteban has organized a bonterfest, and this man apparently intends to be on hand."

"Very good; learn his name, and watch what goes on. If their activities exceed simple talk then I can act."

Jantiff grumbled: "That's like waiting for the rain before you start to fix the roof."

The cursar chuckled. "The rain at least shows us where the leaks are. I'll do this much. Tomorrow I leave for Waunisse to confer with the Whispers. I'll report what you have told me and they can take what steps they think necessary. They're a sensible group and won't automatically dismiss the matter. For your part, try to assemble more facts."

Jantiff gave a glum assent. He finished his tea and departed the Centrality.

The man-way took him toward the space-port. Jantiff looked back at the Centrality with the uneasy sense of lost opportunity. But what more could he say or do? And, under the circumstances, what more could the cursar say or do?"

At the space-port exchange office he converted five ozols into tokens, and returned toward Old Pink. His thoughts turned to Kedidah. She would certainly be pleased at the change; Sarp, after all, could not be the easiest person in the world to live with. Still, Jantiff reflected uneasily, she had expressed herself quite definitely on the subject. Probably not in all seriousness, Jantiff assured himself. In due course he arrived at Old Pink.

Skorlet was out. Jantiff packed his belongings. At last the tide of events was flowing in his favor! Kedidah! Marvelous feckless delightful Kedidah! How surprised she'd be! . . . Jantiff's mental processes became sluggish. A future without Kedidah seemed dark and lorn, but—and why deny it?—a future with her seemed impossible! Nonetheless, they'd work it out together. They'd naturally move out of Uncibal, but where? It was hard to imagine Kedidah and her flamboyant habits in the context of, say, Frayness. A contrast indeed! Kedidah would simply have to restrain herself . . . The absurdity caused Jantiff to wince. He paced back and forth across the sitting room, three steps this way, three steps that. He stopped short, looked at the door. The die was cast: Sarp was coming; he was going. Oh, well, it might turn out for the best. Kedidah thought well of him; he was certain of this. No doubt they'd work out a happy accommodation of some kind . . . The door opened; Skorlet entered the room. She stood just inside the doorway, glowering at him "All right; it's done. Are you packed?"

"Well, yes. Actually, Skorlet, I've been thinking that maybe I might not move after all."

"What!" cried Skorlet. "You can't be serious!"

"I've been thinking that maybe—"

"I don't care what you've been thinking! I've made the arrangements and you're going. I don't want you here!"

"Please, Skorlet, be reasonable. Your 'wants' are not altogether relevant to the matter."

"Yes they are!" Jutting out her head, Skorlet took an abrupt step ahead; Jantiff moved a corresponding pace backward. "You're a trial, Jantiff, I won't conceal it! Always peering and lurking and listening."

Jantiff tried to protest, but Skorlet paid no heed. "Quite honestly, Jantiff, I've had it with you! I'm sick of your namby-pamby postures, your ridiculous paintings, your eccentricities! You can't even copulate without counting your fingers! By all means move in with that shrick*; that's two of you. If you're a voyeur you'll have plenty to see; she's quite tireless! Time and time again I've seen the Ephthalotes stagger away on limp legs. Perhaps she'll allow you a turn or two at the end—"

"Stop, stop!" cried Jantiff. "I'll move if only to get away from your tirades!"

"Then give me the money! Nine hundred and twenty tokens!"

"Nine hundred and twenty!" exclaimed Jantiff. "I thought you said five hundred!"

"I've had to take three places: for you, me and Tanzel. At three hundred tokens apiece, plus twenty tokens for minor expenses."

"But you said you had a hundred tokens!"

"I'm not spending them! Come now, the money!" She lurched forward; Jantiff stared fascinated into the round face, congested with emotion like a bruise with blood. He shuddered: how could he ever have fondled this appalling woman?

"The money!"

Jantiff numbly counted over nine hundred and twenty tokens; Skorlet thrust a yellow card at him. "There's your place; go or stay as you like."

* Untranslatable.

The door slid aside; Sarp thrust his head into the room. "Is this home? Good enough; one crib is much like another. Show me my bed."

Jantiff quietly took his belongings and departed. Kedidah, arriving home an hour later, found him in her sitting room, arranging his painting equipment on one of the shelves. Kedidah, abstracted, failed to notice what he was doing. "Hullo, Janty, nice to see you, but you'll have to scamper; I've no time at all today."

"Kedidah! There's lots of time! I've succeeded."

"Magnificent. How?"

"I pawned old Sarp off on Skorlet! We're living together at last!"

Kedidah thrust her arms stiffly down, fingers outspread, thumbs to her hips, as if galvanized by an electric shock. "Jantiff, this is the most idiotic behavior; I don't know what to say!"

"Say: 'Jantiff, how wonderful!' "

"Not quite. How can it be wonderful when my teammates are here and you stand in the corner glowering?"

Jantiff's jaw dropped. "Did you say 'teammates'?"

"Yes, I did. I'm the new Ephthalote sheirl. It's absolutely marvelous and I love it! We're going to play in the tournament and we're going to win; I feel it in my bones, and there'll be nothing but gay times forever!"

Jantiff somberly seated himself. "Who was the last sheirl?"

"Don't mention her, the catrape*! She carried bad luck on her back; she infested everyone with despair! The Ephthalotes say so themselves! Don't sneer, Jantiff, you'll see!"

"Kedidah, my dear, listen to me. Seriously now!" Jantiff jumped to his feet, ran across the room and took her hand. "Please, don't be sheirl! What's to be gained? Just think, if you and I share life together, how happy we'll be! Give up the Ephthalotes! Say no to them! Then we'll start making plans for the future!"

Kedidah patted Jantiff's cheek, then gave him a grim little slap. "When do you drudge?"

"I'm done for the week."

"A pity. Because I'm entertaining friends tonight and you'll be in the way."

There was a brief silence. Jantiff rose to his feet. "You need only specify when you need the apartment and I'll

---

* Offensive epithet signifying bedragglement, offensive odor and vulgarity of manner.

leave you free to exert yourself as thoroughly as you like."

Kedidah said: "Sometimes I think that in my heart of hearts I despise you, Jantiff. Also don't ask me to change the door code to suit your convenience, because I won't."

Not trusting himself to speak, Jantiff stormed from the room, out of Old Pink and away into the late afternoon. Along Uncibal River he rode, as far as Marchoury Lateral, bowing his head to gusty winds, striding ahead through the crowds careless of whom he shouldered aside. The folk so treated moaned in outrage and hissed epithets, which Jantiff ignored. He collided with a fat woman wearing flamboyant orange and red; she tottered, lurched and fell with a great thrashing of limbs and a fluttering of garish garments. Raising her head she bawled a horrid curse at Jantiff's back. Jantiff hurried away, while the woman heaved herself to her feet. No one paused to help her; all passed by with preoccupied expressions, nor did anyone so much as glare at Jantiff, nor call out censure, of which in any event he had had a surfeit. Through Jantiff's mind passed the melancholy reflection: this is precisely the pattern of life! One moment a person rides Uncibal River, comfortable with his or her thoughts, serenely proud of his or her orange and red costume; the next instant an insensate force sends one head over heels, rolling and tumbling under the feet of the passersby.

Jantiff thoughtfully strode along Uncibal River. With the toppling of the fat woman his fury had waned, and he looked along the current of oncoming faces in a spirit of moody detachment.

What strange people these were, and also, for a fact, all other people of the Gaean universe! He studied the faces carefully, as if they were clues to the most profound secrets of existence. Each face alike and each face different, as one snowflake both simulates and differs from all others! Jantiff began to fancy that he knew each intimately, as if he had seen each a hundred times. That crooked old man yonder might well be Sarp! The tall thin woman with her head thrown back could as easily be Gougade, who lived on the Sixteenth level of Old Pink. And Jantiff amused himself with the fancy that along Uncibal River might come a simulacrum of himself, exact in every detail. What kind of person might be this pseudo-Jantiff, this local version of his own dreary self?

The idea presently lost whatever glimmer of interest it might have possessed, and Jantiff returned to his immediate circumstances. The options open to him were pitifully few however, and gratefully, they included immediate departure. No question about it; he'd had his fill of insults and tirades, not to mention gruff, deedle and wobbly. He felt a new spasm of resentment, most of it directed against himself. Was he such a sorry creature then? Jantiff, shame on you! Let's have no self-pity! What of all those wonderful plans? They depend on no one but yourself! Must they be tossed aside like so many scraps of trash just because your feelings have been hurt? As if to point up the issue, the setting sun passed behind a wisp of cloud, which instantly showed fringes of glorious color, and Jantiff's heart turned over within him. The Arrabins might be dense, obscure and impenetrable, but Dwan shone as clear and pure as light across mythical Heaven.

Jantiff drew a deep regenerative breath. His work must now absorb him. He would prove himself as rigid as any Arrabin; he would show regard for no one. Courtesy, yes. Formal consideration, yes. Warmth, no. Affection, no. As for Kedidah, she could be sheirl to four teams at once, with his best wishes. Skorlet? Esteban? Whatever their sordid plot he could only hope that they should fall over backwards and break their heads. The yellow card and the bonterfest? The group might include a massive black-haired man with a husky-harsh voice; it would certainly be interesting to learn his identity and pass the information along to Bonamico. And why should he not attend the bonterfest? After all, he had paid for it, and Esteban certainly would refuse to refund his money. So be it! From now on the primary concern of Jantiff Ravensroke was Jantiff Ravensroke, and that was all there was to it! Perhaps he should once more change apartments, and make a clean break with his problems. And leave Kedidah? The thought gave him pause. Charming, foolish Kedidah. Fascinating Kedidah. No doubt about it, she had befuddled him. There was always the possibility that she might change her ways. Devil take her! Why should he inconvenience himself to any slightest degree? He would take up his rightful residency; she would notice his detachment and possibly, from sheer perversity, begin to take an interest in him. Such a pattern of events was not impossible, at the very least! Jantiff diverted to a lateral and was carried north to the mud flats. On the outskirts of Disjerferact he purchased a dozen water-puffs, and so fortified, returned to Old Pink. With careless bravado he let himself into his new apartment. Kedidah was not at home. On the wall someone had scrawled a memorandum in chalk:

GAME TOMORROW! EPHTHALOTES AGAINST
THE SKORNISH BRAGANDERS! PRACTICE
THIS AFTERNOON! VICTORY TOMORROW!
EPHTHALOTES FOREVER!

Jantiff read the notice with a curled lip, then set about arranging his belongings in those few areas where Kedidah had not strewn her own gear.

Late the following afternoon Kedidah brought an exultant party of teammates, friends and well-wishers to the apartment. She ran across the sitting room and ruffled Jantiff's hair. "Janty, we won! So much for all your grizzling and croaking! On five straight power drives!"

"Yes," said Jantiff. "I know. I attended the game."

"Then why aren't you cheering with the rest of us? O hurrah everyone! The Ephthalotes are the best ever! Jantiff, you can come along to the party! There'll be swill by the crock and you'll quite get over your dudgeon."

"No dudgeon whatever," said Jantiff coldly. "Unfortunately I have work to do and I don't think I had better come."

"Don't be such an old crow! I want you to do a picture of the Ephthalotes with their glorious good-luck sheirl!"

"Some other time," said Jantiff. "At a party it would be totally impossible."

"You're right! In a day or so then. For now—pour out the swill! A lavish hand there, Scrive! Here's joy for the Ephthalotes!"

The hubbub became too much for Jantiff. He left the apartment and went up to the roof garden where he sat brooding under the foliage.

After an hour he returned to find the apartment empty but in a terrible state of disorder; chairs were overturned; crockery mugs lay broken on the floor and someone had spilled a cup of swill on his bed.

He was only vaguely aware of Kedidah's return to the apartment, and somehow ignored the subsequent sounds from her side of the curtain.

In the morning Kedidah was ill, and Jantiff lay stiffly on

his cot while Kedidah uttered small plaintive moans of distress. At last she called out: "Jantiff, are you awake?"

"Naturally."

"I'm in the most fearful condition; I don't think I can stir."

"Oh?"

"Yes, really, Janty! I'm sore everywhere; I can't imagine what happened to me."

"I could guess."

"Jantiff, I've got drudge and I'm simply not up to going out. You'll trade off with me, won't you?"

"I'll do nothing of the sort."

"Jantiff, please don't say no! This is an emergency; I absolutely can't make it out of the apartment. Be kind to me, Janty!"

"Certainly I'll be kind to you. But I won't take your drudge. In the first place you'd never pay me back. Secondly, I've got my own drudge today."

"Dog defile all! Well I'll have to bestir myself; I don't know how I'll manage. My head feels like a big gong."

During the next two days Kedidah left the apartment early and returned late and Jantiff saw little of her. On the third day, Kedidah remained at home, but the Ephthalotes' forthcoming game against the well-regarded Vergaz Khaldraves had put her in a trembling state of nerves. When Jantiff suggested that she sever her connection with the team she stared at him in disbelief. "You can't be serious, Janty! We've only got to beat the Khaldraves and then we're into the semi-finals, and then the finals and then—"

"Those are many 'and thens.'"

"But we can't lose! Don't you realize, Janty, that I'm a lucky talisman? Everyone says so! After we win we're established forever! We can chwig it in the bonter, not to mention a total end to drudge!"

"Very nice, but wouldn't you like to visit other places on other worlds?"

"Where I'd have to kowtow to all the plutocrats, and drudge eight days a week forever? I can't envision such a life. It must be appalling!"

"Not altogether. Many folk around the Cluster live this way."

"I prefer egalsim; it's much easier on everyone."

"But you really don't prefer egalism! You want to be triumphant so that you'll have bonter and never any drudge. That's elitism!"

"No, it's not! It's because I'm Kedidah and because we're going to win! Say what you like but it's not elitism!"

Jantiff gave a sad chuckle. "I'll never fathom the Arrabins!"

"It's you who are illogical! You don't understand the simplest little things! Instead you dabble all day in those ridiculous colors. Which reminds me: when will you do our picture, as you promised?"

"Well, I don't know. I'm not really sure—"

"It can't be today; we're practicing; nor tomorrow, that's game day; nor the next day, because we'll be recovering from the celebration. You'll just have to wait, Jantiff!"

Jantiff sighed, "Let's forget the whole thing."

"Yes; that will be best. Instead, you can make a fine bold poster for the wall: 'Ephthalotes Triumphant' with titans and cockaroons and darting thunderbolts—all in orange and red and smashing green. Please do, Janty; we'll all be thrilled to see such a thing!"

"Really, Kedidah—"

"You won't do it? Such a trifling favor?"

"Go arrange the pigments and paper. I refuse to waste my own on something so ridiculous."

Kedidah uttered a yelp of sick disgust. "Jantiff, you're really extreme! You niggle over such trivial things!"

"Those pigments were sent to me from Zeck."

"Please, Jantiff, I can't bear to bicker with you."

Summoning all his dignity, Jantiff vacated the apartment.

In the ground level foyer he encountered Skorlet. She greeted him with unconvincing affability. "Well, Jantiff, are you honing your appetite? The bonterfest is all arranged." She turned him a sly sidelong glance. "I suppose you're surely coming?"

Jantiff did not care for her manner. "Certainly; why not? I paid for the ticket."

"Very good. We leave early the day after tomorrow."

Jantiff calculated days and dates. "That will suit me very well. How many are going?"

"An even dozen; that's all the air-car will take."

"An air-car? How did Esteban promote such a thing?"

"Never underestimate Esteban! He always lands on his feet!"

"Quite so!" said Jantiff coldly.

Skorlet suddenly became gay—again a patently spurious

display. "Also very important: be sure to bring your camera! The gypsies are quaint; you'll want to record every incident!"

"It's just something more to carry."

"If you don't bring it you're sure to be sorry. And Tanzel wants a remembrance. You'll do it for her, won't you?"

"Oh, very well."

"Good. We'll meet here in the lobby directly after wump."

Jantiff watched her cross to the lift. Skorlet obviously wanted mementos of the great occasion and expected Jantiff to provide them. She could expect in vain.

He went out upon the loggia and sat on a bench. Presently Kedidah emerged from the foyer. She paused, stretched her arms luxuriously to the sunlight, then set off at a pace somewhere between a skip and a trot toward the man-way. Jantiff watched her disappear into the crowd, then rose to his feet and went up to the apartment. Kedidah as usual had left disorder in her wake. Jantiff cleaned up the worst of the mess, then went to lie on his bed. No doubt in his mind now: it was time to be leaving Uncibal . . . Skorlet's manner in regard to the camera had been most odd. She had never shown any interest in photographs before . . . He dozed and woke only when Kedidah returned with a group of swaggering Ephthalotes, who chaffed each other in raucous voices and discussed tactics for tomorrow's game. Jantiff turned on his side and tried to cover his ears. At last he rose, stumbled up to the roof garden where he sat until time for the evening meal.

Kedidah came into the refectory, still aglow with excitement. Jantiff averted his eyes.

Kedidah bolted her food and departed the refectory. When Jantiff returned to the apartment she was in bed and asleep, without having troubled to draw the curtain. How innocent and pure she looked, thought Jantiff. Turning sadly away, he undressed and went to bed. Tommorrow: the dangerous Khaldraves, in combat against the Ephthalotes and their glorious sheirl!

Late the next afternoon Jantiff returned to Old Pink. The day had been warm; the air even now seemed heavy. Black thunderheads rolled across the city; the sky to westward glistened like fish skin. Jantiff grimaced: was his imagination far, far, too vivid, or did a sickly odor indeed hang in the air? He suppressed the thought with a shudder: what revolting tricks one's mind played on oneself! Sternly ordering his thoughts he went up to the apartment. He halted outside the door, to stand rigidly in an odd posture: head down, right hand half-raised to the lock. He stirred, opened the door, entered the empty apartment. The lights were low; the room was dim and still. Jantiff closed the door, crossed to his chair and seated himself.

An hour passed. Out in the corridor sounded a soft footstep. The door slid aside; Kedidah entered the room. Jantiff silently watched her. She went to her chair and sat down: stiffly, laboriously, like an old woman. Jantiff dispassionately studied her face. The jawbones glimmered pale through her skin; her mouth drooped at the corners.

Kedidah appraised Jantiff with no more expression than his own. She said in a soft voice: "We lost."

"I know," said Jantiff. "I was at the game."

Kedidah's expression changed, if only by a twitch of her mouth. She asked in the same soft voice: "Did you see what they did to me?"

"Yes, indeed."

Kedidah, watching him with a queer twisted smile, made no comment.

Jantiff said tonelessly: "If you had to bear it, I could be brave enough to watch."

Kedidah turned away and looked at the wall. Minutes passed. A gong sounded along the corridor. "Ten minutes to wump," said Jantiff. "Take a shower and change your clothes; you'll feel better."

"I'm not hungry."

Jantiff could think of nothing to say. When the second gong sounded, he rose to his feet. "Are you coming?"

"No."

Jantiff went off to the refectory. Skorlet, arriving a moment later, brought her tray to the place opposite him. She pretended to look up and down the room. "Where's Kedidah? Isn't she here?"

"No."

"The Ephthalotes lost today." Skorlet surveyed Jantiff with a tart smile. "They took a terrible trouncing."

"I saw the game."

Skorlet gave a curt nod. "I'll never understand how anyone can put herself into such a position. It's unnatural display! Presently the team loses, and then it's the most grotesque display of all. No one can tell me that it's not purposeful! Criminal sexivation, really; I wonder that it's not banned."

"The stadiums are always full."

Skorlet gave a sour snort. "Be that as it may! The Ephthalotes and Khaldraves and all the other foreign teams mock us in our own stadium. Why won't they bring in their own sheirls? Never! They prefer to suborn anti-egalism. At the core, that's what sexivation is; don't you agree?"

"I've never thought much about it," said Jantiff listlessly.

Skorlet was not satisfied with the response. "Because in your heart of hearts you're not truly egal!"

Jantiff had nothing to say. Skorlet became heavily jovial. "Still, cheer up! Think of tomorrow: the bonterfest! All day you can be as anti-egal as you like, and no one will deny you your fun."

Jantiff sought phrases to suggest that Skorlet's zest for the occasion was far greater than his own. He chose simple candor. "I'm not altogether sure that I'll be going."

Skorlet jerked up her black eyebrows and stared hard across the table. "What! After you've paid all those tokens? Of course you're going."

"Really, I'm not in the mood."

"But you promised!" Skorlet blurted. "Tanzel expects you to take photographs! So do I! So does Esteban! We're counting on you!"

Jantiff began a grumbling counter-argument, but Skorlet refused to listen. "You'll come then, in absolute certainty?"

"Well, I don't like—" Skorlet leaned balefully forward; Jantiff stopped short. He remembered his conversation with the cursar. "Well, if it makes all that much difference I'll come."

Skorlet relaxed back into her chair. "We leave directly after wump, so don't go mooning off in all directions. Remember: bring your camera!"

Jantiff could think of no dignified retort. He swallowed the last of his deedle, rose and marched from the refectory, with the weight of Skorlet's gaze against his back.

He returned to his apartment and quietly entered. The sitting room was empty. He looked into the bedroom. The curtain was drawn around Kedidah's couch.

Jantiff stood uncertainly a moment, then returned to the sitting room. He lowered himself into his chair and sat staring at the wall.

In the morning Jantiff awoke early. Behind the curtain Kedidah lay inert. Jantiff dressed quietly and went to the refectory. Skorlet arrived a moment later, to stand by the doorway in an almost swashbuckling posture: legs apart, head thrown back, eyes glittering. She searched up and down the tables, spied Jantiff and came marching across the room. In annoyance Jantiff raised his eyes to the ceiling. Why must Skorlet be so bumptious? Skorlet either ignored or failed to notice his attitude, and swung herself into the chair beside him. Jantiff glanced sourly at her from the corner of his eye. This morning Skorlet was not at her best. She had obviously dressed in haste, perhaps not troubling to wash. When she leaned over to pluck Jantiff's sleeve, a rank sebaceous waft followed her gesture, and Jantiff drew fastidiously away. Skorlet again failed to notice, either through callousness or inattention. "It's the great day! Don't eat your gruff; save it for swill; you'll be so much the hungrier at the feast!"

Jantiff looked dubiously at his tray. Skorlet, as if at a sudden recollection, reached over and scooped up Jantiff's gruff. "You've got no hand for swill; I'll take care of it."

Jantiff tried to recover his gruff, but Skorlet dropped it into her pouch. "I'm hungry now!" cried Jantiff.

"There's bonter ahead! Take my advice: don't wad your gut solid with gruff!"

Jantiff moved his deedle and wobbly out of Skorlet's reach. "All very well," he growled, "but maybe I won't like the bonter."

"No fear on that score! The gypsies are marvelous cooks; nowhere in the Cluster will you eat better. First, tidbits: pastels of spiced meat, chobchows, fish sausages, pepper pancakes, borlocks. Next course: a pie of diced morels, garlic and titticombs. Next course: wild forest greens with musker sauce and toasted crumbs. Next course: meat grilled over coals with onions and turnips. Next course: cakes in flower syrup. And all washed down in Houlsbeima wine! Now then, what of that?"

"A most impressive menu; in fact I'm amazed—where do they get their materials?"

Skorlet made an airy gesture. "Here, there; who cares so long as it sits well on the tongue?"

"No doubt they rob the farm cattle for the meat."

Skorlet scowled sidewise. "Really, Jantiff, what is to be gained by all this careful analysis? If the meat is savory, don't concern yourself as to its source."

"Just as you say." Jantiff rose to his feet. Skorlet eyed him in speculation. "Where are you going?"

"To my apartment. I want a word with Kedidah."

"Hurry, because we leave at once. I'll meet you downstairs. And don't forget your camera."

With defiant deliberation Jantiff strolled around to his apartment. The curtains were still drawn around Kedidah's bed. She'll miss her breakfast, thought Jantiff, unless she moves very briskly indeed. "Time to get up!" he called out. "Kedidah, are you awake?"

No answer. Jantiff went to the bed and pulled back the curtains. Kedidah was not there.

Jantiff stared down at the empty bed. Had she passed him in the corridor? Might she be bathing? Why leave the curtain drawn? A horrid suspicion sprang full-blown into his mind. He turned to the cupboard. Her newest costume and sandals were gone. Jantiff opened the drawer where she kept her tokens. Empty.

He ran from the apartment, rode down to the lobby, raced out, ignoring Skorlet's hoarse call. Boarding the man-way, he thrust himself through the crowds, ignoring angry curses, searching right and left for the glint of golden brown hair.

Arriving at Disjerferact he ran dodging and sidling to the Pavilions of Rest, paid his token and entered the area.

On the Pier of Departure a red haired man read a valedictory ode to a small audience. Kedidah was nowhere to be seen; she would render no declamations in any event. The Perfumed Voyage? Jantiff peered into the floral atrium. Six folk silently waited for boats: he recognized none of them. Jantiff ran to Halcyon House and walked around the arcade, peering into the golden prisms. From time to time a reflection reached him: a flutter of garments, a groping hand, and suddenly the glimpse of a familiar and dear profile. Jantiff frantically rapped on the glass. "Kedidah!" The prisms moved; the face, just as it turned toward Jantiff, was lost in the golden shimmer.

Jantiff stared and called to no avail. "She's gone," said an annoyed voice. "Come along now; we're all waiting."

Looking over his shoulder Jantiff saw Skorlet. "I can't be sure," he muttered. "It looked like her, still. . . ."

"We can easily find out," said Skorlet. "Come over to the booth." She took Jantiff by the elbow and led him to the wicket. She called through the aperture: "Anyone from Old Pink been through this morning? That's 17-882."

The clerk ran his finger down a list. "Here's a tag from Apartment D6 on the 19th."

Skorlet said to Jantiff, "She's been here, but she's gone now."

"Poor Kedidah!"

"Yes, it's sad, but we haven't time to mope. Do you have your camera?"

"I left it at the apartment."

"Oh bother! Why can't you be more thoughtful? Everyone's hopping from one foot to the other on your account!"

Jantiff silently followed Skorlet to where Esteban stood waiting. "Kedidah went through the prisms," said Skorlet.

"A pity," said Esteban. "I'm sorry to hear that; she was always so gay. But we'd better get in motion. The day's not all that long. Where's Tanzel?"

"I left her at Old Pink. We've got to go for Jantiff's camera in any case."

"Well then, let's meet where Uncibal River crosses Tumb Flow, on the north deck."

"Very good. Give us twenty minutes and we'll be there. Come along, Jantiff."

Jantiff and Skorlet returned to Old Pink. Jantiff felt curiously light-headed. "I'm almost happy!" he told himself, marveling. "How can it be when darling Kedidah is gone? . . . It's because she was never mine. I never could have her, and now I'm free. I'll go on this bonterfest; I'll identify the fourth man; then I'll leave Arrabus, most definitely . . . Peculiar, Skorlet's insistence on the camera! Quite odd, really. What can it mean?"

In the lobby Skorlet said in a crisp voice, "I'll find Tanzel; you run up for your camera, and we'll meet here."

Jantiff spoke with dignity: "Please, Skorlet, try to be just a trifle less domineering."

"Yes, yes; just hurry; the others are waiting."

Jantiff rode the ascensor to the nineteenth floor, entered his apartment, opened the strongbox, brought out the camera. He weighed it on his hand, thought a moment; then, removing the matrix he replaced it with a spare, and locked the first crystal into the strongbox.

Returning to the lobby he found Skorlet and Tanzel awaiting him. Skorlet's eyes went instantly to the camera. She gave a brisk nod. "Good; we're off at last."

"Hurry, hurry!" cried Tanzel, running ahead, then turning to run backwards, the better to signal Jantiff and Skorlet to haste. "The flibbit will go and we'll be left behind!"

Skorlet gave a grim laugh. "No chance of that. Esteban

will wait for us, never fear. We're all most important to the success of the bonterfest."

"Hurry anyway!"

The lateral took them to Uncibal River, where they diverted and rode east. Tanzel spoke in awe. "Think of all these people, millions and millions, and we're the only ones going out on a bonterfest! Isn't that marvelous?"

"It's a bit anti-egal to think of it so," Skorlet reproved her. "More properly, you should say: 'Today is our turn for the bonterfest.' "

Tanzel screwed up her face into a grimace of quaint frivolity. "Just as you like, so long as we are going, and not someone else."

Skorlet ignored the remark. Jantiff watched Tanzel's impish quirks with detached amusement. In some manner she reminded him of Kedidah, even though her hair was short, dark and curling. Kedidah also had been silly and gay and artless . . . Jantiff blinked back tears and looked up into the sky, where shoal after shoal of herringbone cirrus floated in the blissful Dwanlight. Somewhere up there in the radiance Kedidah's spirit drifted: such, at least, was the doctrine of the True Quincunx Sect accredited by his father and mother. Wonderful, if only he could believe as much! Jantiff scrutinized the clouds for even the most subtle sign, but saw only that ravishing interplay of nacreous color which was the special glory of Wyst. Skorlet's voice sounded in his ear: "What are you staring at?"

"The clouds," said Jantiff.

Skorlet inspected the sky, but apparently saw nothing out of the ordinary and made no comment.

Tanzel called back over her shoulder: "There's Tumb Flow Lateral; I see Esteban on the north deck and all the other people!"

Jantiff, suddenly mindful of his mission, became alert. He inspected Esteban's companions with the keenest interest. They numbered eight: four men and four women; Jantiff recognized only Sarp. None displayed the broad-shouldered bulk of the man Jantiff had glimpsed in the apartment.

Esteban wasted no time on introductions; the group continued westward along Uncibal River. Jantiff, having discovered no massive black-haired man among the party once again became apathetic and rode somewhat behind the others. For a moment or two he considered leaving the group, inconspicuously of course, and returning to Old Pink. But what then?

Only the empty apartment awaited him. The idea lacked appeal. Skorlet and Esteban, so Jantiff noticed, had taken themselves somewhat apart from the others, and rode with their heads together in earnest conversation. From time to time they glanced back toward Jantiff, who became convinced that the two were talking about him. He felt a tremor of uneasiness: perhaps he was not, after all, among friends.

Jantiff stirred himself from his listlessness and examined the others of the party. None had given him any particular attention, save for Sarp who periodically turned him glances of crooked amusement, no doubt inspired by the news of Kedidah's journey into the prisms.

Jantiff sighed and fatalistically decided to continue with the party; after all, the day had only begun and there still might be much to be learned.

At the Great Southern Adit the group diverted to the left, and rode away through District 92: finally through the fringes of the city and out upon a soggy wasteland, grown over with salt grass, tattersack and burdock. The land was utterly deserted save for a pair of small boys flying a kite who only served to emphasize the desolation of the area.

The adit climbed a long gradual slope; behind, Uncibal could be seen as a pattern of rectangular protuberances, the colors dulled by distance. The way swung into Outpost Valley and Uncibal was blotted from view. In the distance, under the first ledges of the scarp Janty saw a cluster of long low buildings. Almost simultaneously he became aware of a grumbling, mumbling roar, which as the group approached became broken into a hundred components: pounding, grating, whistling screams, the trundling of iron wheels, low-pitched thuds and impacts, grinding vibrations, flutings and warbles. A tall prong-bar fence angled across the flat, then turned sharply to parallel the man-way. The message of the prongs was emphasized by bolts of blue-white energy snapping at random between the strands. Behind the fence gangs of men and women crouched over a pair of long slide belts burdened with rock. Jantiff took a step forward and put a question to Sarp: "What goes on yonder?"

Sarp inspected the activity with placid and almost benevolent contempt. "Alas, Jantiff, there you see our nursery for bad children: in short, the Uncibal Penal Camp, which both of us, so far, have fortuitously evaded. Still, never become complacent; never let the Mutuals prove you at your sexivation."

106   *Jack Vance*

Jantiff stared in astonishment. "These folk are all sexivators?"

"By no means; they run the criminal gamut. You'll find shirkers there and shiftills, not to mention flamboyants, performers and violeers."

Jantiff watched the prisoners a moment and could not restrain a sneer. "The murderers go free but the flamboyants and sexivators are punished."

"Of course!" declared Sarp with relish. "We've got lots of folk to be murdered, but only one egalism to be suborned. So never waste your pity: they all befouled our great society and now they sort ore for the Metallurgical Syndicate."

Skorlet snapped over her shoulder: "There's Jantiff for you, full of pity, but always for the deviates. Well, Jantiff, that's how such persons fare in Arrabus: double-drudge, no swill and they're tapped three times a year besides. Hard lives, eh, Jantiff?"

"What's it to me?" Jantiff asked shortly. "I'm not an Arrabin."

"Oh?" inquired Skorlet in a voice of silken mockery. "I thought you had come to Wyst to enjoy our egalistic achievements."

Jantiff merely shrugged and turned back toward Sarp. "And what is this Metallurgical Syndicate?"

"It's the facility of the five High Contractors, so naturally it is here that the deviates learn egalism." Sarp gave a cackle of wild laughter. "Let me name these eminent teachers: Commors, Grand Knight of the Eastern Woods. Shubart, Grand Knight of Blale. Farus, Grand Knight of Lammerland. Dulak, Grand Knight of Froke. Malvesar, Grand Knight of the Luess. There're five good plutocrats for you despite subservience!* And Shubart, who contracts the Mutuals, is the most arrant of all."

"Come now, if you please," said Esteban shortly. "Don't castigate Shubart, who is good enough to fly us out to Ao River Meadow; otherwise we'd all be for the bumbuster." **

---

* Subservience: In the Arrabin world view, the contractors, their technicians and mechanics are a caste of interplanetary riffraff, quite outside all considerations of egalistic dignity. The Arrabins like to think of the contractors as servile work masters, eager to oblige the noble egalists and at all times conscious of their inferior status. Hence the word "subservience" often appears in conversations concerning the contractors.

** Omnibus.

A man named Dobbo called out jocularly: "What's wrong with the old bumbuster? How better to see the countryside?"

"And if you fall asleep you're carried all the way to Blale," snapped Esteban. "No, thanks. I'll ride the flibbit, and let's offer Contractor Shubart a soft lip."

Sarp, who seemed to take a positive delight in baiting Esteban, would not be daunted. "I'll fly Shubart's flibbit and hold never a grudge. He lives in manorial style at Balad; why shouldn't he call himself 'Grand Knight' and go forth in pomp?"

"I'd do the same," said Dobbo, "given opportunity, of course. I'm egal, certainly, because I hold no other weapon against drudgery. Still, give and I'll take."

Ailas said: "Dobbo takes even when no one gives. When he takes his title, it should properly go: 'The Grand Knight of Snergery.'"

"Oh, ho!" cried Dobbo, "you wield a most wicked tongue! Still I admit I'll use anything available, including that title!"

The man-way proceeded past the sorting belts, then curved toward the foundries and fabricating plants, glided beside slag dumps, hoppers where barges unloaded raw ore, and a pair of maintenance hangars. The man-way split; Esteban led the group to a terminus in front of the administration complex, then around to the side where a dozen vehicles rested on a landing plat . . . Esteban stepped into the dispatcher's office, reappeared a moment later and signaled the group toward a battered old carry-all. "All aboard for the bonterfest! Transportation courtesy of Contractor Shubart whom I happen to know!"

"While you were scrounging, why didn't you promote a Kosmer Ace or a Dacy Scimitar?" called out Sarp.

"No complaints from the infantry!" Esteban retorted. "This is not absolutely deluxe, but isn't it better than traveling by bumbuster? And here comes our operator."

From the administration office came a heavily muscled man with black hair, a sagging portentous visage. Jantiff leaned forward: could this be the fourth party to the cabal? Not impossibly, although this man seemed burly, rather than massive.

Esteban addressed the group: "Bonterfesters, allow me to introduce the Respectable Buwechluter, factotum and aide indispensable to Contractor Shubart, more commonly known as 'Booch.' He has kindly agreed to fly us to our destination."

Intoxicated with excitement, Tanzel cried out: "Three cheers for the Respectable Booch! Hurrah, hurrah, hurrah!"

Esteban threw up his hands in facetious admonition. "Not too much adulation! Booch is a very suggestible man and we don't want him to become vainglorious!"

Jantiff cocked his ears as Booch gave a not altogether amiable snort. Inconclusive. Jantiff studied Booch's features: narrow heavy-lidded eyes, ropy jowls, a heavy mouth pouting over a creased receding chin. Booch was not a prepossessing man, though he exuded a coarse animal vitality. He muttered inaudibly to Esteban and swung up to the operator's station. "Everybody aboard!" called Esteban. "Briskly, now! We're an hour late."

The bonterfesters climbed into the carry-all and took seats. Esteban bent over Booch and gave instructions. Jantiff studied the back of Booch's head. Almost definitely, Booch was not the fourth conspirator.

Esteban seated himself behind Booch, who with contemptuous familiarity flicked fingers across the controls: the carry-all rose into the air and flew south over the scarp. In the seat behind Jantiff Ailas and a woman named Cadra seemed to be discussing Esteban. Cadra said, "This carry-all enhances a bonterfest beyond description; suddenly all the tedium disappears! As a scrounger Esteban ranks supreme."

"Agreed," said Ailas sadly. "I wish I knew his technique."

"There's no mystery whatever," said Cadra. "Combine persistence, ingenuity, charm, an exact sense of timing, persuasiveness: you've created a scrounger."

"For best effect, include bravado and a quantum of sheer brashness!" noted a man named Descart, to which Rismo, a tall plain woman, replied rather sarcastically: "What about simple ordinary luck? Has that no meaning?"

Cadra chuckled. "Most significant of all: Esteban is acquainted with the Contractor Shubart!"

"Oh, give the devil his due!" Ailas said. "Esteban definitely has a flair. Out in the Bad Places he'd be a top-notch entrepreneur!"

"Or a tycoon."

"Or a starmenter," suggested Rismo. "I can just see him swaggering about in a white uniform and a gold helmet—great cudgers in his harness, bluskin at his hip."

"Esteban, come listen to this!" Descart called. "We're trying to establish your previous incarnations!"

Esteban came aft. "Indeed? What indignities are you putting me to now?"

"Nothing extreme, nothing outrageous," said Cadra. "We just consider you a monster of anti-egalism."

"So long as you don't accuse me of anything sordid," said Esteban with suave equanimity.

"Today we're all anti-egal!" Ailas declared grandly. "Let's wallow in our shortcomings!"

"I'll drink to that!" called a man named Peder. "Esteban! Where's the swill?"

"No swill aboard," said Esteban shortly. "Control your thirst till we put down at Galsma. The gypsies are providing an entire keg of Houlsbeima wine."

Cadra asked mischievously: "Does anyone know that song: 'Anti-Egalists Eat Roast Bird, While Arrabins Get Only Feathers in the Mouth'?"

"I know it but I don't intend to sing it," said Skorlet.

"Oh, come! Don't be stuffy, today of all days!"

"I know the song," said Tanzel. "We sing it at the crèche. It goes like this." In an earnest voice she sang the scurrilous ditty. One by one the others joined in—all except Jantiff, who had never heard the song and in any case was in no mood to sing.

The landscape slid past below: the long southern slopes of the scarp, forests and high moors, then valleys opening down upon a rolling plain. The Great Dasm river, smooth as an eel, coiled across the landscape. Near a bend where the river turned southeast appeared a village of a hundred small houses, and the carry-all started to descend. Jantiff at first assumed that the village was their destination, but the carry-all flew another twenty miles: over a marsh overgrown with reeds, then a forest of gray and russet spider-leg, then a sluggish tributary of the Great Dasm, then another forest and at last down into a clearing from which rose a wisp of smoke.

"We've arrived!" Esteban announced. "At this point a word or two of caution, no doubt unnecessary to so many veteran bonterfesters, but I'll say them anyway. Tanzel, take special note! The gypsies are a peculiar race, and all very well in their own way, no doubt, but they have callous habits and they are by no means egalists. As Arrabins, we mean no more to them than so many shadows! Don't drink too much wine: if for no other reason than you'll lose zest for your bonter. And naturally—it goes without saying!—don't stray off by yourself—for unknown reasons!"

"Unknown reasons?" An odd phrase, thought Jantiff. If "reason" were "unknown," why had everyone's face gone bland and blank? Jantiff decided that when opportunity offered, he would put a question to Sarp. Meanwhile, whether for reasons known or unknown, he would heed Esteban's warning.

The carry-all touched ground; the passengers, pushing rather rudely past Jantiff, alighted. He followed with ostentatious deliberation, which, however, no one noticed.

The gypsies waited across the meadow, beside a row of trestle tables. Jantiff first saw a flutter of rich costumes striped in ocher, maroon, blue and green. Upon closer inspection he noted four men in short loose pantaloons, and three women swathed in ankle-length gowns: slender dark-haired folk, quick of motion, fluid of gesture, sallow-olive of complexion, with straight narrow noses, eyes tilted mournfully down at the corners and shadowed under dark eyebrows. A handsome people, thought Jantiff, but in some inexplicable fashion rather repellent. And once again he was assailed by second thoughts in regard to his participation at the bonterfest, though again for no definable reason: perhaps because of the gypsies' expressions as they regarded the Arrabins: a coolness distinguished from contempt only by virtue of indifference. Jantiff wondered whether he cared to eat gypsy food: surely they would feed the Arrabins anything palatable, without regard to fastidiousness. Jantiff managed a wry grin for his own qualms; after all, he had eaten ration after ration of Arrabin wump, prepared from sturge, with hardly more than a grimace or two. He followed the other bonterfesters across the meadow.

Despite Esteban's warnings all hurried to the keg, where the youngest of the gypsy women dispensed wooden cups of wine. Jantiff approached the keg, then moved back because of the crush. Turning away he appraised the other arrangements. The tables supported pots, tureens and trenchers, all exuding odors which Jantiff despite his reservations found undeniably appetizing. To the side hard knots of timber burnt to coals under a metal rack.

Esteban and the oldest of the gypsy men went to the table. Esteban checked items off against his list, and apparently found all to his satisfaction. The two turned and surveyed the group at the wine keg and Esteban spoke with great earnestness.

Tanzel tugged at Jantiff's sleeve. "Please, Jantiff: get me a cup of wine! Every time I step forward someone reaches past me."

"I'll do my best," said Jantiff dubiously, "although I've had the same experience. This group of egalists seems unusually assertive."

Jantiff managed to obtain two cups of wine, one of which he brought to Tanzel. "Don't drink it too fast or your head will swim, and you won't want to eat."

"No fear of that!" Tanzel tasted the wine. "Delicious!"

Jantiff cautiously sipped from the mug, to find the wine tart and light, with a faintly musky redolence. "Quite decent, indeed."

Tanzel drank again. "Isn't this fun? Why can't bonterfests be for every day? Everything smells so good! And, no argument, I'm ravenous!"

"You'll probably overeat and get sick," said Jantiff morosely.

"I have no doubt!" Tanzel drained her wine cup. "Please—"

"Not just yet," said Jantiff. "Wait a few minutes; you might not want another."

"Oh, I'll want another, but I suppose there's no great hurry. I wonder what Esteban is talking about; he keeps looking over toward us."

Jantiff turned his head, but Esteban and the gypsy had completed their conversation.

Esteban came over to the group. "Appetizers will be served in five minutes. I've had an understanding with the hetman. Courtesy and freedom have been guaranteed; everyone is safe from molestation so long as he doesn't stray too far from the clearing. The wine is of prime quality, as I specified; you need fear neither agues nor gripes. Still, moderation, I beg of all of you!"

"But not too much of it!" Dobbo called out. "We'd be defeating only ourselves. Moderation must be practiced in moderation."

Esteban, now in the best of moods, made a gesture of concession. "Well, no matter. Enjoy yourself in your own fashion. That's the slogan for today!"

"Here's to Esteban and future bonterfests!" called out Cadra. "Damnation to all croakers!"

Esteban smilingly accepted the congratulations of his friends, then gestured toward the table. "We can now enjoy our appetizers. Don't overeat; the meat is just now going on the grill."

And again Jantiff stood back as the group surged toward the table.

Never, for so long as Jantiff lived, was the bonterfest far from his memory. The recollections came always in company with a peculiar throat-gripping emotion which Jantiff's mind reserved for this occasion alone, and always in swirling clots of sensation: the gypsy gowns and breeches, in striking contrast to the pallid faces; flames licking up at the spitted meat; the table loaded with post and tureens; the bonterfesters themselves: in Jantiff's memory they became caricatures of gluttony while the gypsies moved in the background, silent as shadows. Ghost odors might drift through his mind: pungent pickles, pawpaws and sweetsops, roasting meat. Always the faces reasserted themselves: Skorlet, at one juncture transcending the imaginable limits of emotion; Tanzel, vulnerable to both pleasure and pain; Sarp with his slantwise leer, Booch, coarse, reeking, suffused with animal essence; Esteban. . . .

Nowhere to be seen was the fourth man to the cabal, and Jantiff lost whatever zest he might have felt for the occasion. Tanzel brought her mug and a heaped platter of food to the bench where he sat. "Jantiff! Aren't you eating?"

"After a bit, when the elbowing subsides."

"Be sure to try the pickles. Here, take this one. Isn't it wonderful? The whole inside of my mouth tingles."

"Yes, it's very good."

"You'd better hurry or there'll be none left."

"I don't care much, one way or the other."

"Jantiff, you are a strange, strange person! Excuse me while I eat."

Jantiff at last went to the table. He served himself a plate of food and accepted a second mug of wine from the impassive woman at the keg. Returning to the bench he found that Tanzel already had devoured the contents of her platter. "You have an excellent appetite!" said Jantiff.

"Of course! I've been starving myself for two days. So now, more chobchows? Or another portion of those delicious pepper pancakes? Or should I wait until the meat is served out?"

"If I were you I'd wait," said Jantiff. "Then you can go back for whatever you like the best."

"I believe you're right. Oh, Jantiff, isn't this exciting? I wish times like these would go on forever. Jantiff! Are you listening?"

"Yes indeed." Jantiff had in fact been distracted by a rather odd incident. Off to the side Esteban stood talking to the gypsy hetman. Esteban gestured with his mug, and both turned to look in Jantiff's direction. Jantiff feigned inattention, but a thrill ran along his nerves.

Someone had approached. Jantiff looked up to find Skorlet standing beside him. "Well, Jantiff? How goes the bonter?"

"Very well. I like these little sausages—although I can't help but wonder what goes into them."

Skorlet gave a bark of harsh laughter. "Never ask, never wonder! If it's savory, eat every morsel! Remember, it all flushes down the same drain in the end."

"Yes, no doubt you're right."

"Eat hearty, Jantiff!" Skorlet returned to the table and filled her platter for the third time. Jantiff watched from the corner of his eye, not altogether happy with her manner. Now he saw Esteban saunter across the clearing to where Skorlet stood devouring her food. Esteban spoke a question into her ear; Skorlet, her mouth full, shrugged, and managed to utter a reply. Esteban nodded and continued his circuit around the fringes of the group.

He halted beside Jantiff. "Well, how goes it? Is everything to your satisfaction?"

"Exactly so," said Jantiff guardedly.

"All I want to know," declared Tanzel, "is when we can come again!"

"Aha! We mustn't become guttricks, with thought for nothing but food!"

"Of course not; still—"

Esteban laughed and patted her head. "We'll make plans, never fear. So far, it's been a great success, eh?"

"It's all wonderful."

"Well, don't fill up too soon. There's more to come. Jantiff, have you taken photographs?"

"Not yet."

"My dear Jantiff! The banquet table: loaded, aromatic, inviting! You missed that?"

"I'm afraid so."

"And our picturesque hosts? Their magnificent faces, so placid and remote? Their boisterous breeches and pointed boots? Ah, then, allow me the use of your camera!"

Jantiff hesitated. "Well, I don't know. In fact I'd prefer not. You might somehow lose it."

"By no means! Put that other small escapade out of your mind; it was only a lark. The camera will be safe, I assure you!"

Jantiff reluctantly brought out the instrument.

"Thank you," said Esteban. "I assume there's still ample scope to the matrix?"

"Take as many pictures as you like," said Jantiff. "It's a new matrix."

Esteban stiffened; his fingers clenched at the camera. "What of the other matrix?"

"It was almost full," said Jantiff. "I didn't want to risk losing it."

Esteban stood silent. "Where is this old matrix? Are you carrying it with you?"

Surprised by the blunt question, Jantiff raised his eyes to find Esteban glowering in obvious annoyance. Jantiff spoke with cold politeness: "Why do you ask? I can't account for your interest!"

Esteban tried to throttle the fury in his own voice, without success. "Because there are pictures of mine on that matrix, as you're perhaps aware."

"You need not worry," said Jantiff. "The matrix is absolutely safe."

Esteban recovered his aplomb. "In that case I'm quite content. Aren't you drinking? This is Houlsbeima wine; they've done famously for us today."

"I'll have more presently."

"Do so, by all means!" Esteban sauntered away. A few minutes later Jantiff saw him conferring first with Skorlet, then Sarp.

Discussing me and the matrix, thought Jantiff. Here was surely the reason for Skorlet's urgency in connection with the camera. She and Esteban were interested in the matrix. But why? Enlightenment broke suddenly upon Jantiff: of course! Upon the matrix were imprinted images of the fourth man!

Jantiff shook his head in sad self-recrimination: after recovering his camera from Esteban he had never thought to examine the matrix. What a foolish oversight! Of course, at the time there had been no particular reason to do so; he lacked all interest in Esteban's activities. Now the situation was different! Lucky the matrix was locked securely in his strong box! Which stimulated a new and chilling thought:

Sarp still knew the code, since Jantiff had never thought to change it. Immediately upon his return to Uncibal he must rectify this oversight!

The gypsies ordered the table, then, taking the meat from the fire, arranged it upon long wooden platters. One of the women poured sauce over the meat; another set out crusty loaves; a third brought forth a great wooden bowl of salad. All then returned to the forest shadows.

Esteban called: "Everyone to the table! Eat as you've never eaten before! For once, we're all guttricks together!"

The bonterfesters surged forward, with Jantiff, as usual, bringing up the rear.

Half an hour later the group sprawled lethargic and sated around the meadow. Esteban roused himself to croak in a rich glottal voice: "Everyone remember: the sweet is still to come! White millicent cake in flower syrup! Don't give up now!"

From the group came groans of protest. "Show us mercy, Esteban!"

"What? Are there no more courses?"

"Bring my ration of gruff!"

"With wobbly to fill in the chinks!"

The gypsies passed among the group serving out portions of pastry with mugs of verbena tea. They then set about packing together their equipment.

Tanzel whispered to Jantiff, "I've got to go off in the woods."

"In that case, go, by all means."

Tanzel grimaced. "That person Booch has been making himself gallant. I don't want to go alone; he's sure to follow."

"Do you really think so?"

"Yes indeed! He watches my every move."

Jantiff, glancing around the clearing, saw that Booch's eyes were fixed upon Tanzel with more than casual interest. "Oh, very well; I'll come with you. Lead the way."

Tanzel rose to her feet and moved off toward the forest. Booch rather sluggishly bestirred himself, but Jantiff quickly went after Tanzel, and Booch glumly subsided into his position of rest.

Jantiff caught up with Tanzel in the shade of the sprawling elms. "Just this way a bit," said Tanzel, and presently: "You wait here; I won't be long."

She disappeared into the foliage. Jantiff sat upon a fallen

tree and looked off through the forest. The sounds from the
clearing already had muted to inaudibility. Bars of Dwan-
light slanted down through the foliage, to shatter upon the
forest floor. How far seemed the vast cities of Arrabus! Jantiff mused upon the circumstances of his life at Uncibal, and
the folk he had come to know: for the most part Old Pinkers. Poor proud Kedidah, going dazed and humiliated to her
death! And Tanzel: whatever might she hope to achieve? He
looked over his shoulder, expecting to see Tanzel returning
from her errand. But the glade was vacant. Jantiff composed
himself to wait.

Three minutes passed. Jantiff became restless and jumped
to his feet. Surely she should have returned by now! He
called: "Tanzel!"

No response.

Odd.

Jantiff went off into the shrubbery, looking left and right.
"Tanzel! Where are you?"

He saw a fresh mark on the turf which might have been a
footprint, and nearby, in damp lichen, what might that series
of parallel scratches signify? Jantiff came to a halt, in utter
perplexity. He looked quickly over his shoulder, then licked
his lips and called once more, but his voice was little more
than a cautious croak: "Tanzel?" Either she was lost, or she
had returned to the bonterfest by a different route.

Jantiff retraced his steps to the clearing. He looked here
and there. The gypsies had departed with all their gear. Tanzel was nowhere to be seen.

Esteban saw Jantiff. His face sagged in blank dismay. Jantiff approached him: "Tanzel went off into the forest; I can't
find her anywhere."

Skorlet came running forward, eyes distended, to show
white rims around the glaring black. "What's this, what's this?
Where's Tanzel?"

"She went off into the woods," stammered Jantiff, awed by
Skorlet's face. "I've looked for her and called but she's gone!"

Skorlet emitted a horrid squeal. "The gypsies have taken
her! Oh, they have taken her! This vile bonterfest, and now
there'll be another!"

Esteban, jerking her elbow, spoke through clenched teeth:
"Control yourself!"

"We have eaten Tanzel!" bawled Skorlet. "Where is the
difference? Today? Tomorrow?" She lifted her face to the sky
and yelled forth a howl so wild that Jantiff's knees went limp.

Esteban, his own face gray, shook Skorlet by the shoulders. "Come along! We can catch them at the river!" He turned and called to the others: "The gypsies have taken Tanzel! Everyone after them! To the river; we'll stop their boat!"

The erstwhile bonterfesters lurched off after Esteban and Skorlet. Jantiff followed a few steps, but could not control the spasmodic pumping of his stomach. He veered off the path, and, only half conscious, fell to his knees, where he vomited, again and again.

Someone nearby was moaning a weird song of two alternating tones. Jantiff presently became aware that the sound proceeded from himself. He crawled a few yards across the dark mold and lay flat. The shuddering in his stomach became intermittent.

His mouth tasted sour and oily; and he remembered the sauce which had been poured over the meat. Again his organs twisted and squeezed, but he could bring up only a thin acrid gruel, which he spat to the ground. He rose to his feet, looked blearily here and there, then returned to the path. From the distance came shouts and calls, to which Jantiff paid no heed.

Through a gap in the foliage he glimpsed the river. He picked his way to the water's edge, rinsed his mouth, bathed his face, then slumped down upon a chunk of driftwood.

Along the trail returned the bonterfesters, mumbling disconsolately to each other. Jantiff hauled himself to his feet, but as he started back toward the trail he heard first Skorlet's voice, then Esteban's baritone mutter; they had turned off the trail and were coming toward him.

Jantiff halted, appalled at the prospect of meeting Skorlet and Esteban face to face in this isolated spot. He jerked himself behind a clump of polyptera and stood in concealment.

Esteban and Skorlet passed by and went to the water's edge, where they peered up and down the river.

"Nowhere in sight," croaked Esteban. "By now they're halfway to Aotho."

"I can't understand," cried Skorlet tremulously. "Why should they hoodwink you; why play you false?"

Esteban hesitated. "It can only be a misunderstanding, a terrible blunder. The two were sitting together. I spoke to the hetman and made my wishes known. He looked across and asked, as if in doubt: 'That young one yonder? The stripling?' Never thinking of Tanzel, I assured him: 'Exactly so!' The hetman took the younger of the two. Such are the bitter facts.

I will now purge them from my mind and you must do the same."

For a space Skorlet said nothing. Then she spoke in a voice harsh with strain: "So what now—with him?"

"First the matrix. Then I'll do whatever needs to be done."

"You'll have to be quick," said Skorlet tonelessly.

"Events are under control. Three days remain."

Skorlet looked out across the river. "Poor little creature. So dear and gay. I can't bear to think of her. But the thoughts come."

"No help for it now," said Esteban, his own voice uncertain. "We can't become confused. Too much hangs in the balance."

"Yes. Too much. Sometimes I am staggered by the scope."

"Now then! Don't create bugbears! The affair is simplicity itself."

"The Connatic is a very real bugbear."

"The Connatic sits in his tower Lusz, brooding and dreaming. If he comes to Arrabus, we'll prove him as mortal as the next man."

"Esteban, don't speak the words aloud."

"The words must be spoken. The thoughts must be thought. The plans must be planned. The deeds must be done."

Skorlet stared out across the water. Esteban turned away. "Put her out of your mind. Come."

"The cursed stranger lives, and poor little Twit is gone."

"Come," said Esteban shortly.

The two went up the path. Jantiff presently followed, walking like a somnambulist.

Chapter 8

•••◦━━━◈━━━◦•••

The bonterfesters returned to Uncibal in a mood greatly in contrast to that in which they had set out. Aside from one or two muttered conversations, the group rode in silence. Skorlet and Esteban sat grimly erect, looking neither right nor left;

Jantiff watched them in covert fascination, his skin crawling at the thought of their conversation. They had meant him to be taken and dragged away by the mournful-eyed gypsies. At the contractor's depot Esteban went off with Booch to the dispatcher's office. Jantiff took advantage of the occasion to slip quietly away from the group. He jumped aboard the man-way and rode north, walking and trotting to increase his speed. Every few moments he looked back even though no one could possibly be so close on his heels. He gave a nervous laugh: in truth he was frightened, and no denying the fact. By sheer chance he had stumbled upon something awful, and now his very existence was threatened: Esteban had left him in no doubt of this.

The Great Southern Adit intercepted Uncibal River; Jantiff diverted eastward, and as before traveled at the best speed possible: pushing through the crowds, sidling and side-stepping, trotting when space opened before him. He diverted from Uncibal River along Lateral 26, and presently arrived at Old Pink.

Jantiff loped into the block, across the foyer, into the ascensor. Its familiar musty reek already seemed alien, and no longer part of his life. He alighted at the nineteenth level, raced around the corridor to his apartment.

He entered, and stood stock-still an instant, to pant and organize his thoughts. He glanced around the room. Kedidah's belongings already appeared to show a thin film of dust. How remote she seemed! A week from now she would be gone from memory; that was the way of Uncibal. Jantiff quietly closed the door and made sure of the lock; then he went to his strongbox in the bedroom and opened the door. Into his pouch he packed ozols, family amulet, pigments, applicators and a pad of paper. Into one pocket he tucked his passage-voucher, personal certificate and tokens; the matrix he hefted in his hand, glancing toward the door. Urgency struggled with curiosity. Surely he had a few moments; the bonter-festers rode Uncibal River far to the west. Time for a quick look. He slid the new matrix from the camera, inserted the old, turned the switch to "Project" and pointed the camera at the wall.

Images: the blocks of Uncibal, dwindling in perspective; the crowds of Uncibal River; the mudflats and Disjerferact. Old Pink: the façade, the foyer, the roof garden. More faces: the Whispers addressing an audience; Skorlet with Tanzel, with Esteban, Skorlet alone. Kedidah with Sarp, Kedidah in the refectory, Kedidah laughing, Kedidah pensive.

Then Esteban's photographs during his custody of the camera: persons known and unknown to Jantiff; copies of pictures from a red reference volume; a sequence of shots of a heavy-shouldered dark-haired man wearing a black blouse and breeches, ankle boots and short-billed cap. This was the man of the secret meeting. Jantiff studied the face. The features were blunt and uncompromising; the eyes, narrow under black eyebrows, gleamed with shrewdness. Somewhere and recently, Jantiff had seen such a face, or one very similar. Frowning in concentration, Jantiff stared at the face. Could it be—

Jantiff jerked around as someone pushed at the door latch and then, failing to secure ingress, rapped sharply on the panel. Jantiff instantly turned off the projector. He removed the matrix, fingered it indecisively, then tucked it into his pocket.

Again a rap at the door, and a voice, muffled behind the panel: "Open up!" Esteban's voice, harsh and hostile. Jantiff's heart sank. How had Esteban arrived so soon?

"I know you're there," came the voice. "They told me below. Open up!"

Jantiff approached the door. "I'm tired," he called out. "Go away. I'll see you tomorrow."

"I want to see you now. It's important."

"Not to me."

"Oh, yes! Important indeed." The words carried sinister import, thought Jantiff. In a hollow voice Jantiff called: "What's so important?"

"Open up."

"Not just now. I'm going to bed."

A pause. Then, "As you like."

Silence from the hall. Jantiff put his ear to the door. Ten seconds passed, twenty seconds, then Jantiff sensed the diminishing pad of steps. He threw a slantwise glance over his shoulder in farewell to the room, with its ghosts and dead voices. Picking up his pouch and camera he slid back the door and peered out into the corridor.

Empty.

Jantiff emerged, closed the door and set off toward the lift, uncomfortably aware that he must pass in front of Apartment D-18, where now lived Skorlet and Sarp.

The door to Apartment D-18 was closed. Jantiff lengthened

his stride and ran past on springing tiptoe paces, like a dancer miming stealth.

The door to D-18 slid back. Esteban and Sarp emerged.

Esteban, looking back into D-18, made a final remark to Skorlet.

Jantiff tried to glide soundlessly up the corridor, but Sarp, peering past Esteban's elbow, noticed him. Sarp tugged at Esteban's arm. Esteban swung about. "Wait! Jantiff! Come back here!"

Jantiff paid no heed. He raced to the descensor, touched the button. The door opened; Jantiff stepped aboard. The door closed almost upon Esteban's distorted face. In his hand shone the glint of metal.

With heart pounding Jantiff descended to the ground floor. He loped across the foyer, out the portal, and away to the man-way.

Sarp and Esteban emerged from Old Pink. They paused, looked right and left, saw Jantiff, and came in pursuit. Jantiff bounded recklessly across to the crowded high-speed lane, where he thrust forward past other passengers, heedless of their annoyance, pouch and camera still gripped in his hand. After came Esteban, with Sarp lagging behind. The blade in Esteban's hand was plainly visible. Jantiff lurched ahead, eyes starting from his head in disbelief. Esteban meant to kill him! On the man-way, in full view of the passengers? Impossible! It wouldn't be allowed! People would help him; they would restrain Esteban! . . . Or would they? As Jantiff lunged forward he looked despairingly right and left but met only expressions of glazed annoyance.

Esteban, shouldering ahead even more roughly than Jantiff, gained ground. Jantiff could see his intent expression, the glitter of his eyes. Jantiff stumbled and lurched to the side; Esteban was upon him, knife raised high. Jantiff seized a tall sharp-featured woman and pushed her into Esteban. In a rage she snatched out at Jantiff and tore away his pouch; Jantiff relinquished pouch and camera and fled, heedful only of his own life. Behind came the remorseless Esteban.

At the diversion upon Uncibal River the way was open and Jantiff gained a few yards, only to lose it almost at once among the crowds. Sidling, elbowing, shoving, buffeting, Jantiff thrust his way through the protesting folk. Twice Esteban approached close enough to brandish his blade; the folk nearby called out in fear and pushed pell-mell to escape. Jantiff on each occasion managed to evade the attack, once through a spasmodic spurt of agility, again by pushing a man into Esteban's path, so that both fell and Jantiff was able to gain ten yards running room. Someone, either inadvertently or through malice, tripped Jantiff; he fell flat and once again Esteban was on him. As the riders of Uncibal River watched to observe the outcome, Jantiff kicked Esteban in the groin, rolled frantically aside. Clambering to his feet he swung a short square woman screaming into Esteban, who fell on top of the woman. The knife jarred free; Jantiff groped to pick it up, but the woman hit him in the face, and Esteban reached the knife first. Croaking in despair Jantiff sprang away and fled along the River.

Esteban was tiring. He called out: "Snerge! Snerge! Hold the snerge!" Folk turned to look back and observing Jantiff stood quickly aside. Esteban's calls therefore worked to Jantiff's benefit, and he lengthened his lead. Esteban presently stopped shouting.

Ahead Uncibal River intersected Lateral 16. Jantiff veered to the side as if intending to divert; instead, he crouched behind a knot of folk and let himself be carried along the River. Esteban, deceived, rushed out the diversion to the lateral and so lost his quarry.

At the next switch-over, Jantiff reversed direction and rode back to the east, keeping sharp lookout to all sides. He discovered no evidence of pursuit: only the faces of Uncibal, rank on rank, back along the River.

His pouch was gone with all his ozols, and likewise his camera. Jantiff gave a great shuddering groan of fury; he cursed Esteban with all the invective at his command and swore restitution for himself. What an abominable day! From now and into the future things would go differently!

Where Uncibal River made its great swerve toward the spaceport, Jantiff continued toward Alastor Centrality. With a sense of deliverance he passed under the black and gold portal, crossed the compound and entered the agency. The clerk, Clode, in the black and biege of the Connatic's Service, rose to his feet. Jantiff cried out: "I am Jantiff Ravensroke of Zeck! I must see the cursar at once!"

"I'm sorry, sir," said the clerk. "This is impossible at the moment."

Jantiff stared aghast. "Impossible? Why?"

"The cursar is not presently in Uncibal."

Jantiff barely restrained a cry of anguish. He looked over

his shoulder. The compound was empty. "Where is he? When will he return?"

"He has gone to Waunisse; he counsels the Whispers before they leave for Numenes. He returns Aensday with the Whispers aboard the *Sea Disk.*"

"Aensday? Three days from now! What will I do till then? I've discovered a dangerous plot against the Connatic!"

Clode looked dubiously sideways at Jantiff. "If such is the case, the cursar must be informed as soon as possible."

"If I survive until Aensday. I have no place to go."

"What of your apartment?"

"It's not safe for me. Why can't I stay here?"

"The chambers are locked. I can't let you in."

Jantiff darted another glance over his shoulder. "Where shall I go?"

"I can only suggest the Travelers Inn."

"But my money is gone; it's been taken from me!"

"You need not pay your bill until Aensday. The cursar will surely advance you funds."

Jantiff gave a glum nod. He thought carefully and brought the matrix from his pocket. "Please give me paper."

Clode tendered paper and stylus. Jantiff wrote:

This is the matrix from my camera. Certain of the pictures indicate a plot. The Connatic himself may be threatened. The people responsible live in Old Pink, Block 17-882. Their names are Esteban, Skorlet and Sarp. There is another unknown person. I will return Aensday unless I am killed.

Jantiff Ravensroke,
Frayness, Zeck.

Jantiff wrapped the message around the matrix and handed the parcel to Clode. "This must be kept safe and delivered to the cursar at the earliest opportunity! In the event that I—" here Jantiff's voice quavered a trifle—"that I am killed, will you do this?"

"Certainly, sir, I'll do my very best."

"Now I must go, before someone thinks to look for me here. Inform no one of my whereabouts!"

Clode managed a strained grin. "Naturally not."

Jantiff slowly turned away, reluctant to leave the relative security of the Centrality. But no help for it: he must immure himself in the Travelers Inn until Aensday, and all would be well.

In the shadows under the portal he halted and surveyed the territory beyond. He spied Esteban immediately, not fifty yards distant, striding purposefully toward the Centrality. Jantiff's jaw dropped in consternation. He shrank back into the compound and pressed himself to the inner surface of the portal. There, holding his breath, he waited.

Footsteps. Esteban marched past and away across the compound. As soon as Jantiff saw the retreating back he slipped through the portal and raced away on long fleet-footed strides toward the man-way.

"Hey! Jantiff!" Esteban's furious cry struck at his back. As Jantiff stepped aboard the man-way he looked over his shoulder, to find that Esteban had halted at the portal to stand swaying, as if in response to conflicting urgencies.

Jantiff wondered what might have ensued had the cursar been on hand.

Jantiff jumped across to the speed lane. He looked back to catch a last glimpse of Esteban, still under the portal, then was carried past the range of vision.

At the Travelers Inn Jantiff signed the register as Arlo Jorum of Pharis, Alastor 458. Without comment the clerk assigned him a chamber.

Jantiff bathed and stretched himself out on his couch, aware of aching muscles and comprehensive fatigue. He closed his eyes; the three days to Aensday would pass most rapidly in sleep.

Jantiff inhaled and exhaled several deep breaths. Circumstances at last were under control. The Travelers Inn at the very least provided security; if Esteban offered offense, Jantiff need merely notify the Mutuals* on duty at the inn.

Jantiff opened his eyes, blinked and grimaced and closed them again. Images from across the terrible day passed before his eyes; Jantiff writhed on the couch.

His stomach began to gripe; Jantiff sat erect. He needed food. Dressing, he went down to the cafeteria where he made a meal of gruff, deedle, and a bowl of wobbly, which he charged to his account.

The public address system, which had been projecting a

---

* Mutuality: a contract police force of non-Arrabins, inconspicuous, small in number, efficient in practice, directed and controlled by the local Panel of Delegates.

series of lethargic popular tunes, suddenly enunciated a bulletin:

"Attention all! Take note of a heinous murder, just reported to the Uncibal Mutuality. The assassin is one Jantiff Ravensroke, a probationary visitor, originally of Zeck. He is a man of early maturity, tall, slender, with dark hair worn nondescript. He has a thin face, a long nose and eyes noticeably green in color. The Mutuals urgently require that he be held in detention, pending full investigation of his foul act. A search at the highest level of intensity is already being prosecuted. Egalists all! Keep a vigilant watch for this dangerous alien!"

Jantiff jumped to his feet to stand quivering in consternation. He went on delicate steps to the arch giving on the lobby. At the registration desk two men in low-crowned black hats loomed over the clerk. Jantiff's heart rose into his throat: Mutuals! Responding with nervous volubility, the clerk waved a long pale finger toward the ascensor and Jantiff's room.

The two men turned from the desk and strode to the ascensor. As soon as they were gone, Jantiff stepped out into the lobby, sidled unobtrusively around the far wall to the door and departed into the night.

Chapter 9

••••——◆——••••

Disjerferact, the carnival strip along the mud flats, had never failed to fascinate Jantiff with its contrasts and paradoxes. Disjerferact! Gaudy and gay, strident and makeshift, trading brummagem for equally valueless tokens, achieving no more than the dream of a dream! By the light of Dwan, and from a distant perspective, the dark red paper pavilions, the tall blue tents, the numberless festoons, banners, and whirligigs conjured a brave and splendid fantasy. By night uncounted flambeaux flared to the sea breeze; the consequent gleams and shadows, darting and jerking, suggested a bar-

baric frenzy—in the end as factitious as all else of Disjerferact. Still, the confusion and helter-skelter provided Jantiff an effective refuge: who at Disjerferact cared a whit for anything other than his own yearnings?

For three days Jantiff skulked through nooks and back passages, venturing never a step without seeking the low black hats of Mutuals or the dread shape of Esteban. During daylight hours he occupied a cranny between the booth of a pickle merchant and a public latrine. By night he ventured forth, disguised by a mustache fashioned from his own hair and a head rag in the fashion of the Carabbas Islanders. His tokens—those remaining to him after paying bonterfest fees—he grudgingly exchanged for poggets and cornucopias of fried kelp. He slept by day in fits and starts, disturbed by the calls of hawkers, the puffworm vendor's bugle, the screeching of child acrobats, and from a booth across the way, the thud of clog-dancing and simulated enthusiasm from shills.

Early Aensday morning, while Jantiff lay half-torpid, the public megaphones spoke loud across the mud flats.

"Attention, all! Today greet the Whispers as they embark on their mission to Numenes! As adumbrated in recent statements, they intend a daring and innovative program, and they have proclaimed a slogan for the next century: *Viable egalism must fulfill both needs and aspirations, and provide scope for human genius!* They go to Lusz Tower to urge the Connatic's sympathetic support for the new scheme, and they will draw strength from your advocacy. Therefore, come today to the Public Zone. The Whispers fly from Waunisse aboard the *Sea Disk*; their time of arrival is high noon and they will speak from the Pedestal."

Jantiff listened apathetically while the megaphones broadcast a second and yet a third repetition of the message. For an instant, while the echoes died, Disjerferact hung suspended in an unnatural silence; then the customary tumult returned.

Jantiff rose to a kneeling position, peered right and left from his cranny, then, finding nothing to foster his anxieties, he stepped out into the flow of pleasure-seekers. At a nearby refreshment booth he exchanged a token for a spill of fried kelp. Leaning against a wall he consumed the crisp, if insipid, strands, then for want of a better destination he wandered eastward toward the Public Zone, or the Field of Voices, as it was sometimes called. The cursar returned with the Whispers aboard the *Sea Disk*; he would not be likely to return to the Centrality before the Whispers departed for Numenes: so there was time enough for Jantiff to hear the remarks of the Whispers, perhaps at close range.

Jantiff sauntered eastward, across Disjerferact and the mud flats beyond, over the Whery Slough Bridge and out upon the Public Zone: an expanse a mile long and almost as wide. At regular intervals poles rose high to support quatrefoil megaphones, each pole likewise displaying a numerical code to assist in the arrangement of rendezvous. Almost against the eastern boundary a pylon held aloft a circular platform under a glass parasol: this was the so-called "Pedestal." Beyond spread the scarred grounds of the space-port.

By the time Jantiff crossed over the Whery Slough Bridge, folk by the thousands were migrating across the field, to pack into a vital sediment around the Pedestal. Jantiff was annoyed to find that he could approach no closer than a hundred yards to the Pedestal, which would hardly allow him an intimate inspection of the Whispers.

As Dwan rose toward the zenith, crowds debouched from Uncibal River in a solid mass, to disperse and sift across the Zone, until presently no further increment was possible: the Zone was occupied to its capacity and past. Those arriving on Uncibal River could not alight, but must continue into the round-about, and return the way they had come. On the Zone folk stood elbow to elbow, chin to shoulder. A sour-sweet odor arose from the crowd to drift away on airs from the sea. Jantiff recalled his first impressions of Arrabus, upon debarking from the spaceship: at last he could identify that odor which then had caused him puzzlement and perhaps a trace of revulsion.

Jantiff attempted to calculate the number of persons surrounding him, but became confused: the number was surely somewhere among the millions. . . . He felt a pang of claustrophobic alarm: he was confined, he could not move! Suppose something prompted these millions of entities into a stampede? A horrifying thought! Jantiff pictured tides of people surging over one another, rising and climbing, at last to topple and break in churning glimpses of arms, faces, legs . . . The crowd produced a sudden mumble of sound, as out over the water appeared the *Sea Disk*, inbound from Waunisse. The vessel veered over the space-port, descended in a smart half-spiral and dropped to a landing near the Public Zone. The port opened; an attendant stepped out, followed by the four Whispers: three men and a woman wearing formal robes. Ignoring the crowd they disappeared into a subsurface walkway. Two minutes passed. Out on the Zone gazes lifted to the platform at the top of the Pedestal.

The Whispers appeared. For a moment they stood looking over the crowd: four small figures indistinct in the shade of the parasol. Jantiff tried to match them with the Whispers he had seen on the screen. The woman was Fausgard; the men were Orgold, Lemiste and Delfin. One of the men spoke— which could not be discerned from below—and a thousand quatrefoil megaphones broadcast his words.

"The Whispers are revivified by this contact with the folk of Uncibal! We take nourishment from your benevolence; it flows in upon us like a mighty tide! We shall bring it forth when we confront the Connatic, and the sheer power of egalistic doctrine shall overcome every challenge!

"Great events are in the offing! At our noble Centenary we celebrate a hundred years of achievement! A new century lies before us, and succeeding centuries in grand succession, each to ratify anew our optimum style of life. Egalism shall sweep Alastor Cluster, and all the Gaean Reach! So much is foreordained, if it be your will! Is it so?"

The Whisper paused; a somewhat perfunctory and even uncertain mutter of approval arose from the crowd. Jantiff himself was puzzled. The tone of the address was not at all consonant with the announcement he had heard that morning in Disjerferact.

"So be it!" declared the Whisper, and a thousand quatrefoil megaphones magnified his words. "There shall be no turning back, or faltering! Egalism forever! Man's great enemies are tedium and drudgery! We have broken their ancient tyranny; let the contractors do the drudge for their lowly pittances. Egalism shall ensure the final emancipation of Man!

"So now: your Whispers go forth to Numenes, impelled by our composite will. We shall take our message to the Connatic and make our three important desires known.

"First: no more immigration! Let those who envy us impose egalism on their own worlds!

"Second: Arrabins are a peaceful folk. We fear no attack; we intend no aggression. Why then must we subsidize the Connatic's power? We require none of his advice, nor the force of his Whelm, nor the supervision of his bureaucrats.

We will therefore require that our annual tax be reduced, or even abolished.

"Third: our exports are sold at the cheap, yet the items we import come dear. Effectually, we subsidize those inefficient systems still in force elsewhere. Believe this: your Whispers shall press for a new schedule of exchange between the token and the ozol; in fact, they should go at par! Is not an hour of our toil equal to that hour worked by some whey-faced diddler of, let us say, Zeck?"

Jantiff jerked his head and frowned in displeasure. The remarks seemed both absurd and inappropriate.

The megaphones rang on.

"Our Centenary is at hand. At Lusz we shall invite the Connatic to visit Arrabus, to join our festival, and appraise for himself our great achievements. If he declines, the loss is his own. In any case, we shall make our report to you at a great rally of the Arrabin egalists. We now depart for Numenes; wish us well!" The Whispers raised arms in salute; the crowd responded with a polite roar. The Whispers stepped back and disappeared from view. Several minutes later they emerged from the ingress kiosk out upon the space-port. A car awaited them; they entered and were conveyed to the great hulk of the spaceship *Eldantro*.

The crowd began to depart the field, but without haste. Jantiff, now impatient, thrust, sidled and slid through the obstructive masses to no great effect, and a full two hours elapsed before he managed to squeeze aboard Uncibal River, sweating, tired and temper at the quick.

He rode directly to Alastor Centrality. Entering the structure he found behind the counter, not Clode, but a woman tall and portly, with an imposing bust and austere features. She wore a severe gown of gray twill over a white blouse; her hair was drawn to the back of her head and held in a handsome silver clip. As in the case of Clode, her place of origin was clearly other than Arrabus. She spoke in a formal voice: "Sir, how may I assist you?"

"I must see the cursar at once," said Jantiff. Out of reflexive habit he darted a nervous glance over his shoulder. "The matter is most urgent."

The woman inspected Jantiff for a long five seconds, and Jantiff was made conscious of his disheveled appearance. She answered in a voice somewhat crisper than before. "The cursar is not in his office. He has not yet returned from Waunisse."

Jantiff stood rigid with disappointment. "I expected him to-day," he said fretfully. "He was to have returned with the Whispers. Is Clode here?"

The woman turned another searching inspection upon Jantiff who became uneasy. She said: "Clode is not here. I am Aleida Gluster, clerk in the Connatic's service, and I can discharge any business which you might have had with Clode."

"I left a parcel with him, a photographic matrix, for delivery to the cursar. I merely wanted to assure myself of its safety."

"There is no such parcel in the office. Clode Morre, I regret to say, is dead."

Jantiff stared aghast, "Dead?" He collected his wits. "How did this happen? And when?"

"Three days ago. He was attacked by a ruffian and stabbed through the throat. It is tragic for us all."

Jantiff asked in a hollow voice: "Has the murderer been apprehended?"

"No. He has been identified as a certain Jantiff Ravensroke, of Zeck."

Jantiff managed to blurt a question: "And the parcel I left is gone?"

"There is definitely no such parcel in the office."

"Has the cursar been notified?"

"Naturally! I telephoned him immediately at the Waunisse Centrality."

"Then call Waunisse now! If the cursar is there I must speak to him. The matter is most important, I assure you."

"And what name shall I announce if he is there?"

Jantiff made a feeble attempt to wave the question aside. "It is really of no great consequence."

"Your name is of considerable consequence," said Aleida crisply. "Is it by any chance 'Jantiff Ravensroke'?"

Jantiff quailed before the searching inspection. He nodded meekly. "I am Jantiff Ravensroke. But I am no murderer!"

Aleida gave him a level glance of unreadable significance and turned to the telephone. She spoke: "This is Aleida, at Uncibal Centrality. Is Cursar Bonamico anywhere at hand?"

A voice responded: "Cursar Bonamico has returned to Uncibal. He departed this morning on the *Sea Disk*, in company with the Whispers."

"Odd. He has not yet looked into his office."

"Evidently there has been some delay."

"Yes, quite likely. Thank you." Aleida Gluster turned back

to Jantiff. "If you are not the assassin, why do the Mutuals insist otherwise?"

"The Mutuals are mistaken! I know the murderer; he has influence with Contractor Shubart, who contracts the services of the Mutuals. I am anxious to lay all facts before the cursar."

"Doubtless." Aleida looked past Jantiff through the glass panels of the front wall. "Here are the Mutuals now. You can place your information before them."

Jantiff turned a glance of startled terror over his shoulder, to see two men in low black hats marching in ponderous certitude across the compound. "No! They will take me away and kill me! I have urgent news for the cursar; they wish to stifle me!"

Aleida nodded grimly. "Step into the inner office: quickly now!"

Jantiff sped through the door into the cursar's chamber. The door closed; Jantiff pressed his ear to the panel to hear a measured thud of footsteps, then Aleida's voice: "Sirs, how may I be of service?"

A resonant baritone voice spoke: "We wish to apprehend a certain Jantiff Ravensroke. Is he on the premises?"

"You are the Mutuals," said Aleida curtly. "You must determine the facts for yourself."

"The facts are these! For three days we have kept close watch on this place, fearful that the assassin might attempt a second murder, perhaps on your own person. Now five minutes ago Jantiff Ravensroke was seen arriving at the Agency. Call him forth, if you please, and we will take him into protective custody."

Aleida Gluster spoke in her coldest tones. "Jantiff Ravensroke has been accused of murder: this is true. The victim was Clode Morre, clerk in the Connatic's service, and the deed occurred upon the extraterritorial grounds of Alastor Centrality. Responsibility for the detection and punishment of this crime, therefore, is beyond the legal competence of the Mutuals."

After a pause of ten seconds, the baritone voice spoke. "Our orders are definite. We must do our duty and search the premises."

"You shall do nothing of the sort," said Aleida Gluster. "At your first move I will touch two buttons. The first will destroy you, through robot sensors; the second will call down the Whelm."

The baritone voice made no response. Jantiff heard the measured thud of retreating footsteps. The door opened; Aleida looked in at him. "Quickly now, go after them; it is your only chance. They are confused and return for orders, and they will find that I waived extraterritoriality when I reported Clode's murder."

"But where shall I go? If I could get aboard a spaceship, I have my passage voucher——"

"The Mutuals will certainly guard the space-port. Go south! At Balad there is a space-port of sorts; go there and take passage for home."

Jantiff grimaced sadly. "Balad is thousands of miles away."

"That may well be. But if you stay in Uncibal, you will surely be taken. Leave now, by the rear exit. When you reach Balad telephone the Agency."

Jantiff had departed. Aleida Gluster gave her head a shake of outrage and indignation, and composed a message:

> To the Connatic at Lusz, from the Alastor Centrality at Uncibal, Arrabus:
>
> Events are flying in all directions here. Poor Jantiff Ravensroke is in terrible danger; unless someone puts a stop, they'll have his blood or worse. He is accused of a vile crime but he is surely as innocent as a child. I have ordered him south into the Weirdlands, despite the rigors of the way. Cursar Bonamico is unfortunately nowhere to be located. I send this off in agitation, and with the hope that help is on the way.
>
> Aleida Gluster, Clerk
> The Alastor Centrality,
> Uncibal.

Chapter 10

••••———◆———••••

With hunched shoulders and smouldering gaze, Jantiff rode
Uncibal River west: away from the space-port, away from
Alastor Centrality, away forever from the detestable Old
Pink, where all his troubles had originated. Fragmented
images whirled through his mind, churned by rage and by
sick misgivings at the prospect of traversing the Weirdlands.
How far to Balad? A thousand miles? Two thousand miles?
An enormous distance, in any event, across a land of forests,
mouldering ruins and great sluggish rivers, gleaming like
quicksilver in the Dwanlight . . . Something tickled Jantiff's
mind: the mention of an omnibus, its terminus at the Metallurgical Syndicate. Someone had joked of riding all the way
to Balad, so presumably a connection existed. Regrettably,
transportation came dear on Wyst when bought with Arrabin
tokens, of which Jantiff had but few in any case. Glumly he
thought of his family amulet: a disk of carved rose quartz on
a stelt armstrap. Perhaps this might buy his passage to Balad.

So Jantiff rode across the waning afternoon, through the
twilight and into the night. Diverting to the Great Southern
Adit he was carried along the route of the bonterfesters. How
far now seemed that occasion, though only four days gone!
Jantiff's stomach twisted at the recollection.

South through the fringes of the city he rode. Night had
fallen in earnest: a damp dark night by reason of a low overcast. Strands of cold mist blew along the avenues of District
92, and the overhead lamps became eerie puffs of luminosity.
Few folk were abroad at this time, and as the adit slanted
away from the city their number dwindled even further, so
that Jantiff rode almost alone.

The way climbed a long slope; Uncibal, behind and below,
became a ribbon of hazy light, streaming far to the right and
far to the left; then the way swung into Outpost Valley and
Uncibal was blotted from sight.

Ahead appeared the lights of the Metallurgical Syndicate.

The fence came to parallel the man-way, and the fat bolts of energy playing among the strands were more sinister than ever through the darkness.

Mounds of ore, slag and sinter loomed against the sky; a barge discharged ore into an underground hopper, to create a clattering roar. Jantiff watched in sudden interest. Presumably, after unloading the ore, the barge would return to the mines, somewhere in Blale, at the southern fringe of the Weirdlands . . . Here was transportation quick and cheap, if he could avail himself of it. Jantiff moved to the side of the way and stepped off. The barge slid off and stationed itself under another hopper; again came a clatter as material poured into the barge. Jantiff appraised the situation. The fence no longer barred the way, but between himself and the barge interposed an area illuminated by overhead lamps; he would surely be seen if he approached from the direction of the man-way.

Jantiff returned to the man-way and rode a hundred yards past the lighted area. Alighting once more, he set off across the dark field, which was dank with seepage from the slag piles; the mud released an acrid reek as Jantiff trudged through. Cursing under his breath, he approached the shadow side of the mound, where the ground became somewhat firmer. Cautiously Jantiff moved to where he could view the field: just in time to see the barge lift and sweep away through the night.

Jantiff looked forlornly after the receding side-lights: there went his transportation south. He hunched his shoulders against the chill. Standing in the shadows he felt more alone than ever before in his life: as isolated and remote as if he were already dead, or floating alone in the void.

He stirred himself. No point standing stupidly in the cold, though indeed he could see small scope for anything better.

Lights slid across the sky: another barge! It settled upon the discharge hopper, the operator leaning from his cab to perceive signals from the hopper attendant.

The compartments tilted; out poured the ore with a rush and a rattle. Jantiff poised himself at the ready. The barge slid to a hopper near the slag pile; slag roared down the chute into the barge. Jantiff bounded at best speed across the intervening area. He reached the barge and climbed upon a horizontal flange at the base of the cargo bins. Grasping for a secure handhold, he found only vertical flanges; he would lose his grip as soon as the barge lurched to a cross gust. Jantiff jumped, caught the upper lip of the ore compartment; kicking and straining he hauled himself up, slid over the lip into the compartment, which just at this moment received its charge from the hopper above. Jantiff danced and trod this way and that, and climbed sprawling across the slag and so managed to avoid burial. In the cab the operator turned his head; Jantiff threw himself flat. Had be been seen? . . . Evidently not. The loaded barge lurched aloft and slid away through the darkness. Jantiff heaved a great shuddering sigh. Arrabus lay behind him.

The barge flew a mile or two, then slowed and seemed to drift. Jantiff lifted his head in perplexity. What went on? A lamp on top of the control cab illuminated the cargo area; the operator stepped from his cab and walked astern along the central catwalk. He called harshly to Jantiff. "Well, then, fellow. What's your game?"

Jantiff crawled across the slag until, gaining his feet, he was able to look up at the menacing figure. He did not like what he saw. The operator was a notably ugly man. His face, round and pale, rested directly upon a great tun of a torso; his eyes were set far apart, almost riding the cheekbones. The nose, no more than a button of gristle, seemed vastly inadequate for the ventilation of so imposing a body. The operator repeated himself, in a voice as harsh as before: "Well then: what's the game: Haven't you read the notices? We're sharp for restless custodees."

"I'm no custodee," cried Jantiff. "I'm trying to leave Uncibal; I only want to ride across Weirdland into Blale."

The operator looked down in sardonic disbelief. "What are you seeking in Blale? You'll find no free wump for certain; everyone earns his keep."

"I'm not Arrabin," Jantiff explained eagerly. "I'm not even an immigrant; I'm a visitor from Zeck. I thought I wanted to visit Wyst, but now I'm anxious only to leave."

"Well, I can believe you're no custodee; you'd know better than to ride the ore-barge. Can you guess how you might have fared, had I not taken pity on you?"

"No, not exactly," mumbled Jantiff. "I intended no harm."

The operator spoke in a lordly tone. "First, to clear Daffledaw Mountains, I raise to three miles, where the air is chill and the clouds are shreds of floating ice. So then, you freeze rigid and die. No, no, don't argue, I've seen it happen. Next. Where do you think I take this slag? To be set into a tiara for the contractor's lady? No indeed. I float over Lake Neman,

where Contractor Shubart builds his ramp. I turn up the
compartments; out pours the slag, and your frozen corpse as
well, to fall a mile into the black water. And what do you
think of that?"

"I was not aware of such things," said Jantiff mournfully.
"Had I known, I would certainly have chosen some other
transportation."

The operator rocked his head briskly back and forth.
"You're no custodee; this is clear. They know well enough
what happens to illicit vagabonds." The operator's voice became somewhat more lenient. "Well then, you're in luck. I'll
fly you to Blale—if you pay a hundred ozols for the privilege. Otherwise you can take your chances with the chill and
Lake Neman."

Jantiff winced. "The Arrabins robbed me of everything I
own. I have nothing except a few tokens."

The operator stared down a long grim moment. "What do
you carry in that sack at your belt?"

Jantiff displayed the contents. "Fifty tokens and some bits
of kelp."

The operator gave a groan of disgust. "What good is such
trash to me?" He wheeled and marched back along the catwalk toward the cab.

Jantiff stumbled and slid in the loose slag as he tried to
keep pace. "I have nothing now, but my father will pay; I assure you of this!"

The operator turned and scrutinized the compartments
with exaggerated care. "I discern no one else; where is your
father? Let him come forth and pay."

"He is not here; he lives at Frayness on Zeck."

"Zeck? Why did you not say so?" The operator reached
down and yanked Jantiff up to the catwalk. "I'm a Gatzwan-
ger from Kandaspe, which is not all that far from Zeck. The
Arrabins? Madmen all, and slovens, as well. Into the cab with
you; I marvel to see a decent elitist in such a plight."

Jantiff gingerly followed the operator's great bulk into the
cab.

"Sit on the bench yonder. I was about to take a bite of
food. Do you care to join me, or would you prefer your
kelp?"

"I will join you with pleasure," said Jantiff. "My kelp has
become a bit stale."

The operator set out bread, meat, pickles, and a jug of
wine, then signaled Jantiff to serve himself.

"You are a lucky man to have fallen in with me, Lemiel Swarkop, rather than certain others I could name. The truth is, I despise the Arrabins and I'll ferry away anyone who wants to leave, custodee or not. There is a certain Booch, now Contractor Shubart's personal chauffeur, but a one-time operator. He shows a kind face only to obliging girls, and even then is fickle—if one is to believe his tales."

Jantiff decided not to mention his acquaintance with Booch. "I am grateful both to you and to Cassadense.*

"Whatever the case," said Swarkop, "the Weirdlands are no place for a person like yourself. No one maintains order; it is every man for himself, and you must either fight, hide, or run, unless you have a submissive disposition."

"I only want to leave Wyst," said Jantiff. "I am going to the Balad space-port for this purpose only."

"You may have a long wait."

Jantiff instantly became alarmed. "Why so?"

"Balad space-port is just a field beside the sea. Perhaps once a month a cargo ship drops down to discharge goods for Balad township and Contractor Shubart; you'd be in great luck if you found a ship to carry you toward Zeck."

Jantiff pondered the information in gloomy silence. At last he asked: "How then should I return to Zeck?"

Swarkop turned him a wondering gaze. "The obvious choice is Uncibal Space-port, where ships depart each day."

"True," said Jantiff lamely. "There is always that possibility. I must give it some thought."

The barge slid south through the night. Overcome by fatigue, Jantiff drowsed. Swarkop sprawled out on a couch to the side of the cab and began to snore noisily. Jantiff went to look out the front windows, but found only darkness below and the stars of Alastor Cluster above. Down to the side a flickering light appeared and passed abeam. Who might be abroad in that dark wilderness? Why were they showing so late a light? Gypsies? Vagabonds? Someone lost in the woods? The light fell astern and was gone.

Jantiff stretched himself out on the bench and tried to sleep. Eventually he dozed, to be aroused some hours later by the thump of Swarkop's boots.

Jantiff blinked and groaned, and reluctantly hunched himself up into a sitting position. Swarkop washed his face at the basin, gurgling, blowing and snorting like a drowning animal.

* See Glossary, #5.

A bleary gray light gave substance to the interior of the cab. Jantiff rose to his feet and went to the forward window. Dwan had not yet appeared; the sky was a sullen mottled gray. Below spread the forest, marked only by an occasional glade, out to a line of hills in the south.

Swarkop thumped a mug of tea down in front of Jantiff. He peered down at the landscape. "A dreary morning! The clouds are dank as dead fish and the Sych is the most dismal of forests, fit only for wild men and witches!" He raised his hand and performed a curious set of signals. Jantiff eyed him askance but delicately forebore comment. Swarkop said heavily: "When a wise man lives in a strange place he uses the customs and believes the beliefs of that place, if only as sensible precaution. Each morning the wild men of the Sych make such signs and they are persuaded of the benefits; why should I dispute them, or despise what, after all, may be a very practical technique?"

"Quite true," said Jantiff. "This seems a sensible point of view."

Swarkop poured out more tea. "The Sych guards a thousand secrets. Ages ago this was a fruitful countryside; can you believe it? Now the palaces are covered with mold."

Jantiff shook his head in awe. "It seems impossible."

"Not to Contractor Shubart! He intends to break the forests and open up the land. He'll establish farms and homesteads, villages and counties, and then he'll make himself King of the Weirdlands. Oh, he has a taste for pomp, does Contractor Shubart; never think otherwise!"

"It seems an ambitious program, to say the least."

"Ambitious and expensive. Contractor Shubart milks a golden stream from the Arrabin teat, so there's no lack of ozols. Oh, I'll fly his barges and work to his orders, and someday I'll be Viscount Swarkop. Booch no doubt will ordain himself Duke, but that's nothing to me, so long as he keeps to his own domain. Ah well, that's all for the future." Swarkop pointed to the southeast. "There—Lake Neman, where Contractor Shubart builds his causeway, and where I must relinquish your company."

Jantiff had hoped for transportation all the way to his destination. He asked despondently, "And then how far to Balad?"

"A mere fifty miles; no great matter." Swarkop put a plate of bread and meat before him. "Eat; fortify yourself against the promenade, and please do not mention my name in

Balad! The news of my altruism would soon reach the Contractor's manse and I might be deprived of my title."

"Naturally, I'll say nothing whatever!" Jantiff glumly addressed himself to the food; the next meal might be long in coming. He voiced a forlorn hope: "Perhaps I can somehow secure passage out of Balad on a cargo ship?"

"Most unlikely. Cargo ships reject all passengers. Otherwise starmenters dressed like tourists would take passage, destroy captain and crew and whisk their booty away across space. Anywhere in the Primarchic* a cargo ship sells for a million ozols and no questions asked. And you may be sure that the shipping lines are well aware of this. I suggest that you dismiss Balad Space-port from your plans."

Jantiff looked out across the dour forest he must traverse afoot: all to no purpose if Swarkop were to be believed. At Balad he was further removed than ever from his passage home. Still, under the circumstances, what better options had been open to him? He said tentatively: "Perhaps I could persuade you to deliver a message to the cursar in Uncibal? The matter is of great importance."

Swarkop's eyes bulged in disbelief. "You suggest that I ride that vile man-way into Uncibal? My dear fellow, not for a hundred ozols! You must transmit your messages by telephone, like everyone else."

Jantiff hastened to agree. "Yes, that's the best idea, of course!" He stood aside as Swarkop manipulated controls; the barge slanted down upon Lake Neman: a great gash across the wilderness brimming with black water and never more than two or three miles wide. Swarkop brought the barge to a halt and thrust a lever: slag poured down upon the end of a dike already half across the lake.

"The plan is to strike a road from Balad across the Sych to Lake Neman, thence to the head of the Buglas River, then across the Dankwold; or perhaps Shubart intends to blast through the Daffledaws; yes, that must be the case, since I've carried six great cargoes of frack north to Uncibal Depot— enough to pulverize Zade Mountain and cut a new Dinklin River gorge."

"It seems a tremendous project."

---

* The Primarchic is an aggregation of stars somewhat lesser than Alastor Cluster, at one time controlled by the Primarch, now in a chronic state of disorder, factionalism and war.

An important function of the Connatic's Whelm is protection against raids from the Primarchic.

"True, and quite beyond my understanding. But then I am Lemiel Swarkop, hireling, while Shubart is Grand Knight and Contractor, and there the matter rests."

Swarkop lowered the barge to the base of the causeway. Throwing open the cab door, he leaned out to inspect the countryside. The air was cold and still; Lake Neman lay flat as a black mirror. "The day will be fine," declared Swarkop with a heartiness Jantiff refused to find infectious. "Trudging the Sych in the rain is not good sport. Good luck to you, then! Fifty miles to Balad: two days' easy journey, unless you are delayed."

Jantiff's ear discovered alarming overtones in the remark. "Why should I be delayed?"

Swarkop shrugged. "I could lay forth a thousand ideas and still fall short of reality. Giampara* will dispose."

"Is there an inn along the way where I might rest the night?"

Swarkop pointed to the shore of the lake. "Notice that tumble of milk-stone; it marks a grand resort of the ancient times, when lords and ladies dallied up and down the lake in barges with carved silver screens and velvet sails. Then there were inns along the road to Balad. Now you'll find only a roadmender's hut just past Gant Gap; use it at your own risk."

" 'Risk'?" cried Jantiff. "Why should there be risk?"

"The roadmenders sometimes set out traps to startle the witches. The witches sometimes leave hallucinations to startle the roadmenders. Build four blazing fires against the gaunch; lie down in the middle and you'll be safe until morning. But keep the fires flaming high."

"What is a gaunch?" asked Jantiff, looking dubiously along the edge of the forest.

"That question is often asked but never answered. The witches know but they say nothing, not even to each other." Swarkop mused a moment. "I suggest that you put the matter out of your mind. You'll know the gaunch when you meet him face to face. If you do not do so the matter becomes moot. Fire is said to be a deterrent, if it blazes higher than the creature cares to step, and there is my best advice."

Swarkop bundled up what remained of his provisions and

---

* Swarkop's reference to Giampara is facetious. Were he in earnest he would no doubt have invoked Corë of the Four Bosoms, who controls his home world Kandaspe. Jantiff perceives this nuance of usage but is not altogether reassured.

thrust the pack upon Jantiff. "You'll find plums, kakajous and honeybuttons along the way. But don't steal so much as a turnip from the farmers: they'll take you for a witch and hunt you down with their wurgles. Once again: good luck." Swarkop backed into the cab and closed the door. The barge lifted and slid off across the lake.

Jantiff watched until the barge disappeared into the distance. Swinging around, he scrutinized the edge of the forest but found only dark foliage and darker shadows. He squared his shoulders to the road and trudged off south toward Balad.

Chapter 11

•••◆◆◆•••

Dawn, rising into the sky, projected Jantiff's shadow along the road ahead of him; as in Arrabus the light seemed to shimmer with an over-saturation of color. In these middle latitudes half around the curve of Wyst, the effect if anything seemed emphasized, and Jantiff fancied that if he were to examine one of the light spatters, where a ray struck down through the foliage, he would find innumerable points of color, as if from ten million miscroscopic dew drops . . . He recalled his first wonder at the light and the stimulation it had worked on him; small benefit had he derived! In fact, to the contrary: his sketches and depictions had set in motion those events which were the source of all his troubles! And the end not yet in sight! At least from Balad he could telephone the cursar, who would certainly provide him transportation back to Uncibal and safe access through Uncibal Space-port. And Jantiff, marching south at a brisk stride, began to take an interest in the landscape. When eventually he returned to Zeck, what wonderful tales he would be able to tell!

The road led up a long slope through sprawling heavy-boled trees, then breasted a low ridge. Ahead lay forest and yet more forest: trees indigenous and exotic, some perhaps tracing a lineage back through the Gaean Reach, all the way to Old Earth itself! Jantiff's imagination was stirred; he imagined himself arriving a Alpha Gaea Space-port on Earth, with fabulous cities and unimaginable antiquities awaiting his inspection! How much would it cost? Two or perhaps three thousand ozols. Where would he ever gain so much money? One way or another; nothing was impossible. First: a safe return to Zeck!

Beguiling himself with fancies and prospects, Jantiff put miles behind him, walking with long steady strides. When Dwan reached its zenith, little more than halfway up the sky to the north, Jantiff halted beside a rivulet and ate a portion of his provisions. For the moment, at least, the forest seemed placid and devoid of menace. How far had he come? Ten miles at least . . . Fifty yards along the road a group of eight folk emerged from the forest. Jantiff tensed, then decided to sit quietly.

Three of the folk were women in long gowns, and three were men, wearing black vests over pale green pantaloons; one was a child and another a stripling. All were blond; the child's hair was flaxen. Upon spying Jantiff the group came to a wary halt, then, neither speaking nor making signals, they turned and went off along the road to the south, the stripling and the child bringing up the rear.

Jantiff watched them go. From time to time the child looked back, whether or not by reason of instruction, Jantiff could not determine, since the child made no comment to its elders. They rounded a bend and were lost to view.

Jantiff immediately jumped to his feet and went to that spot where the witches had emerged from the forest. A few yards off the road he saw a tree burdened with plump purple fruit. Jantiff restrained himself. The witches might or might not have been eating the fruit; perhaps it carried a venom which must be dispelled by cooking or other treatment . . . Jantiff proceeded on his way, and at his previous gait, unconcerned whether or not he might overtake the witches. They had shown no hint of hostility, and surely they could apprehend no threat from him. But when presently he commanded a view along the road the witches were nowhere to be seen.

Jantiff walked steadily onward, his strides becoming slower and his legs beginning to ache as the afternoon waned. As Dwan angled low into the northwest the land heaved up ahead in a line of stony juts and retreating gullies. On a promontory overlooking the road the ruins of a great palace lay tumbled among a dozen black tzung trees: a dolorous place, thought Jantiff, no doubt a rendezvous for melancholy ghosts. He hastened past with all the speed his legs could provide: up a gulch where a small river bounded back and forth between rocks—Gant Gap, Jantiff decided. It was a place dark and cold; he was pleased to emerge upon a meadow.

Dwan almost brushed the horizon. Jantiff looked in all directions for the shed Swarkop had mentioned, but no such structure could be seen. Lowering his head he set off once more along the road, as the last rays of Dwan-light played across the meadow. The road entered a new forest, and Jantiff hunched along in the gathering darkness, assured that he had passed the shed by.

A waft of smoke reached his nostrils: Jantiff stopped short, then walked slowly forward and presently saw a spark of firelight fifty yards ahead.

Jantiff approached with great caution and looked out upon a small meadow. Here, in fact, was the shed: a crude structure set thirty yards back from the road. Around the fire sat eight folk: three men of widely disparate age; three women, equally various; a boy of four or five and a girl somewhat past her adolescence. These were evidently the folk Jantiff had seen earlier in the day: how had they arrived so soon? Jantiff could not fathom their speed; they clearly had been at rest for at least an hour. He studied them from the shadows. They seemed neither uncouth nor horrid, after the reputed witchling style; indeed they seemed quite ordinary. Jantiff recalled that their far ancestors were the nobility whose palaces lay shattered across the Weirdlands. All were blond, their hair ranging from flaxen through pale brown to dusty umber. The girl in particular seemed almost comely. A trick of the firelight? Perhaps one of her hallucinations or glamours?

None spoke; all stared into the fire as if deep in meditation.

Jantiff stepped forward. He attempted a hearty greeting, but achieved only a rather reedy "Hallo!"

The small boy troubled to turn his head; the others paid no heed.

"Hallo there!" called Jantiff once more, and stepped forward. "May I join you at your fire?"

Certain of the folk gave him a brief inspection; none spoke.

Accepting the absence of active hostility as an invitation, Jantiff knelt down beside the blaze and warmed his hands. Once again he essayed conversation: "I'm on my way to

Balad where hopefully I'll take passage offplanet. I'm a
stranger to Wyst, actually; my home is Zeck, out along the
Fiamifer. I spent a few months in Uncibal but had quite
enough of it. Too many people, too much confusion . . . I
don't know if you've ever visited there. . . ." Jantiff's voice
dwindled off to silence; no one seemed to be listening. Odd
conduct, to be sure! Well, if they preferred silence to conversation they were well within their rights. If these were truly
witches, they might know mysterious means to communicate
without sound. Jantiff felt a tingle of awe; covertly he inspected the group, first left, then right. Their garments, woven
from bast and dyed variously green, pink or pale brown, were
serviceable forest wear; in the place of hats the men wore
kerchiefs, the women's hair fell loosely over the ears. Each
had gilded his or her fingernails so that they glinted in the
firelight. Otherwise they displayed no ornaments, talismans or
amulets. Whatever mysteries they controlled, their methods
were not obtrusive. Apparently they had supped; a cooking
pot rested upside down on a bench, and also a platter with
fragments of skillet cake.

Emboldened by the acceptance of his presence, Jantiff put
forward: "I am very hungry; I wonder if I might finish off
the skillet cake?"

No one seemed to care one way or another. Jantiff took a
modest portion of the cake and ate with good appetite.

The fire began to burn low; the girl rose to her feet and
went to fetch logs. She was slender and graceful, so Jantiff
noticed; he leapt to his feet and ran to assist her, and it
seemed that her lips twitched in an almost imperceptible
smile. None of the others paid any heed, save the small boy
who watched rather sternly.

Jantiff ate another piece of skillet cake, wondering meanwhile whether the group planned to sleep in the shed. . . .
The door was closed; perhaps they feared the roadmenders'
tricks.

The fire glowed warm; the silence soothed; Jantiff's eyelids
drooped. He fell asleep.

By slow and fitful degrees Jantiff awoke. He lay on the
ground, cramped and cold; the fire had burnt down to embers. Jantiff peered through the darkness; no one was visible:
the witches were gone.

Jantiff sat up and hunched over the coals. A spatter of cold
rain fell against his face. Laboriously he rose to his feet and

stood swaying in the darkness. Shelter would be most welcome. Dubiously he considered the shed; it should be in yonder direction.

Groping through the darkness, he found the plank walls, and sidled to the door. The latch moved under his hand; the door creaked ajar. Jantiff's heart jerked at the sound, but no one, or nothing, seemed to notice. He listened. From inside the hut: silence. Neither breathing, nor movement, nor any of the sounds of sleep. Jantiff tried to step forward, but found that he could not do so: his body thought better of the idea.

For a minute Jantiff stood wavering, every instant less disposed to enter the hut. There was something within, said a mid-region of his brain; it would seize him with a horrible babbling sound. So in his childhood had gone a remembered nightmare, perhaps an anticipation of this very moment. Jantiff backed away from the door. He stumbled off to where he and the girl had gathered firewood, and presently found dead branches which he brought to the embers. After great effort he blew up the fire and finally achieved a heartening blaze. Warm once more he sat down, resolved to remain awake. He turned to look at the hut, now visible in the firelight. Through the open door nothing could be seen. Jantiff quickly averted his gaze, to avoid giving offense. . . . His mind wandered; his eyes closed. . . . A creaking sound brought him sharply awake. Someone had closed the door to the shed.

Jantiff jerked up to his knees. Run! Take wild and instant flight! The hysterical animal within himself keened and raved. . . . But run where? Off into the darkness? Jantiff fetched more wood and built up the fire, and no longer was he urged to sleep.

A dank light seeped into the sky. The meadow took on substance. Beside the guttering fire Jantiff was like a figure carved from wood. He stirred up the fire, feeling ancient as the world itself, then rose stiffly to his feet and ate the last of his bread and meat. He turned a single incurious glance toward the shed, then trudged somberly away toward the south.

Halfway through the morning the overcast lifted. Lambent Dwan-light burst down upon the landscape and Jantiff's spirits lifted. Already the events of the previous night were sliding from his mind, like the episodes of a dream.

The road crossed a river; Jantiff drank, bathed his face,

and ate berries from a low-growing thicket. For ten minutes he rested, then once again went his way.

Gradually the land altered. The forest thinned and sheered back from stony meadows. At noon Jantiff encountered a lane leading away to the right, and thereafter similar lanes left the road every mile or so. Jantiff walked across a wild stony land, grown over with coarse shrubs and land corals. To his left the forest continued into the southeast dark and heavy as ever.

During the middle afternoon he came upon a farmstead of modestly prosperous appearance. A young man of his own age worked behind a fence whitewashing the trunks of young fruit trees. He stood erect at Jantiff's approach, and came to the fence to secure a better view: a sturdy fellow with a narrow long-nosed face and sleek black hair tied in three tufts. Jantiff gave him a courteous greeting, then, not caring for the farmer's expression of sardonic bewilderment, continued along his way.

The farmer's curiosity, however, was not to be denied. "Hola there! Hold up a minute!"

Jantiff paused. "Are you addressing me?"

"Naturally. Is anyone else present?"

"I believe not."

"Well, then! You're not of these parts certainly."

"True," said Jantiff coldly. "I am a visitor to Wyst. My home is Frayness on Zeck."

"I don't know the place. Still I daresay there are millions of chinks and burrows about the Cluster of which I know nothing."

"No doubt this is the case."

"Well then—why are you walking the Sych Road which leads nowhere but to Lake Neman?"

"A friend flew me out from Uncibal and put me down at Lake Neman," said Jantiff. "I walked the road from there."

"And what of the witches: did you see many? I am told a new tribe just moved over from the Haralumilet."

"I encountered a group of wandering folk, yes," said Jantiff. "They troubled me not at all; in fact, they seemed quite courteous."

"So long as they forebore to feed you their tainted* food you're in luck."

---

* Inexact translation. Uslak is "devil's dross"; the adjective *uslakatn* means *unholy, unclean, profane, repulsive.*

Jantiff managed a smile. "I am fastidious about such things, I assure you."

"And what will you do in these parts?"

Jantiff had prepared an answer to such a question: "I am a student traveling on a research fellowship. I wanted to visit Blale before returning home."

The farmer gave a skeptical grunt. "You'll find nothing here to study; we are quite ordinary folk. You might have studied to better effect at home."

"Possibly so." Jantiff bowed stiffly. "Excuse me; I must be on my way."

"As you like, so long as you don't wander into the orchard among my good damsons, whether to study or to meditate or just to stroll, because I'll believe you're there to pilfer, and I'll loose Stanket on you."

"I have no intention of stealing your produce," said Jantiff with dignity. "Good day to you."

He continued south where the road skirted the damson orchard; he noted clusters of fruit dangling almost within reach. He marched resolutely past, even though he was apparently not under observation.

The land became settled. To the west spread cultivated lands: farmstead after farmstead, with orchards and fields of cereal. To the east the forest thrust obdurately south, as heavy, tall and dense as ever. Jantiff presently saw ahead a cluster of ramshackle structures: the town Balad. To the right a group of warehouses and workshops indicated the site of the space-port. The field itself was barren of traffic.

Jantiff urged his weary legs to a final effort and moved at his best speed.

A slow full river swung in from the east; the road veered close to the Sych. Jantiff, chancing to look off into the forest, stopped short, on legs suddenly numb. Twenty yards away, camouflaged by the light and shadow, three men in black vests and pale green pantaloons stood motionless and silent, like fabulous animals.

Jantiff stared, his pulse pounding from the startlement; the three gazed gravely back, or perhaps beyond.

Jantiff released his pent breath; then, thinking to recognize the men of the night before, he raised his hand in an uncertain salute. The three men, giving back no acknowledgment, continued to gaze at, or past, Jantiff, as before.

Jantiff trudged wearily onward, away from the forest,

across the river by an ancient iron bridge, and finally arrived at the outskirts of Balad.

The road broadened to become an avenue fifty yards wide, running the length of the town. Here Jantiff halted, to look glumly this way and that. Balad was smaller and more primitive than he had anticipated: essentially nothing more than a wind-swept village on the dunes beside the Moaning Ocean. Small shops lined the south side of the main street. Opposite were a marketplace, a dilapidated hall, a clinic and dispensary, a great barn of a garage for the repair of farmers' vehicles, and a pair of taverns: the Old Groar and the Cimmery.

Lanes angled down to the river, where half a dozen fishing boats were moored. Cottages flanked the lanes and overlooked the river which, a half-mile after leaving Balad, became a shallow estuary and so entered the ocean. A few pale dark-haired children played in the lanes; half a dozen wheeled vehicles and a pair of ground-hoppers were parked beside the Old Groar and as many near the Cimmery.

The Old Groar was the closest: a two-story structure, sinter blocks below and timber painted black, red, and green above to produce an effect of rather ponderous frivolity.

Jantiff pushed through the door and entered a common room furnished with long tables and benches and illuminated by panes of dusty magenta glass set high in the side wall. At this slack hour of the day the room was vacant of all but seven or eight patrons, drinking ale from earthenware vessels and playing sanque.*

Jantiff looked into the kitchen, where a portly man, notable for a shining bald pate and a luxuriant black mustache stood with a knife and brush, preparatory to cleaning a large fish. His attitude suggested peevishness, provoked by conditions not immediately evident. Upon looking up and seeing Jantiff he lowered knife and brush and spoke in a brusque voice: "Well, sir? How may I oblige you?"

Jantiff spoke in an embarrassed half-stammer: "Sir, I am a traveler from off-world. I need food and lodging, and since I have no money, I would be pleased to work for my keep."

The innkeeper threw down the knife and brush. His manner underwent a change, to become what was evidently a

---

* A complicated game of assault and defense, played on a board three feet square, with pieces representing fortresses, estaphracts and lancers.

normal condition of pompous affability. "You are in luck! The maid is hard at it, giving birth, the pot-boy is likewise ill, perhaps in sympathy. I lack a hundred commodities but work is not one of them. There is much to be done and you may start at once. As your first task, be so good as to clean this fish."

Chapter 12

•••◦━━◆━━◦•••

Fariske the innkeeper had not deceived Jantiff: there was indeed work to be accomplished. Fariske, himself inclined to ease and tolerance, nevertheless, through sheer force of circumstances, kept Jantiff constantly on the move: scouring, sweeping, cutting, paring, serving food and drink; washing and cleaning pots, plates and utensils; husking, shelling and cleaning percebs.*

Jantiff was allowed the use of a small chamber at the back of the second floor, whatever he chose to eat and drink and a daily wage of two ozols. "This is generous pay!" declared Fariske grandly. "Still, after you perform the toil that I require, you may think differently."

"At the moment," said Jantiff feelingly, "I am more than satisfied with the arrangement."

"So be it!"

On the morning after his arrival in Balad, Jantiff took himself to the local post and communications office and there telephoned Alastor Centrality at Uncibal—a call for which, by Cluster law, no charge could be levied. On the screen appeared the face of Aleida Gluster. "Ah ha ha!" she exclaimed in excitement. "Jantiff Ravensroke! Where are you?"

"As you suggested, I came to Balad; in fact I arrived yesterday afternoon."

---

* Percebs: a small mollusk growing upon sub-surface rocks along the shores of the Moaning Ocean. The percebs must be gathered, husked, cleaned, fried in nut oil with *aiole*, whereupon they become a famous local delicacy.

"Excellent! And you will now take passage from the space-port?"

"I haven't applied yet," said Jantiff. "It may well be useless. Only cargo ships put down here; and they take no passengers, or so I'm told."

Aleida Gluster's jaw dropped. "I had not considered this aspect of affairs."

"In any event," said Jantiff, "I must speak to the cursar. Has he returned to Uncibal?"

"No! Nor has he called into the office! It is most strange."

Jantiff clicked his tongue in disappointment. "When he arrives, will you telephone me? I am at the Old Groar Tavern. My business is really important."

"I will give him your message, certainly."

"Thank you very much."

Jantiff left the post office and hurried back to the Old Groar, where Fariske had already become petulant because of his absence.

The custom of the Old Groar comprised a cross-section of local society: farmers and townspeople, servants from the manor of Grand Knight Shubart (as he was locally known), warehousemen and mechanics from the space-port and the port agent himself: a certain Eubanq. Jantiff found most of these folk somewhat coarse and not altogether congenial, especially the farmers, each of whom seemed more positive, stubborn and curt than the next. They drank Fariske's compound ale and smoky spirits with zeal and ate decisively. They derived neither expansion nor ease from their drinking, and when drunk became torpid. As a rule Jantiff paid little heed to their conversation; however, overhearing mention of the witches, he asked a question: "Why do they never speak? Can anyone tell me this?"

The farmers exchanged smiles at Jantiff's ignorance. "Certainly they can speak," declared the oldest and most amiable of the group, a person named Skorbo. "My brother trapped two of them in his barn. The first got away; the other he tied to the farrel-post and took the truth out of her; I won't say how. The witch agreed that she could talk as well as the next person, but that words carried too much magic for ordinary occasions; therefore they were never used unless magic was to be worked, as at that very moment, so said the witch. Then she sang out a rhyme, or whatever it might be, and Chabby—that's my brother—felt the blood rush to his ears in a burst

and he ran from the bar. When he came back with his vyre*
the creature was walking away. He took aim, and would you
think it? The vyre exploded and tore open his hands!"

A farmer named Bodile jerked his head in scorn for the
folly of Chab the brother. "No one should use a vyre, nor
any complex thing, against a witch. A cudgel cut from a
nine-year-old hawber and soaked nine nights in water which
has washed no living hand: that's the best fend against
witches."

"I keep a besom of prickle-withe and it's never failed me
yet," said one named Sansoro. "I've laid it out ready for use
and I'm smarting up my wurgles; there's a new coven into
Inkwood."

"I saw some yesterday," said Duade, a lanky young man
with a great beak of a nose and crow-wing eyebrows. "They
seemed on the move toward Wemish Water. I shouted my
curse, but they showed no haste."

Skorbo drained his mug and set it down with a rap. "The
Connatic should deal with them. We pay our yearly stiver**
and what do we get in return? Felicitations and high prices.
I'd as soon spend my tax on ale. Boy! Bring another pint!"

"Yes, sir."

Nearby sat a man in a suit of fawn-colored twill, to match
his sparse sandy hair. His shoulders were heavy, but narrow
and sloping above a pear-shaped torso. This was Eubanq, the
port agent, an outworlder appointed by Grand Knight
Shubart. Eubanq, a regular of the Old Groar, came every afternoon to sip ale, munch percebs and play sanque at a dinket*** a game, with whomever chose to challenge him. His
manner was equable, humorous, soft and sedate; his lips constantly pursed and twitched as if at a series of private amuse-
ments. Eubanq now called from a nearby table. "Never
scurrilize the Connatic, friends! He might be standing among
us at this very minute. That's his dearest habit, as we all
know quite well!"

Duade uttered a jeering laugh. "Not likely. Unless he's this
new serving boy. But somehow I don't see Janx in the part."

"Janx" was a garbled mishearing of "Jantiff," which had
gained currency around the tavern.

"Janx is not our Connatic," Eubanq agreed, with humorous

* A light weapon used for the control of rodents, the hunting of
wild fowl, and like service.

** Colloquialism for the Connatic's head tax.

*** A coin worth the tenth part of an ozol.

emphasis. "I've seen his picture and I can detect the difference. Still, never begrudge the Connatic's stiver. Have you ever looked up into the sky? You'll see the stars of Alastor cluster, all protected by the Whelm."

Bodile grunted. "The stiver is wasted. Why should starmenters come to Blale? There's nothing for them to take; certainly not at my house."

"Grand Knight Shubart is the bait," said Skorbo. "He surrounds himself with richness, as is his right; but by the same token he now must fear the starmenters."

Duade grumbled: "We both pay the same stiver! Who does the Whelm protect? Shubart? Or me? Justice is remote."

Eubanq laughed. "Take comfort! The Whelm is not allpowerful! Perhaps they will fail to guard the Grand Knight, then your stivers are equally misspent, so there you have your justice after all. And who is for a quick go at the sanque board?"

"Not I," said Duade sourly. "The Connatic takes his stiver; you take our dinkets, Bahevah only knows by what set of artifices. I'll play no more with you."

"Nor I," said Bodile. "I know a better use for my dinkets. Boy! Are the percebs on order?"

"In just a few minutes, sir."

Eubanq, unable to promote a game, turned away from the farmers. A few minutes later, finding a lull in his work, Jantiff approached him. "I wonder, sir, if you'd be good enough to advise me."

"Certainly, within the limits of discretion," said Eubanq. "I should warn you, however, that free advice is usually not worth its cost."

Jantiff ignored the pleasantry. "I wish to take passage to Frayness on Zeck; this is Alastor 503, as no doubt you know. Is it possible to arrange this passage from the Balad spaceport?"

Eubanq shook his head. "Ships clearing Balad invariably make for Hilp and then Lambeter, to complete a circuit of the Gorgon's Tusk."

"Might I make connections from either Hilp or Lambeter to Zeck?"

"Certainly, except for the fact that the ships putting down here won't carry you; they're not licensed to do so. Go to Uncibal and take a Black Arrow packet direct."

"I am bored with Uncibal," Jantiff muttered. "I don't want to set foot there again."

"Then I fear that you must reconcile yourself to residence in Blale."

Jantiff considered a moment. "I hold a passage voucher to Zeck. Could you issue me a ticket from Balad directly through to Frayness, so that I could board the packet without going through Uncibal Terminal?"

Eubanq's glance became shrewd and inquisitive. "This is possible. But how would you travel from Balad to Uncibal?"

"Is there no connecting service?"

"No scheduled commercial flights."

"Well, suppose you were making the trip: how would you go?"

"I would hire someone with a flibbit to fly me. Naturally it wouldn't come cheap, as it's a far distance."

"Well then—how much?"

Eubanq pulled thoughtfully at his chin. "I could arrange it for a hundred ozols; that's my guess. It might come more. It won't come less."

"A hundred ozols!" cried Jantiff in shock. "That's a vast sum!"

Eubanq shrugged. "Not when you consider what's involved. A man with a sound flibbit won't care to work on the cheap. No more do I, for that matter."

A call came from the farmers: "Boy! Service!"

Jantiff turned away. A hundred ozols! Surely the figure was excessive! At two ozols a day and not a dinket wasted, a hundred ozols meant fifty days; the Arrabin Centenary would have come and gone!

No doubt the hundred ozols included a substantial fee for Eubanq, thought Jantiff glumly. Well, either Eubanq must reduce his fee or Jantiff must earn more money. The first proposition was far-fetched: Eubanq's parsimony was something of a joke around the Old Groar. According to Fariske, Eubanq had arrived at Balad wearing his fawn twill costume and never had worn anything else. So then: how to earn more money? No easy accomplishment in view of the demands Fariske made upon his time.

So Jantiff reflected as he cleared a vacated table. He glanced resentfully toward Eubanq, who was deep in colloquy with a person newly arrived at the Old Groar. Jantiff froze in his tracks. The new arrival, a person large and heavy, with coarse black hair, narrow eyes, a complexion charged with heavy reeking blood, commanded local importance, to judge from Eubanq's obsequious manner. His garments by Balad standards were rather grand: a pale blue suit (somewhat soiled) cut in military style, black boots, a black harness and a cap of black bast set off with a fine panache of silver bristles. He now looked around the room, saw Jantiff, signaled. "Boy! Bring ale!"

"Yes, sir." With a beating heart Jantiff served the table. Booch glanced at him again without any trace of recognition. "Is this Fariske's old Dark Wort? Or the Nebranger?"

"It's the best Dark Wort, sir."

Booch dismissed Jantiff with a brusque nod. If he had so much as noticed Jantiff at the bonterfest, the recollection apparently had dissolved. More reason than ever to leave Balad, Jantiff told himself through gritted teeth. A hundred ozols might turn out to be a dramatic bargain!

Eubanq presently rose to his feet and took leave of Booch. Jantiff accosted him near the door. "I don't have a hundred ozols now, but I'll make up the amount as soon as possible."

"Good enough," said Eubanq. "I'll check the Black Arrow schedule, and we can set up definite arrangements."

Jantiff made a half-hearted proposal: "If you could get me away sooner, I'd pay you as soon as I arrived on Zeck."

Eubanq gave an indulgent chuckle. "Zeck is far from Balad; memories sometimes don't extend such distances."

"You could trust me! I've never cheated anyone in my life!"

Eubanq raised his hand in a laughing disclaimer. "Nevertheless and not withstanding! I invariably do business in proper fashion, and that means ozols on the barrel head!"

Jantiff gave a morose shrug. "I'll see what I can do. Er— who is your friend yonder?"

Eubanq glanced back across the room. "That's the Respectable Buwechluter, usually known as Booch. He's factotum to Grand Knight Shubart, who happens to be offplanet at the moment, so Booch takes his ease at the manor and regales us all with his blood-curdling anecdotes. Step smartly when he calls his order and you'll find no difficulties."

"Boy!" called out Booch at this moment. "Bring a double order of percebs!"

"Sorry, sir! No percebs left; we've had a run on them today."

Booch uttered a curse of disgust. "Why doesn't Fariske plan more providentially? Well then, bring me a slice of good fat grump and a half-pound of haggot."

Jantiff hastened to do Booch's bidding, and so the evening progressed.

The patrons departed at last and went their ways through the misty Blale night. Jantiff cleared the tables, set the room to rights, extinguished lights and gratefully retired to his room.

Taking all with all, Jantiff had no fault to find with the Old Groar. But for his anxiety and Fariske's importunities, he might have taken pleasure in Balad and its dim, strange surroundings. He was aroused early by Palinka, Fariske's robust daughter, who then served him a breakfast of groats, sausage and blackmold tea. Immediately thereafter he swabbed out the common room, brought up supplies from the cellar and smartened up the bar in preparation for the day's business. After his third day a new task was required of Jantiff. In rain or shine, mist or storm, he was sent out with a pair of buckets to gather the day's supply of percebs from the offshore rocks. Jantiff came to enjoy this particular task above all others, in spite of the uncertain weather and the chill water of the Moaning Ocean. Once beyond the immediate precincts of Balad, solitude was absolute, and Jantiff had the shore to himself.

Jantiff's usual route was eastward along Dessimo Beach, where half-sunken platforms of rock alternated with pleasant little coves. Dunes along the shore-side supported a multitude of growths: purple gart, puzzle-bush, ginger-tufts, creeping jilberry, which squeaked when trod upon. Interspersed were patches of silicanthus: miniature five-pronged radiants of a stuff like frosted glass, stained apparently at random in any of a hundred colors. Here and there granat trees twisted and humped to the wind, with limbs wildly askew like harridans in flight. When Jantiff looked south across the ocean, the near horizon never failed to startle him with the illusion that he stood high in the air. The wet days were undeniably dreary; and when the wind blew strong, the ocean swells toppled ponderously over the rocks; and sometimes Jantiff slouched empty-bucketed back to the Old Groar.

On fine days the ocean sparked and scintillated to the Dwan light; the gart glowed like purple glass; and the sand beneath Jantiff's feet seemed as clean and fresh as at the beginning of time; and Jantiff, swinging his buckets and breathing the cool salt air, felt that life was well worth living, despite every conceivable tribulation.

Halfway along the Dessimo headland an arm of the Sych swung out and approached the ocean. Here Jantiff discovered a dilapidated shack, half-hidden in the shadows of the forest. The roof had dropped; one wall had collapsed; the floor was buried under the detritus of years. Jantiff prodded here and there with a stick, but found nothing of interest.

One day Jantiff walked to the end of the headland: a massive tongue of black rock protecting a dozen swirling pools of chilly water in its lee. Exploring these pools Jantiff found quantities of excellent percebs, including many of the prized coronel variety, and thereafter Jantiff visited the area daily. Passing the old hut, he occasionally troubled to fit a stone or two back into the wall, or clear an armload of litter from the interior. One sunny morning he circled the headland and returned to Balad along the shore of Lulace Sound, and so obtained a view of Lulace, Grand Knight Shubart's manor, at the back of an immaculate formal garden. Jantiff paused to admire the place, of which he had heard a dozen marvelous tales. Immediately he noticed Booch sunning himself on a garden bench, and as he watched, a young maid in black and red livery came out from the kitchen with a tray of refreshments. Booch seemed to make a facetious invitation, but the maid sidled nervously away. Booch reached out to haul her back and caught one of the red pompoms of her livery. The girl protested, pleaded and at last began to cry. Booch's gallantry instantly vanished. He gave the girl a buffet across the buttocks, to send her stumbling and weeping toward the manor. Jantiff took an impulsive step forward, ready to call out a reprimand, but thought twice and held his tongue. Booch, chancing to notice him, jumped to his feet in a fury; Jantiff was relieved that sixty yards of water lay between them. He took up his percebs and hurried away.

Halfway through the evening Booch appeared at the Old Groar. Jantiff went about his duties, trying to ignore Booch's glowering glances. At last Booch signaled and Jantiff approached. "Yes, sir?"

"You were spying on me today. I've half a mind to shove your head in the cesspool."

"I was not spying," said Jantiff. "I happened to be walking along the shore with percebs for today's custom."

"Don't walk that way again. The Grand Knight likes his privacy, and so do I."

"Did you wish to order?" asked Jantiff with what dignity he could muster.

"When I see fit!" growled Booch. "I have the feeling that I've seen your unwholesome face before. I did not like it then, nor do I like it now, so have a care."

Jantiff went stiffly off about his duties.

In the corner of the room sat Eubanq, who presently signaled to Jantiff. "What's your difficulty with Booch?"

Jantiff described the episode. "And now he's in a rage."

"No doubt, and the whole situation has curdled, since I intended Booch to fly you to Uncibal in one of the Grand Knight's flibbits."

Booch loomed over the table. "This is the person you want flown to Uncibal?" A grin spread over his face. "I'll be happy to take him aloft, at no payment whatever."

Neither Jantiff nor Eubanq made response. Booch chuckled and departed the tavern.

Jantiff said bleakly: "I certainly won't fly to Uncibal with Booch."

Eubanq made one of his easy gestures. "Don't take him seriously. Booch is bluff and bluster, for the most part. I've consulted the schedule and now I'll need your passage voucher. Do you have it with you?"

"Yes, but I don't care to let it out of my hands."

Eubanq smilingly shook his head. "There's no way to negotiate a firm reservation without it."

Jantiff reluctantly surrendered the certificate.

"Very good," said Eubanq. "You will depart Uncibal in three weeks aboard the *Jervasian*. How much money do you have now?"

"Twenty ozols."

Eubanq clicked his tongue in vexation. "Not enough! In three weeks you'll have at most eighty ozols! Well, I'll simply have to reschedule you for the *Serenaic*, in about six weeks."

"But that will be after the Arrabin Centenary Festival!"

"What of that?"

Jantiff was silent a moment. "I have business at Uncibal, but before the Centenary. Can't you trust me for twenty ozols? As soon as I'm home I'll send back whatever money is lacking. I swear it!"

"Of course!" said Eubanq wearily. "I believe you, never doubt it! You are deadly in earnest—now. But on Zeck there might be needs more urgent than mine here at this dismal little outpost. That is the way things go. I fear that I must have the money in hand. Which shall it be? The *Jervasian* or the *Serenaic*?"

"It will have to be the *Serenaic*," said Jantiff hollowly. "I simply won't have the money sooner. Remember: under no circumstances will I fly with Booch."

"Just as you say. I can hire Bulwan's flibbit and fly you myself. We'll plan on that basis."

Jantiff went off about his work. Six weeks seemed a very long time. What of the Arrabin Centenary? He must telephone Alastor Centrality again, and yet again, until finally he had unloaded all his burden of facts and suspicions upon the cursar. . . From the distance of Balad, his notions seemed strange and odd: incredible, really—even to Jantiff himself. Might he have suffered a set of vivid paranoid delusions? Jantiff's faith in himself wavered, but only for a moment or two. He had not imagined Esteban's murderous attempts, nor the overheard conversation, nor the camera matrix, nor the death of Clode Morre.

During the course of the evening Jantiff noticed a plump pink-faced young man in the kitchen, and just before closing time, Fariske called him aside. "Jantiff, conditions have more or less returned to normal, and I'm sorry to say that I must let you go."

Jantiff stared aghast. At last he managed to stammer: "What have I done wrong?"

"Nothing whatever. Your work has been in the main satisfactory. My nephew Voris, nevertheless, wants his position back. He is an idler; he drinks as much as he serves; still, I must oblige him, or risk the rough edge of my sister's tongue. That is the way we do things in Balad. You may use your chamber tonight, but I must ask you to vacate tomorrow."

Jantiff turned away and finished the evening's duties in a fog of depression. Two hours before he had been disturbed by a delay of six weeks; now how blessedly fortunate seemed that prospect!

The patrons departed. Jantiff set the room to rights and went off to bed, where he lay awake into the small hours.

In the morning Palinka awoke him at the usual time. She had never been wholly cordial, and today even less so. "I have been ordered to feed you a final breakfast, so bestir yourself; I have much else to do."

Defiance trembled upon Jantiff's tongue, but second thoughts prevailed. He muttered a surly acknowledgment, and presented himself to the kitchen as usual.

Palinka put before him his usual gruel, tea, bread and conserve; Jantiff ate listlessly and so aroused Palinka's impatience. "Come, Jantiff, eat briskly, if you please! I am waiting to clear the table."

"And I am waiting for my wages!" declared Jantiff in sudden fury. "Where is Fariske? As soon as he pays me, I will leave!"

Then you will be waiting the whole day long," Palinka retorted. "He has gone off to the country market."

"And where is my money? Did he not instruct you to pay me?"

Palinka uttered a coarse laugh. "It is too early for jokes. Fariske has made himself scarce hoping that you would forget your money."

"Small chance of that! I intend to claim every dinket!"

"Come back in the morning. For now, be off with you!"

Jantiff left the Old Groar in a sullen mood. For a moment he stood in the street, hands tucked into the flaps of his jacket, shoulders hunched against the wind. He looked east along the street, then west, where his eyes focused upon the Cimmery. Jantiff grimaced; he had lost all zest for the taverns of Balad. Nonetheless, he settled his jacket and sauntered down the street to the Cimmery, where he found Madame Tchaga, a short stout woman with an irascible manner, employed at a task Jantiff knew only too well: scrubbing out the common-room. Jantiff addressed her as confidently as possible, but Madame Tchaga, pausing not a stroke of the push broom, uttered a bark of sour amusement. "The ozols I take in are not enough for me and mine; I've no need for you. Seek elsewhere for work; try the Grand Knight. He might want someone to pare his toenails."

Jantiff returned to the street, where he considered Madame Tchaga's suggestion.

From one of the side lanes came Eubanq on his way to his office at the space-port. At the sight of Jantiff he nodded and would have proceeded had not Jantiff eagerly stepped forward to accost him. Here, after all, was the obvious solution to his problems!

Eubanq greeted him politely enough. "What brings you out in this direction?"

"Fariske no longer needs me at the Old Groar," said Jantiff. "This may be a blessing in disguise, since you can surely put me to work at the space-port, hopefully at a much better wage."

Eubanq's expression became distant. "Unfortunately not.

In truth, there's little enough work to keep my present crew busy."

Jantiff's voice rose in frustration. "Then how can I earn a hundred ozols?"

"I don't know. One way or another, you must discover the money. Your voucher has been sent to Uncibal and you are booked aboard the *Serenaic*."

Jantiff stared in consternation. "Can't the passage be postponed?"

"That's no longer possible."

"Can't you suggest something? What of the Grand Knight? Could you put a word in for me?"

Eubanq started to make small sidling moves, preparatory to moving on past Jantiff. "The Grand Knight is not in residence. Booch now rules the roost, when he's not wenching or witch-chasing or drinking dry the Old Groar vats, and he's not likely to assist you. But no doubt your dilemma will resolve itself: happily, I hope. Good day to you." Eubanq went his way.

Jantiff slouched eastward along the street: past the Old Groar to the edge of town and beyond. Arriving at the seashore, he sat upon a flat stone and looked out across the rolling gray water. Morning light from Dwan, collecting in the wave hollows, washed back and forth like quicksilver. Silver foam broke around the rocks. Jantiff stared morosely at the horizon and pondered his options. He might, of course, try to return to Uncibal and his refuge behind the Disjerferact privy—but how to cross the thousand miles of wilderness? Suppose he were to steal one of the Grand Knight's flibbits? And suppose Booch caught him in the act? Jantiff's shoulder blades twitched. His best hope, as always, lay with the cursar. To this end he must make daily telephone calls to Alastor Centrality. In the morning he would collect his wages from Fariske: a not too satisfactory sum which nonetheless would feed him for an appreciable period. Of more immediate concern was shelter. An idea crossed his mind. He rose to his feet and walked along the shore to the ruined fisherman's shanty, if such it were. Without enthusiasm he examined the structure, although he knew it well already, then set to work clearing the interior of trash, dead leaves, and dirt.

From the forest he brought saplings which he arranged over the walls in a mat which was strong and resilient but hardly waterproof. Jantiff considered the problem carefully. He had no money to spare for conventional roofing; a solution, therefore, must be improvised. The obvious first attempt must be thatch—and even thatch involved financial outlay.

Returning into Balad, Jantiff invested an ozol in cord, knife, and a disk of hard bread, then trudged back to the shack. The time was now afternoon; there was no time to rest. From the beach he brought armloads of seaweed, and laid it out into bundles. Some of the stalks were old and rotten, and smelled of fetid sea life; before Jantiff had fairly started he was cold and wet and covered with slime. Doggedly ignoring discomfort he tied up the bundles and fixed them to his roof in staggered layers.

Sunset found the job still short of completion. Jantiff built a fire, washed himself and his garments in the stream, and before the light had died, gathered a quart of percebs for his supper. He hung up his clothes to dry, then huddled naked in the firelight, trying to keep warm on all sides at once. Meanwhile the percebs baked in their shells, and Jantiff presently ate his supper of bread and percebs with a good appetite.

Night had come; darkness cloaked both land and sea. Jantiff lay back and studied the sky. Since he had never learned the constellations as seen from Wyst, he could name none of the stars, but surely some of these blazing lights above him were famous places, home to noble men and beautiful women. None could even remotely suspect that far below, on the beach of the Moaning Ocean, sat that entity known as Jantiff Ravensroke!

Letting his mind wander free, Jantiff thought of all manner of things, and presently decided that he had divined the soul of this odd little planet Wyst. On Wyst nothing was as it seemed: everything was just a trifle askew or out of focus, or bathed in a mysterious quivering light. This quality, Jantiff reflected, was analogous to the personality of a man. Undoubtedly men tended to share the personality of that world to which they were born. . . . Jantiff wondered about his own world, Zeck, which had always seemed so ordinary: did visitors find it odd and unusual? By analogy, did Jantiff himself seem odd and unusual? Quite conceivably this was the case, thought Jantiff.

The fire burned down to embers. Jantiff rose stiffly to his feet. His bed was only a heap of leaves, but for tonight, at least, it would have to serve. Jantiff made a final survey of the beach, then took shelter in his hut. Burrowing into the leaves, he contrived to make himself tolerably comfortable and presently fell asleep.

At sunrise Jantiff crawled out into the open air. He washed his face in the stream, and ate a few mouthfuls of bread and cold percebs, by no means a heartening breakfast. If he were to stay here even so long as a week he would need pot, pan, cup, cutlery, salt, flour, a few gills of oil, perhaps an ounce or two of tea—at considerable damage to his meager store of ozols. But where was any rational alternative? Sleep had clarified his thinking: he would make a temporary sojourn in the hut and telephone Alastor Centrality at regular intervals; sooner or later he must reach the cursar: perhaps today!

Jantiff rose to his feet, brushed the chaff and twigs from his clothes, and set out toward Balad. Arriving at the Old Groar, he went around to the back and knocked at the kitchen door.

Palinka looked forth. "Well, Jantiff, what do you want?"

"I came for my money; what else?"

Palinka threw back the door and motioned him within. "Go talk to Fariske; there he sits."

Jantiff approached the table. Fariske puffed out his cheeks and, raising his eyebrows, looked off to the side as if Jantiff thereby might be persuaded to go away. Jantiff seated himself in his old place and Fariske was obliged to notice him. "Good morning, Jantiff."

"Good morning," said Jantiff. "I have come for my money."

Fariske heaved a weary sigh. "Come back in a few days. I bought various necessities at the market and now I am short of cash."

"I am even more short than you," cried Jantiff. "I intend to sit in this kitchen and take my meals free of charge until you pay me my wages."

"Now, then!" said Fariske. "There is no cause for acrimony. Palinka, pour Jantiff a cup of tea."

"I have not yet taken breakfast; I would be glad to accept some porridge, were you to offer it."

Fariske signaled Palinka. "Serve Jantiff a dish of the coarse porridge. He is a good fellow and deserves special treatment. What is the sum due you?"

"Twenty-four ozols."

"So much?" exclaimed Fariske. "What of the beer you took and the other extras?"

"I took no beer, and no extras, as you well know."

Fariske glumly brought out his wallet and paid over the money. "What must be must be."

"Thank you," said Jantiff. "Our relationship is now on an even balance. I assume that the situation is like that of yesterday? You still have no need for my services?"

"Unfortunately true. As a matter of fact, I have come to regret your departure. Voris suffers a distension of the leg veins, and is unable to collect percebs. The task therefore devolves upon Palinka."

"What!" cried Palinka in a passion. "Can I believe my ears? Am I suddenly so underworked that I can now while away my hours among the frigid waves? Think again!"

"It is only for today," said Fariske soothingly. "Tomorrow Voris will probably feel fit."

Palinka remained obdurate. "Voris does not lack ingenuity; when his leg veins heal, he will contrive new excuses: the counter needs waxing; ale has soured his stomach; the waves thrash too heavily on the rocks! Then once more the cry will ring out: 'Palinka, Palinka! Go out for percebs! Poor Voris is ill!'" Palinka struck a pan down upon the table in ringing emphasis. "For all Jantiff's oddities, at least he fetched the percebs. Voris must learn from the example."

Fariske attempted the cogency of pure logic. "What, after all, is the fetching of a few percebs? The day contains only so many minutes; it passes as well one way as another."

"In that case, go fetch them yourself!" Palinka took herself off to indicate that the subject was closed.

Fariske pulled at his chin, then turned toward Jantiff. "Might you oblige me, for today only, by bringing in a few percebs?"

Jantiff sipped his tea. "Let us explore the matter in full detail."

Fariske spoke pettishly: "My request is modest; is your response so hard to formulate?"

"Not at all," said Jantiff, "but perhaps we can proceed further. As you know, I am now unemployed. Nevertheless I am anxious to earn a few ozols."

Fariske grimaced and started to speak, but Jantiff held up his hand. "Let us consider a bucket of percebs. When shelled and fried a bucket yields twenty portions, which you sell for a dinket per portion. Thus, a bucket of percebs yields two ozols. Two buckets: four ozols, and so forth. Suppose every day I were to deliver to you the percebs you require, shelled and cleaned, at a cost to you of one ozol per bucket? You would thereby gain your profit with no inconvenience for Palinka, or yourself, or even Voris."

Fariske mulled over the proposal, pulling at his mustache. Palinka, who had been listening from across the kitchen, once again came forward. "Why are you debating? Voris will never fetch percebs! I also refuse to turn my legs blue in the swirling water!"

"Very well, Jantiff," said Fariske. "We will test the system for a few days. Take another cup of tea, to signalize the new relationship."

"With pleasure," said Jantiff. "Also, let us agree that payments will be made promptly upon delivery of the percebs."

"What do you take me for?" Fariske exclaimed indignantly. "A man is only as large as his reputation; would I risk so much for a few paltry mollusks?"

Jantiff made a noncommittal gesture. "If we settle accounts on a day-to-day basis, we thereby avoid confusion."

"The issue is inconsequential," said Fariske. "A further matter: since you evidently intend to pursue this business in earnest, I will command four buckets of percebs from you, rather than the usual two."

"I intended to suggest something of the sort myself," said Jantiff. "I am anxious to earn a good wage."

"You will of course provide your own equipment?"

"For the next few days, at least, I will use the buckets, pries and forceps which you keep in the shed. If there is any deterioration, I will naturally make good the loss."

Fariske was not inclined to let the matter rest on a basis so informal, but Palinka made an impatient exclamation. "The day is well advanced! Do you expect to serve percebs tonight? If so, let Jantiff go about his business." Fariske threw his hands into the air and stalked from the kitchen. Jantiff went to the shed, gathered buckets and tools, and went off down the beach.

The day before he had marked a ledge of rock twenty yards offshore which he had never previously explored, because of the intervening water. Today he contrived a raft from dead branches and bits of driftwood, upon which he supported the buckets. Immersing himself to the armpits, with a shuddering of the knees and a chattering of the teeth, Jantiff pushed the raft out to the ledge and tied it to a knob of rock.

His hopes were immediately realized: the ledge was thickly encrusted with percebs and Jantiff filled the buckets in short order.

Returning to the shore he built a fire, at which he warmed himself while he shelled and cleaned the percebs.

The sun had hardly reached the zenith when Jantiff made his delivery to the Old Groar. Fariske was somewhat puzzled by Jantiff's expedition. "When you worked for me, you used as much time to gather two buckets, and they were not even shelled."

"The conditions are not at all comparable," said Jantiff. "Incidentally, I notice that the shed is cluttered with broken furniture and rubbish. For three ozols I will order the confusion and carry the junk to the rubbish dump."

By dint of furious argument, Fariske reduced Jantiff's price to two ozols, and Jantiff set to work. From the discards Jantiff reserved two old chairs, a three-legged table, a pair of torn mattresses, a number of pots, canisters and dented pans. The ownership of these items, in fact, had been his prime goal, and he suspected that Fariske would have put an inordinate value upon the items had he requested them directly. With considerable satisfaction Jantiff calculated the yield of his day's employment: six ozols and the furnishing of his hut.

On the following day, Jantiff went early to work. He gathered, shelled and cleaned seven buckets of percebs. After delivering the stipulated quota to Fariske, he took the remaining percebs to the Cimmery, where he found no difficulty in selling them to Madame Tchaga for three ozols.

Madame Tchaga was notable for her verbosity. Lacking any better company, she served Jantiff a bowl of turnip soup and described the vexations inherent in trying to gratify the tastes of a fickle and unappreciative clientele.

Jantiff agreed that her frustrations verged upon the insupportable. He went on to remark that the prosperity of an inn often depended upon its cheerful ambience. Possibly a profusion of floral designs upon the Cimmery's façade and a depicted procession of jolly townsfolk on a long panel, perhaps to be hung over the door, might enhance the rather bleak atmosphere of the establishment.

Madame Tchaga dismissed the idea out of hand. "All very well to talk about designs and depictions, but who in Balad is capable of such cleverness?"

"As a matter of fact, I am gifted with such talent," said Jantiff. "Possibly I might find time to do certain work along these lines."

During the next hour and a half Jantiff discovered that Madame Tchaga, as a shrewd and relentless negotiator, far surpassed even Fariske. Jantiff, however, maintained a detached and casual attitude, and eventually won a contract on essentially his own terms, and Madame Tchaga even advanced five ozols for the purchase of supplies.

Jantiff went immediately to the general store where he bought paint of various colors and several brushes. Returning to the street he noticed a plump heavy-faced man in fawn-colored garments approaching at a leisurely splay-footed gait. "Eubanq! Just the person I want to see!" called Jantiff in a jovial voice. "We now return to our original plan!"

Eubanq halted and stood in apparent perplexity. "What plan is this?"

"Don't you remember? For a hundred ozols—an exorbitant sum, incidentally—you are to convey me to Uncibal spaceport in time for me to board the *Serenaic*."

Eubanq gave a slow thoughtful nod. "The hundred ozols naturally are to be paid in advance: You understand this?"

"I foresee no difficulty," said Jantiff confidently. "I have on hand something over thirty ozols. My arrangement with Madame Tchaga will net another twenty-two ozols, and I regularly earn six or seven ozols a day."

"I am pleased to hear of your prosperity," said Eubanq courteously. "What is your secret?"

"No secret whatever! You could have done the same! I simply wallow around the ocean until I have gathered seven buckets of percebs, which I clean and shell and deliver to the Cimmery and the Old Groar. Might you need a bucket or two for your own use?"

Eubanq laughed. "My taste is amply satisfied at the Old Groar. You might make your proposal to Grand Knight Shubart. He is back in residence with a houseful of guests. He'll certainly require a supply of percebs."

"A good idea! So then it's all clear for the *Serenaic*!"

Eubanq smiled his somewhat distant smile and went his way. Jantiff paused to consider a moment. The sooner he earned a hundred ozols the better. The Grand Knight's ozols were as good as any, so why not hazard a try?

Jantiff left off his paints in Fariske's shed, then set out along the northern shore of Lulace Sound to the Grand Knight's manor. Approaching Lulace he sensed bustle and activity where before there had been somnolence. Keeping a wary eye open for Booch, Jantiff went to the service entrance at the back of the building. A scullion fetched the chief cook, who made no difficulty about placing a continuing order for two buckets every third day, at two ozols the bucket; double Jantiff's usual price, for a period of twenty-four days. "The Grand Knight entertains important guests until the Centenary at Uncibal," explained the cook. "Thereafter, all will return to normal."

"You can rely upon me to satisfy your needs," said Jantiff.

In a mood almost buoyant, Jantiff returned up the road to Balad. The hundred ozols were well within his reach; he could confidently look forward to a comfortable passage home. . . . He heard the whir of driven wheels and jumped to the side of the road. The vehicle, guided by Booch, approached and passed. Booch's expression was rapt and glazed, his ropy lips drawn back in a foolish grin.

Jantiff returned to the road and watched the vehicle recede toward Balad. Where would Booch be going in such a fervor of anticipation? Jantiff proceeded thoughtfully into town. He went directly to the telephone and once again called the Alastor Centrality of Uncibal.

Upon the screen appeared the face of Aleida Gluster. Her cheeks, once plump and pink, sagged; Jantiff thought that she seemed worried and even unwell. He spoke apologetically. "Once again it's Jantiff Ravensroke, and I fear that I'm a great nuisance."

"Not at all," said Aleida Gluster. "It is my duty to serve you. Are you still at Balad?"

"Yes, and temporarily at least all seems to be going well. But I must speak to the cursar. Has he returned to Uncibal?"

"No," said Aleida in a tense voice. "He has not yet returned. It is most remarkable."

Jantiff could not restrain a peevish ejaculation. "My business is absolutely vital!"

"I understand as much from our previous encounters," said Aleida tartly. "I cannot produce him by sheer effort of will. I wish I could."

"I suppose that you've tried the Waunisse office again?"

"Of course. He has not been seen."

"Perhaps you should notify the Connatic."

"I have already done so."

"In that case there is nothing to do but wait," said Jantiff reluctantly. "A message to the Old Groar Tavern will reach me."

"This is understood."

Jantiff went out to stand in the wide main street. The weather had changed. Clouds hung heavy and full, like great black udders; huge raindrops struck into the sandy dust. Jantiff hunched his shoulders and hurried to the Old Groar. With a confident step he entered the common-room, seated himself at a table, and signaled Voris for a mug of ale.

Fariske, glancing through the kitchen door, saw Jantiff, and approached in a portentous manner. "Jantiff, I am vexed with you."

Jantiff looked up in wonder. "What have I done?"

"You are supplying percebs to the Cimmery. This is not conceivably a benefit to me."

"It is neither a benefit nor a hindrance. Her patrons eat percebs like your own. If I failed to supply them, someone else would do so."

"Using my buckets, my pry-bars, my forceps?"

Jantiff contrived a negligent laugh. "Really, a trivial matter. The equipment is not damaged. I reserve all the best coronels for the Old Groar. No matter what fault your patrons may find, they will always say: 'Fariske's percebs, at least, are superior to those at the Cimmery.' So why do you complain?"

"Because I had hoped for your loyalty!"

"That you have, naturally."

"Then why do I hear that you are about to paint that ramshackle old place, so that it presents an impression of sanitary conditions?"

"I will do the same for the Old Groar, if you will pay my wage."

Fariske heaved a sigh. "So that is how the wind blows. How much does Madame pay?"

"The exact amount is confidential. I will make a general statement to the effect that forty ozols is quite a decent sum."

Fariske jerked around in astonishment. "Forty ozols? From old Tchaga, who carries every dinket she has ever owned strapped to the inside of her legs?"

"Remember," said Jantiff, "I am an expert at the craft!"

"How can I remember something you never told me?"

"You gave me hardly enough time to clear my throat, much less describe my talents to you."

"Bah!" muttered Fariske. "Forty ozols is an outrageous sum, just for a bit of daubing."

"How would you like a series of ten decorative plaques to hang on your walls, at five ozols each? Or for six ozols I will use silver-gilt accentuations. It will put the Cimmery to shame."

Fariske made a cautious counter-proposal and the discussion proceeded. Meanwhile Booch came into the tavern with a number of burly young men: farmhands, fishermen, laborers and the like. They seated themselves, commanded ale and discussed their affairs in boisterous voices. Jantiff could not evade their conversation: "—with my four wurgles through the Sych—"

"—out to Wamish Water; that's where the creatures collect!"

"Careful, Booch! Remember the yellows!"

"No fear: I'll get none in my mouth!"

At last Jantiff complained to Fariske. "What are those people shouting about?"

"They're off for a bit of witch chasing. Booch is famously keen."

"Witch-chasing? To what end?"

Fariske considered the group over his shoulder. "Herchelman farms his acres like a priest growing haw; last year someone stole a bushel of wattledabs, and now he punishes the witches. Klaw ate witch-tainted food; he underwent the cure and now he carries a great club when he goes on a hunt. Sittle is bored; he'll do anything novel. Dusselbeck is proud of his wurgles and likes to put them to work. Booch specializes in witch kits; he chases them down and forces his body upon them. Pargo's case is absolutely simple; he enjoys witch killing."

Jantiff darted a lambent glance toward the witch chasers, who had just commanded additional ale from the sweating Voris. "It seems a vulgar and brutal recreation."

"Quite so," said Fariske. "I never relished the sport. The witches were fleet; I continually blundered into bogs and thickets. The witches enjoy the game as much as the chasers."

"I find this hard to believe."

Fariske turned up the palms of his hands. "Why else do they frequent our woods? Why do they steal wattledabs? Why do they startle our nights with witchfires and apparitions?"

"Nevertheless, witch chasing seems an ugly recreation."

Fariske gave a snort of rebuttal. "They are a perverse folk; I for one cannot understand their habits. Still, I agree that the chases should be conducted with decorum. Booch's conduct is vulgar; I am surprised that he has not come down with the yellows. You know how the disease is cured? Booch, for his risks, must be considered intrepid."

Jantiff, finding the topic oppressive, tilted his mug but

found it dry. He signaled, but Voris was busy with the witch chasers. "If we are entirely agreed upon the decorative panels and their cost—"

"I will pay twenty ozols, no more, for the ten compositions, and I insist upon a minimum of four colors, with small touches of silver-gilt."

Jantiff squared around as if to depart. "I can waste no more time. With works of aesthetic quality one does not niggle over an ozol or two."

"The concept works in a double direction, like an apothecary's tremblant. Remember: it is you, not I who will experience the joys of artistic creation. This is no small consideration, or so I am told."

Jantiff refuted the remark and eventually the two reached agreement. Fariske served Jantiff a pint of old Dankwort and the two parted on good terms.

Jantiff returned to his hut with Dwan low in the west and the pale light slanting over his shoulder down Dessimo Beach. The clouds had scattered to blasts of wind from the south which had now abated to random gusts of no great force. The Moaning Ocean still churned in angry recollection, and pounded itself to spume on the offshore rocks; Jantiff was grateful that he need collect no more percebs this day. Passing the forest, he halted to listen to the far hooting of wurgles, a mournful throbbing sound which sent tingles of ancient dread along Jantiff's back. More faintly came whoops and ululations from the throats of men. Hateful sounds, thought Janiff. He walked more quickly along the beach, shoulders hunched, head low.

The outcry of the wurgles waxed and waned, then suddenly grew loud. Jantiff stopped short and stared in apprehension toward the Sych. He glimpsed movement under the trees, and a moment later discerned a pair of human figures scurrying through the shadows. Jantiff stirred his numb limbs and proceeded on his way. A frightful outcry sounded suddenly loud: the wailing of wurgles, gasps of human horror and pain. Jantiff stood frozen, his face wrenched into a contorted grimace. Then, crying out wordlessly, he ran toward the sound, pausing only to pick up a stout branch to serve as a cudgel.

A brook, issuing from the Sych, widened into a pond. The wurgles bounded back and forth across the brook and splashed into the pond, the better to tear at the woman who had mired herself in the mud. Jantiff ran screaming around the pond, to halt at the edge of the mire. Two wurgles hanging on the woman's shoulders had borne her down to press her head into the water. One gnawed at her scalp; the other rent the nape of her neck. Blood swirled out to darken the pond; the woman made spasmodic motion and died. Jantiff backed slowly away, sick with disgust and fury. He turned and lurched away toward the road. The wurgles keened again; Jantiff swung around with ready cudgel, hoping for attack, but the wurgles had flushed forth the second member of the pair. From the Sych ran a girl with contorted features and streaming brown-blond hair; Jantiff instantly recognized the girl-witch he had met at the roadmender's shed. Four wurgles bounded in pursuit, massive heads out-thrust to display gleaming fangs. The girl saw Jantiff and stopped short in dismay; the wurgles lunged and she fell to her knees. But Jantiff was already beside her. He swung his cudgel, to break the back of the foremost wurgle; it slumped and lay kinked on the trail, bending and unbending in agonized jerks. Jantiff struck the second wurgle on the head; it somersaulted and lay still. The two survivors backing away, set up a desolate outcry. Jantiff chased them but they leapt smartly away.

Jantiff returned to the girl, who knelt gasping for breath. From the Sych came the calls of the witch chasers, ever more distinct; already different voices and different cries could be detected.

Jantiff spoke to the witch-girl. "Listen carefully! Do you hear me?"

The girl lifted a face bloated with despair; she gave no other sign.

"Up! To your feet," cried Jantiff urgently. "The chasers are coming; you've got to hide." He seized her arm and hauled her erect. The third wurgle suddenly darted close; Jantiff was ready with his cudgel and struck hard. The animal ran screaming in a circle, snapping at its own mouse-colored hind quarters. Jantiff struck again and again in hysterical energy until the creature dropped. He stood panting a moment, listening. The chasers had become confused; Jantiff could hear them calling to each other. He thrust the dead wurgle into the brook, then did the same with the other two bodies. The current swung them away, and they drifted toward the sea.

Jantiff turned back to the witch-girl. "Come, quickly now! Remember me? We met in the forest. Now, this way, at a run!"

Jantiff tugged her into a trot; they ran beside the brook,

across the road, over the shore stones to the water's edge. The girl stopped short; by main force Jantiff pulled her out into the surf and led her stumbling and tottering for fifty yards parallel to the shore. For a moment they rested, Jantiff anxiously watching the edge of the forest, the girl staring numbly down at the surging water. Jantiff lifted her into his arms and staggered up the beach to his hut. Kicking open his makeshift door he carried her to one of his rickety chairs. "Sit here until I come back," said Jantiff. "I think—I hope—you'll be safe. But don't show yourself, and don't make any noise!" This last, so Jantiff reflected, as he went back along the beach, was possibly an unnecessary warning; she had uttered no sound from the moment he had seen her.

Jantiff went back to where the brook crossed the path. From the Sych came three men, the first two led by leashed wurgles. The third man was Booch.

The wurgles, sniffing out the witch-girl's track, paused where she had fallen, then strained toward the sea.

Booch caught sight of Jantiff. "Hallo, you, whatever your name! Where are the witches we chased through the Sych?"

"I saw but one," said Jantiff, contriving a meek and eager voice. "I heard the wurgles as I came from town. She crossed the path and led them yonder." He pointed toward the sea, in which direction the wurgles already strained.

"What did she look like?" rasped Booch.

"I barely saw her, but she seemed young and agile: a witch kit, for sure!"

"Quick then!" cried Booch. "She's the one I've ranged the forest to find!"

The wurgles followed the trail to the water's edge where they halted and made fretful outcries. Booch looked up and down the beach, then out to sea. He pointed. "Look! There's something out there: a body!"

"It's a wurgle," one of his fellows said. "Damnation and vileness!* I believe it's my Dalbuska!"

"Then where's the kit?" bellowed Booch. "Did she drown herself? Hey, fellow!"—this to Jantiff—"What did you see?"

"The kit and the wurgles. She led them down to the water and when I came to look she was gone."

"And my good wurgles! Pastola put a curse on her; the witches swim underwater like smollocks!"

---

* The oath spoken in Blale idiom exerts considerably more impact: *Shauk chutt!*

Booch shouldered Jantiff aside and returned to the road. The other two followed.

Jantiff watched as they marched to the pool and there observed the corpse of the witch-woman. After a few minutes' muttered conversation they called up their wurgles and tramped off toward Balad into the last lavender rays of the setting sun.

Jantiff returned to his hut. He found the witch-girl where he had left her, sitting wan and still.

"You're safe now," said Jantiff. "Don't be frightened; no one will harm you here. Are you hungry?"

The girl responded by not so much as quiver. *In a state of shock*, thought Jantiff. He built a good blaze in his fireplace and turned her chair toward the heat. "Now: warm yourself. I'll cook soup, and there'll be roast percebs as well, with scallions and oil!"

The girl stared into the fire. After a few moments she listlessly held out her hands to the blaze. Jantiff, preparing the meal, watched her from the corner of his eye. Her face, no longer contorted by terror, was pinched and pale; Jantiff wondered about her age. It was certainly less than his own, still he could not regard her as a child. Her breasts were small and round; her hips, while unmistakably feminine, were slender and unobtrusive. Perhaps, thought Jantiff, she was of a constitution naturally slight. He bustled here and there, and presently served up the best meal his resources allowed.

The girl showed no diffidence about eating, though she took no great quantity of food. Jantiff from time to time attempted conversation: "There, now! Are you feeling better?"

No response.

"Would you like more soup? And here: a nice perceb."

Again no answer. When Jantiff tried to serve out more food, she pushed the plate away.

Her conduct was almost that of a deaf-mute, thought Jantiff. Nonetheless, something about her manner left him in doubt. Perhaps his language was strange to her? This consideration bore no weight: at the clearing in the woods there had likewise been no conversation.

"My name is Jantiff Ravensroke. What is your name?"

Silence.

"Very well then; I must supply a name for you. What about 'Pusskin'? or 'Tickaboo'? or 'Parsnip'? Even better, 'Jilliam';* that would do nicely. But I mustn't make jokes. I shall call you 'Glisten' because of your hair and your golden fingernails. 'Glisten' you shall be."

But "Glisten" would not acknowledge her new name, and sat leaning forward, arms on knees, staring into the fire. Presently Jantiff saw that she was weeping.

"Come, come, this won't do! You've had a miserable time, but. . . ." Jantiff's voice trailed off. How could he console her for the loss of someone who might have been her mother? Indeed, her self-control was marvelous in itself! He knelt beside her and gingerly patted her head. She paid no heed, and Jantiff desisted.

The fire burnt low. Jantiff went outside, to fetch wood and look around the night. When he returned within, Glisten—so he had resolved to call her—had lain herself on the damp floor with her face to the ground. Jantiff surveyed her a moment, then bent over and with a bit of undignified stumbling, carried her to the bed. She lay limp and passive, eyes closed. Jantiff somberly banked the fire with three green logs and removed his boots. After a moment's hesitation he diffidently removed Glisten's sandals, noting that she had also gilded her toenails. A curious vanity! A symbol perhaps of caste, or status? Or an ornamental convention, no more? He lay down beside her and pulled up the ragged old coverlet—an item also rescued from Fariske's shed. For a long time he lay awake until finally the witch-girl's breathing indicated sleep.

* In the traditional fables of Zeck, Jilliam is a talkative girl who is captured by a starmenter and almost immediately set free because of her incessant prattle.

Chapter 13

••••————◆▶————••••

The light of dawn entered Jantiff's makeshift window. He cautiously raised himself on his elbow. Glisten was awake, and lay with her eyes fixed on the ceiling.

"Good morning," said Jantiff. "Are you speaking to me today? . . . I thought not. . . . Well, life goes on and I must gather my percebs. But first, breakfast!"

Jantiff blew up the fire, boiled tea and toasted bread. For five minutes Glisten watched apathetically, then—abruptly, as if prodded—she sat up, swung her legs to the floor. She slipped on her sandals and with an inscrutable sidelong glance toward Jantiff, walked from the hut. Jantiff sighed and shrugged and turned his attention back to the food. Glisten doubtless longed for the company of her own kind. He could offer only temporary security, at best. She was better off in the Sych. Nevertheless he felt a pang of regret; Glisten had invested his hut with something heretofore lacking: companionship? Perhaps.

Jantiff prepared to eat a solitary breakfast. . . . Footsteps. The door swung open. Glisten entered, her face washed, her hair ordered. She carried in her skirt a dozen brown pods which Jantiff recognized as the fruit of the turnover vine. Glisten deftly husked the pods, dropped them into a pan. Five minutes later, Jantiff gingerly tasting, found them a most savory adjunct to the toasted bread.

"I see that you are a wise girl, indeed," said Jantiff. "Do you like the name 'Glisten'? If you do, nod—or better, smile!" He watched her closely and Glisten, whether or not responding to his instruction, seemed to manage a twist of the lips.

Jantiff rose to his feet and gazed out over the dreary ocean. "Well, no avoiding it. The percebs must be harvested, and now I need nine bucketloads! Oh, my clammy skin; can it tolerate such abuse?"

Luckily for Jantiff his shoal of rocks had lain fallow for years and the outer face was heavily encrusted. Jantiff

175

worked with an energy born of discomfort, and in record time gathered his nine buckets. Glisten meanwhile had wandered about, often looking toward the forest, as if listening for a summons or a call, which evidently she failed to hear. At last she came down to the shore, and seating herself primly on a rock, watched Jantiff at his work. When Jantiff began to shell and clean his catch, she helped him: listlessly at first, then with increasing deftness. Well before noon, Jantiff was ready to make his deliveries.

"I must leave you," he told Glisten. "If you decide to go away then you must do so, without regrets. Of course if you care to stay, you are more than welcome. But above all remember: if you see anyone, hide, and quickly!"

Glisten listened soberly and Jantiff went off about his business.

The Old Groar was full of gossip about the witch chasing, which by general consensus had gone well. "They're cleared from the Sych, this end at least," declared one man. "Cambres caught his two garden thieves and downed them on the spot."

"Ha! That will soothe his soul!"

"Booch is in an awful state; he missed his young kit. He swears she ran out on the water and led Dusselbeck's good Feigwel wurgles to their death."

"Ah, the thing!"

"Still the wurgles tore a witch-mother properly to bits!"

"Now they'll have to take the treatment!"

This last was evidently a jocularity; everyone laughed, and at this point Jantiff departed the tap room.

During the afternoon he started his decoration of the Cimmery, working with great intensity and so completed perhaps a third of his job. He might have accomplished more had he not found himself fretting and anxious to return to his hut. Along the way he stopped by the general store and bought new bread, oil, a packet of dehydrated goulash and another of candied persimmon slices.

When he returned to the hut, Glisten was nowhere to be seen, but the fire was burning, the bed had been put in order and the hut seemed unaccountably tidy. Jantiff went out to look this way and that. "Better, far better, if she's gone," he muttered. "After all, she can't stay here after I've gone off to Uncibal." Even as he turned to enter the hut, Glisten came trotting across the meadow, looking back over her shoulder.

Jantiff seized up his cudgel but whatever had alarmed her made no appearance.

At the sight of Jantiff, Glisten slowed her pace to a demure walk. She carried a cloth sling full of green finberries. Ignoring Jantiff as if he were invisible, she put down the berries, then stood looking pensively back toward the forest.

"I'm home," said Jantiff. "Glisten! Look at me!"

Somewhat to his surprise—by coincidence, so he suspected—the witch-girl turned her head and studied him sombery. Half in frustration, half in jest, Jantiff asked: "What goes on in your mind? Do you see me as a person? or a shadow? or a chattering moon-calf?" He took a step toward her, thinking to arouse some flicker of reaction: surprise, alarm, perplexity, anything. Glisten hardly seemed to notice, and Jantiff rather sheepishly contented himself with handing over the packet of sweetmeats. "This is for you," he said. "Can you understand? For Glisten. For dear little Glisten, who refuses to talk to Jantiff."

Glisten put the packet aside, and began to clean the berries. Jantiff watched in a warm suffusion. How pleasant this might have been under different circumstances! But in a month he would be gone and the hut would again fall into ruins, and Glisten must return to the forest.

Jantiff, contriving fanciful arabesques in red, gold, dark blue and lime green across the front of the dreary old Cimmery, looked around to find Eubanq shuffling quietly past. Jantiff jumped down from the trestle. "Eubanq, my good fellow!"

Eubanq halted somewhat reluctantly, shoving his hands into the pockets of his fawn-colored jacket. He cast an eye over the decorated timbers. "Ah, Jantiff. You're doing fine work, getting the old Cimmery ready for the fair. Well, you'll want to get along with your work, and I mustn't disturb your concentration."

"Not at all!" said Jantiff. "This is no more than improvisation; I can do it in my sleep. I have a question for you: a business matter, so to speak."

"Yes?"

"I'm paying a hundred ozols for transportation to Uncibal space-port, in time to catch the *Serenaic*; correct?"

"Well, yes," said Eubanq guardedly. "That was the proposal we discussed, I believe."

"A hundred ozols is a large sum of money and naturally

pays all costs for the trip. I may want to bring a friend along; the hundred ozols will of course suffice. I mention this now to avoid any possible misunderstanding."

Eubanq's pale blue eyes flicked across Jantiff's face, then away. "What friend might this be?"

"No matter; it's really all hypothesis at the moment. But you agree that the hundred ozols will cover our costs?"

Eubanq considered, pursing his thick lips, and at last shook his head. "Well, Jantiff, I should hardly think so. In this business we've got to work to rules; otherwise everything goes topsy-turvy. One passage: one fare. Two passages: two fares. That's the universal rule."

"Another hundred ozols?"

"Correct."

"But that's an enormous amount of money! I'm renting the flibbit on a trip basis, not by fares."

"That's one way of looking at it. On the other hand, I've got a hundred expenses to consider: overhead, maintenance, depreciation, interest on the initial investment—"

"But you don't own the boat!"

"It's all to the same effect. And never forget, like anyone else I hope to gain a bit of profit from the transaction."

"A very generous profit," cried Jantiff. "Have you no human feelings or generosity?"

"Very little of either," Eubanq confessed with his easiest grin. "If you don't like my price, why not try elsewhere? Booch might be persuaded to borrow the Grand Knight's Dorphy for the afternoon."

"Hmf. I expect that you've received confirmation of my passage aboard the *Serenaic*?"

"Well, no," said Eubanq. "Not yet. Apparently there's been some sort of mix-up."

"But time is getting short!"

"I'll surely do my best." Eubanq waved his hand and went on his way.

Jantiff continued painting, using furious emphatic strokes which lent a remarkable brio to his work. He calculated his assets. A hundred ozols was well within his reach, but two hundred? Jantiff counted forward and backward, but in every case fell short by fifty or even sixty ozols.

Later in the day at the Old Groar, Jantiff cut and primed the panels he would paint for Fariske. There was still talk of the witch-chasing, to which Jantiff listened with a curled lip. Someone had noted remnants of the band straggling north toward the Wayness Mountains. All agreed that the Sych had been effectively cauterized, and talk turned to the forthcoming Market Fair. A certain portly fisherman went to watch Jantiff at his work. "What will you paint on these panels?"

"I haven't quite decided. Landscapes, perhaps."

"Bah, that's no entertainment! You should paint a humorous charade, with all the Old Groar regulars dressed in ridiculous costumes!"

Jantiff nodded politely. "An interesting idea, but some might object. Also, I'm not being paid to paint portraits."

"Still, put my picture somewhere in the scene; that's easy enough."

"Certainly," said Jantiff. "At a charge of, say, two ozols. Fariske, of course, must agree."

The fisherman drew back his head like a startled turtle. "Two oxols? Ridiculous!"

"Not at all. Your image will hang on this wall forever, depicting you in all your joviality. It is a kind of immortality."

"True. Two ozols it is."

"You may also paint my image," said another. "I'll pay the two ozols now."

Jantiff held up a restraining hand. "First Fariske must be consulted."

Fariske made no difficulties. "These fees will naturally reduce your payment from me."

"By not so much as a dinket!" Jantiff declared stoutly. "In fact, I want half of my fee now, so that I may buy proper pigments."

Fariske protested, but Jantiff held firm and finally had his way.

As he returned to the hut Jantiff once again totted up his expectations. "Ten panels. . . . I can crowd five faces into each panel, if necessary. That's fifty faces at two ozols each: one hundred solid ringing ozols, and my difficulties vanish like smoke!" Jantiff arrived home in an unusually optimistic mood.

As usual, Glisten was nowhere to be seen; apparently she did not care to stay alone in the hut. But almost immediately upon Jantiff's return she came from the forest with a bundle of shaggy bark, which when scraped and washed yielded a nourishing porridge.

Jantiff ran to take her bundle. He put his arm around her waist and swung her up and around in a circle. Setting her down, he kissed her forehead. "Well, young Glisten, my lovely little sorceress: what do you think! Money pours in by the bucketful! Faces for Fariske's panels, at two ozols per face! So then: would you like to live at Frayness on Zeck? It's a long way and there's no wild forest like this, but we'll find what's wrong with your voice and have it fixed, and there'd be no witch chasing, I assure you, except the kind of pursuit every pretty little creature enjoys. What about it? Do you understand me? Away from Wyst, off across space to Zeck? I don't quite know how I'll manage the fare, but no doubt the cursar will help. Ah, that elusive cursar! Tomorrow I must telephone Uncibal!"

At the moment he was more interested in Glisten. He sat on the bench and pulled her down upon his lap, so that he was looking directly into her face. "Now then," said Jantiff, "you must really concentrate. Listen closely! If you understand, nod your head. Is this understood?"

Glisten seemed to be amused by Jantiff's earnestness, though her lips twitched by no more than an iota.

"You wretched girl!" cried Jantiff. "You're absolutely frustrating! I want to take you to Zeck and you show not a flicker of interest. Won't you please say something or do something?"

Glisten comprehended that somehow she had distressed Jantiff. Her mouth drooped and she looked off across the sea. Jantiff groaned in exasperation. "Very well then; I'll take you willy-nilly and if you want to come back to your dank black forest you shall do so!"

Glisten turned back; Jantiff leaned forward and kissed her mouth. She gave no response, but neither did she draw away. "What a situation," sighed Jantiff. "If only you'd give me some little inkling, just a hint, that you understand me."

Glisten once again produced her wisp of a smile. "Aha!" said Jantiff. "Perhaps you understand me after all, and only too well!"

Glisten became restive; Jantiff reluctantly allowed her to leave his lap. He rose to his feet. "Zeck it is then, and please, at the last minute, don't cavort and hide like a wild thing."

During the night a storm blew in from the south; in the morning long combing breakers pounded the rocks and Jantiff despaired of gathering percebs. An hour later the wind moderated. A black rain sizzled upon the surface of the ocean, somewhat moderating the surf. Jantiff forced his shrinking flesh into the water, but was unmercifully swept back and forth, and finally retreated to the shore.

Taking his buckets he set off eastward along the beach, hoping to find a sheltered pool. At the far end of Isbet Neck, with the ocean on the right hand and Lulace Sound on the left, he found a spot where the currents swung past two long fingers of rock, and created a still deep pool between. Here the percebs grew large and heavy, with a large proportion of the prized coronels, and Jantiff harvested a day's quota in short order. Glisten appeared from nowhere; together they shelled the catch and carried the yield back to the hut for cleaning. "Everything seems to work for the best," declared Jantiff. "A storm drives us from our rocks and we find the home of all percebs!"

And it seemed that Glisten gave a nod of endorsement for Jantiff's opinions.

"If only you could speak!" sighed Jantiff. "The local folk wouldn't dare to chase you, since you could go to the telephone and notify the cursar. . . . Ah, that cursar! where can he be? He is duty bound to hear petitions, but he has become thin air!"

Chapter 14

••••——◆▷——••••

Jantiff finished the Cimmery decorations and even Madame Tchaga was pleased with the effect. At the Old Groar, Jantiff began to paint his panels. Not a few of Fariske's patrons paid two ozols each to gain Jantiff's version of immortality. Eubanq declined to lend his own visage to the decorations. "I'll spend my two ozols on ale and percebs. I have no desire to see myself as others see me."

Jantiff took him aside. "Another hypothetical question. Suppose one of my friends decided to visit Zeck: what might be the fare aboard the *Serenaic*?"

"Sixty or seventy ozols, or in that general area. Who is this friend?"

"Just one of the village girls; it's no great matter. But I'm surprised that the interstellar voyage to Zeck comes so much cheaper than the hop, skip and jump to Uncibal."

"Odd indeed, on the face of it," Eubanq agreed. "Still, what is money to you, prosperous perceb merchant that you are?"

"Ha! When, or if, I pay you your two hundred and seventy ozols, I will consider myself fortunate. By the way, I'm sure that passage aboard the *Serenaic* has now been confirmed?"

"Not quite yet. I must jostle them along."

"I would hope so! Perhaps I should call them myself!"

"Leave it to me. Do you seriously plan to take someone else to Zeck?"

"It's just a notion. But surely there would be no difficulty, if I were to pay over the ozols?"

"None that I can envision."

"I must give the matter serious thought." Jantiff returned to his panels.

As he worked he heard talk of the Fair, an occasion which this year would occur only a week before the Arrabin Centenary. Jantiff suddenly saw how he might earn a goodly sum of money, perhaps enough to pay Eubanq his requirements.

That night, as he sat by the fire with Glisten, he explained his scheme. "Hundreds of folk come to the fair, agreed? All will be hungry; all want percebs, so why not satisfy this need? It will mean a great deal of work for both of us, but think! Perhaps we can pay your passage to Zeck! What do you think of that?" Jantiff searched Glisten's face as he was wont to do, and she responded with her glimmer of a smile.

"You're so pretty when you smile," said Jantiff with feeling. "If only I weren't afraid that I'd frighten you and drive you away. . . ."

Toiling long hours Jantiff gathered twenty buckets of percebs and penned them into a quiet pool near his hut. On the day before the fair he set up a booth not far from the Old Groar and provided himself with a kettle, salt and cooking oil. Early on the morning of the fair he delivered his usual quota of percebs to the Cimmery and the Old Groar, then, starting his fire and warming the oil, he began to sell percebs to the farm folk arriving from the outer districts.

"Come buy, come buy!" called Jantiff. "Fresh percebs from the briny deep, cooked to a crisp and appetizing succulence! Come buy! A dinket for a portion, percebs to your taste!"

Jantiff became very busy, so that he found time to cry his wares only at odd intervals. Halfway through the morning

Eubanq stopped by the booth. "Well, Jantiff, I see that you intend to prosper one way or another."

"I hope so! If business continues I'll be able to pay you off either today or tomorrow, as soon as I collect from Fariske. And then, mind you, I want the tickets, all confirmed, most definitely with a written guarantee of passage to Uncibal."

Eubanq put on his easy grin. "These are meticulous precautions. Don't you trust me?"

"Did you trust me to pay after I arrived home on Zeck? Am I less honorable than you?"

Eubanq laughed. "A good point! Well, we'll arrange the matter one way or another. In the meantime, give me a dinket's worth of those percebs. They look to be exquisite; where do you find such excellent quality?"

"Aha! That's my little secret!" To a farmer: "Yes, sir; three packets, three dinkets!" Back to Eubanq: "I'll say this, that we came upon, that is to say, I came upon a ledge that has obviously lain fallow for years. And here you are; one dinket, if you please."

Eubanq, taking the packet, chanced to notice Jantiff's hands. He became rigid, as if arrested by a startling thought. Slowly he raised his eyes to Jantiff's face. "One dinket," said Jantiff. "Hurry, please! Others are waiting."

"Yes, of course," said Eubanq in an odd choked voice. "And cheap at the price!" He paid over his coin and turned away, carrying the packet gingerly between forefinger and thumb. Jantiff watched him go with a puzzled frown. What had come over Eubanq?

Outside the Old Groar, Eubanq met Booch. They talked earnestly for a period. Jantiff watched them from the corner of his eye as he worked. Something, so his sensitive instincts assured him, was in the wind.

One of Eubanq's remarks startled Booch. He swung around and stared toward Jantiff. Eubanq quickly took his arm and the two men entered the Old Groar.

Business became even brisker. An hour later his stock of percebs ran out. He hired a boy to stand by the booth; then, chinking up his earnings and taking his sacks, he set off toward his hut for fresh stock.

Halfway along the beach he noticed Eubanq approaching at a rapid stride, his loose fawn shoes scuffing up little eruptions of sand. A parcel dangled from his right hand.

Eubanq swerved aside and vanished momentarily from

sight behind a granat tree. When he reappeared he walked at his usual saunter and carried no parcel.

The two drew abreast; Jantiff asked in an edgy voice: "What are you doing out here? Just an hour ago I saw you go into the Old Groar."

"Occasionally I take a stroll to ease my lungs of the town air. Why aren't you tending business?"

"I sold out of percebs." Jantiff looked Eubanq up and down without cordiality. "Did you pass by my hut?"

"I went nowhere near so far. . . . Well, I'll be getting along." Eubanq strolled back toward Balad.

Jantiff hastened along the beach, and presently broke into a trot. There ahead, his hut. Glisten was nowhere to be seen. Near the water's edge a pair of buckets indicated where she had been working; one of the buckets was half full of cleaned percebs. But no Glisten.

Jantiff looked up and down the beach, then went to his hut. Glisten was not within, which caused him no surprise. In the corner of the hut stood the old pot where he kept his money. He crossed the room to unburden himself of the morning's take. The pot was quite empty.

Jantiff stared at the cracked old vessel with shoulders sagging and mouth agape.

Jantiff went outside to stand in the pale sunlight. Serene detachment blanketed his mood: a fact which puzzled and disturbed him. "Why am I not more shocked?" he asked himself. "Very odd! I would expect to be sick with anguish, yet I seem quite unmoved. Evidently I have transcended ordinary emotion. This, of course, is remarkable. A notable achievement, I should say. I have instantly seized upon the proper way to deal with catastrophe, which is to ignore it. And meanwhile, my customers wait for percebs. By all precepts of decency I ought not deny them their treat because of a personal matter, which in any event I have dealt with most efficiently. Yes, most curious. The worlds seems far away."

Jantiff loaded himself with percebs from the pool and marched stiff-legged back up the beach and to his booth. Once more he began to serve his customers.

"Percebs!" cried Jantiff to the passersby. "Choice morsels direct from the ocean! I guarantee quality! A dinket for a generous portion! Come buy these excellent percebs!"

From the Old Groar came Eubanq. He turned a smiling glance toward Jantiff and started up the street. Words burst up Jantiff's throat of their own volition; Jantiff was surprised to hear them. "Eubanq! I say, Eubanq! Step over here, if you please!"

Eubanq paused and looked back with an expression of polite inquiry. "You called to me, Jantiff?"

"Yes. Bring me my money at once. Otherwise I will notify the Grand Knight, and lay all particulars before him."

Eubanq turned his smiling glance around the circle of onlookers. He muttered a few quiet words to a strapping young farmer who, a moment before, had purchased a packet of Jantiff's percebs. The farmer gaped down at the half-empty packet, then shouldered through Jantiff's waiting customers to the booth. "Show me your hands!"

"What's wrong with my hands?" demanded Jantiff.

The farmer and the customers stared at Jantiff's fingernails. Jantiff looked also and saw a glint of that golden sheen which he had often noted upon Glisten's fingernails.

"The yellows!" roared the farmer. "He's given us all the yellows!"

"No, no!" cried Jantiff. "My fingernails are stained because of working in the cold water with the percebs . . . Or perhaps my gamboge pigment. . . ."

"Not true," Eubanq explained. "You have eaten witches' food, and now we have eaten your food and all of us are infected, and all of us must undergo the treatment. I assure you that any money which might have changed hands is no compensation."

The farmer began to shout curses. He kicked over Jantiff's booth and tried to seize Jantiff, who backed away and then, turning, walked quickly off down the street. The farmer and others came in pursuit; Jantiff broke into a run and so proceeded from town, along the familiar beach road. The road forked; to avoid being trapped on the headland, Jantiff swung to the left, toward Lulace Sound and Lulace, the Grand Knight's manor. Behind came his pursuers, bawling threats and curses.

Jantiff pushed through the ornate front gate at Lulace, and ran at a failing lope through the garden. He staggered across the verandah, leaned against the front door. Along the road came his enemies.

Jantiff tugged at the massive latch. The door swung aside; Jantiff staggered into the mansion.

He stood in a tall reception room, paneled in pale wood and furnished a trifle too elaborately for Jantiff's taste, had he been in a mood to exercise his faculties.

To the left a pair of wide steps gave upon a salon carpeted in green and illuminated by high windows facing to the north. Jantiff went to the steps and looked into the salon. A dark-haired man with heavy shoulders conversed with two other men and a woman. Jantiff timidly stepped forward. The woman turned; Jantiff looked into her face. "Skorlet!" he cried in a voice of wonder.

Skorlet, sleek and well-fed, froze into an almost comical rigidity, mouth half open, one hand aloft in a gesture. The others turned; Jantiff looked from Sarp to Esteban to Contractor Shubart, as he was known in Uncibal.

Skorlet spoke in a strangled voice, "It's Jantiff Ravensroke!"

Contractor Shubart marched forward and Jantiff retreated into the foyer.

The Contractor spoke in a heavy voice: "What do you want? Why weren't you announced? Can't you see I'm entertaining guests?"

Jantiff responded in a stammer: "Sir, I intend nothing wrong. My life is threatened by the folk in the road. They say that my percebs gave them a disease, but it's not true; at least not purposeful. Eubanq, the shipping agent, stole my money and incited them to attack me. I didn't mean to intrude upon your guests." Jantiff's voice faltered as he considered the identity of these guests. "I will return when you are less busy."

"Wait a minute. Booch! Where is Booch?"

A footman stepped forward and murmured a few quiet words.

Contractor Shubart growled: "Be damned to his wurgles and witch-kits! Why isn't he on hand when I need him? Take this fellow to the gardener's shed and keep him safe until Booch returns."

"Yes, sir. Come along, please." But Jantiff lurched backward to the door, groped for the latch, threw open the door and ran out into the garden.

The footman came running after, calling: "Here, fellow! Stop! By the Grand Knight's orders, halt!"

Jantiff ran around the manor and with a cunning born of desperation, waited at the corner. When the footman lunged past, Jantiff held out his foot. The footman sprawled; Jantiff struck him with a stake and the footman lay limp. Jantiff continued around to the back of Lulace, through the kitchen garden and out into the park. Behind a tree he caught his breath. No time now for crafty or complicated planning. "I shall go directly to Eubanq's house," Jantiff told himself. "I will kill and rob Eubanq, or perhaps force him to provide me an air-car. I will then fly him high over the Sych and throw him out; then I will continue on to Uncibal and demand protection from the cursar. If, of course, the cursar has returned. If not, I will hide once more in the Disjerferact."

Jantiff set off at once toward Balad. Unfortunately his exaltation caused him to ignore elementary caution; he was seen and identified as he came along the river road. Sullen folk surrounded him. The women began to call out invectives; the crowd pressed closer and Jantiff was backed up against a wall. He cried out in anguish: "I have done nothing! Leave me be!"

A dockworker named Sabrose, whom Jantiff had often served at the Old Groar, bellowed him down: "You have given us all the yellows, and we must now undergo the treatment, unless we want to be deaf and dumb witches. Do you call that nothing?"

"I don't know anything about it! Let me pass!"

Sabrose gave a ferocious laugh. "Since all Balad must be treated, you shall be the first!"

Jantiff was dragged up to the main street and across to the apothecary's shop. "Bring out the treatment!" bawled Sabrose. "Here's the first patient; we'll cure him on the cheap, without the headbangers."

The treatment device was wheeled from the shop. The apothecary, a mild old man who had frequented neither of the taverns nor Jantiff's booth, dropped two pills in a mug of water and held it to Jantiff's face. "Here; this will dull the pain."

Sabrose brushed away the mug. "Take away your headbangers! Let him know what he's done to us!"

Jantiff's hands were fixed into metal gloves, with loose joints over the fingernails. Sabrose wielded a mallet to crush Jantiff's fingertips. Jantiff croaked and groaned.

"Now then!" said Sabrose. "When the nails drop off, apply black niter of argent; maybe you'll be cured."

"He's getting off too easy!" screamed a woman. "Here: my frack sludge! Turn his face about; he'll never see his mischief."

Sabrose said: "Enough is enough; he's beyond knowing anything."

"Not yet! Let him pay to the full. There! Now! Right in the face!"

A thick acrid fluid was flung into Jantiff's face, scalding his skin and searing his vision. He gave a strangled cry and tore at his eyes with mutilated fingers.

The apothecary threw water into Jantiff's face and wiped his eyes with a rag. Then he turned in fury on the crowd. "You've punished him beyond all justice! He's only a poor sad lout."

"Not so!" cried a voice which Jantiff recognized as that of Eubanq. "He housed himself with a witch-woman; I saw her at his hut, and he poisoned us knowingly with witch food!"

Jantiff mumbled: "Eubanq is a thief; Eubanq is a liar." But none heard him. Jantiff opened his eyes a crack, but a granular fog obscured his vision. He moaned in shock and grief. "You've blinded me! I will never see the colors!"

One of the women cried out: "Where now the horrid witch? Do her like the others!"

"No fear," said Eubanq. "Booch has taken her in hand."

Jantiff gave a call of mindless woe. He struggled to his feet, flailed his arms to right and left, an act which the crowd considered ludicrous. They began to bait Jantiff, shoving him, prodding his ribs, hissing into his face. Jantiff at last threw up his hands and staggered off down the street.

"Catch him!" screamed the most vindictive. "Bring him back and deal with him properly!"

"Let him go," growled an old fisherman. "I've seen enough."

"What? After he has given us all the yellows?"

"And all must take the treatment?"

"He fed us witch food; never forget it!"

"Today let him go; tomorrow we will put him on a raft."

"Quite right! Jantiff! Can you hear? Tomorrow you float south across the ocean!"

Jantiff lurched heedlessly down the street. For a space children followed him, jeering and throwing stones; then they were called back and Jantiff went his way alone.

Out to the beach he stumbled, and along the familiar track. With his eyes wide and staring he could see only a vague luminosity; he walked a good distance but could not find his hut. Finally he dropped down upon the sand and turned his face to the sea. He sat a long time, confused and listless, his hands throbbing with a pain to which he gave no heed. The fog across his vision grew thick as Dwan set and night came to Dessimo Beach and the Moaning Ocean. Still Jantiff sat, while water sucked across the offshore ledges.

A breeze drifted in from the ocean: at first a chilly breath which tingled Jantiff's skin, then gusts which penetrated his threadbare garments.

Jantiff saw himself as if in a clairvoyant vision: a gaunt creature crouched on the sand, all connections to the world of reality broken. He began to grow warm and comfortable; he realized that he was about to die. Images formed in his mind: Uncibal and Old Pink; the human tides along Uncibal River; the four Whispers on the Pedestal. He saw Skorlet and Tanzel, Kedidah and the Ephthalotes; Esteban and Booch and Contractor Shubart. Glisten appeared, facing him from a distance of no more than an arm's length, and gazed steadfastly into his eyes. Miracle of miracles. He heard her speak, in a soft quick voice: "Jantiff, don't sit in the dark! Jantiff, please lift yourself! Don't die!"

Jantiff shuddered and blinked, and tears ran from his eyes. He thought of his cheerful home at Frayness; he saw the faces of his father and mother and sisters. "I don't want to die," said Jantiff. "I want to go home."

With a prodigious effort he hauled himself to his feet and stumbled off along the beach. By chance he encountered an object he recognized: the branches of a misshapen old cod-mollow tree. His hut stood only fifty yards beyond; the ground was now familiar.

Jantiff groped his way to the hut, entered, carefully closed the door. He stood stock still. Someone had only recently departed; his odor, rank and heavy, hung on the air. Jantiff listened, but heard no sound. He was alone. Tottering to his bed, he lay himself down and instantly fell asleep.

Jantiff awoke, jarred to consciousness by an awful imminence.

He lay quiet. His blinded eyes registered a watery gray blur: daylight had arrived. A rank harsh odor reached his nostrils. He knew that he was not alone.

Someone spoke. "So, Jantiff, here you are after all. I looked for you last night, but you were out." Jantiff recognized the voice of Booch. He made no response.

"I looked for your money," said Booch. "According to Eubanq, you control quite a tidy sum."

"Eubanq took my money yesterday."

Booch made an unpleasant nasal sound. "Are you serious?"

"I don't care about money now. Eubanq took it."

"That cursed Eubanq!" groaned Booch. "He'll make an accounting to me!"

"Where is Glisten?"

"The kit? Ha, don't worry about her, not a trifle. In five minutes you'll be past caring for anything. I've had my orders. I'm to put a wire around your neck, without fail. Then I'll settle with Eubanq. Then I'm off to Uncibal, where I can take any woman I see for a dish of tripes. . . . Raise your head, Jantiff. This won't take long."

"I don't want to die."

"No use to whine. My orders are strict. Jantiff must definitely be dead. So then——now none of your kicking or flailing about! Hold now."

Jantiff scuttled sideways like a crab and through some mad accident, pushed Booch off balance and rolled out the door. From far up the beach came a jeering cry: "Mad Jantiff: there! You see him now!"

Jantiff heard Booch's heavy tread. Two steps, then an uncertain halt and a mutter of annoyance. "Now, in the name of Gasmus, who can that be? A stranger, an off-worlder. Does he plan to interfere? I'll stop him short."

Steps approached. A boy's voice cried out in glee: "That's Mad Jantiff on the ground, and there's Constable Booch, who'll give it to him properly; you'll see!"

"Good morning to you both," said a pleasant voice. "Jantiff, you seem to be in poor condition."

"Yes, I've been blinded, and my fingers are all broken."

The boy cried out in eager fury: "Never fear, there's more to come! Sir, he gave us all the yellows, and he consorted with a witch! May I strike him with this stick?"

"By no means!" said the newcomer. "You are far too ardent; calm yourself! Jantiff, I am here in response to your numerous messages. I am the Respectable Ryl Shermatz, a representative of the Connatic."

Jantiff sat dazed on the ground. "You are the cursar?"

"No. My authority considerably exceeds his."

"Then ask Booch what he did with Glisten. He may have killed her."

"Utter nonsense," said Booch in jovial, if uneasy, tones. "Jantiff, you have peculiar notions about me."

"You brought your wurgle and hunted her down! Where is she now?"

Ryl Shermatz said: "Constable Booch, I suggest that you respond to Jantiff's question, in all candor."

"Lacking facts, how can I answer? And why all the anxiety? She was just a witch-kit."

"You speak in the past tense," noted Ryl Shermatz. "Is this significant?"

"Of course not! I chanced to stroll past with my wurgle, admittedly, and she ran off, but what's that to me? Or to you, for that matter?"

"I am the Connatic's agent. I am required to adjust situations such as this."

"But there is no situation to adjust! Look yonder; even now she's coming out of the Sych!"

Jantiff struggled to his knees. "Where? Tell me where. But I can't see."

The boy gave a screech of panic; there came an odd sequence of sounds: a stamping of feet, a whisper as if of spurting gas, a thud, a gasp, a scuffling sound; then, for a moment, silence.

The boy babbled: "He's dead! He tried to kill you! How did you know?"

Ryl Shermatz spoke without perturbation: "I am sensitive to danger, and well trained to deal with it."

"Who came from the forest?" cried Jantiff. "Was it Glisten?"

"No one came from the forest; Booch attempted a ruse."

"Then where can she be?"

"We shall do our best to find her. But now: tell me why you sent so many urgent messages."

"I will tell you," mumbled Jantiff. "I want only to talk; I must do hours and hours of talking—"

"Steady, Jantiff. Come, sit here on the bench. Boy, run to town; bring back new bread and a pot of good soup. Here: an ozol for your pains. . . . Now, Jantiff, talk, if you are able."

Chapter 15

Dwan, halfway up the sky, shone from behind films of shifting mist. Jantiff sat on the bench, leaning back against his ramshackle stone and seaweed hut. Ryl Shermatz, a person of medium stature, with well-formed features and short brown hair, stood beside him, one leg propped upon the bench. He had dragged the dead hulk around to the side; only Booch's black boots, extending past the edge of the hut, bore witness to his presence.

Jantiff spoke at length, in a voice which presently dwindled to a husky croak.

Ryl Shermatz said little, inserting only an occasional question. From time to time he nodded as if Jantiff's remarks reinforced opinions of his own.

Jantiff's account came to an end: "My only uncertainty is Glisten. Last night I dreamt of her, and in my dream she spoke; it was strange to hear her, and even in my sleep I felt as if I would weep."

Ryl Shermatz gazed south over the gray ocean. "Well, Jantiff," he said at last, "it is clear that you have endured hard times. Let me summarize your statement. You believe that Esteban, looking over your drawings of the four Whispers, noticed the resemblance between three of the Whispers, and himself, Skorlet and Sarp. You theorize that Esteban, with his devious and supple mind, inevitably recognized the potentiality of the situation, and began, idly at first, to consider methods for making the possible real. A fourth member of the cabal was needed: who better than a man of wealth, power and motivation; in short, a contractor? Esteban searched the reference book, and there, made for the part, he discovered Contractor Shubart.

"Esteban, Skorlet and Sarp were motivated by their lust for food and luxury. Shubart had long enjoyed the good things of life, but now was threatened by the Whispers who intended to free Arrabus from the contractors and already had informed

192

the Connatic of their plans. Shubart needed funds to implement his grand plans for the Weirdlands; he readily joined Esteban, Skorlet and Sarp.

"They contrived a bold and very simple scheme. Here you assert that Skorlet, Esteban, Sarp and Shubart journeyed to Waunisse and there boarded the airship on which the Whispers would return to Uncibal. During the flight the Whispers were killed with all their entourage and dropped into the sea. When the *Sea Disk* landed, Esteban, Skorlet, Sarp and Shubart had become the Whispers. They showed themselves briefly on the Pedestal. No one inspected them closely; no one could have suspected their deed: except you, who were disturbed and perplexed.

"The new Whispers traveled to Numenes, where they consulted the Connatic at Lusz. He found them an unsympathetic group: insincere, evasive and tawdry. Their statements rang false, and failed to accord with their purported mission, as proposed by the original Whispers. The Connatic decided to look more closely into the matter, especially since he had received urgent messages concerning a certain Jantiff Ravensroke.

"I was assigned to the task and arrived at Uncibal two days ago. Immediately I tried to find Cursar Bonamico. I learned that he had flown to Waunisse, on business connected with the Whispers, that he had boarded the same aircraft on which the Whispers returned to Uncibal.

"He never alighted from this aircraft, and the inference is clear. He was murdered and thrust into the Salaman Sea. I naturally took note of the messages you had dispatched from Balad. Last night a final message arrived. The voice was that of a woman—a girl, according to the clerk Aleida Gluster. The woman, or girl, spoke in great agitation: 'Come quickly, come quickly to Balad; they're doing terrible things to Jantiff!' And that was all."

"A girl spoke?" muttered Jantiff. "Who could that have been? Glisten can't speak, except in dreams. . . . Might the clerk have been asleep and dreaming?"

"An interesting conjecture," said Ryl Shermatz. "Aleida Gluster said nothing in this regard, one way or the other. . . . Here we are at Balad. We shall go to the Old Groar Tavern and refresh ourselves. Then we shall try to subdue these obstreperous folk."

"Eubanq is more than obstreperous," Jantiff muttered. "He stole my money and told Booch about Glisten."

"I have not forgotten Eubanq," said Ryl Shermatz.

The two men entered the Old Groar. At the tables sat a considerable number of customers: double the usual for this hour of the day. Fariske came hurriedly forward, his round white forehead glistening with droplets of sweat. "This way, gentlemen," he cried in brave joviality. "Be seated! Will you drink ale? I recommend my Old Dankwort!"

Clearly the boy who had guided Ryl Shermatz to Jantiff's hut had returned to Balad bearing large tales. "You may bring us ale and something to eat," said Shermatz. "But first: is the person known as Eubanq present in the room?"

Fariske darted a series of nervous glances along the tables. "He is not here. You will probably find him at the depot, where he serves as general agent."

"Be good enough to select three reliable men from among your customers and bring them here."

" 'Reliable'? Well, let me consider. That is a hard question. I'll summon the best of the lot. Garfred! Sabrose! Osculot! Step over here, at once!"

The three men approached with varying degrees of truculence.

Ryl Shermatz appraised them with an impassive gaze. "I am Ryl Shermatz, the Connatic's agent. I appoint you my deputies for the period of one day. You are now, like myself, invested with the inviolable authority of the Connatic, under my orders. Is this clear?"

The three men shuffled their feet and signified their understanding: Garfred with a surly grunt; Sabrose making an amiable gesture; Osculot showing a grimace of misgiving.

Ryl Shermatz spoke on. "Proceed at once to the depot. Place Eubanq under the Connatic's arrest. Bring him here at once. Under no circumstances allow him freedom from your custody: not so much as a minute. Be on the guard for any weapons he may carry. Go in haste!"

The three men departed the tavern. Ryl Shermatz turned to Fariske, who stood anxiously to the side. "Send other men to summon all the folk of Balad to an immediate assembly in front of the Old Groar. Then you may serve us our refreshment."

Jantiff sat in the dark, listening to the mutter of voices, the clink of mugs, the scrape of feet. Warmth and relaxation eased his limbs; lassitude came upon him. Ryl Shermatz spoke quietly to someone who made no response: perhaps by means of a transceiver, thought Jantiff. A moment later Shermatz sent Voris to fetch the apothecary, who arrived within the minute.

Shermatz took the apothecary aside; the two conferred and the apothecary departed. Shermatz spoke to Jantiff: "I have specified a treatment to restore a certain fraction of your vision. Later, of course, we will arrange a thorough therapy."

"I will be grateful for any improvement."

The apothecary returned. Jantiff heard muted voices as his case was discussed; then the apothecary addressed him directly. "Now, Jantiff, here is the situation. The surfaces of your eyes have been frosted by the caustic, and are no longer transparent to light. I am about to attempt a rather novel treatment: I coat the surface of your eyes with an emulsion, which quickly dries to a transparent film. Perhaps you will feel discomfort, perhaps you will notice nothing whatever. With the irregularities smoothed out, light should once again reach your retina. I will mention that the film is microscopically porous to allow passage of oxygen. Please lean back, open your right eye wide and do not move. . . . Very good. Now the left. Do not blink, if you please."

Jantiff felt a cool sensation across the front of his eyes, then an odd not unpleasant constriction across the eyeballs. Simultaneously the blur before his vision began to dissipate as if a wind blew through the optic fog. Objects loomed, assumed density; for a time they wavered in a watery medium and presently stilled. Jantiff once more could see, with almost the old clarity.

He looked around the room. He saw the grave faces of Ryl Shermatz and the apothecary. Fariske stood by the counter, abdomen bulging out ahead. Palinka peered from the kitchen, annoyed by the disruption to her daily routine. Hunched over the tables, for the most part glowering and surly sat the regular Old Groar customers. Jantiff looked this way and that, entranced by the wonder of this miraculous faculty which he thought that he had previously exploited to the fullest. He studied the umber-black shadows at the back of the room, the sheen of pewter mugs, the sallow milkwood tables, the shafts of pale lavender light streaming down through the high windows. Jantiff thought: *In later years, when I look across my life, I will mark well this moment in the Old Groar Tavern at Balad on the planet Wyst.* . . . A shuffle of activity distracted Jantiff from his musing. Ryl Shermatz sauntered to the door. Jantiff, hauling himself erect, threw back his shoulders and in unconscious imitation of Shermatz's confident stride, went to the door.

A crowd had gathered before the Old Groar: the entire population of Balad, except for Madame Tchaga who stood peering from the Cimmery. Along the street came Sabrose and Garfred, with Eubanq between them and Osculot bringing up the rear. Eubanq wore his fawn-colored suit, and today a hat with a jaunty pointed bill. His expression, however, was not at all jaunty. His cheeks sagged, his mouth hung in a lugubrious droop. Before Jantiff's inner vision came a remembered illustration from a story-book, depicting a worried brown rat being brought before a tribunal of stately cats by a pair of bulldog sergeants.

After a single glance, Shermatz turned away from Eubanq and spoke to the crowd. "I am Ryl Shermatz, the Connatic's agent, and I am here at Balad in an official capacity.

"The Connatic's policy is to allow all possible independence of thought and action. He welcomes diversity and rules with restraint.

"Nonetheless, he cannot tolerate a disregard for basic law. Such occurs here at Balad. I refer to the persecution of certain forest wanderers, whom you miscall witches. It now must terminate by the Connatic's edict. The ailment known as 'the yellows' results from a fungus-like growth; it can be cured by a pill taken with water. The so-called witches are deaf-mute not because of 'the yellows' but through a hysterical obsession. Organically they are quite normal, and sometimes, under stress of emergency, they can force themselves to speak. As for hearing, my advisers tell me that sound enters their brain at a subliminal level; they do not know they are hearing, but nevertheless are invested with information, much as telepathy affects the mind of an ordinary person.

"Conditions at Balad are unsatisfactory. The Grand Knight seems to act as an informal magistrate and dispenses such justice as he sees fit through his constable. On other occasions, as when unforgivable violence was done to the person of Jantiff Ravensroke, the community is guided by irresponsible fury.

"A cursar will presently arrive to arrange a more orderly system. He will right certain wrongs, and certain persons will regret his coming; especially those who have taken part in the recent witch chasing. They may expect severe penalties. At the moment I intend to deal only with the assault performed upon Jantiff. Constable Sabrose, bring forward the woman who blinded Jantiff."

"It was Nellick, yonder."

"Your Lordship, I acted not from malice; indeed, I thought I held simple and wholesome water in my bucket. I am a laughing woman; I acted in fun and only to ease the situation for the general benefit."

"Jantiff, does this match your recollection?"

"No. She said, 'Here, turn his face about; he will never see the results of his mischief, even though I waste my frack.' "

"Well then: which version is correct? Constable?"

Sabrose grunted. "I don't like to say. I was holding Jantiff when she flung the stuff. It burnt my arms as well."

Jantiff grimaced. "Don't bother with any of them; there were twenty or thirty people, all doing me harm. Except Grandel the apothecary, who wiped my eyes."

"Very well. Grandel, I instruct you to make a careful list of those people who participated in the episode, and to fine them in proportion to their guilt. The sum collected must be paid over to Jantiff. I suggest a fine of five hundred ozols for the woman Nellick."

Grandel looked uncomfortably around the crowd. "I will do my best, though my popularity will not be enhanced."

Fariske called out: "Not so! I took no part in the assault, even though Jantiff sold percebs in competition with me. I believe that stern fines are necessary to redeem the honor of Balad! I will help Grandel discover each name and I will counsel him against leniency. If Grandel suffers unpopularity, I will join him!"

"Then I will entrust the matter to the two of you. Now, another matter. Your name is Eubanq?"

Eubanq nodded and smiled. "Sir, that is my name."

"It is your entire name?"

Eubanq hesitated only the fraction of an instant. "Eubanq is the name by which I am known."

"Where is your place of birth?"

"Sir, as to that I cannot be sure. I was orphaned as a child."

"That is a tragic circumstance. Where were you reared?"

"I have visited many worlds, sir. I call no place home."

"The Connatic's cursar, when he arrives, will examine your background with great care. At this moment I will only concern myself with events of the recent past. First, I believe that you cashed in Jantiff's passage voucher and pocketed the money."

Eubanq considered a moment, then, no doubt reflecting that the matter was susceptible to quick verification, one way or the other, he gave a slow polite nod. "I feel sure that Jantiff would never use the ticket, and I saw no need to waste the money."

"Then, when you learned that Jantiff indeed had earned the fare, you stole his money from him?"

"Do you assert this, sir, or is it the Connatic's justice that a man must incriminate himself from his own mouth?"

"That is a clever reply," said Shermatz graciously. "But the matter is not quite so intricate. Jantiff's information makes it clear that you are the robber beyond all reasonable doubt. My question gave you the opportunity for denial. Secondly, it is clear that you informed Booch in regard to the forest waif whom Jantiff had befriended, in full knowledge of what must occur, your motive being to destroy Jantiff. The cursar will undertake an investigation. If you deny the charges, you will undergo mind-search and the truth will be made known. In the meantime, your possessions are totally confiscated. You are now a pauper, lacking so much as a single dinket."

Eubanq's jaw dropped; his eyes became moist. In a voice musical in its poignancy he cried: "This is most unreasonable! Will you sequester all my poor savings?"

"I suspect that you will fare even worse. I believe that you provoked Booch to assault and murder. If this is so demonstrated the cursar will show you no leniency."

"Take me to Lulace! The Grand Knight will prove my good character!"

"The Grand Knight is no longer at Lulace. He and his guests departed last night. In any event, he is not a trustworthy guarantor; his troubles may exceed your own." Shermatz signaled Garfred and Osculot. "Take Eubanq to a place of security. Make certain that he cannot escape. If he does so, you will each be fined one thousand ozols."

"Smartly then, Eubanq," said Osculot. "We will take you to my root cellar, and if you escape, I will pay both fines."

"One moment!" Jantiff confronted Eubanq. "What happened to Glisten? Tell me if you know!"

Eubanq's expression was opaque. "Why ask me? Put your questions to Booch."

"Booch answers no questions; he is dead."

Eubanq turned away without comment. The two constables marched him up the street and out of sight.

Ryl Shermatz once more addressed the people of the town. "The new cursar will arrive within three days. Remember: he represents the Connatic and he must be obeyed! You may now go about your affairs. Jantiff, come along. We have no further need to remain at Balad."

"But what of Glisten? I can't leave until I know what has happened!"

"Jantiff, let us face the sad facts. Either she is dead or she has returned to the forest. In either case she is beyond our reach."

"Then who was the woman who notified you of my trouble?"

"This is another affair which the cursar must look into. But let us be off to Arrabus. There is nothing more to be accomplished here."

Chapter 16

In a black space-car the two men rode north from Balad: over the gloomy Sych, across Lake Neman and the Weirdlands beyond.

Jantiff sat brooding and made no effort at conversation. Ryl Shermatz finally said: "I suspect that you are still disturbed by recent events—understandably so. Unfortunately, by the very nature of my position I can achieve only an approximate justice. The witch-killing farmers, for instance: are they not murderers? Why are they not punished? Truthfully, I am less interested in punishment than setting things to rights. I make one or two dramatic examples, hoping to frighten all the others into regeneracy. The method works unevenly. Often the most iniquitous are the least inconvenienced. On the other hand an absolutely exact justice may well destroy the community; this might have been the case at Balad. By and large, I am satisfied."

Jantiff said nothing.

Ryl Shermatz continued: "In any event we must now turn our attention to Arrabus and the Whispers. Their conduct puzzles me. Do they intend to live in isolation? If they attend the Centenary fête, or speak before a television audience, their identity must instantly become evident to their old intimates: all those residents of Old Pink, for example."

"They probably rely upon the close similarity," said Jantiff. "When no one suspects, no one notices."

Ryl Shermatz remained dubious. "I can't believe that the similarities are that close. Perhaps they plan cosmetic devices or facial surgery: in fact this may already have occurred."

"At Lulace they were the same as ever."

"And this is the great puzzle! Clearly they are not fools. They must recognize obvious dangers, and they must have prepared for them. I am amazed and fascinated; there is grandeur to their scheme."

Jantiff put a diffident question: "How will you deal with them?"

"Two options, at least, are open. We can denounce them publicly and create an enormous sensation, or we can secretly dispose of the whole affair, and presently nominate a new set of Whispers. I am inclined to the first concept. The Arrabins will enjoy the drama—and why should we not give pleasure to these essentially decent, if indolent, folk?"

"And how will this drama be managed?"

"No difficulty whatever; in fact the event has already been arranged, and by the Whispers themselves. At a Grand Rally they intend to address a select group of notables, while all the rest of Arrabus watches by television. This is an appropriate time to set matters right."

Jantiff mulled over the situation. "They will speak as before from the Pedestal, remote and obscure so that no one can recognize them, and no cameras will be allowed close views."

"I expect that you are right," said Ryl Shermatz. "At the denouement they will be seen clearly enough."

The space-car crossed over the scarp, and Uncibal lay sprawled before them, with the Salaman Sea beyond, flat and listless, the color of moonstone. Ryl Shermatz veered toward the space-port and landed close beside the depot.

"Tonight we will rest at the Travelers Inn," Said Shermatz. "As an elitist monument, it has suffered decay; still we can do no better, and you will no doubt prefer it to your lair behind the privy."

"I intend to revisit this lair, for old time's sake," said Jantiff. "My hut on the beach was actually not much better. . . . Still, it felt like home. As I think back, I was happy there. I had food; I had Glisten to look at; I had goals, impractical though they might have been, and for a time I thought I was realizing them. Yes! I was truly alive!"

"And now?"

"I am old and dull and tired."

Shermatz laughed. "I have felt the same way many times. Life goes on, despite all."

"I find life to be a very peculiar affair."

At the Travelers Inn Shermatz bespoke a suite of six rooms, specifying a high standard of cuisine and service.

Jantiff grumbled that his expectations were not likely to be realized in view of the Arrabin attitude.

"We shall see," said Ryl Shermatz. "As a rule I make few demands, but here, at the Travelers Inn, for non-egalistic prices I insist upon non-egalistic value. Unlike the ordinary traveler, I can instantly avenge sloth, slights and poor service. It is a perquisite of my job. I think that you will notice a distinct improvement over your previous visit. Now I have a few trifles of business, and I will leave you to your own devices."

Jantiff went to his rooms, where, as Shermatz had predicted, he discovered remarkably better conditions. He reveled in a hot bath, donned fresh garments and dined upon the most elaborate repast available. Then, bone-weary but not yet ready for sleep, he wandered out into the city and rode the man-ways as he had done so often in the past. Perhaps by unconscious design he passed Old Pink. After a moment's indecision he stepped off the way, crossed the yard and entered the foyer. The air hung heavy with familiar old odors, compounded of gruff, deedle, wobbly and swill; the sourness of old concrete; the condensed exhalations of all those who across the years had called Old Pink home.

Recollections swept over Jantiff: events, adventures, emotions, faces. He went to the administration desk, where a man, strange to him, sat sorting slips of paper.

Jantiff asked: "Does Skorlet still occupy Apartment D18, on the Nineteenth level?"

The clerk spun an index, glanced at a name. "No longer. She's transferred out to Propunce."

Jantiff turned to the bulletin board. A large placard composed in an eye-catching yellow, white, blue and black read:

In regard to the
GRAND RALLY:

Hail, all, to our second century! May it exceed the grandeur of the first!

The Centenary celebrates our confident advocacy of egalism. From the ends of the Cluster pour congratulations, sometimes couched in candid admiration, sometimes through the tight teeth of bombahs biting back dismay.

On Onasday next: the Grand Rally! at the Field of Voices the Panel of Delegates and many other notables will gather to partake of a ceremonial banquet and to hear the Whispers propose startling new concepts for the future.

The Connatic of Alastor Cluster will definitely be on hand, to share the Pedestal with the Whispers, in comradeship and egality. He is at this moment consulting with the Whispers and hearing their wise counsel. At the Grand Rally he will reveal his program for an augmented interchange of goods and services. He believes that Arrabins should export ideas, artistic creations and imaginative concepts in exchange for goods, foodstuffs and automatic processing devices. At the Grand Rally, Onasday, on the Field of Voices, he and the Whispers will make concrete the details of this proposal.

Only persons with entry permits will be admitted to the Field. All others will participate at this epochal occasion by television in the social halls on their apartment levels.

Jantiff reread the placard a second and a third time. Odd and wonderful! He stood pondering the garish type. At the back of his mind milled fragments of information, small disparate ideas, echoes of half-remembered conversations: all jumbled like the elements of a puzzle shaken in a box.

Jantiff turned away from the placard and departed Old Pink. He rode out Lateral 112 to Uncibal River and diverted into the human flood. For once, with nervous guesses and suspicious conjectures whirling through his head, Jantiff ignored the panorama of faces; as blank and withdrawn as any of the others, he returned to the Travelers Inn.

Back in his rooms, he discovered that a supper had been laid out on the parlor buffet. Jantiff poured out a goblet of wine and took it to a settee. The window overlooked a corner of the space-field and, beyond, the dancing lights of Disjerferact. Jantiff watched with a smile half bitter, half wistful. Would he ever be able to escape his recollections? Vividly now they passed before his inner mind: the House of Prisms; Kedidah's haunted countenance. The flavor of toasted kelp and poggets. The squeaking fifes, the tinkle of pilgrim bells, the calls and importunities, the whirling lights and park fountains . . . Ryl Shermatz emerged from his chambers.

"Aha, Jantiff, you have returned in good time. Have you noticed this array of bonter?"

"Yes. I am amazed. I had no idea that so many good things were available."

"Tonight we are bombahs for sure! I see wines from four different worlds, a noble assortment of meats, pastas, rissoles, salads, cheeses, and all manner of miscellaneous confections. A far more elaborate meal than is my usual habit, I assure you! But tonight let us revel in the ignobility of it all!"

Jantiff served himself such items as met his fancy, and joined Ryl Shermatz at the table. "An hour ago I visited Old Pink, the block where I once lived. In the lobby I saw an amazing placard. It advertised that the Connatic will definitely appear at the Grand Rally, to endorse the Whispers and all their programs."

"I saw a similar placard," said Ryl Shermatz. "I can assert even more definitely that the Connatic plans nothing of the sort."

"In that case I am relieved, but how can the Whispers make such promises? When the Connatic fails to appear, they will be left with lame excuses by the mouthful, and no one will be deceived."

"I have become fascinated by the Grand Rally," said Ryl Shermatz. "Half a dozen courtesy tickets were left at Alastor Centrality. I availed myself of two; we shall not fail to witness this remarkable occasion."

"I am absolutely bewildered," said Jantiff. "The Whispers must know that the Connatic will not appear; it follows, therefore, that they have contrived a plan to cope with this contingency."

"Admirably put, Jantiff! That is the situation in a nutshell, and I admit to curiosity. Might they go so far as to put forward a purported Connatic, to speak as they might wish the real Connatic to speak?"

"It is well within their audacity. But how could they hope

to gain? When the news arrived at Lusz, the Connatic could not fail to be annoyed."

"Exactly so! The Connatic is always amused by verve and sometimes by brashness; still he would be forced to take harsh and definite action. Well, on Onasday the event will be revealed, and we will watch carefully before we put our own program into effect."

Jantiff made a cautious observation: "You persist in using the words 'we' and 'our,' but I must admit that I am confused as to the details of our program."

Ryl Shermatz chuckled. "Our plan is simple. The Whispers appear on the Pedestal. They make their address to the notables, and by television to all the other Arrabins. A purported Connatic may appear on the Pedestal; if not, the Whispers may repair the lack by methods yet unknown, and we will watch with interest. Then, at an appropriate moment, four Whelm corvettes of the *Amaraz* class drop from the sky. They maneuver close to the Pedestal and officers jump across. They place the Whispers under arrest. The cursar now appears. He explains to all Arrabus the crimes perpetrated by the Whispers. He reveals that Arrabus is bankrupt, and he makes a rather harsh announcement to the effect that the Arrabins must awake from their century-long trance and return to work. He announces that he is assuming authority as interim governor, until a proper set of local officials once more assume responsibility.

"The four corvettes then rise to an elevation of a thousand feet, each trailing a long line with a noose at the end. A noose is fitted about the neck of each Whisper; the corvettes rise once more until they and the suspended Whispers are out of sight in the upper atmosphere. The program is crisp, decisive and sufficiently spectacular to command attention." Ryl Shermatz glanced sideways at Jantiff. "You take exception to the plan?"

"Not at all. I am uneasy, for a reason I find hard to define."

Shermatz rose to his feet and went to look out across Disjerferact. "The plan is too forthright, perhaps?"

"There is nothing wrong with the plan. I wonder only why the Whispers seem so confident. What do they know that we do not?"

"That is a provocative concept," said Shermatz. He mused a moment. "Short of asking the Whispers, I can't see how to arrive at an explanation."

"I will try to put my ideas in an orderly sequence," said Jantiff. "Perhaps something will occur to me."

"You have infected me with your uneasiness," Shermatz grumbled. "Well—there is tonight and tomorrow for conjecture. On the day after: the Grand Rally, and then we must act."

Chapter 17

The night passed by, and Dwan rose pale as a frozen tear into the sky. The day ran its course. Jantiff remained at the suite in the Travelers Inn. For a time he paced the parlor back and forth, trying to define his qualms, but the thoughts fled past before he could analyze them. He seated himself with paper and stylus and found no better success; his mind persisted in wandering. He thought of the early days at Old Pink, his dismal romance with Kedidah, the bonterfest, his subsequent flight to Balad. . . . The flow of his thoughts suddenly became viscous and slowed to a halt. For a moment Jantiff thought of nothing whatever; then, with great caution, as if opening a door from behind which something awful might leap, he reconsidered his flight across the Weirdlands, and his association with Swarkop.

Jantiff presently relaxed, indecisively, into the settee. Swarkop's conversation had been suggestive but no more. He would mention the matter and Shermatz could make of it what he chose.

During the afternoon, bored and uneasy, he walked across the mudflats to Disjerferact, and as he had promised himself, made a pilgrimage to his old lair behind the privy, and for old time's sake bought a spill of fried kelp, which he ate dutifully but without enthusiasm. There had once been a time, he reflected sadly, when he could not get enough of this rather insipid delicacy.

At sundown Jantiff returned to the Travelers Inn. Ryl Shermatz had not returned. Jantiff ate a pensive supper, then went to his rooms.

In the morning he awoke to find that Ryl Shermatz had come and gone, leaving a note on the parlor table.

For the notice of Jantiff Ravensroke:

A good morning to you, Jantiff! Today we resolve all mysteries and bring our drama to its climax and then its close. Details press upon me; I have gone off unavoidably early to brief the cursar, and so will be unable to take breakfast with you. Please allow me to issue instructions in regard to the Grand Rally. I have our two tickets and will meet you to the right of Hanwalter Gate, where the Fourteenth Lateral terminates, at half-morning, or as close thereafter as possible. This is not as early as I had hoped; still we shall no doubt find positions of advantage. Take breakfast with a good appetite! I will see you at half-morning.

Shermatz

Jantiff frowned and put the note aside. He went to the window where he could see people already arriving upon the Field of Voices, hastening to take up places as close as possible to the Pedestal. Turning away, he went to the buffet, served himself breakfast, which he ate without appetite.

The time was still early; nevertheless he threw a cape over his shoulders and departed the inn. He walked to Uncibal River, rode a half-mile, diverted upon the Fourteenth Lateral, which discharged him directly before Hanwalter Gate: a three-wicket passage through a tall fence of supple louvres. Half-morning was yet an hour off; Jantiff was not surprised to find Shermatz nowhere on the scene. He stationed himself at the stipulated place to the right of the gate, and stood watching the arrival of the "notables" who had been invited to the Field to hear the Whispers and the Connatic at first hand, and to partake of the festive banquet. An odd assortment of "notables," thought Jantiff. They were persons of all ages and types. Presently he noticed a man whom he thought to recognize; their eyes met and the man halted to exchange greetings: "Aren't you Jantiff Ravensroke from Old Pink? With Skorlet?"

"Precisely right. And you are Olin, Esteban's friend. I forget your block exactly: wasn't it Fodswollow?"

Olin made a wry grimace. "Not for months. I transferred to Winkler's Hovel out along Lateral 560, and I must say I'm pleased with the change. Why don't you move out from Old Pink? We could use someone like you, clever with his hands!"

Jantiff said in a noncommittal voice: "I'll have to call on you one of these days."

"By all means! It's often been remarked how a block stamps its nature on those who live there. Old Pink, for instance, seems so intense, always seething with intrigue. At the Hovel we're a raffish hell-for-leather crew, I assure you! The garden simply vibrates! I've never seen such a flow of swill! It's a miracle that we survive starvation, with the wump all going into jugs."

"Old Pink is somber in comparison," said Jantiff. "And, as you say, the intrigues are extraordinary. Speaking of intrigues, have you seen Esteban lately?"

"Not for a month or more. He's involved in some scheme or other that takes up all his time. An energetic fellow, Esteban! He never fails the game."

"Yes, he's quite a chap!" Jantiff agreed. "But how is it that you're invited to the Field? Are you a notable?"

"Hardly! You know me better than that! The invitation came as quite a surprise! Not an unpleasant one, of course, if there's a banquet of bonter at the other end of it. Still, I can't help but wonder whose invitation I've been tendered by mistake. But what of you? Surely you're not a notable?"

"No more than you. We both know Esteban; that's the only notable thing about us."

Olin laughed. "If that's what brings us bonter, all glory to Esteban! I'll be going on in; I want to place myself as close to the tables as possible. Are you coming?"

"I must wait for a friend."

"A pleasure seeing you again! Come visit Winkler's Hovel!"

"Yes indeed," said Jantiff in a pensive voice. "As soon as possible."

Olin presented his ticket and was admitted to the field. In Jantiff's mind the pieces of the puzzle had dropped together to form a unit, of startling proportions. Surely a flaw marred the pattern? But where? Jantiff thought first one way, then another. The concept stood unchallenged, noble in its simplicity and grandeur.

Half-morning approached: where was Ryl Shermatz? The "notables" poured onto the field by the hundreds! Jantiff scanned their faces with furious intensity. Would Shermatz never arrive?

The time became half-morning. Jantiff glared into the on-coming faces, trying to evoke the presence of Shermatz by sheer force of will.

To no avail. Jantiff began to feel listless. Peering over his shoulder through the louvres, he saw that the Field had become crowded: there were "notables" from everywhere in Arrabus. "Notables" and persons like Olin! But no one from Old Pink! The idea froze his thoughts; they began again only sluggishly. Was this the flaw in the pattern? Perhaps. Again, perhaps not.

A fanfare sounded across the field, then the Arrabus an-them. The ceremonies had begun. A few hurrying late-comers jumped off the lateral to push through the gates. Still no Shermatz!

The field megaphones broadcast a great voice: "Notables of Arrabus! Egalists across all our nation! The Whispers give you greetings! They will shortly arrive on the Pedestal to communicate their remarkable plans, despite furious efforts by the forces of reaction! Hear this, folk of Arrabus, and remember! The Whispers are disputed by enemies to egalism, and events will demonstrate the evil scope of the opposition! But be of brave heart! Our path leads to—"

Jantiff ran forward, as Shermatz stepped from the man-way. Shermatz called out: "My apologies, Jantiff! I could not avoid the delay. But we are still in time. Come along; here is your ticket."

Jantiff's tongue felt numb; he could only stammer discon-nected phrases. "No, no! Come back! No time remains!" He took Shermatz's arm to halt his motion toward the gate. Sher-matz turned on him a look of surprise. Jantiff blurted: "We can't stay here; there's nothing we can do now. Come, we've got to leave!"

Shermatz hesitated only an instant. "Very well; where do you want to go?"

"Your space-car is yonder, by the depot. Take us up, away from Uncibal."

"Just as you say, but can't you explain?"

"Yes, as we go!" Jantiff set off at a run, throwing bits of sentences over his shoulder. Shermatz, jogging alongside be-came grim. "Yes; logical. . . . Even probable. . . . We can't take the chance that you're wrong. . . ."

They boarded the space-car; Uncibal fell away below: row after row of many-colored blocks receding into the haze. To the side spread the Field, dark with the "notables" of Arrabus. Shermatz touched the telescreen controls; the voice spoke "—delay of only a few minutes; the Whispers are on their way. They will tell you how bitterly our enemies resent the success of egalism! They will name names and cite facts! . . . The Whispers are still delayed; they should be on the Pedestal now. Patience for another minute or two!"

"If the Whispers appear on the Pedestal I am wrong," said Jantiff.

"Intuitively I accept your conclusion," said Shermatz. "But I am still confused by your facts. You mentioned a certain Swarkop and his cargoes, and also a person named Olin. How do they interrelate? Where do you start your chain of logic?"

"With an idea we have discussed before. The authentic Whispers were known to many folk; the new Whispers as well. There is a strong similarity between the two groups, but not an identity. The new Whispers must minimize the risk of recognition and exposure.

"Olin came to the Field; someone sent him a ticket. Who? He is a friend of Esteban, but hardly a notable. There are legitimate notables present: the Delegates, for instance. They are well acquainted with the old Whispers. I imagine that all Esteban's acquaintances are at the Field, and all those of Skorlet and of Sarp: all received tickets, and all wondered why they were considered "notable." I saw no one from Old Pink, but they would arrive by a different lateral. Again, six tickets were sent to Alastor Agency. Assume that the Connatic was visiting Arrabus. His curiosity might well be piqued by the placards. He certainly would not have joined the Whispers on the Pedestal, but he very likely would have used one of the tickets."

Shermatz gave a curt nod. "I am happily able to assure you that the Connatic definitely did not use one of these tickets. So now, what of Swarkop?"

"He is a barge operator who carried six cargoes of frack. . . ." Jantiff had the odd sensation that his words triggered the event. Below them the landscape erupted. The Field became an instant seethe of white flame, then disappeared under a roiling cloud of gray dust. Other blurts of white flame with subsequent billows of dust appeared elsewhere across Uncibal. The craters they left behind marked the sites of Old Pink and six other blocks, the Travelers Inn and Alastor Centrality. In the cities Waunisse, Serce and Propunce thirteen other blocks, each with its full complement of occupants, in like fashion became columns of dust and hot vapor.

"I was right," said Jantiff. "Very much too right."

Shermatz slowly reached out and touched a button. "Corchione."

"Here, sir."

"The program is canceled. Call down hospital ships."

"Very well, sir."

Jantiff spoke in a dreary voice: "I should have understood the facts sooner."

"You understood in time to save my life," said Shermatz. "I am pleased on this account." He looked down across Uncibal, where the dust was drifting slowly south. "The plan now becomes clear. Three classes of people were to be eliminated: persons who knew the old Whispers, persons who knew the new Whispers, and a rather smaller group, consisting either of the Connatic or the Connatic's representative, should either be on hand. But you survived and I survived and the plan has failed.

"The Whispers will not know of the failure. They will consider themselves secure, and they will be preparing the next stage of their plan. Can you guess how this will be implemented?"

Jantiff made a weary gesture. "No. I am numb."

"Scapegoats are needed: the enemies of egalism. Who on Wyst is still acquainted with one of the Whispers?"

"The Contractors. They know Shubart."

"Exactly. Within hours all contractors will be arrested. The Whispers will announce that the criminals have made abject confessions, and that justice has been done. All future contracting will be managed by a new egalistic organization, at improved efficiency; and the Whispers will share the wealth of Arrabus between them. Any moment now we can expect their first indignant outcries." Shermatz fell silent; the two sat looking across battered Uncibal. A chime sounded. On the screen appeared the four Whispers: Skorlet, Sarp, Esteban and Shubart, their images blurred as if seen through wavering water.

"They still are afraid to exhibit themselves in all clarity," Shermatz observed. "Not too many people survive who might recognize them but there are probably a few. In the next week or so they would no doubt disappear. Quietly, mysteriously: who would trouble or wonder why?"

Esteban stepped forward a half-pace and spoke, his voice ringing with dull passion: "Folk of Arrabus! By the chance

of a few minutes delay, your Whispers have survived the cat-
aclysm. The Connatic hopefully has also escaped; he never
arrived to the stipulated place of rendezvous, and we as yet
have no sure knowledge. Unless he went incognito out upon
the Field, he escaped, and the assassins failed in double
measure! We are not yet able to make a coherent statement;
all of us are grief-stricken by the loss of so many cherished
comrades. Be assured, however, the demons who planned this
frightful deed will never survive—"

Shermatz touched a button. "Corchione."

"Here, sir."

"Trace the source of the message."

"I am so doing, sir."

"—a day of sorrow and shock! The Delegates are gone, all
gone; by the caprice of Fate we ourselves escaped, but by
sheerest accident! Our enemies will not be pleased: be sure
that we will hunt them down! That is all for now; we must
attend to acts of mercy." The screen went dead.

"Corchione?"

"The transmission originated from Uncibal Central. We
could not fix upon the feed-in."

"Seal off the space-port. Allow no egress from the planet."

"Yes, sir."

"Send a team down to Uncibal central; determine the
source of the transmission. Notify me at once."

"Yes, sir."

"Monitor all air traffic. If anyone is moving, discover his
destination."

"Yes, sir."

Shermatz leaned back in his seat. He spoke to Jantiff: "After today your life may seem pallid and uneventful."

"I won't complain as to that."

"I am alive only through your common sense, of which I
myself showed a dismal lack."

"I wish this 'common sense' had come to life sooner."

"Be that as it may. The past is fixed, and the dead are
dead. I am alive and thankful for the fact. In reference to the
future, may I inquire your goals?"

"I want to repair my vision. It is starting to blur. Then
I will go back to Balad and try to learn what happened to
Glisten."

Shermatz gave his head a sad shake. "If she is dead, you'll
search in vain. If she is alive, how will you find her in the

Weirdland forests? I have facilities for such a search; leave the matter in my hands."

"Just as you say."

Shermatz turned back to his control panel. "Corchione."

"Sir?"

"Order the *Isirjir Ziaspraide* down to Uncibal space-port, and also a pair of patrol cruisers. The *Tressian* and the *Sheer* are both at hand."

"Very good, sir."

Shermatz said to Jantiff: "In times of uncertainty, it is wise to display symbols of security. The *Isirjir Ziaspraide* admirably suits this purpose."

"How will you deal with the Whispers?"

"I can't quite make up my mind. What would you suggest?"

Jantiff shook his head in perplexity. "They have committed awful deeds. No penalty seems appropriate. Merely to kill them is an anticlimax."

"Exactly! The drama of retribution should at least equal that of the crime: in this case an impossible undertaking. Still something must be contrived. Jantiff, put your fecund mind to work!"

"I am not skilled at inventing punishments."

"Nor are they to my taste. I enjoy creating conditions of justice. All too often, however, I must ordain harsh penalties. It is the disagreeable side to my work. The preferences of the criminal, of course, can't be considered; as often as not, he will opt for leniency or even no punishment whatever."

A chime sounded. Shermatz touched a button; Corchione spoke.

"The transmission originated at a lodge owned by Contractor Shubart, on the upper slopes of Mount Prospect, eighteen miles south of Uncibal."

"Send out an assault force; seize the Whispers and bring them to the *Ziaspraide*."

"At once, sir."

Chapter 18

·····━━◆━━·····

The *Isirjir Ziaspraide*, flagship of the Thaiatic* Fleet, and a
vessel of awesome magnitude, served less as a weapon of war
than as an instrument of policy. Wherever the *Isirjir Ziaspraide* showed itself, the majesty of the Connatic and the
force of the Whelm were manifest.

The great hull, with its various sponsons, catwalks and ro-
tundas, had long been regarded as a masterpiece of the naae-
tic** art. The interior was no less splendid, with a main saloon
a hundred feet long and thirty-seven feet wide. From the ceiling, which was enameled a warm lavender-mauve, hung five
scintillants. The floor, of a dead-black substance, lacked all
luster. Around the periphery white pilasters supported massive silver medallions; depictions of the twenty-three goddesses, clothed in vestments of purple, green and blue, occupied the spaces between. Jantiff, upon entering the saloon,
studied the intricacy of these designs with wondering envy;
here were subtle skills, of draughtsmanship and understated
color, beyond his present capacity. Sixty officers of the
Whelm, wearing white, black and purple dress uniforms, followed him into the saloon. They ranged themselves along the
walls to either side and stood in silence.

A far sound broke the silence: a drum roll, and another,
and another, in fateful slow cadence. The sound grew loud.
Into the hall marched the drummer, somberly costumed after
the ancient tradition, with a black mask across the upper half
of his face. Behind came the Whispers, each accompanied by
a masked escort: first Esteban and Sarp, then Skorlet and
Shubart. Their faces were bleak; their eyes glistened with
emotion.

---

* From Thaia, one of the twenty-three goddesses.
** From naae: a set of aesthetic formulae peculiar to the Space Ages:
that critique concerned with the awe, beauty and grandeur associated
with space ships. Such terms are largely untranslatable into antecedent
languages.

The drummer led the way to the end of the hall. He ceased drumming and stepped aside. The ensuing silence tingled with imminence.

The Commander of the *Isirjir Ziaspraide* stepped out upon a raised platform, and seated himself behind a table. He addressed the Whispers: "By the authority of the Connatic, I fix upon you the guilt of multiple murders, in yet unknown number."

Sarp clenched his fingers together; the others stood rigid. Esteban spoke out in a brassy voice: "One murder, many murders: what is the difference? The crime is not multiplied."

"The point is of no consequence. The Connatic admits himself in a quandary. He feels that in regard to your case, death is an almost trivial disposition. Nevertheless, after taking advice, he has issued the following decree. You shall immediately be housed in spheres of transparent glass twenty feet above the Field of Voices. The spheres shall be twenty feet in diameter, and furnished with a minimum of facilities. One week hence, after your crimes have been elucidated in full detail to all Arrabus, you shall be taken into a vehicle. At the hour of midnight this vehicle will rise to an altitude of seven hundred and seventy-seven miles and there explode with a spectacular effulgence of light. Arrabus will thereby be notified that your deeds have been expiated. That is to be your fate. Take your farewells of each other; you will meet again but only briefly, one week hence."

The Commandant rose to his feet and departed the hall. The four stood stiffly, showing no desire to exchange sentiments of any sort whatever.

The drummer stepped forward, and ruffled his drums; again, again, at a portentous tempo. The escorts led the four back down the length of the hall. Esteban's eyes darted this way and that, as if he intended a desperate act; the escort at his elbow paid no heed. Esteban's gaze suddenly became fixed. His head thrust forward; he stopped short and pointed a finger. "There stands Jantiff! Our black demon! We have him to thank for our fate!"

Skorlet, Sarp and Shubart turned to look; their gazes struck into Jantiff's face. He stood coldly watching.

The escorts touched the arms of their charges; the group moved on, at the tempo of the drum roll.

Jantiff turned away, to find Shermatz at his side.

"Events have run their course, so far as you and I are concerned," said Shermatz. "Come; the commander has assigned us comfortable quarters, and for a period we can relax without startlements or dismal duties."

An ascensor lifted them to a high rotunda. Entering, Jantiff stopped short, taken aback by opulence on a scale which exceeded all his previous concepts. Shermatz could not restrain a laugh; he took Jantiff's arm and led him forward. "The appointments are perhaps a trifle grand," said Shermatz, "but, adaptable as you are, you will quickly find them comfortable. The view, especially when the *Ziaspraide* coasts quietly among the stars, is superb."

The two seated themselves on couches upholstered in purple velvet. A mess boy, stepping from an alcove, proffered a tray from which Jantiff took a goblet carved from a single topaz crystal. He tasted the wine, looked deep into the swimming depths, tasted again. "This is very good wine indeed."

Shermatz took a goblet of the same vintage. "This is the Trille Aegis. As you see, we who labor in the Connatic's service enjoy perquisites as well as hardships. On the whole it is not a bad life; sometimes pleasant, sometimes frightening, but never monotonous."

"At the moment I would enjoy a certain level of monotony," said Jantiff. "I feel almost inanimate. There is still a single matter which gnaws at my mind: probably something which is futile to think about. Still. . . ." He fell silent.

Shermatz reflected a moment. "I have made certain arrangements. Tomorrow your eyes will be repaired; you will see better than ever. In about a week's time the *Ziaspraide* leaves Wyst, and will cruise down the Fayarion. Zeck is not far to the side, and so you shall be delivered to your very doorstep. In fact, we will have the *Ziaspraide* hover over Frayness and send you down in the gig."

"That is hardly necessary," mumbled Jantiff.

"Perhaps not, but you are spared the inconvenience of finding your own way home from the space-port. So shall it be done. Along the way of course you will use these chambers.

"What of yourself? Why not come visit me at our house in Tanglewillow Glen? My family will make you most welcome and you would very much enjoy our houseboat, especially when we moor it among the reeds on the Shard Sea."

"The prospect is appealing," said Shermatz. "But to my vast distaste I must remain at Uncibal, and help put together a new Arrabin government. I expect that the cursars, in all discretion, will manage Arrabus perhaps for decades, until the Arrabins regain their morale. They are now confirmed city-dwellers, and generally indecisive. Each person is isolated; among the multitudes he is alone. Detached from reality he thinks in abstract terms; he thrills to vicarious emotions. To ease his primal urges he contrives a sad identification with his apartment block. He deserves better than this; so does anyone. The blocks of Arrabus will come down, and the folk will go north and south to reclaim the Weirdlands and again they will become competent individuals."

Jantiff drank from his goblet. "I remember the farmers of Blale: famous witch-chasers all."

Shermatz laughed. "Jantiff, you are unkind! You would have these poor folk moving from one extreme to the other! Are there no farmers on Zeck? Surely they are not witch-chasers!"

"That's true. Still, Wyst is quite a different world."

"Precisely so, and these concepts must be carefully weighed when one works in the service of the Connatic. Does such a career attract your interest? Don't tell me 'yes' or 'no' at this instant; take time to collect your thoughts. A message sent to my name in care of the Connatic at Lusz will always be delivered."

Jantiff found difficulty in expressing himself. "I very much appreciate your kind interest."

"Nothing of the sort, Jantiff; the thanks are on my side. Were it not for you, I would be part of the atmospheric dust."

"Were it not for you, I would be blind and dead on the beach beside the Moaning Ocean."

"Well then! We have traded good deeds, and this is the stuff of friendship. So now, your immediate future is arranged. Tomorrow the opthalmologists will repair your eyes. Shortly thereafter you depart for home. As for the other matter which preys on your mind, I have a dreary suspicion that all is finished, and that you must turn your mind away."

Jantiff said: "Quite candidly, I still feel impelled to go south and search the Sych. If Glisten is dead: well then, she is dead. If she escaped Booch and still lives, then she is wandering alone in the forest, a poor lost little waif."

"I half expected such an intention on your part," said Shermatz. "Now I see that I must reveal a plan which I kept secret for fear of arousing your hopes. Today I am sending a team of experienced trackers south. They will probe all circumstances and make a definite determination one way or another. Will this satisfy you?"

"Yes, of course. I am more than grateful."

Chapter 19

The *Isirjin Ziaspraide* hovered over Frayness, and while all came out to watch, a gig descended into Tanglewillow Glen and delivered Jantiff to his front door.

"Jantiff, what does all this mean?" gasped his father.

"Not a great deal," said Jantiff. "I may go into the Connatic's service, and on this account was accorded the courtesy of transportation to my home. But I will tell you all about it, and I assure you there is a great deal to tell!"

One morning two months later a set of chords announced the presence of a visitor. Jantiff went to the door and slid it aside. On the porch stood a slender blonde girl. Jantiff's voice stuck in his throat. He could manage only a foolish grin.

"Hello, Jantiff," said the girl. "Don't you remember me? I'm Glisten."

Glossary

1. Wyst is the single planet of Dwan, the Eye of the Crystal Eel, in Giampara's Realm*, low to the side of Alastor Cluster. Wyst is small, damp, cool and unremarkable except for its history, which is as extravagant, desperate and strange as any of the Cluster.

   The four continents of Wyst: Zumer and Pombal, Trembal and Tremora, had been settled by different fluxes of peoples. Each evolved in isolation with little interaction until the Great Hemispheric War between Trembal and Tremora, which destroyed the social order of both continents and reduced the lands to wilderness.

   Trembal and Tremora faced each other across the narrow Salaman Sea, a drowned rift valley. The littoral strip between palisades and water—mud flat and swamp for the most part—was the land of Arrabus, inhabited only by a few farmers, bird trappers and fishermen. To Arrabus now, for want of better destination, migrated refugees from both continents: for the most part members of the gentry. These folk, with neither training nor inclination for agriculture, organized small factories and technical shops, and within three generations were the privileged class of Arrabus, while the native Arrabins became a caste of laborers. With a great increase in population, food was imported for the new gentry and synthesized for the laboring classes.

   The social contrasts necessarily created dissatisfactions, ever more acerb. A certain Ozzo Disselberg presently published a tract, "Protocols of Popular Justice," in which he

---

* Alastor Cluster is divided into twenty-three realms, each nominally ruled by one of the twenty-three mythical goddesses, and the Connatic is formally styled: "Consort to the Twenty-three." In early times each realm selected a maiden to personify its tutelary goddess, with whom the Connatic, during his ceremonial visits, was expected to cohabit.

not only codified the general discontent, but went considerably further, into allegations which might or might not be accurate, and in any event were scarcely susceptible to proof. He asserted that the Arrabin industries were purposefully operated at low efficiency, that enormous toil was wasted upon archaic flourishes and unnecessary refinements, in order to restrict real production. By this callous policy, declared Disselberg, the carrot was suspended tantalizingly just beyond the nose of the worker, so that he would strive for rewards always to be denied him. He further asserted that the Arrabin industries could easily provide everyone with the goods and services now enjoyed only by the privileged few, at a cost of half as much human toil.

The gentry predictably denounced Disselberg as a demagogue, and refuted his arguments with statistics of their own. Nevertheless, the Protocols gained wide currency and, for better or worse, altered the attitudes of the working population.

One dismal morning, on a date later to be celebrated as the "Day of Infamy," Disselberg was discovered dead in his bed, apparently the victim of assassination. Ulric Caradas* immediately called for a massive demonstration, which escalated first into violence, then disintegration of the old government. Caradas organized the First Egalistic Manifold and proclaimed Disselberg's principles to be the law of the land; overnight Arrabus was transformed.

The erstwhile gentry responded variously to the new conditions. Some emigrated to worlds where they had providentially invested funds; others integrated themselves into the new order; still others took themselves north or south into the Weirdlands**, or districts beyond, such as Blale and Froke.

Thirty years later, Ozzo Disselberg might have considered himself vindicated. The labor force, striving under the exhortations of Caradas and the Egalistic Manifold, had performed prodigies of construction: a magnificent system of sliding roadways, that the folk might be freely transported; a complex of food synthesizers, to ensure ev-

---

* Historians (non-Arrabin) are generally of the opinion that Caradas strangled Disselberg during an ideological dispute.

** Weirdlands: those areas of Trembal and Tremora to the north and south of Arrabus, once civilized and cultivated, now wilderness inhabited only by nomads and a few isolated farmers.

eryone at least a minimum diet; row after row, sector after sector, of apartment blocks, each to house three thousand folk. The Arrabins, emancipated from toil and need at last, were free to exercise those prerogatives of leisure once solely at the disposal of the gentry.

2. From *Owl-thoughts of a Peripatetic Pedant*

Arrabus makes few if any concessions to the visitor, and the casual tourist is not likely to discover much comfort or convenience, let alone luxury. At Uncibal City a single hotel serves the needs of transients: the rambling old Travelers Inn at the space-port, where ordinary standards of hospitality are for the traveler no more than a pious hope. Immigrants encounter an even more desolate welcome; they are hustled into a great gray barracks where they wait, perforce with stoicism, until they are assigned to their blocks. After a few meals of "gruff" and "deedle" they are likely to ask themselves: "Is this why I came to Wyst?" and many hurry back the way they came. On the other hand, the visitor who has firmly established his departure date may well find Arrabus exhilarating. The Arrabins are gregarious, extroverted, and dedicated to pleasure; the visitor will make dozens of friends, who as often as not will dispose themselves for his erotic recreations. (As a possible irrelevance, it may be noted that in an absolutely egalistic society, the distinction between male and female tends to become indistinct.)

The visitor, despite the animation of his friends and the insistent gaiety of their company, will presently begin to notice a pervading shabbiness, only thinly disguised under coats of color-wash. The original "sturge" plants have never been replaced; it is still nothing but "gruff" and "deedle" "with wobbly to fill up the cracks," as the popular expression goes. The folk work thirteen hours a week at "drudge," high and low, but they hope to reduce the stint to ten hours and eventually six. "Low" toil—anything to do with machinery, assembly, repair, cleaning or digging—is unpopular. "High" toil—records, calculation, decoration, teaching—is preferred. Essential maintenance and major construction are contracted out to companies based elsewhere. Foreign exchange is earned through the export of fabric, toys, and glandular extracts, but production is inefficient. Machinery falters; the labor force constantly

shifts. Management ("high" drudge shared in turn by all),
by the nature of things, lacks coercive power. Critical jobs
are left to the contractors, whose fees absorb all the foreign exchange. Arrabin money, therefore, is worthless elsewhere.

How can such an economy survive? Miraculous to state,
it does: unevenly, veering and jerking, with surprises and
improvisations; meanwhile the Arrabins live their lives
with zest and charming ingenuousness.

Public spectacles are popular. Hussade assumes an exotic and even grotesque semblance, where catharsis super-
sedes skill. "Shunkery" includes combats, trials, races and
games involving enormous ill-smelling beasts from Pombal.
The shunk riders have recently become disaffected and are
demanding higher wages, which the Arrabins resist.

Naturally, despite general gaiety and good cheer, all is
not positive in this remarkable land. Frustration, annoyance, inconvenience are endemic. Bizarre and incessant
erotic activity, petty thievery, secret malice, stealthy nuisances: these are commonplaces of the Arrabin scene, and
the Arrabins are certainly not a folk of strong psychological fiber. Each society, so it is said, generates its char-
acteristic set of crimes and vices. Those of Arrabus exude
the cloying stink of depravity.

3. Asteroids, stellar detritus, broken planets and the like, afford bases to the pirates and raiders whom even the
Whelm seems unable to expunge.

Andrei Simić, the Gaean philosopher, has theorized that
primitive man, evolving across millions of years in chronic
fear, pain, deprivation and emergency, must have adapted
intimately to these excitations. In consequence, civilized
men will of necessity require occasional frights and
horrors, to stimulate their glands and maintain their
health. Simić has jocularly proposed a corps of dedicated
public servants, the Ferocifers, or Public Terrifiers, who
severely frighten each citizen several times a week, as his
health requires.

Uncharitable critics of the Connatic have speculated
that he practices a version of the Simić principle, never
eradicating the starmenters once and for all, to ensure
against the population becoming bland and stolid." He
runs the Cluster as if it were a game preserve," declares
one of these critics. "He stipulates so many beasts of prey

to so many ruminants, and so many scavengers to devour the carrion. By this means he keeps all his animals in tone."

A correspondent of the *Transvoyer* once asked the Connatic point-blank if he subscribed to such a doctrine. The Connatic replied only that he was acquainted with the theory.

4. For a detailed discussion of hussade see *TRULLION: Alastor 2262*. Like most, if not all, games, hussade is symbolic war. Unlike most games, hussade is played at a level of intensity transcending simple competitive zeal. At hussade, the penalties of defeat are extremely poignant, comparable to the penalties of defeat at war. A team, when defeated at a ploy, or play series, pays a financial indemnity to ransom the honor of its sheirl. The game proceeds until a team is defeated in so many successive ploys that its game fund is exhausted, whereupon the sheirl of the defeated team undergoes a more or less explicit ravishment at the hands of the victors, depending upon local custom. The losers suffer the humiliation of submission. Hussade is never played in lackadaisical style. Spectators, victors and vanquished alike experience a total emotional discharge: hence the universal popularity of the game.

Hussade puts a premium not only on strength, but on skill, agility, fortitude, and careful strategy. Withal, hussade is not a violent game; personal injury, aside from incidental scrapes and bruises, is almost unknown.

5. According to the canons of Alastrid mythology, twenty-three goddesses rule the twenty-three segments of the Cluster. Each goddess is a highly individual entity; each expresses a different set of attributes. Discord often results from the disparities. None of the goddesses is content to confine herself to her own realm; all constantly meddle in the affairs of other realms. When a man encounters an extraordinary circumstance, he more or less jocularly cites the influence of a goddess. Jantiff hence gives thanks to Cassadense, whose realm includes Zeck. For this reason she is presumably concerned with Jantiff's welfare, especially since he travels the realm of her great rival Giampara.

Presenting JACK VANCE in DAW editions:

The "Demon Princes" Novels

- [ ] STAR KING   #UE1402—$1.75
- [ ] THE KILLING MACHINE   #UE1409—$1.75
- [ ] THE PALACE OF LOVE   #UE1442—$1.75
- [ ] THE FACE   #UJ1498—$1.95
- [ ] THE BOOK OF DREAMS   #UE1587—$2.25

The "Tschai" Novels

- [ ] CITY OF THE CHASCH   #UE1461—$1.75
- [ ] SERVANTS OF THE
      WANKH   #UE1467—$1.75
- [ ] THE DIRDIR   #UE1478—$1.75
- [ ] THE PNUME   #UE1484—$1.75

Others

- [ ] SPACE OPERA   #UE1457—$1.75
- [ ] EMPHYRIO   #UE1504—$2.25
- [ ] THE FIVE GOLD BANDS   #UJ1518—$1.95
- [ ] THE MANY WORLDS OF
      MAGNUS RIDOLPH   #UE1531—$1.75
- [ ] THE LANGUAGES OF PAO   #UE1541—$1.75
- [ ] NOPALGARTH   #UE1563—$2.25
- [ ] DUST OF FAR SUNS   #UE1588—$1.75
- [ ] TRULLION: ALASTOR
      2262   #UE1590—$2.25
- [ ] MARUNE: ALASTOR 933   #UE1591—$2.25

If you wish to order these titles,

please see the coupon in

the back of this book.

The really great fantasy books
are published by DAW:

Andre Norton

- [ ] LORE OF THE WITCH WORLD   UE1634—$2.25
- [ ] SPELL OF THE WITCH WORLD   UJ1645—$1.95
- [ ] QUAG KEEP   UJ1487—$1.95
- [ ] PERILOUS DREAMS   UE1405—$1.75

Lin Carter

- [ ] LOST WORLDS   UJ1556—$1.95
- [ ] UNDER THE GREEN STAR   UW1433—$1.50
- [ ] THE WARRIOR OF WORLD'S END   UW1420—$1.50

Michael Moorcock

- [ ] ELRIC OF MELNIBONE   UJ1644—$1.95
- [ ] STORMBRINGER   UE1574—$1.75
- [ ] THE JEWEL IN THE SKULL   UE1547—$1.75
- [ ] THE GOLDEN BARGE   UE1572—$1.75

C. J. Cherryh

- [ ] WELL OF SHIUAN   UJ1371—$1.95
- [ ] FIRES OF AZEROTH   UJ1466—$1.95
- [ ] GATE OF IVREL   UE1615—$1.75

Tanith Lee

- [ ] VOLKHAVAAR   UE1539—$1.75
- [ ] SABELLA   UE1529—$1.75
- [ ] KILL THE DEAD   UE1562—$1.75
- [ ] DEATH'S MASTER   UJ1441—$1.95

Many more by the above and other famous fantasy writers. Ask for a copy of the DAW catalog.

DAW BOOKS are represented by the publishers of Signet and Mentor Books, THE NEW AMERICAN LIBRARY, INC.

THE NEW AMERICAN LIBRARY, INC.,
P.O. Box 999, Bergenfield, New Jersey 07621

Please send me the DAW BOOKS I have checked above. I am enclosing
$_____ (check or money order—no currency or C.O.D.'s).
Please include the list price plus 50¢ per order to cover handling costs.

Name _____

Address _____

City _____ State _____ Zip Code _____

Please allow at least 4 weeks for delivery